BELOW
THE
RADAR

D0557148

BELOW

THE

RADAR

DANA
RIDENOUR

Print ISBN 13: 978-1-63489-224-7

Library of Congress Catalog Number: 2019907454

Printed in the United States of America
First printing: 2019

23   22   21   20   19   5   4   3   2   1

Cover and interior design by James Monroe Design, LLC.

Wise Ink,
807 Broadway St. NE, Suite 46
Minneapolis, MN 55413

Visit: DanaRidenour.net

To my husband, Bill.
Our life together has truly been one adventure after another.
Here's to the next adventure, my love.

"Sentiment without action
is the ruin of the soul."

—Edward Abbey

1

New Orleans, Louisiana

FBI Special Agent Alexis Montgomery paced Dr. Susan Levering's office, examining the numerous psychiatric licenses and degrees displayed on the wall.

Miniature shrines to herself and her purported greatness, Lexie thought.

The office occupied what once had been the library of a historic Victorian-style home located in the French Quarter. Lexie ran her hand along the wood shelf that held Dr. Levering's collection of psychiatric books—the slightly musty smell reminded her that most of the furnishings in the office were antiques. Her favorite thing in the room was the elaborate fireplace at center stage.

"You seem anxious, Lexie," Dr. Levering said. "What's on your mind?"

Lexie stretched her neck from side to side, trying to alleviate the tightness in her shoulders. Her throat felt like sandpaper; she plucked a hard peppermint from the dish on the coffee table, removed it from the noisy wrapper, and popped it into her mouth. Without making eye contact,

Lexie said, "The FBI has another undercover assignment for me. It's overseas."

The therapist stared incredulously at Lexie. "I assume you told them no." When her patient didn't answer, Dr. Levering put down her pen and leaned forward. "Let's talk this through, Lexie."

Dr. Levering's unusual green eyes and the soft precision of her speech reminded Lexie of her mother. Her pearl necklace with matching earrings accentuated her fair skin and fine-boned features. Halting her pacing, Lexie made eye contact with the doctor and said, "I don't think I have a choice." She plopped down on the leather couch and ran her hands through her hair.

"You do have a choice. You can say no. It's that simple."

Lexie fought to keep her eyes from rolling. *Here we go.* "You don't understand."

"Help me to understand. Let's talk about your options. There are always options."

"I need to take this assignment," Lexie replied firmly.

Shifting in her oversized wingback chair and crossing her legs, Dr. Levering leaned forward. "Why do you feel you have to accept the assignment? We've made so much progress over the past few months."

"Because I do."

"That's a child's answer, Lexie. Tell me the real reason you would go back into undercover work." Dr. Levering counted off on her fingers. "During your last undercover assignment, you were taken hostage, severely beaten, shot, and left for dead."

"Oh, come on, Doc. It was only a flesh wound."

"Lexie, I'm trying to help you, but you're minimizing again."

Good thing I've never mentioned the nightmares. She'd never let me outta here.

"Time may have healed your physical wounds, but your psychological wounds are still raw. You've made great strides in the time we've been working together, but quite frankly, you have a long way to go in the recovery process."

Lexie pulled her knees up into her chest and wrapped her arms around them. "This isn't about me. This is about a Dutch police constable who's gone missing while working undercover. It's possible he's been killed, but if he's alive, then he needs help." She tried to impart the urgency of the situation through her voice. "The thing is, I'm in a perfect position to help find this guy. He has a family who deserves to know the truth. If he were your son or brother, wouldn't you want to know what happened to him?"

"Of course I would. But Lexie, I'm telling you, you're not ready for this assignment. You still haven't completely processed the trauma of the *last* one."

"Do you think I don't know that, Doc? I relive those horrors every time I close my eyes. This could be my chance to make things right."

Shifting in her chair, Levering once again leaned closer to Lexie. "Let's talk about what you just said. What do you feel you need to make right?"

A sudden rush of tears threatened to spill from Lexie's eyes; she rested her forehead on her knees, fighting to keep them at bay.

"Lexie," the doctor said softly, "listen to me. I know in

your mind you're trying to make amends for what happened to Logan Burkhart. We've discussed the difference between fault and responsibility—you still think it's your fault that Logan was killed."

"It *was* my fault," Lexie murmured.

"No, it wasn't your fault. That's like saying it's a person's fault that they were born into a home with an alcoholic, abusive father. Human beings have a deep-seated need for fairness and justice, especially people like you who choose law enforcement as a profession. You feel the need to assign fault in every situation, even if it means blaming yourself. But this world isn't fair. Logan was in the wrong place at the wrong time and was killed by ruthless criminals. It wasn't your fault, but it *is* your responsibility to take the pain from that event and put your life back together. You don't have to make amends for his death. Putting your life in jeopardy won't bring him back."

Lexie closed her eyes. A memory surfaced: Logan's soulful eyes, the color of molten chocolate. She remembered the bouquet of white daisies and yellow roses he had given her on their first date. Her body trembled as she recalled the sensation of his lips on hers—like a phantom limb, no longer present but still felt. When she opened her eyes and lifted her head, the vision disappeared. She felt her throat thicken. Logan was dead, his life cut short because of their relationship.

"I know I can't bring him back, but maybe I can help find the missing constable so another family won't suffer like Logan's did."

The therapist folded her hands and rested them on the

notepad in her lap. "Lexie, I hear what you're saying and I understand your desire to help, but there has to be someone else who can do this."

Why can't I make this woman understand?

"That's the thing. There isn't. I'm not thought of too highly in the Bureau right now. I barely escaped with my job intact. The only reason they've asked for me now is because there's no one else who can do it. I'm it."

"I don't believe that. You're not the only undercover agent in the FBI."

"You're right, I'm not. But I'm the only undercover agent who's lived with the eco-extremists. They're the ones responsible for the constable's disappearance. I understand their mindset and their methods."

"And someone can't be trained in those methods?"

"There isn't time, Doc. I'm the only one who can get close enough to these people to find out what's happened to this guy."

"I can't believe your supervisor has approved you."

"He hasn't yet. In fact, he doesn't even know about it. The request came directly to me from FBI headquarters. I'm meeting with my supervisor after I leave here."

Sighing, Dr. Levering picked up her pen and looked at her notes. "You're in therapy as a condition of your continued employment by the FBI."

"I'm aware, Doc."

"Why do you think you were ordered to undergo therapy?"

"Oh, that's an easy one—my last assignment met with

what the FBI termed 'negative results.'" Lexie chuckled bitterly. "Most people would have called it a disaster."

"I don't want to be a box that you check to get back to work, Lexie," Levering said, her tone a mix of frustration and empathy. "I want to help you. I *can* help you, but only if you let me."

"I know you mean well, but the best thing for me right now is to get back on the horse. I need to find the missing constable."

"Finding the constable isn't going to solve everything. We need to get to the origin of your problems."

"We can do that when I get home. I won't be gone forever."

Dr. Levering joggled her pen between her thumb and first finger. "I'm sorry, but I'm recommending that you not be cleared for this assignment. Going back into an undercover role is not in your best interest."

A wave of frustration washing over her, Lexie raised her voice before she was able to stop herself. "Doctor, the Bureau doesn't give a rat's ass what's in my best interest. The FBI is going to do what's in the best interest of the FBI."

"I don't care what's in the best interest of the FBI. I care what's in your best interest. And you should too."

This is pointless. Without another word, Lexie stood, smiled at Dr. Levering, and walked toward the five-panel Victorian door.

"Thank you for all you've done for me, Doc. You can cancel my upcoming sessions. I'm going back to work. I'll call and schedule another appointment when I return from overseas."

As Lexie reached for the door handle, she heard Dr. Levering mutter, "*If* you return from overseas."

* * * * *

"Absolutely not!" Supervisory Special Agent Mark Clarkson yelled.

"But Mark—" began Lexie, perched on the edge of the chair opposite her supervisor's desk.

"No, Lexie. Not this time. You're not gonna railroad me. You're lucky to have a job right now—you're lucky to be *alive*. If you think I'm going to let you gallivant around Europe on your own this soon after your last undercover debacle, then—"

"But the Dutch police need our help."

"I don't care. How did you even find out about this?"

Lexie stood and walked over to the window that overlooked the parking lot, glancing down at the sea of cars below. "Someone at HQ called me."

"Who, Lexie? I want to know who contacted you."

Still staring out the window, Lexie replied, "Adam Harper."

"Harper? Of course. I should've known."

Lexie turned to face her supervisor. "He's in the Undercover and Sensitive Operations Unit now. It's his job to find undercover agents for ongoing cases."

"I'm well aware of his job, Lexie," barked Mark, "and how he got there. This isn't how things are done in the FBI. There's a chain of command and a protocol for this type of thing." He stopped and straightened his back, his eyes narrowing as he stared at her. "To be clear, he called you. You didn't call him looking for another undercover mission."

"He called me."

Her supervisor's glare intensified.

"He did!" Returning from the window, Lexie sat back in her chair, then leaned forward and locked eyes with her supervisor. "Mark, I need this."

"No, you don't. You're my responsibility and I have the final say. My answer is no. You promised me that if I saved your job you would forget all about the undercover program and work narcotics cases for me. Remember that, Lexie?"

"Yes, but—"

"No buts. This discussion is over. Go back to your desk."

Lexie didn't move.

"*Now*, Agent Montgomery."

Clenching her jaw, she said through her teeth, "Yes, sir."

As Lexie was walking out of Clarkson's office, his phone rang. "Clarkson," he said into the handset.

Lexie closed the door behind her. A few minutes later, her supervisor stormed out of his office, glared at her, and bolted down the long hallway toward the Special Agent in Charge's office.

* * * * *

"*Agent Montgomery, report to the SAC's office,*" blared from the overhead speakers.

Oh shit, that can't be good. Wonder if I need to box up my belongings.

Lexie strolled down the long, narrow hallway that led to the office of Tyrese Evans, the Special Agent in Charge of the New Orleans Division. Photographs of the SACs who'd come before Evans adorned the stark white walls. The secretary was not at her desk, so Lexie approached the closed door and knocked firmly.

A gravelly voice from behind the door boomed, "Come in."

Lexie opened the door to find Clarkson sitting across from SAC Evans. Clarkson shot Lexie an icy stare, his nostrils flaring and his eyes narrowing.

"Sit down, Agent Montgomery," Evans demanded.

Lexie took the empty chair beside Clarkson. Her right knee bounced as she waited for the SAC to continue.

Evans loosened his tie and crossed his arms over his starched, white Oxford shirt. Sweat beaded on his shiny, bald head; his eyebrows furrowed as he made eye contact with Lexie.

"Agent Montgomery, would you like to guess who I received a telephone call from this morning?"

Lexie lowered her eyes, but didn't answer.

"I'll tell you. I received a call from the director of the FBI. I shouldn't have to tell you that when an SAC receives a telephone call from the director, the news is usually not good. Do you know why the director was calling?"

Lexie glanced up.

"The director told me that he received word the New Orleans Division has a highly specialized undercover agent assigned to the field office who is needed immediately for a very important case, and that *I* was impeding the investigation by not allowing this agent to proceed in the matter. You can imagine my surprise, Agent Montgomery, since I had no fucking idea what the director was referring to."

Mark tried to intervene. "That's my fault, sir."

"Shut up, Clarkson. You already gave me your input. I want to hear from Montgomery now."

Lexie looked up. She concentrated on the SAC's gold nameplate, embossed with his name and the FBI seal.

"I . . . " Her voice cracked; she cleared her throat. "I received a call from Supervisory Special Agent Adam Harper, who works in the Undercover and Sensitive Operations Unit at HQ. He asked if I would consider an overseas mission. I told him that I had removed myself from the undercover program after what happened with my last . . . ahh . . . my last mission."

Pausing for a deep breath, she continued. "SSA Harper explained that the Dutch police have a well-placed undercover constable within the animal rights extremist movement. The undercover has been missing for several days. The Dutch think he's been kidnapped or killed."

"I'm still not sure how this warranted me receiving a phone call from the director," Evans replied, lowering his eyebrows.

"After I told SSA Harper no, he pressed the issue. He assumed that it was my supervisor who wouldn't allow me to work the case, because of how things went on my last assignment. I told him that it was strictly my decision, but I don't think he believed me."

Evans stared at her for several moments, silent, then growled: "If I find out that you aren't telling me the truth, I'll bury you, Agent Montgomery. If you, in any way, manipulated this situation so you could travel to Amsterdam—"

"What?" Clarkson interrupted. "You can't allow her to accept this mission, sir. She's not ready to go back to undercover work. She needs time to recover."

"Neither you nor I has a say in this matter, Clarkson. The director of the FBI has said that the New Orleans Division will cooperate fully in this matter. That means Agent Montgomery leaves for Amsterdam next week. Do you have an undercover passport, Agent Montgomery?"

Lexie straightened and made eye contact with the SAC. "I do, sir."

"Sir, you can't let her do this," Clarkson protested. "She's not mentally ready to work undercover. I'm her supervisor. I know what she's capable of handling, and she's not ready for this assignment."

Ignoring Clarkson, Evans glared across the desk at Lexie. "Agent Montgomery, are you willing and able to take this undercover assignment?"

Lexie looked over at Clarkson. He shook his head, his eyes pleading with her.

Turning her attention back to Evans, she said, "I am, sir. I'll do my best to locate and rescue the missing constable."

"It's decided, then," replied Evans, leaning back in his chair. "I'll let the director know. You two are dismissed."

Clarkson stomped down the narrow hallway, Lexie in tow.

"Text me Adam Harper's cell phone number," he spat at her. "I want to talk to that son of a bitch."

With that, he disappeared into his office, slamming the door behind him.

2

FBI Field Office —
Louisville, Kentucky

Special Agent Blake Bennett stared at the enormous pile of documents on his desk, not sure where to start.

"Nice of you to grace us with your presence, Bennett," Squad Supervisor Harold Post said from across the desk.

"Yeah, great to be back," Blake grumbled, laying a hand on top of the pile. It looked to be in imminent danger of toppling over.

"Your file review is past due," Post said. "I need it completed and on my desk by the end of the day."

"Are you kidding me? Come on, Harold. It's my first day back."

Post's sunken cheeks reddened, drawing attention to the protruding eyes normally hidden behind his thick-rimmed eyeglasses. "I don't care. Your casework is behind, and I need that file review."

"What's the problem here? I'm back in the office for five minutes and you're jumping my shit."

Post paused, slammed his beat-up leather briefcase on

Blake's desk, and said, "Damn it, Bennett. I allowed you to let your work slide while you worked your undercover case. Now you're bitching about having to put forth a little effort when you return to real work."

"I don't mind work. I just want—"

"What? You want to continue to ride motorcycles all day and drink beer with a bunch of criminals all night, like you were doing? Do you think you deserve a commendation or something for hanging out with common thugs?"

Blake took a deep breath and blew it out before answering. "I don't expect a commendation or even a congratulations, but it would be nice for someone to at least acknowledge the work that I've done."

Post shook his head. "I'm sorry if you feel you aren't *appreciated*, but I have a squad to run and I was short an agent for an entire month. Your fellow squad members had to pull double duty while you were gone. It's my job to take care of the entire squad, not just you."

"Okay, Harold," Blake said tersely, grabbing a slab of papers that had been dislodged by the briefcase's impact and sliding them to an open spot on the desk. "I'll get you my file review by the end of the day."

"And cut your hair and shave that beard. You're an agent, not a criminal—dress the part." Snatching his briefcase off Blake's desk, Post turned and walked away.

Blake shook his head and went back to his emails. Almost immediately, his phone rang. Exhaling in frustration, he considered letting the call go to voicemail. When he saw that the incoming call was from Headquarters in Washington, DC, he decided he'd better take it.

"Bennett," he answered curtly, tucking the phone against his shoulder while typing on his keyboard.

"Agent Bennett, this is Supervisory Special Agent Adam Harper from the Undercover and Sensitive Operations Unit. Is this a good time to talk? I'd like to discuss an undercover opportunity with you."

"Yeah, sure. Call me Blake."

"Blake, I'm responsible for finding agents to fill undercover slots across the United States and overseas missions. I've been following your undercover work for the last few years. I'd like to congratulate you on your outstanding work. You've been a great asset to the Bureau."

This guy wants something, Blake thought.

"I'm in desperate need of a secondary undercover agent for a case that involves travel overseas," the voice continued.

"What kind of case and where?" Blake asked gruffly.

"The Dutch police have requested the assistance of the FBI to locate a constable who disappeared while working undercover. You'd need to travel to the Netherlands."

"Why would the Dutch police need our assistance?"

"The missing constable had infiltrated an extremist cell and was communicating with an American known to be involved in dangerous terrorist actions."

"What kind of extremist cell?"

"Are you familiar with the Animal Liberation Front?"

Abandoning his attempt to multitask, Blake shifted his phone back to his hand. "You mean like the PETA people?"

"No. PETA is child's play. These guys are extremists. The ALF is an international, clandestine resistance group that engages in various forms of illegal direct action, purportedly to save animals. They operate in cells and can be extremely dangerous and destructive."

"Look . . . what was your name again?"

"Harper. Adam Harper."

"Look, Adam. I appreciate the interest, but I may not be the right guy for this case. I've never heard of these ALF people and I just returned from a monthlong undercover gig."

"I saw that in your file. It was a biker case, right?"

"That's correct."

"I was hoping the case required you to have a rough street look."

Blake smirked briefly and ran his free hand through the beard sprouting from his chin. "Funny you should say that. My asshole supervisor just jumped my shit for not looking like an agent. I was told to shave my beard and cut my hair."

"Don't do anything yet. The scruffier the better for this assignment."

"Hey, I haven't said I'm interested yet. You said I would be the secondary undercover agent. Who's the primary?"

"Her name is Lexie Montgomery. She's worked a couple long-term cases and has extensive experience dealing with extremists and anarchists. Lexie would take the lead and teach you about the extremist culture. It'd be on-the-job training."

"When would you need me?"

"Immediately."

"That could be a problem. I've literally just returned after being gone for a month. Today is my first day in the office. I'm pretty sure my supervisor will nix this idea."

"If you agree to work this case, I'll handle your management team. This case is a priority with the FBI director."

"The director?"

"Yes. He expects an FBI team to be on the ground in the Netherlands as soon as possible. This is a big case."

"Big cases, big problems," Blake mumbled, tilting the receiver downward.

"What was that?"

"Nothing. Look, I don't have any experience dealing with animal rights extremists. Why can't the primary undercover handle the case alone?"

"I'm going to be honest with you, Blake." Adam lowered his voice, his whisper hissing across the line. "Agent Montgomery's last case was hard on her, both physically and mentally. I don't feel comfortable with her working alone, especially in a foreign country."

"What happened to her?"

"I don't want to get into that right now."

Things were crossing the line from intriguing to irksome very quickly. "Well," Blake said, endeavoring to keep his irritation at being stonewalled out of his tone, "I'm not willing to agree to the assignment without having all the facts."

The line crackled with Adam's sigh. "Let's just say that she's not mentally where I would like for her to be for this assignment."

"Wait, what are you saying? Is she mentally unstable?" Blake asked.

"I wouldn't say that, but she's definitely fragile. I need eyes on her at all times."

"So you want me to babysit her?"

"Just keep a watch over her. Make sure she keeps her mind in the game."

"If you're so concerned over her fragility, why send her?"

"Because her experience allows her to hit the ground running—she already knows the animal rights extremist culture. She's our best hope of infiltrating this group in a timely manner and finding the missing constable."

"What else do I need to know about her?" Blake asked.

"During a couple of her recent cases, Agent Montgomery became quite empathetic toward the animal rights activists."

"What exactly does that mean?"

"I really don't want to get into this with you," Adam said.

Of course you don't. Prick. "I don't care what you want," replied Blake, the bite of annoyance in his voice. "If I'm going to travel to a foreign country and put my life on the line, then I need all the facts."

"Okay. But this has to stay between the two of us." Adam was silent for a moment, then continued. "Before I was promoted, I was a case agent on a long-term undercover investigation in Los Angeles—Operation Blind Fury. Lexie was the full-time undercover agent on the case. Between you and me, she got too close to the subjects. She related a little too well to their mission."

"Are you saying she went over to the other side?"

"No, nothing like that. I'm saying that she and I had differing opinions on how the case was handled. She formed what I considered *inappropriate* relationships with some of the activists."

"What, sexually?"

"No, but by the end of the investigation Lexie seemed to care more about saving animals than the mission of the FBI."

"And you want me to go the Netherlands with this crazy chick and immerse myself in a terrorist cell to find a missing undercover officer?"

"I wouldn't call her crazy."

Blake let out a mirthless chuckle, shaking his head. "Oh, that's right, she's *fragile*."

"Look, Blake. I wouldn't ask if this weren't a dire situation. I need someone who I can trust to go with Lexie and be my eyes and ears. I've heard good things about you. I think you're the right man for the job. What do you say? Are you up for the challenge?"

"All my instincts are telling me to say no to you, Adam."

"Does that mean you'll go?"

Blake looked down at the pile of papers on his desk, then up at his bearded reflection in the computer monitor. "Let me think about it."

"I need an answer by tomorrow." The line clicked off.

3

Two days after the meeting with the SAC, Lexie and Mark entered the J. Edgar Hoover Building in Washington, DC, showed their FBI credentials at the front window, and waited for Adam Harper to come and get them.

Adam strode into the lobby, his face brightening as he caught sight of Lexie. He beelined over to embrace her. In his navy suit, starched white dress shirt, and tie, he looked like the quintessential FBI agent. "It's good to see you, Lexie."

"It's nice to see you too, Adam," she said, breaking away from the embrace. "This is my supervisor, Mark Clarkson. Mark, this is Adam Harper."

"I'm not happy about this whole situation," Mark noted bluntly as he squeezed Adam's hand harder than necessary.

"You mentioned that over the phone, Supervisor Clarkson. Let's go to the conference room so we can talk in private. We can discuss your concerns, and I can show you what we have so far on this investigation."

The three agents walked through an endless maze of poorly lit, dreary hallways.

"Is this the first time that you've been to HQ?" Adam asked Lexie.

"Yep, and hopefully the last. Feels like an insane asylum."

Adam laughed. "You're not far off."

Eventually, the winding hallways gave way to their destination: a large conference room. The colorful FBI seal hung prominently on the large center wall, behind a podium.

"I have the video conference equipment up and running for our meeting with the Dutch police," Adam said, his voice echoing in the cavernous space.

"What's the time difference between here and the Hague?" Lexie asked.

"They're six hours ahead of us," Adam said, instinctively looking at his wristwatch. "We have a little time to kill before our call, so have a seat and let's talk."

Although Adam still looked in top condition, Lexie noticed the fine lines around his eyes and the deepening wrinkles on his forehead, both accentuated by his thinning hair. He had aged since she last saw him. "First of all," he said as they took their places, "thank you for agreeing to help with this matter."

"Let's get a few things straight," Mark said, cutting him off. "First, don't ever go behind my back and get the director involved in a situation that involves my squad. You could've contacted me first. I don't appreciate getting blindsided and being called into the SAC's office to have my ass chewed out over a case that I've never been briefed on. Second, I am 100 percent against Lexie taking this assignment. You know what happened during her last undercover mission. She's not ready to be involved in another deep-cover investigation."

Before Lexie could object, Adam answered. "Sorry this came out of nowhere, Mark, but you may need to reassess your place in the chain of command here. I didn't realize that the director would contact your SAC and the shit would roll downhill, but in the end the decision is not yours to make."

"Well, Adam, down is the only direction shit can roll in the FBI, and it rolled right over top of me."

"And for that," Adam said, raising his voice by the slightest degree, "I'm truly sorry. I know Lexie has work to do on her recovery from her last assignment, but she's the only undercover agent in the FBI who has experience infiltrating animal activist extremist cells. If this situation weren't so urgent, I wouldn't even consider sending her in this soon."

"I'm sitting right here," Lexie snapped, glaring from one man to the other. "Stop talking about me like I'm not here."

Mark's face reddened as he narrowed his eyes at Lexie. Looking back at Adam, he asked, "How in the hell do you plan to ensure Lexie's safety while she's overseas? It seems to me you're risking the life of one agent in an attempt to save another."

"That's one of the topics we need to discuss with the Dutch today."

"So, in other words, you don't have anything in place?"

"The plan is fluid right now. I plan to hammer out some of the details with today's call."

"I've got a bad feeling about this," Mark said. "What time is the call?"

Adam looked down at his watch. "In ten minutes."

"I think I need a bathroom break before we begin," Lexie said. *Anything to get away from these two and their pissing contest.*

"There's one outside the door to the left," Adam said.

"Great," she said, rising and stretching her legs. "Be right back."

* * * * *

Lexie stared into the bathroom mirror. The tip of a small, thin white scar peeked out from her hairline—a reminder of her last mission.

Are you ready for this?

She inhaled deeply to calm the fluttery feeling in her stomach.

You can do this. Just breathe.

Lexie wandered back to the conference room, but before entering she heard Adam and Mark engaged in a heated conversation. She knew it was unseemly to eavesdrop, but she also knew the conversation was about her, so she chose to listen.

"This is really fucked up," Mark was saying. "The only reason we are here is because the director of the FBI basically told our SAC that Lexie *will* participate in this investigation. She couldn't have said no, even if she wanted to."

"I'm going to make sure that she's protected," Adam shot back.

"How? How are you going to protect her?"

"I have an idea."

"Tell me this great idea."

"Not yet."

"Why are you being so cryptic?" Mark asked. It sounded like he was talking through clenched teeth.

"Give me a couple of days. Everything will work out."

"You're going to get Lexie killed. Even if she's not killed, this case could mess her head up even worse than it is now."

"I'll make sure she doesn't end up with any more scars. She'll be safe."

Lexie instinctively reached up with her right hand and pulled her hair down to cover the scar.

"How can you say that?" Mark snapped. "You have no idea what could happen to her. You've never spent a day of your life undercover. I have. She'll be operating without backup in a foreign country where she's not able to speak or understand the language. The extremist culture in other countries makes the extremists in America look like the Girl Scouts. She's out of her league, and you know it."

"Maybe you should have a little faith in her," Adam said, bristling at the insult against his experience. "I think she can handle herself just fine overseas. She's a smart and innovative undercover agent. She'll make do."

"She's a remarkable undercover agent, but she's only human, and she's not ready."

"I appreciate your concern for Lexie, Clarkson," Adam replied, his voice laced with condescension, "but the bottom line is, this ship has sailed and you and I have no control over it. The director has ordered us to assist the Dutch. We need to work together to make sure Lexie completes the mission and walks away unharmed."

"That's your job, Harper. Once Lexie leaves this country, she's your responsibility. You better make sure she stays safe, or—"

"Or what?"

I'd better stop this testosterone showdown.

Lexie barged into the conference room. "What did I miss?"

Adam and Mark stood face-to-face, their noses only a few inches from one another.

"Nothing," Mark said, keeping his eyes locked on the other man's. "Adam has the video equipment up and running." Without breaking eye contact, he yanked out a chair and sat.

Adam placed the call; a few moments later, an image of two uniformed men appeared on the large screen.

"Good afternoon," the younger of the two said. "I'm Constable Connor Rowan of the National Police Force Central Unit. I guess it's actually 'good morning' for you. How is the reception?"

"Good afternoon, Constable Rowan," Adam replied. "We can hear you loud and clear. I'm Supervisory Special Agent Adam Harper. To my left is Supervisory Special Agent Mark Clarkson, and this is Special Agent Alexis Montgomery," he finished, motioning to Lexie at his right.

Constable Rowan smiled into the camera. Even sitting down, Lexie could tell the gentleman was tall. His perfectly coiffed, chestnut-brown hair gave him a youthful appearance.

"Please call me Connor. If it is acceptable to you, we would prefer to skip formalities and use first names."

"That works for us," Adam said.

Connor nodded and continued. "As you know, we are requesting assistance from the FBI to help locate a missing undercover constable. If you are not familiar with our rank system, a constable is what you would refer to as a senior police officer."

Leaning forward on his elbows, he continued. "While acting in an undercover capacity, Constable Jonas Hummel infiltrated a violent extremist cell. This is a long-term investigation, so he has been undercover nearly two years. Over the past several months, Jonas's communication with his contact agent became sporadic. At first, we were not worried. However, two weeks ago, we lost all communication with Jonas. His cell phone has been turned off or destroyed, and we have no way to track him. His last location was a makeshift activist camp outside Amsterdam. The tactical team raided the campsite but found it abandoned. There was no sign of Jonas."

"What's your plan to move forward?" Mark asked.

"We plan to use an informant to introduce your undercover agent to cell members."

"Does this informant have a criminal history?" Lexie asked. "Why is he willing to cooperate?"

"Like most good informants, he does have a criminal history. Nothing horrible, but pretty lengthy. Our informant and his brother found themselves in a bit of trouble last year and both got arrested and locked up. Robert got out early; now he provides us with information in hopes of getting his brother released."

"Do you have any other operatives working the extremists?" Adam asked.

"We have a female undercover in another region. The plan is to bring her to this area for the Gathering. Do you know what the Gathering is?"

"I've never heard of it," Mark said.

"The Gathering is an international animal rights workshop which teaches the use of illegal direct action, such as bomb making, countersurveillance, and bypassing security systems. The courses are taught in English because most Europeans speak English as a second language. The event is always held in rural, off-the-grid areas. Admission is by invitation only. Everyone is subject to search prior to being allowed into the campsite. To make things even more complicated, no cameras, tablets, or phones are allowed into the campsite."

Mark ran his hands through his hair. "I don't understand. If you have a female undercover in place, then why do you need assistance from the FBI?"

"We think that an American would be better suited for this role for two reasons. First, because America is so far away, there are very few American activists who attend the Gathering; that gives any American who does attend immediate credibility. Second, before he disappeared, Jonas had befriended an American activist by the name of Holden Graham. We don't know if it's his real name or an alias. Graham is an American expat who told Jonas that he hated what America has become; at some point he planned to return to America and cause major destruction. Jonas was assessing the terrorist threat to the United States when he went missing. It's likely that Holden Graham has information regarding the whereabouts of Jonas, and he might open up to another expat who shares his disgust for America. Graham told Jonas that he planned to attend the Gathering."

Connor took a breath and continued. "We know that the violent underground extremists and anarchists use the Gathering for recruitment purposes. The workshop provides an opportunity for them to watch and talk with activists from all over the world. We're hoping your undercover can get herself recruited and find our missing constable."

"This is ludicrous," Mark said. "You're asking a lone American FBI agent to travel to a foreign country and participate in criminal activity in the hopes of joining a violent extremist cell who may have already murdered a Dutch constable."

"Would you feel better if we sent Lexie overseas with a partner?" Adam asked, making eye contact with Mark.

"Who?" Lexie and Mark asked simultaneously.

"I have an agent in mind. He's a really good undercover agent, but he doesn't have any experience with these kind of extremists. Lexie would have to teach him."

"Why didn't you mention this before?" Mark asked.

"He hasn't agreed to the plan yet. But I'm pretty sure I can get him on board. I didn't want to mention him until it was a done deal, but since you're pushing the issue . . ."

Mark lowered his head and pinched the bridge of his nose.

"I'll handle any paperwork that needs to be done through Interpol," Connor added in an attempt to defuse the argument.

"We'll need a small support team to accompany the undercover agents," Adam said. "The team will stay far away from the camp, but in case something happens, we want agents available to assist in the response."

"That's acceptable," Connor replied. "I'll coordinate with your agent stationed in the Hague."

"The support team will be myself and a contact agent," Adam said.

Connor nodded. "We'll make sure that our female undercover attends the Gathering. If possible, we'll arrange a discreet meeting between her and your undercover agents once your team arrives in the country."

"I like that plan," Lexie said. "Another ally never hurts. Gives us another possible target for recruitment."

"I hate to sound pushy, but the Gathering starts in ten days," Connor said. "How quick can you get here?"

Adam let out a low whistle. "That's a short deadline. We'll get organized as quickly as possible."

"Will I be allowed to record conversations using a body wire?" Lexie asked. "I know some countries have restrictions on making recordings."

"You will be allowed to record any and all conversations that you deem relevant," Connor said. "However, be careful with equipment. Your bags will be thoroughly searched before you're allowed into the campsite."

The group ended the call with assurances from each side to work on establishing safety measures for the undercover agents.

Adam turned off the video system and turned to face Mark and Lexie. "Thoughts?"

"I don't like it," Mark said.

Lexie snorted. "Oh, that's shocking."

Shooting her a disapproving look, Mark directed Adam, "Tell us about this second undercover."

"His name is Blake Bennett. He's been in the FBI for fifteen years. He's almost forty but, like Lexie, looks young for his age."

"What kind of undercover work has he done?" Lexie asked.

"He's been in the undercover program six years. He's done gambling cases, motorcycle gang cases, and even posed as an international arms dealer. He's rugged and knows his way around weapons and explosives."

Lexie raised her eyebrows. That was an impressive list. "And where is he assigned?"

"He's in the Louisville Division."

"When can we meet?"

"You might not get a chance to meet in person until you're en route to the Netherlands."

"That sounds like a bad idea," Mark interjected. "What if they're incompatible? Meeting on a plane on the way to Europe is a hell of a way to find that out."

"They're both highly trained professionals," Adam replied, the faintest trace of a patronizing smirk tugging at his mouth. "I'm sure they can work it out."

"I'll need a contact agent, right?" Lexie asked.

"You will," said Adam. "Do you have anyone in mind?"

Lexie nodded. "Kate Summers," she said.

"The detective from the LAPD who was your contact agent during Operation Blind Fury?"

"Yes. The last time I spoke with her, she was still assigned to the FBI's Joint Terrorism Task Force. She would be perfect."

"But Los Angeles doesn't have any ties to this case."

"Why should that matter? Like me, she has a specialty. Unlike your male undercover agent, Kate won't require any training. She could be brought up to speed on the investigation in minutes. We know for a fact she's a highly efficient contact agent. She and I have a built-in trust from our previous work together. I can't see her department denying her the opportunity to assist a foreign country. If we're successful, the LAPD can say that they helped the Dutch police thwart a terrorist plot intended to harm Americans." She raised an eyebrow. "Come on, Adam. It's all how you write it up. Use your creative writing skills."

Adam rolled his eyes and shook his head. "I'm suddenly remembering how big a pain in the ass you can be."

"Welcome to my world," Mark said, sounding amused.

Adam sighed. "Okay. Call Kate and give her a heads-up. I'll work on everything else."

"Thanks, Adam." Rising from her seat, Lexie injected a chipper note into her voice, willing herself to feel it. "This is going to be great. The Operation Blind Fury team, back together again." A question occurred to her: "What'll we call this one?"

"How about Operation Below the Radar?" Mark suggested. "What you're going to be doing, after all."

"I like it," Lexie said. "I guess Operation Below the Radar is officially underway."

4

Three days later— Washington, DC

Lexie opened her hotel room door. Standing in the hallway was a man who, even to her trained eyes, looked nothing like an FBI agent. The wavy, dark hair that hung to his shoulders emphasized the intense blue of his eyes; his goatee, with just a hint of gray, completed his laid-back, self-confident look. "Blake Bennett," he said, extending his hand.

Lexie shook Blake's hand and opened the door wider. "I'm Lexie Montgomery. Please come in."

So far, so good. At least he doesn't look like a cop.

Blake entered and surveyed the room. "Is that our equipment?" he asked, motioning toward the bed.

Hmm, so much for social niceties.

"Yeah. The tech team did a great job. Have a seat. Can I get you something to drink?"

"Only if you have bourbon."

"Nope, sorry, just water."

"I'm good, then."

Lexie couldn't help but notice Blake's smooth, flat stomach under his black, fitted Gaslight Anthem T-shirt. "I like your shirt," she said, grabbing her bottle of water from the nightstand. "You have good taste in music."

"Thanks. Since you recognized the band, I'll assume you do too."

Blake opted to sit in the large, overstuffed chair. Lexie took a swig from her bottle of water and sat on the sofa across from him. "I can make you a cup of coffee or hot tea," she offered, motioning to a coffee maker sitting in the corner.

"I'm fine—we should get down to business," he replied, shaking his head. "I'll be honest, I don't know the first thing about animal rights extremists. I'm not sure why I got selected for this wild goose chase in the first place."

"You do know there is a missing Dutch undercover officer, right?" she asked, adding more emphasis than necessary. This guy seemed entirely too casual about his lack of experience.

"Yeah, I know. Seems like a problem for the Dutch police to handle, not the FBI."

"This is a voluntary assignment. You didn't have to come."

"The way Adam put it to me, I didn't have much of a choice. So I guess we better get started. Tell me everything I need to know about these fools."

Lexie bristled. "Well, first of all, they're *not* fools. Most animal and environmental activists are well-educated and extremely intelligent."

"Whoa, lighten up," Blake said, raising his hands. "I didn't mean to insult your *friends*."

"What the fuck does that mean?"

"I've heard that you have a soft spot for these activists."

"Who told you that? Did Adam say something to you?"

"It doesn't matter who said it. Is it true?"

Lexie leaned back and crossed her arms. "It's not true. Just because I understand the activists doesn't mean I have a soft spot for them. Adam never took the time to learn and truly understand their ideology, so he assumes that someone who understands them has some kind of weakness when it comes to investigating them. I don't have a problem arresting subjects who are guilty of committing crimes. I do have a problem targeting people who haven't done anything wrong."

"Fair enough," he conceded, nodding—if not in apology, at least in acknowledgment of her point. "Give me the CliffsNotes version of the animal rights movement and how you see this unfolding overseas."

"First of all, animal rights goes beyond simply a philosophy. It's a social movement. Animal activists believe that nonhuman animals were not put on this planet for human use. They believe that animals deserve to live their lives free from suffering and exploitation. For them, this means no consuming meat or dairy, no wearing leather, and no going to circuses and zoos. Quite simply, if it has a face, we don't eat, drink, or wear it."

"Wait," Blake interjected, brow creasing as he leaned forward. "You said *we*. You consider yourself one of them?"

"No," Lexie said hastily, cursing herself for the loose word choice. "I don't. Stop putting words in my mouth."

"You said it, not me."

"I *meant* because I'm vegan. You'll be vegan too for this assignment, so you better get familiar."

"Isn't it about the same as being a vegetarian?" Blake asked.

"Veganism goes beyond diet. It's an avenue of resistance that wages war on capitalism as well. The goal is to obtain a self-sustainable world in which humans don't rely on animals for a food source."

"If it's all so peaceful, what makes the activists resort to criminal behavior?"

"Frustration, mainly. I think most of the activists start out with good intentions, trying to rescue suffering animals. They try to bring about change using legal means, but the wheels of justice are slow-moving, so they get more aggressive. Activists become members of the Animal Liberation Front—ALF—an international clandestine resistance that uses illegal direct action to get the attention of animal abusers by removing animals from laboratories and farms and destroying facilities and equipment."

Blake leaned farther forward, resting his elbows on his knees. This was where things got interesting for him, evidently. "Do they resort to murder? This missing constable, do you think he's dead?"

Lexie stared at the stained, patterned carpet. "I think he may be dead, but his family and the police need to know for sure."

"I agree." He hesitated, then added, "Look, this shit is

all new to me. I didn't mean to be a dick about the subject matter."

She waved her hand dismissively. "I'll teach you what you need to know, but don't underestimate the cell members. They take their security culture and commitment to the movement very seriously and can be manipulative and dangerous." Rising from her chair, she gestured at the bed. "Want to see our equipment?"

The two walked over and surveyed the neatly organized gear. Lexie continued, "We needed equipment that we could carry onboard an airplane and then smuggle into the campsite. Since everyone at the camp will be environmentally conscious, the tech agents provided us with two concealed recorders, one in a water bottle and the other in a travel mug."

"I wondered why Adam needed my shoe size," Blake said, picking up a well-worn boot.

"Yeah, my boots were too small to use. Check it out," Lexie said, picking up the other shoe. "One boot has a compartment for a small cell phone and the other for a battery. The boots are vegan as well."

"Nice touch, making them look worn out."

Dropping the boot back on the bed with a muted *thump*, Lexie said, "I hope you don't mind, but I elected to use my own camping equipment. I'm familiar with the tent assembly, and nothing screams *law enforcement* like showing up with brand-new, shiny toys."

"Good thinking. So you're a camper?"

"I enjoy hiking and backpacking. What about you?"

"Not so much. I like a warm, comfy bed, preferably near a good restaurant and a bar."

Lexie's eyes widened. *Are you* kidding *me?*

"Don't worry," Blake added. "I've camped. It's just not one of my favorite things to do."

"I get it."

Fiddling with the boot in his hands, her colleague suddenly asked, "Are you married?"

"What?"

"Married. Yes or no? It's not a difficult question."

"You switched gears on me."

"Since we're gonna be spending so much time together, maybe we should get to know one another."

Maybe I'm being too defensive. "You're right. No, I'm not married. You?"

"Divorced."

"What about children?" Lexie asked.

"I have a fourteen-year-old daughter."

"I detect a little bit of a Southern twang in your voice, but I can't place it," she said.

"I grew up in Kentucky," replied Blake. "I've bounced around with the Bureau, and I've recently been transferred to the Louisville Division."

"So you made it home."

"I did. What about you?"

"I grew up in Mobile and was assigned to the New Orleans Division out of the Academy. I'm only two hours from Mobile, so I can see my family whenever I want."

"That's good. I wasn't as lucky. My first office was New York."

"Yikes. A Kentucky boy in New York."

"To complicate the problem, I had a very unhappy wife and a young daughter. Trying to make ends meet on a new agent's salary was pretty stressful."

"Is that what ended your marriage?"

Blake shifted in his chair and ran his hands through his hair. "It was one of the factors. Let's talk about you. How long have you been in the Bureau?"

Lexie suppressed a snort. *Not so talkative when the shoe is on the other foot.* "Nine years. You?"

"Fifteen years. You must've come in young if you've already done nine years. You don't look old enough to be an agent."

"I get that a lot. That's part of the reason why I'm good at this kind of case. I don't look my age. I'm thirty-three."

Blake grinned. "You don't look thirty-three. Me, on the other hand, the gray in my goatee gives me away."

"You don't have that much gray. By the way, how do you get away with the long hair? Not exactly clean-cut FBI material."

"I just came off an undercover assignment where I was working a biker gang that was running drugs and illegal firearms across state lines."

"How'd it go?"

"We ended up arresting seven gang members, including the leader. Not to mention the seizure of tens of thousands of dollars in money and motorcycles."

"That's fantastic. Congratulations."

He shrugged. "It got me exactly zero respect in my office. You know how it is."

Lexie nodded. "I do. So, how old are *you*?"

"You changed the subject."

"You're avoiding the question," she shot back, smirking.

"This is the last year that I can say that I'm in my thirties."

"You don't look thirty-nine."

A smirk to match her own developed on his face. "Now you're just flirting with me."

Lexie felt heat rush to her cheeks.

Blake laughed. "You're blushing."

"What? I didn't blush."

"You sure as hell did. Say, are you hungry? Let's finish this conversation over dinner. I missed lunch, and I'm starving."

The way he shot from subject to subject without any sort of transition was disorienting, and Lexie didn't like being disoriented—but at least they'd left the topic of flirting behind. "Dinner sounds good," Lexie said, willing the red to leave her face. "You'll find that I'm almost always hungry."

Grinning, Blake replied, "We're going to get along just fine."

* * * * *

Lexie and Blake walked to a nearby restaurant, selected a quiet corner table, and perused the menu.

"So, how do you think you're going to do as a vegan?" Lexie asked.

"I have no idea. I'm going to follow your lead when it comes to food."

"Always remember, nothing with a face."

"Does a cheeseburger have a face? Just kidding," he added at the expression on her face.

The server arrived with a pad in hand. "What can I get you?"

Lexie smiled at the server. "I'll have the shrimp wrap with fries."

"Bring me the half-pound burger, loaded," Blake said.

"How would you like your burger cooked?"

"Medium well, please."

"I'll get this order right in."

Lexie glared at Blake as their server walked off.

"What? We're not vegan yet." He smirked and jabbed at her with an index finger. "Besides, the last time I checked, shrimp had faces. Ugly little crustacean faces, but still faces."

She laughed. "Touché."

"Tell me about your last assignment. Adam said you had a pretty rough time."

Lexie picked up her water glass and took a sip. "I don't want to talk about it."

"That bad?"

"Worse."

"Are you sure you're up for *this* assignment?" he asked, eyebrows drawing together in concern.

Doing her best to keep her voice steady, she asked, "Did Adam tell you to ask me that question?"

"No, I'm asking for myself. You and I are getting ready

to travel overseas together and possibly end up in a hornets' nest. I want to make sure the person I'm working with is stable."

Lexie slammed down her glass, sloshing water over the rim. "Screw you. If I weren't stable, then I wouldn't be here. I could be asking you the same question. I don't know the first thing about you either, and you seem pretty damn unqualified for this assignment if you ask—"

"What do you want to know?" he cut her off.

Leaning across the table, she asked, forcing her voice down to a loud whisper, "Why did you agree to this mission? It seems pretty far out of your wheelhouse."

"I told you, Adam asked me to do it and it seemed like a great opportunity to work overseas. Why are you so paranoid?"

"Let's just say Adam and I don't always see eye to eye when it comes to cases."

"You don't trust Adam, therefore you don't trust me?"

"I don't *know* you."

"And I don't know you either," he hissed back. "Isn't that what the next few days are for? Building trust?" Pulling himself a few inches further away from her face, he continued, "Lexie, I don't know any of the details, but I know that your last case was pretty traumatic. I'm not here to judge you. I know undercover work is a bitch. I've been down the same road. Like it or not, you and I are stuck with one another, and we need to make the best of the situation."

Lexie leaned back in her chair and cocked her head to the side. *It's not worth it,* she thought to herself. *He's right about that if nothing else. You're stuck with him.*

Blowing out a long breath, she said, "I agree. I think we got off on the wrong foot. Let's start over."

"Sounds good to me."

They sat in silence for a while. Finally, Blake asked, "Since we've got some time, would you like to hear about my first undercover operation? It might make you feel better about your last case."

"I would."

He clapped his hands together and leaned back. "So, it's a Friday night and I'm at my desk in the squad area gathering up all my stuff, getting ready to face that awful New York commute. I'm literally just standing up to leave when two guys from the gang squad rush in and say they need me to do an undercover buy and it needs to happen tonight.

"Now, I'd just gotten back from undercover school and knew this really wasn't how these things were supposed to go. They'd taught us there's supposed to be a planning and preparation phase and then the whole thing's supposed to be run up the chain to be signed by management. But here I was, young and inexperienced, and I knew if I turned them down or asked too many questions, word would get around the office and no one would ask me to do UC work. So I told them I'd be glad to help."

Lexie nodded.

Blake paused to take a sip of water, then continued. "They said they'd just talked with their snitch and he'd set up a deal to buy a crate full of fully automatic AR-15s. This was red flag number one—they'd let the snitch make the deal on his own. They told me they'd heard I knew a lot about guns and could put on a good show of examining them at the buy to make sure they were fully functional, just like anyone purchasing them off the street would. So now they're stroking me, and I'm letting myself fall for it because I want to do some real UC work.

"They hand me $5,000 in hundreds and say, 'Let's go meet the snitch.' We went to the parking garage and the three of us got into the car. At this point, I asked if the rest of the backup team would be meeting us at another location. One of them replied that they'd used this snitch before against the same gang with no problems, so the two of them would handle the backup duties. That was red flag number two. Only two guys for backup for a gun buy with a New York gang."

"Oh no," Lexie said. "I have a feeling this is gonna go bad."

"So we cross the bridge and turn into the docks in Jersey. It's starting to get dark and this whole thing is starting to feel like a really bad idea. But every new undercover has been there. You want to work and you want people to ask you to work. If you start to protest too much, no one will ask you to work for them."

"Exactly."

"We pull into a secluded area. We drive up to the snitch's car, which is a tinted-out black Firebird straight from *Smokey and the Bandit*. As soon as we stop, the snitch bails out of his car, runs to our car, and dives into the backseat like he's being chased by hornets. He sits up and says, 'So you think anyone saw me?'

"I can see this guy is tweaking. His eyes are shining in the New Jersey moonlight and both his knees are bouncing like he's going to come apart at the seams. He looks at me and asks me if I know about guns. I reply that I do. He says, 'Okay, let's do this thing.'

"Red flag number three. These guys are letting the snitch run the show . . . and he's high on meth."

Lexie's jaw dropped open as she shook her head back and forth.

"I know, I know. Just wait, it gets worse. Finally, the two agents in the front seat turn around and ask the snitch a few questions about where and when this meet will take place. I'm listening to every detail because I haven't been told shit. The meet is set to take place just a couple of miles away in the dock area around a bunch of cargo crates. There'll be three gang guys transporting the crate of guns. We'll meet with them. I'll verify the guns are as represented. We pay them, load them into the snitch's car, and everyone goes their own way."

Wow, either this guy has some serious balls or he's plain crazy.

Blake smirked. "I see you shaking your head over there. What? Nice, simple, easy plan, right?"

"I'm counting how many ways this plan can go wrong," Lexie replied.

"I'm getting to that. At this point, I tell everyone that I have a gun in my boot in case things go south. Immediately they all jump my shit and say these guys always pat everyone down before they do a deal. Okay, good to know. It might have been something they wanted to mention earlier." Blake rolled his eyes. "So, I remove my gun and one of the agents hands me a sweater that looks like it's been stolen from Mister Rogers's closet. My comment was something like, 'What the fuck is this?' They tell me to put it on as it has recording equipment sewed into it. I can record the meeting even though they've patted me down. Now we're to red flag number four. While the idea is sound, how in the hell can I look natural? I'm supposed to be a streetwise gun guy, but the vest makes me look like I just escaped from a retirement home."

"No way," Lexie said. "What did you do?"

"I put it on, get into the snitch's car, and we go to the meet. Of course, when we arrive, there are seven gang guys standing around instead of the three. The last time I counted, I've got two FBI guys about four hundred yards away to protect me from seven gangbangers if things go bad. Not an ideal situation, but at this point I just want to get it over with and get the hell out of there.

"The actual meet seems to go surprisingly well. They do their pat-downs. I pretend to object. We do the usual back-and-forth on the price of the guns, even though every-one knows the price has been agreed on. I take my time examining the guns, which are, in fact, fully automatic and fully functional AR-15s."

Lexie leaned forward, absorbed in the story; the back-ground chatter of the restaurant had faded away into nothingness.

"We're about to close the deal when one of the gang guys pulls a large wand out of his back pocket. It looks like one of those wands the TSA uses on you at the airport. He comes over to me and waves the wand down my body, and the thing lights up like a frickin' Christmas tree. Bells and whistles are going off like I'm in a parade. I'd seen these things in spy shops before but didn't know gang-bangers used them. They can detect all kinds of recording equipment."

Lexie put her fingers to her parted lips.

"There it is," Blake said, pointing to Lexie. "That *oh shit* look on your face. Welcome to my world. You can imagine my pucker factor at this point. Now I've got fourteen hands on me, feeling me up and down for recording equipment. I have to hand it to the vest people; try as they might, those bangers couldn't feel any equipment. So now they order me to disrobe.

"What in the hell do I do now? I've been in my share of fights and like to think I'm a pretty tough guy, but with these odds, there's no way things go well for me if I start something. I look at the snitch and he's just standing there like nothing out of the ordinary is happening. I know I'll get no help from him. So I strip down to my boxers. Now, they're all staring me up and down, trying to figure out where the recording equipment is."

"What did you do?"

"I'm trying to think ahead. I usually think pretty fast on my feet, but I can't think of a lie I can spin to justify what's happening here. I do know between the New Jersey night and the adrenaline flowing through my veins, I'm start-ing to shake. So I use that and ask if I can at least put my boots back on. They wand my boots and nothing happens, so they throw them to me—but in return, they tell me to remove my boxers."

Unable to suppress her emotion, Lexie gasped, then laughed at her own outburst.

"And now, Miss Lexie, your smile returns. You're laughing, but this is some serious shit. As you probably guessed, between the cold night and being scared shitless, there's a little shrinkage happening here. But that's the least of my worries at this point."

"Just so I'm clear," Lexie said. "You're standing at the New Jersey docks, surrounded by gangbangers and fully automatic rifles, wearing nothing but a smile and a pair of boots? That's quite an image. I'm horrified and fascinated at the same time."

"That about sums it up. I'm sure my backup guys don't even see me at this point, so there'll be no cavalry coming to save my lily-white ass. I can see from their faces they're starting to figure out that if the recorder isn't on my body, that leaves only my clothes. All at once, they turn away from me and start walking toward the pile of clothes with wand in hand. As soon as they turn to wand the clothes, I take off like a cat with his tail on fire. And I run, and I run, and I run, until my legs and lungs won't carry me any further."

"Holy shit," Lexie said, trying and failing to suppress her laughter. "Did they catch you?"

"Darlin', Usain Bolt couldn't have caught me that night. I was so full of adrenaline I must have run for three miles before slowing down. After the adrenaline wore off, however, I was reminded of why my fifth-grade physical education teacher required all the boys to purchase a jock before they attended class. There was a whole lot of shakin' going on down below, if you know what I mean. I had a stomachache for a week."

Lexie laughed softly, then harder, and then uncontrollably, until she almost fell off her chair. Once she'd recovered, she asked, "Is that all true, or did you just make it up to make me feel better?"

"How could I ever make that shit up? It's not like you'll ever see an FBI agent do that on TV or in the movies."

"Oh my, I hope not," Lexie said, choking back tears.

The server arrived with the entrees. "Anything else I can get you?" she asked, looking at a wheezing Lexie in bemusement.

Blake grinned. "I think we're good."

"I'll be back to check on you in a little while. Enjoy." She left, shooting a look back at the two of them before vanishing into the kitchen.

Blake could barely get his mouth around the huge burger. He took a bite, then wiped the grease from his chin. "Well, that's delicious. How's your wrap?"

Lexie finished chewing before answering. "It's really good. Great choice of restaurant."

Blake leaned forward so she could hear him better. "So, when it comes to you and me, what's our legend? Are we a couple or just two friends traveling together? How do you want to play it?"

The transition back to business took Lexie a few seconds. After some consideration, she said, "Since you don't know a lot about the activist culture, it might make more sense for us to be a couple, but newly dating. You're trying to assimilate into my world. That way, if you get tripped up on something, you can fall back on the fact that you're new to the lifestyle."

"Sounds like a good plan," Blake said. "In case we need it, I had the FBI undercover unit set up a fake company and show me as the owner. It might come in handy if anyone asks where I work."

"What kind of company?"

"A printing equipment and supply business," he said. "After dinner, we'll work on our legend. When we met, how we met, and how long we've been dating." He picked up his burger and took another bite.

"Enjoy that burger, dude," Lexie said through a mouthful of her wrap. "Your meat-eating days are numbered."

5

The next morning

Waiting for Kate, Lexie felt like a little girl on the first day of school. It had been so long since she'd seen her old friend.

Lexie spotted Kate as soon as she entered the hotel lobby, trailing a bell captain who pushed a jangling luggage cart piled with her bags to the registration desk. Immediately, the FBI agent ran over and threw her arms around her dear friend.

"I've missed you so much!" Lexie exclaimed.

"Good morning to you too," Kate replied, laughing.

Lexie stepped back to take a good look at her friend's dark hair and smooth skin. "You look fantastic. Love your new hairstyle."

"Thank you," Kate said. "It's so good to see you."

"How was the red-eye?"

"It was good, but I'm starving."

"Let's get you checked in and go to breakfast."

They found a retro diner not far from their hotel. Seated in a booth nestled against the wall, Lexie examined the daily specials written on the whiteboard. The smell of freshly brewed coffee and bacon filled the air.

After they placed their orders, Kate leaned forward, crossed her arms, and placed them on the table. "Are you sure you're up for this assignment, Lex?"

Lexie returned the laminated menu to the holder on the end of the table, then took a swig of ice water from a red, pebbled tumbler. "That seems to be the question everyone is asking these days. If I weren't ready, then I wouldn't be doing it. I have to get back on the horse at some point."

"Do you? Undercover work is a voluntary assignment. You don't have to go back to it."

"I know, but this case is special."

"Is that the only reason you're accepting this assignment?" Kate asked.

"What do you mean?"

Lowering her voice, Kate chided, "Come on, Lex, it's me you're talking to. I know what happened to you in South Carolina."

Lexie sighed. "My therapist thinks I may be trying to atone for Logan's death."

"Are you?"

"Maybe, but it's not the only reason."

Reaching across the table, Kate placed her hand on top of her friend's. "It wasn't your fault, Lexie. What happened to Logan was a tragedy, but you can't continue to blame yourself. And you can't take unnecessary risks to try to right some kind of cosmic wrong. You need to think of yourself and your well-being. If you're not 100 percent sure you can do this, then there's no shame in dropping out."

"I can't drop out, Kate. That's the problem. There's no one else who can do this case."

"I have trouble believing that there isn't another person, either from the FBI or some other country, who can take on this mission. What about the secondary agent who's going with you?"

"Blake? He's going along as backup. He doesn't have the background in the movement to do the assignment alone."

Kate withdrew her hand and settled back into her chair. "As your contact agent, you know I had to ask."

Lexie nodded gratefully. "I know. I appreciate your concern, but I can do this, Kate."

"I know you can. But I'll be there if for any reason you need to be pulled out. You let me know and I'll send in the cavalry to get you."

"I know you will. That's why I wanted you as my contact agent. I'm sure you heard that the contact agent situation in my last case wasn't ideal."

"That's one way of putting it," Kate said, shaking her head. "I heard you didn't *have* a contact agent. What the hell were you thinking operating solo?"

"I wasn't thinking. That was the problem."

"Well, you have one for this case. I'll be right there arguing with Adam. Just like old times."

Chuckling, Lexie leaned back in her chair. "That's the other reason I wanted you. You see through Adam's bullshit."

"You better believe it." After a few moments of silence, Kate said, "So, tell me about this Blake guy. What's he like?"

Lexie shrugged. "Jury's still out. He seems competent, but also a little cocky."

"Really? A cocky male FBI agent?"

Both women laughed.

"I know. Hard to believe, right?" Sobering, Lexie confided, "To be honest, I'm a little worried about his demeanor. He's used to working biker gangs, so he's rough around the edges. He doesn't seem very empathetic toward the animal rights movement. I'm not sure he's a good fit for the vegan activist culture." Smirking, she added, "On the bright side, he may fit in well with the anarchists."

"Do you think you can smooth out the rough edges?"

"I hope so. He's eager to meet you. I would've invited him for breakfast, but I was selfish and wanted some girl time."

"I'm glad. We needed some time to catch up."

After the two old friends had eaten their fill and downed several cups of coffee, they made their way back to the hotel.

"You ready to meet Blake?" Lexie asked.

"I am."

Blake opened the door to his room and invited the two women in.

"Blake, this is Kate Summers. Kate, this is Blake Bennett."

Blake extended a hand to Kate. "Nice to meet you. I have some coffee made. Either of you want a cup?"

Lexie and Kate looked at one another and grinned. "We just drank a pot each," Lexie replied. "But thanks."

Letting out a long whistle, Blake motioned toward his couch. "Have a seat."

While Blake poured a cup of coffee for himself, Kate tilted her head and made a gesture toward him with her eyes. Lexie rolled her eyes and shrugged her shoulders. *Yes, he's good looking. And?*

Blake sat down in the big chair across from the two female agents. "So, you're from LAPD?" he asked Kate.

"I am," she replied. "Been with the department seventeen years."

"You don't look old enough to have seventeen years under your belt," he said with a slight Southern lilt.

"Unfortunately, I am."

"You must've been a baby when you entered on duty."

"I was." Kate stopped short of giving him any further clues. Lexie snorted, amused. Kate's slender build and flawless, silky skin concealed her age. Her flowing dark hair showed no signs of gray. Lexie knew her friend would turn forty at the end of the year, but she had no intention of disclosing that information to Blake.

After the getting-acquainted time ended, Kate got down to business. "Blake, Lexie and I have a history together, but I'm your contact agent as well. I understand the seriousness of my assignment and I want you to know that I will do everything in my power to keep the two of you safe and protected. If for any reason you feel that your safety has been compromised, all you have to do is let me know. I'll make sure that you're both extracted. My sole responsibility is your safety and well-being. I don't answer to the FBI, so I'm not afraid to make the hard decisions if they need to be made."

"Thank you. I appreciate your dedication to the case."

"Not to the case," she corrected, emphasizing her words carefully. "To you and to Lexie."

"I understand."

"Excellent." She rubbed at her eyes. "Well, I think that all-night flight finally caught up with me. If you guys will excuse me," she said, rising from the sofa, "I'm in need of a nap and a shower. I'm looking forward to working with you, Blake."

"Me too," he said as he walked her to the door. "And thanks again for dropping everything and joining us on this little adventure."

After Kate had left, Blake turned to Lexie. "She takes her contact agent role very seriously."

"She does. Which is good for us. She'll do all she can to make sure we're safe."

"Is she married?"

Lexie raised her eyebrows. "Are you interested?"

"What? No," he protested, shaking his head. "I just like to know all I can about the people who hold my fate in their hands. I asked the same of you, remember?"

Lexie rolled her eyes and shook her head in turn. "She's divorced, but she has a boyfriend."

"Wanna take a walk?" Blake asked suddenly, their conversation apparently closed. "I need a decent cup of coffee. This hotel coffee sucks."

"Sure, I could use another cup."

"Oh, I don't know about that."

"What?"

"You've been talking a mile a minute."

Lexie dropped her head, feeling her cheeks start to flush.

"I'm just kidding," Blake said, chuckling. "You're cute

when you've had too much coffee. Besides, I get more info out of you once you're caffeinated."

"So you use coffee to get me caffeinated, then pump me for information."

"Yep. Coffee seems to work on you like truth serum." Blake's two rows of perfectly straight, pearly white teeth flashed when he smiled. He gathered his wallet and hotel key.

"What're you thinking?" he asked when he turned back to look at her, cocking his head. "You were looking at me funny."

"You have a nice smile, Blake Bennett," Lexie said with a smile of her own.

Blake grinned. "Why thank you, Lexie Montgomery."

5

The next morning

The two women spent the eight-hour flight to the Hague sandwiched between Blake and Adam, who'd seized the end seats. Blake enjoyed the feel of Lexie's head on his shoulder as she slept. It had been a long time since he'd been in a relationship; an undercover girlfriend was better than none.

He felt Lexie twitch. A small moan escaped her throat. When her breathing became irregular and choked, he opted to wake her. "Lexie," he said, gently shaking her. "Lexie, wake up."

Lexie jerked, then straightened up. She wiped the corner of her mouth and looked around. "What happened?"

"Are you okay?"

"I think so." Reaching for her throat and swallowing hard, Lexie said, "Someone was choking me."

"Who?"

"Someone from the past."

"Do you want to talk about it?"

She shook her head. "I don't remember much about it.

He had dirty fingernails, yellow teeth . . . and a hell of a stare. He was choking me, but that's all I remember."

"I hate nightmares," Blake said. "When I have a bad one, it affects my whole day."

Lexie nodded. "Sorry I fell asleep on you."

"No worries. Your snoring kept me awake so I could finish my book."

"Did I snore?"

Blake laughed. "No, I'm just kidding. You *did* mutter something about Blake being the best partner ever."

Rolling her eyes, she punched his shoulder. "Now I know you're lying."

Grinning, he motioned toward Kate and Adam. "Those two have been asleep nearly the whole trip. I wish I could sleep on a plane."

"You can't?"

"No. I'm a light sleeper. Everything wakes me up."

"I usually am too, but I didn't seem to have any problems on this trip."

After a few moments of slightly uneasy silence, Blake decided to change gears. "I have contraband," he whispered, bending over and pulling his backpack from under the seat in front of him. He rummaged around in it and pulled out a bag of M&Ms. "After the crash course in veganism you gave me, I know these are against the rules. Guess that means we need to eat them before we land. Want some?"

"Well," she said, "since we have to get rid of the evidence, I can't leave you hanging." She put down her raggedy paperback and dug out a handful of M&Ms.

"What're you reading?" Blake asked, his mouth full of candy.

"*The Prince of Tides* by Pat Conroy," she said as she showed him the worn-out cover. "It's my favorite book. I carry it with me almost everywhere I go. It's kind of a security blanket. I didn't have it with me on my last case in South Carolina, and things went bad. I wasn't taking any chances this time."

"Kind of a good-luck charm?"

Lexie smiled. "Yeah. Kind of."

Blake reached over and rubbed the tattered cover of the book. "Well, maybe it'll bring us both luck."

* * * * *

Adam and Kate were traveling overtly, both carrying surveillance equipment in their bags. Since every country had its share of airport personnel on the take, Blake and Lexie waited until everyone else was off to deplane. The more distance between them and Adam and Kate at the customs checkpoint, the better.

Blake's huge backpack rolled off the baggage carrier first, with Lexie's not far behind. The two walked to the customs checkpoint together and handed their alias passports to the customs officer.

Looking up with tired eyes, the officer droned in a monotone, "What is the purpose of your travel?"

Blake blurted out "Work" at the same time that Lexie said "Vacation."

Oh, shit, Blake thought. *Of all the simple things, we forgot to get our initial story straight. Lexie is going to think I'm completely incompetent.*

The customs officer put down the two passports and glared at the couple. "Are you traveling together?"

"We are," Lexie said. "We're on vacation, but I'm also a travel writer. I'm planning to write an article about the Netherlands, so our trip is both vacation and work."

Blake's heart palpitated as the customs officer scrutinized their passports.

"Where are you staying?"

"The Hague," Blake answered.

"What hotel?"

"We don't have one yet," he said. "We figured we would find a hotel once we arrived."

"What are you carrying in your packs?"

"Clothes, sleeping bags, some camping supplies, and a tent," Lexie answered. "We plan to camp while we're here."

His eyes narrowing further, the officer said, "Your travel companion said you were looking for a hotel. Are you staying in a hotel or camping?"

"Both," Lexie said. "We plan to stay in a few hotels along the way, but mostly camp to save money. We're on a tight budget."

The customs officer held the two passports up and carefully compared the photographs to the two persons standing in front of him. He put the documents on the counter and forcefully stamped each of them.

"Enjoy your stay."

"Thank you," Blake and Lexie said in unison.

With their first test barely passed, they walked out of the airport.

"Work? Really?" Lexie hissed as they emerged into the Dutch air.

"I wasn't thinking," Blake said defensively. "Hey, you dropped the ball too. We discussed every aspect of this case *except* why we're in the country."

"Vacation works for me," Lexie said, shifting her bag on her shoulders.

"Okay," he said, scanning the surroundings for their ride. "Vacation it is."

* * * * *

Supervisory Special Agent Jack Webster waited for Blake and Lexie in a black van parked outside the customs area. He hopped out of the driver's seat when he saw the two emerge from the building.

"I'm Jack Webster. You must be Lexie and Blake." He threw their bags into the hatch and hauled the van door open. Adam and Kate were waiting inside.

"Welcome to the Hague," Jack continued as he helped Lexie get her backpack into the van. "I'm sure you guys are tired, so I'll take you to your hotel. You can have the rest of the day to relax and unwind from the trip. We're meeting with Constable Rowan and Sergeant Eldridge tomorrow morning at ten." Sliding into the driver's seat, he took a moment to observe all four of his passengers through the rearview mirror. "They're good investigators and nice guys.

I think you'll enjoy working with them. We're meeting at a covert location to avoid having to deal with the security nightmare at the US embassy."

"Sounds good," Adam said. "Do you have a particular timeline in mind?"

Gunning the motor, Jack pulled out into the departing traffic. "Lexie and Blake will leave here the day after tomorrow and travel to Amsterdam. That's where they'll meet the informant. On Thursday, the three of them will move to the Gathering camp location while the support team moves to a nearby town. Because of the rural area, the team will be a half-hour drive from where Lexie and Blake will be staying. We'll know more tomorrow when we meet with our Dutch counterparts."

"Lotta moving parts," Kate said.

"I know," Jack replied. "The plan has to remain fluid— circumstances can turn on a dime."

Blake observed the broad avenues, parks, and public gardens through the van window as they drove past buildings dating from the fifteen to the eighteenth century. "This is a beautiful country," he said. "Wish we were vacationing for real. How do you like living here?"

"I love it here. It's been a great experience." A moment later, Jack directed his charges, "If you look out the window, you'll see we are now entering the Hague, which is the seat of the cabinet of the Netherlands, the States General, the Supreme Court, and the Council of State. Most of the foreign embassies are located here, including ours."

"The architecture is gorgeous," Lexie said.

"I've booked you guys into the Hotel Novotel Den Haag

City Centre. It's a nice hotel, and it's walking distance to the lake and museums."

"How about food?" Blake asked.

Lexie giggled. Her colleague smiled at her and shrugged. "You were wondering too," he whispered.

"There are plenty of great restaurants surrounding your hotel as well," Jack assured them.

Through the mirror, he watched Blake watch Lexie. The man was staring almost unabashedly. It was a wonder she didn't notice. It wasn't Jack's job to say anything; he just drove the van. *Still,* he thought to himself, *he'd better be careful. An undercover mission isn't the best time for personal affairs.*

7

The next morning, Jack drove the FBI team out of the city and through the countryside. He pulled up to a nondescript industrial-looking building and pushed the intercom button.

A voice answered in Dutch. *"Hoe kan ik u helpen?"*

"Goedemorgen. Jack Webster to see Connor Rowan."

"Please come in," the voice answered, this time in English.

"It amazes me how many people speak English," Lexie said. "I wish I could speak a second language. How did you learn Dutch, Jack?"

"My maternal grandmother was Dutch, so I grew up speaking both languages."

The giant gate opened and allowed access into the parking lot. The group was greeted at the front door by a young, blonde woman and escorted to a conference room. As the FBI team entered, the two Dutch officers within stood.

Jack took over the introductions. "Gentlemen, this is the FBI team: Supervisory Special Agent Adam Harper,

Special Agent Lexie Montgomery, Special Agent Blake Bennett, and Task Force Agent Kate Summers."

"Very nice to meet you. I'm Constable Connor Rowan, and this is Sergeant Benjamin Eldridge," the taller of the two Dutch agents said, motioning toward his coworker. Sergeant Eldridge's thick shock of silver hair and matching eyebrows were a contrast to his espresso-colored eyes.

"We have provided coffee and traditional Dutch pastries," Connor said as the group shook hands. "Please help yourselves." Lexie and Kate each took a cookie that resembled a small waffle before finding a seat at the table. The men elected to try a flaky, log-shaped pastry.

"In case you are unfamiliar with our pastries, the ladies have stroopwafels," said Connor, indicating the chewy cookies with a sticky syrup filling in the middle. "The stroopwafel is traditionally placed on top of your coffee cup. The heat from the coffee will soften the cookie and the filling will melt. It's delicious. I see the gentlemen decided to try banketstaaf, which is a puff pastry shell with almond paste filling."

Lexie's eye widened. "That sounds delicious. I might have to try the bank . . . a . . . st . . . how did you say it?"

"Banketstaaf."

"That one," she said, a sardonic grin crooking her mouth.

"She has a bit of a sweet tooth," Kate said.

Shrugging, Lexie dug into her pastry. "Guilty as charged."

"I like a woman who likes to eat," Connor said, laughing.

"Well, you're gonna love Lexie," replied Adam.

"Hey, hey, hey," she protested through a mouthful of stroopwafel, "I don't eat that much."

"You're so tiny," Connor said. "I can't believe you eat more than a small bird."

"A pterodactyl, maybe," scoffed Adam.

Lexie shook her head. "I get no respect from these guys."

After the group shared a few more laughs, Connor formally started the meeting.

"We would like to start by saying thank you to the FBI for sending such a large contingent to help with our investigation. Jonas Hummel's family deserves to know what has happened to him." Connor looked down and cleared his throat before continuing. "Jonas isn't simply my coworker, he is also my dear friend. We are in your debt."

"We're happy to help," Adam said. "Plus, this gives us an opportunity to determine if this scenario poses a terrorist threat to the United States."

Sergeant Eldridge took over for Connor, clearing his throat. "Hello, everyone. I'm Ben. I've been assisting Connor with the investigation from the start. I think he told you in the conference call that we have an informant who has agreed to help with this matter. His name is Robert, and I spoke with him yesterday. He is willing to introduce Lexie and Blake to his old girlfriend, Jade Acker. We know that Jade is active in the underground movement, but we haven't been able to catch her doing anything illegal. We believe that Jade is friends with Holden Graham, the American activist."

"As of now, a top priority is to fully identify Holden Graham," Adam said. "Especially since your intelligence indicated that Graham may be planning a terrorist attack on US soil."

Everyone in the room nodded.

"Can we trust Robert?" Blake asked.

"He's been reliable so far, and he has a great deal riding on his level of cooperation," Ben replied. "We've arranged for him to meet you and Lexie in Amsterdam. You'll have a day and a half together to come up with your backstory; then the three of you will attend the Gathering and he will make the introductions."

Finishing her first pastry, Lexie surreptitiously reached for a second. "How will we get to Amsterdam?"

"By train," Ben replied. "It takes less than an hour. I think it is important that once you leave the Hague, the two of you are no longer seen with any law enforcement personnel."

Her mouth full, Lexie nodded in agreement.

Ben pulled out a photo from a file folder marked *GEKLASSEERD* in red on the front. Lexie assumed this meant *classified*.

"This is a photo of Robert," the sergeant said as he handed the photo to Lexie. She and Blake examined the photo. The young man's green eyes were highlighted by his bushy eyebrows and tousled hair, both the color of paprika.

"He looks young," Blake said.

"He's twenty-four years old." Ben pulled out a second photo, a bit fuzzier than the first one. "This is a photo of Robert with Jade. It was taken last year at an animal rights protest. She changes her hair color almost weekly, so there is no telling what color it will be when you meet her. That said, she has a preference for bright pink."

Lexie closely scrutinized the photo, then passed it to Blake.

"This," Ben said, unveiling yet another image, "is a photo of our undercover agent who will be at the Gathering. Her alias is Tess Haas, but she goes by Bug."

"Why Bug?"

"Because she's small and has big eyes."

The girl in the photo was indeed small in stature, with pale skin and large eyes so dark they were almost ebony. She had spiked hair, and both her lip and her right eyebrow were pierced.

"She knows the two of you will be attending the Gathering. She will be there but will maintain a discrete distance for operational purposes."

Ben placed the last photo in front of Lexie and Blake.

"This is Constable Jonas Hummel. His undercover name is Jonas Hurley."

The photo showed a decorated young constable wearing his dress uniform. He had deep-set, dark eyes and short, cropped brown hair.

Connor glanced over at the photograph and said, "The last time I saw Jonas, his hair was longer than in this photograph and he had a beard."

Lexie studied the photograph of Constable Hummel, trying to memorize his features.

"Where will the Gathering be held?" Kate asked.

Ben answered. "We know the campsite will be near the village of Appelscha, which is in the province of Friesland."

"Is there a nearby town where we can set up and not look suspicious?"

"The closest you will be able to get to the campsite is Assen. It's a thirty-minute drive from Assen to Appelscha. Any closer and you will be jeopardizing the safety of the undercover agents."

Frowning, Blake leaned forward. "How will we meet up with Robert?"

"There is a room at the Hotel Old Quarter in Amsterdam held under the name Lexie Lancaster," Ben said. "Robert will meet you in the hotel lobby tomorrow afternoon at four o'clock." He handed Lexie an envelope. "Here are some important addresses that will help you while you are in Amsterdam, as well as a map of the city."

"Thank you," Lexie said. "We appreciate the help."

"It's the other way around," replied the sergeant. "We appreciate your help. You are both courageous undercover agents. You volunteered for a dangerous mission in a foreign country, and now you find out that your backup team will be far away. I wish we could do more to ensure your safety."

"Every mission is different," Blake said. "We understand the risks."

"We'll do our best to find Constable Hummel," Lexie added.

The FBI agents left the meeting, departing for lunch at a busy restaurant. It would be their last meal together as a group.

* * * * *

After dinner, Lexie and Blake returned to the hotel and conducted one final equipment check. Satisfied, they packed their backpacks. Blake watched as Lexie shrugged hers on.

"All I can see is a giant rucksack with two little legs sticking out the bottom. You look like you're about to topple over."

"This stuff fit better the first time I packed it," she groused. "I haven't added anything, so why does it seem so much bulkier?"

"Let me carry the tent. It will fit on my pack easier and I'm taller. Plus," he said, raising an eyebrow and smirking, "a gentleman should always carry a lady's tent."

Lexie dropped her pack and untied the tent. She looked up at Blake, who was staring at her.

"Oh, I'm not gonna argue with you if that's what you're waiting for." She gestured at the pile on the ground. "Take it."

Laughing, he took the tent and secured it to the bottom part of his pack.

"I almost forgot," Lexie added, "I have a gift for you." She pulled a small paper bag out of her dresser drawer.

"A gift?"

"Open it."

Blake opened the bag and pulled out a black T-shirt. The front showed a pair of bolt cutters, a Molotov cocktail, and a raging fire. Printed under the picture was the slogan *Don't just be sorry. Do something. —The Animals.*

"I figured you probably didn't have any activist clothing," Lexie explained.

"It's great," Blake replied, running a thumb over the worn printing. "Thank you."

"You're welcome."

Blake folded the T-shirt and placed it into his pack. Without looking up he asked, "Are you nervous?"

"A little. You?"

He nodded. "I've done a lot of undercover roles, but this is so different from anything that I've done in the past."

"You'll be fine," Lexie said, briskly patting his head and laughing when he swatted at her hand. "Be mellow and go with the flow."

"That's easy for you to say. That isn't exactly suited to my personality. I'm just glad this isn't your first rodeo." Looking up, he winced. "See, I probably shouldn't have said rodeo. I'm sure that's taboo in the animal rights world."

Lexie giggled. "You're learning. For the record, I'm glad you're with me on this one."

"I'll do my best to not say the wrong thing. Or eat the wrong thing."

"We'll get through it together, partner."

Lexie noticed that Blake's eyes twinkled when he grinned. It looked . . . nice.

A sudden knock on the door made her jump; hurrying to the door, she looked through the peephole. "It's Kate," she called to Blake before opening the door.

Ambling in, the other agent brushed a strand of black hair away from her eyes. "Hey guys, anything I can do to help?"

"I think we have everything covered," Blake replied, slinging a newly packed bag up and onto the bed. Kate sat down on the couch and watched as he and Lexie make final adjustments.

"Call me tomorrow after you meet with Robert," she instructed them. "I'll be curious to know your thoughts."

"We will," Lexie said.

"And be careful. If you get that feeling that something isn't right, pull out." Sighing, she added, "I would feel better if we had some kind of backup communication plan. I don't completely trust cell phone coverage in this country."

"Like what?" Blake asked. "Telegraph?"

Glaring, Kate replied, "I don't know. This camp seems like it's out in the middle of nowhere. What if you get there and you have no cell phone coverage and you can't get a message out?"

"If that happens, you'll just have to trust us. We'll contact you as soon as we leave the camp," Lexie said. "I know it's not ideal, but it may be our only choice. Besides, it's four days at the Gathering. What could happen?"

"I don't like it," Kate insisted.

"Kate," Blake said. "If the worst happens and we don't have cell phone service, then we'll try to walk to a town to get better service."

"The closest town might be miles away!"

Lexie reached over and touched Kate's shoulder. "We'll be all right."

Kate pulled her into a hug; then, over his protests, she did the same to Blake.

"Look at it this way," Lexie told her after they broke apart. "This can't go as bad as my last case."

"That's not funny," Kate said.

"It's a little funny."

Rolling her eyes, their contact agent raised her hand in a wave and left the hotel room.

"So just how bad did your last case go?" Blake asked, doing his best to sound casual.

"Bad," Lexie replied, in a tone that told him not to take things further.

8

As the train surged forward, Blake checked his watch. "Right on time. Europe has an exceptional rail system."

Lexie watched the unspoiled Dutch landscape roll by. Small herds of cattle grazed in the peaceful country pastures. A picturesque little church stood near an old, wooden windmill, the perfect image of tranquility.

Closing her eyes, she settled back and listened to the lulling sound of the train. She thought about Logan and how much she missed his smile. He'd been an uncomplicated guy with simple dreams and a love of boats—the kind of man who could've made her happy. She'd never had the chance to tell him that she was an FBI agent. *How would he have responded?*

Suddenly, a vision of Logan lying on a gurney, his skin an eerie shade of gray, void of life, jolted Lexie back to reality. She drew in a breath and opened her eyes.

"You okay?" Blake asked, looking up from the Amsterdam map he was studying.

She yawned and stretched her arms above her head. "Yeah. Why?"

"You seemed far away."

"I'm okay," she said, smiling.

Lexie returned to watching the countryside as Blake continued to study the map. So many questions rolled around her head. Was she ready for this? Should she have listened to Mark and Dr. Levering? *After all, the nightmares seem to be getting worse instead of better.* Had she taken on this case for the right reasons?

She knew it was too late to withdraw. The life of the Dutch undercover might depend on her. She had to make sure her head was in the game.

"You sure you're okay?" Blake asked, concern coloring his voice.

"If we have time in Amsterdam, I'd like to take a canal ride," Lexie said, the segue out of her mouth before she could think of a better one.

Blake folded the map and smiled, though she could still see worry behind his eyes. "Sure. Whatever you want."

After a few moments watching green landscape pass by across the glass, she thought of a better topic of conversation. "Sure hope this Robert guy isn't a pain in the ass."

Blake nodded. "Relying on a source goes against everything I've been taught, but I guess we don't have a choice at this point. Makes me nervous, though."

"Yeah, he could be leading us into a real shitstorm—"

Before she could continue, an announcement over the intercom system informed the passengers the next stop was Amsterdam. After Blake helped Lexie get her backpack on, she followed him off the train.

"Wow!" Lexie said. "This station is amazing."

Amsterdam Central Station was a gothic, renaissance revival building with a cast-iron platform roof spanning nearly half the length of a football field. Brightly colored coats of arms ran across the top of the building; lions and all manner of humans were sculpted into the walls. The two agents found their way to the street, taking time to appreciate the beauty of the station.

"Look at the turrets," Blake said.

"And all the ornamental details," Lexie added.

Blake touched Lexie's shoulder and pointed to an area that housed more bicycles than she had ever seen. "There must be ten thousand over there," she said. "It looks like a beehive of bikes."

"I read somewhere that Amsterdam has more bikes than people," Blake said.

"I believe it," Lexie said, watching parents on bikes loaded with children weave their way quickly and easily through the city, businesspeople pedaling to get to important meetings.

After they finished gawking, Blake led the way toward the hotel, map in hand.

"I can't believe how cool Amsterdam is," Lexie panted, out of breath from hauling her pack. "Look at the facade on that building. It actually has gargoyles on it."

"That building is older than our country," Blake said. "I can't wait to explore."

The hotel, it turned out, was a tall historic building in the heart of the tourist area. Their room, tiny but clean, had two twin beds and a private bathroom.

"Not much room in here," Blake said as he struggled to

find a place to store their large backpacks. While it wasn't cramped enough to be claustrophobic, the room had definitely been designed with minimalist travelers in mind. Lexie turned and slammed into him—the two stood chest to chest for an awkward moment, each trying to figure out which direction to move.

"I guess this is a good way to get used to sleeping in close quarters," Lexie said.

"Speaking of that," Blake said, "you sure you're okay with the two of us sharing that small tent?"

"Do you snore?" she asked.

"I haven't been *told* that I snore," he replied, grinning.

Lexie shook her head and smirked. "Then I'm fine with sharing a tent."

"Well," Blake said, finally giving up and dumping his bag on his bed, "the day is ours until we have to meet Robert at four o'clock. How about we do some exploring and find a place to have lunch?"

"Sounds good. I could use a coffee."

Blake showed Lexie his map. "The city is laid out in the shape of a fan, with three main canals forming concentric half-circles around the center."

"You lead the way," she replied.

The two wandered the streets, enjoying the sights and sounds of the bustling city. They stopped to enjoy a coffee and watch the locals navigating the thoroughfares filled with tourists; sun streamed down from above, mingling perfectly with the breeze.

"I like the feel of this place," Lexie said. "It's weird but cool." She flipped through the tourist map while they sipped their coffees. "*Speaking* of weird, there's a museum of prostitution and a sex museum."

"I've never been a museum kind of guy, but I may need to take in a little culture."

Lexie raised an eyebrow and snickered. "Look at that, the trip's already broadening your horizons."

After this, banter fell by the wayside. Blake was mostly quiet and kept glancing off in the distance. About halfway through her coffee, Lexie finally asked, "Is something wrong?"

"I know it sounds crazy," he said, keeping his eyes on the horizon, "but I think somebody is following us."

Frowning, Lexie tried to look where he was looking. "We just arrived. Who would be following us?"

"I don't know. Maybe it's my imagination."

She squinted through the myriad of bicycles and pedestrians. "Male or female?"

"A man. I noticed him in our hotel lobby when we checked in. I've seen him twice since then."

"That doesn't sound like a coincidence. What's he look like?"

"White male, looks to be in his early thirties. He's wearing jeans, a red T-shirt, and a blue baseball cap. The last time I saw him, he had on a pair of sunglasses. Like I said, it might be my imagination."

"We can't be too careful. I'll watch for him."

Nodding, Blake finally turned back to the table. "You ready for lunch?"

"I could eat."

* * * * *

On the way to the restaurant, Blake leaned over and whispered to Lexie. "Our tail is back."

"Where?" she asked, resisting the immediate impulse to turn her head.

"Your three o'clock. He took off the baseball cap, but still has on the red T-shirt."

Lexie used her peripheral vision; a flash of scarlet darted across it. "I see him. What's our plan?"

"Let's walk down an alley and see what happens."

"Do you think our cover is blown?" she asked.

"I don't know. I guess it depends on who this guy is and why he's following us."

"I wonder if the agent at customs put him on us."

"I don't know, but there's an alley coming up on the right. Let's take it and see if he follows us."

The two ducked down the alley, then quickly hid behind a large, foul-smelling trash receptacle. Minutes later, the man who had been following them appeared at the mouth of the alley. He looked around for a few moments, shoes scraping against the pavement, then turned to leave.

Blake rushed up behind him, grabbed his wrist, and thrust it upward, folding the man's arm into a chicken wing. He propelled the subject forward, slamming his chest and left cheek into the brick wall with a gritty thud.

Lexie moved in close, ready to assist if the man managed to escape Blake's hold.

"Hey asshole, why are you following us?" Blake asked

through clenched teeth, his face inches from the unknown man's right eye.

"I'm not following you," the subject replied as best he could with his face grinding against a wall, trying to jerk away from Blake. Even under the circumstances, his accent was noticeable—Irish, Lexie thought.

Blake wrenched the subject's arm upward, causing him to cry out in pain. "Answer me. Why are you following us?"

"Let me go! You're hurting me."

"I'll let you go when you tell me who you are and why you're following me and my girlfriend."

After a few seconds of further pressure on his arm, the man slumped. "I'm Robert," he said, barely audible.

Blake lessened the pressure on the man's arm. "What?"

The man caught his breath before answering. "I'm Robert. We were supposed to meet later today. At your hotel."

Lexie recognized the man from the photo she had been shown at the briefing.

"Why in the hell are you following us?" Blake asked.

Robert kept his right eye locked on Blake. "I'm putting my life on the line for you two. I wanted to make sure you were cool and looked the part," he said. "I *also* wanted to make sure no one else was following you. Looks like you have that part covered."

Blake released his hold and helped Robert to stand up straight. He turned to face them.

"We're trained professionals," Lexie said.

Robert rubbed his shoulder and looked at her. "I needed to see for myself."

"What if you didn't like what you saw?" Blake asked.

"I wasn't going to show up for our meeting at your hotel." Brushing himself off further, he glared at Blake. "Look, the people I'm introducing you to are serious about their cause and can be extremely dangerous. I needed to know if you two would fit in at the Gathering."

"Following us wasn't a smart move," Lexie said. "You could've gotten yourself hurt or blown our cover."

"I see that now," Robert said, rotating his shoulder and his wrist with a grimace. "I'm sorry. I didn't mean to give you a scare."

"So you followed us from our hotel?" Lexie said.

"Yeah. I staked out your hotel and waited for you to check in. I guess I'm not great at surveillance." Robert stretched his neck from side to side. "Or self-defense."

"Are you all right?" Blake asked.

"I'm fine, mate. Can we start over?" He extended his hand. "I'm Robert."

Blake shook his hand. "I'm Blake, and this is Lexie."

Taking his hand in her own, Lexie said, "I'm glad that mystery is solved."

"Let's go someplace quiet to talk," Robert said. "I know a nearby pub that'll be quiet this time of the day."

"Lead the way," Blake replied.

* * * * *

Tucked into a cozy street, the traditional Dutch pub was elegantly decorated and furnished in dark woods and velvet.

The bar was nearly empty except for two patrons sitting at the bar sampling the local whisky and a small group of middle-aged men huddled around a table, each with a pint of dark beer.

Robert selected a table in a back corner away from prying ears. The men ordered a beer, Lexie a glass of wine. After the drinks arrived, they got down to business.

"This is what's going to happen," Robert said. "On Thursday morning at eight o'clock, a bus will pick up all the activists in Amsterdam and take us to the Gathering. It's about a two-hour ride to the camp. The bus will bring everyone back to Amsterdam on Monday. I've already made a reservation going and returning for all three of us on the bus. It's seven euros each way. Do you have cash?"

"We do," Lexie replied, taking a sip of her wine.

"The organizers will require you to turn in your cell phone for the duration of the training. If you leave the camp you can get it back, but I wouldn't recommend doing so. It raises suspicions if you claim your cell phone, leave, then return. Don't try to smuggle a phone into the camp. They will search you and your belongings. You don't want to get caught smuggling electronics."

"Anything else?" Blake asked.

"Be accepting and understanding of all people, no matter their background, religion, race, or sexual orientation. The Gathering is a safe zone for all individuals."

"We're not idiots," Blake said. "Do you think we're going to go to the camp and act like assholes?"

Robert shook his head. "I didn't say that. Just be respectful of others. I'll introduce you to Jade when it seems natural. She's a powerful influence in the movement and a good person to get to know. She's also acutely perceptive. She can easily ferret out a cop, so be savvy around her."

"This isn't our first undercover mission," Blake said. "You get us in, make the introductions, and let us worry about the rest."

"Look, mate," Robert said, leaning across the table, "it's not just your life on the line here. If you fuck this up, I go down with you."

"Let's all calm down," Lexie said. "We need to figure out how we know each other. Our stories have to match, and we need to know them like the backs of our hands."

Robert nodded. "Last year I spent the entire summer traveling in the United States. That would've been the perfect time for us to meet and become friends."

"Great idea," Lexie said. "Where did you go?"

"All over. I started in California and ended up in New York City."

"Did you travel to any of the southern states?"

"I visited New Orleans."

"Perfect. That's where we met."

Over the next two hours, the three meticulously constructed the story of how they'd met and become friends. After a couple of drinks, the tension between Robert and Blake had started to ease, though the former still rubbed at his shoulder periodically

"What's the plan for tomorrow?" Lexie asked, draining her second glass of wine.

"I'll show you around Amsterdam," Robert said. "That way, if people who are attending the Gathering see us, it'll be natural that we're together. During that time, we can keep practicing our story."

"How many will be attending?" Blake asked.

"About three hundred."

His eyes widened. "I had no idea there would be that many people."

"It's a big deal in the animal rights world. That's the whole point, isn't it? It's my understanding that you hope to make connections here, go deeper into the underground movement."

"That's the plan," Lexie said.

Nodding, Robert finished his drink and stood. "I'll be leaving at the conclusion of the Gathering, so you'll be on your own. I have to warn you"—he dropped his voice to a low whisper—"be careful. You'll be swimming in dangerous waters, my friends. Sometimes people go missing. It's not like in the United States. You're playing in a whole different league."

His speech finished, he laid some cash on the table, turned on his heel, and departed.

"Fun guy," Blake said, motioning to the server for a refill.

9

The next day, Robert showed Lexie and Blake around Amsterdam, the three of them spending time getting to know each of their legends in preparation for the Gathering. Eventually, they stopped for a coffee break. Even sitting at an outside table, the aroma of fresh-brewed coffee and ground beans filled the air. The sweet scent of warm caramel made Lexie crave a fresh-baked dessert. Since none of the desserts were vegan, she settled for a piece of dark chocolate.

"Are you ready for tomorrow?" Robert asked.

"I think so," Lexie replied, the steam from the coffee warming her face.

"Anything else that we need to be aware of before going into the camp?" asked Blake.

Robert rubbed his chin as he considered the question. "Don't be pushy when you're trying to get information. Remember, everyone is suspected of working for the police until proven otherwise. So be cool."

"We'll be cool," Lexie said.

"You do know not to wear anything leather, right?"

"Of course."

"I figured as much, but thought I would double-check."

"Have you ever met the American activist?" Blake asked.

"Holden?" Robert shrugged. "Not directly, but I've heard Jade talk about him."

"What has Jade told you about him?"

"He's a charismatic leader. From what I understand, he's a bit of a ladies' man as well."

"Has Jade hooked up with him?" Lexie asked.

"Not that I know of, but she probably wouldn't tell me if she had. I'm sure he'll be around this weekend. The other activists treat him like some sort of a god."

"Can you show me on the map where we'll be going for the Gathering?" Blake asked, smoothing out the folded paper on the table.

Robert stood up to get a better look. He put his right index finger on a spot and his left index finger on another spot. "This is where we are now, and this is where we're going."

Lexie leaned over so she could see.

Blake whistled. "It's really out in the middle of nowhere, huh?"

"That is the point, now, isn't it?" Robert said.

"What happens if the police show up?"

"The police know better. They'll leave us alone. Speaking of police, you two better stay cool for all our sakes. If they find out you two are coppers, all three of us are in big trouble. I won't be able to protect you."

"Has that ever happened?"

"Oh, sure. Undercover operatives attempt to infiltrate the camp every year."

His brow furrowing, Blake folded the map back up. "How do they get discovered?"

"Usually because they do something stupid, like trying to sneak a cell phone or a camera into the camp. You're not going to do anything like that, are you?"

"Of course not," Lexie said. "We know what we're doing, Robert. Let's talk about something else."

"I don't think it hurts to know what's happened in the past," Blake said, holding up his hand. "What happened to the infiltrators once they were discovered?"

"Some were beaten up. Others were stripped naked and thrown out of the camp."

Lexie rolled her eyes. "Don't get spooked, Blake. I'm sure you'll do fine—and remain fully clothed."

"I'm not spooked, but you seem overconfident. Are you sure you're up for this assignment? Adam said—"

"Adam said what? Do you really want to have this conversation here?"

"Forget it," Blake said.

"Adam is a—"

"Hey!" Robert snapped. "You two need to get your shit together. I'm putting my neck on the chopping block for you two."

"Give me a break, dude," Blake said. "We all know why you're doing this, and it's not out of the kindness of your heart."

"Blake," Lexie warned, grabbing him by the arm.

Sneering briefly, Robert stared at Blake. "He's right. I'm

doing this because I have to, not because I want to. That being said, I want to make it out of this thing alive. Like it or not, the three of us have to work together."

Blake nodded. "I agree."

"Me too," Lexie said. "We need to all be on the same sheet of music."

"Friends, then?" asked Robert.

She nodded. After a slight pause, Blake did the same.

Examining the bottom of her empty mug, Lexie sighed contentedly. "One thing's for certain—the Dutch sure have wonderful coffee."

"Would you like another cup?" Blake asked.

"Maybe later. Right now, I wanna go on a canal tour."

"The best way to get around the Amsterdam canals is to use the Hop On and Hop Off boats," Robert said. "You can get a pass for twenty-four hours, then go anywhere you like."

"That sounds like fun," Lexie said. "Are you coming with us?"

Robert checked his watch. "I better get home. I still have to pack for the trip."

"Do you feel confident with our stories?" Blake asked.

"I do. I think we'll be fine. Anything else you want to discuss before I leave?"

"Nope." Lexie said. "I feel ready."

"I'll be in your hotel lobby tomorrow morning at fifteen after seven. It's only a fifteen-minute walk to the bus, but I don't want to take any chances."

* * * * *

The couple cruised the legendary canals, getting on and off at their leisure.

Lexie reached over and touched Blake's forearm, allowing her hand to linger. "This is spectacular. Look at that building over there."

Blake craned his neck to see where Lexie was pointing. "According to the map, that's the Bartolotti house, built in the seventeenth century," he said, struggling to keep the paper from being tossed about by the breeze.

"It's gorgeous. The facade is actually curved."

Blake moved in close and whispered in Lexie's ear. "Too bad we have to go to the Gathering tomorrow. You and I could have a great time exploring this city."

Lexie playfully bumped Blake's leg with her hip. "You wanna play hooky?"

"I wish."

"Me too. Two days in Amsterdam isn't nearly enough time."

"Maybe we can come back someday," Blake said. "On vacation. Not for work. Without Robert."

"That would be nice."

They ate dinner at a quaint little Indian restaurant, then stopped for drinks at the Skylounge Amsterdam. The trendy rooftop bar with a panoramic view of the unique metropolis was the perfect way to end the day.

Lexie stared at the flickering candle, watching it dance and cast shadows. She looked up to see Blake gazing at her. She felt her face warm.

"You're blushing," Blake said.

"It's the wine," she replied.

"Is it?" he asked with a mischievous grin.

Looking back down at her wine glass, she took a fortifying sip. "Did you enjoy dinner?"

"You have a way of changing the subject when a topic gets uncomfortable."

"You noticed."

"I did. You're cute when you're nervous. But to answer your question, dinner was good."

"Are you ready to convert to veganism?" she asked, looking back up.

Her colleague made a face. "Never. I don't eat a ton of meat, but I like having the option. Every once in a while, I have to have a big juicy burger."

"The kind that drips down your chin," Lexie added.

"Exactly."

They both exhaled simultaneously, then laughed.

"Maybe I'm not such a great vegan after all," Lexie said. "You have me fantasizing about burgers."

"And here I was hoping to have you fantasizing about me."

Lexie felt her cheeks heat up again. Blake laughed out loud.

The waiter brought the couple a second round of drinks. Neither wanted to leave the utopian atmosphere of the lounge.

Blake's demeanor became serious. "Lexie, I'm sorry about this afternoon with Robert. Things got kind of got weird."

"It wasn't your fault. You were right to try to get as much information as possible from him. I don't know why I was acting so strange. I guess I was in a mood."

"Are we good, then?" he asked, concern lingering on his face.

"Yeah, we're good."

The two left the lounge and wandered the streets of the ancient city. As night fell, things took on a whole new life. The streets teemed with young people walking hand in hand. Couples sat at outside tables and drank wine.

"Oh, wow," Blake said. "I read about this bridge." He took Lexie's hand and pulled her along at a quicker pace. "Check it out. It's called Magere Brug, which means *skinny bridge*."

Lexie gasped at the beauty of the picturesque bridge, which was romantically illuminated with thousands of lights twinkling against the white stone. "I've never seen anything like it. It's gorgeous."

The two agents stood, hand in hand, staring at the spectacular site. Lexie looked down at their interwoven fingers and felt her stomach flutter.

"Oh, I'm sorry," Blake said, releasing Lexie's hand. "I guess I got caught up in the moment."

"I don't mind," she replied, taking Blake's hand. "Maybe we should practice for the role."

Blake smiled. "Practice is good."

The two strolled back to their floating chariot, fingers intertwined, indistinguishable from all the other young couples out for the evening.

* * * * *

Lexie and Blake repacked their backpacks and got into their respective beds. The small room reminded Lexie of her college dorm—their twin beds were each pushed against opposite walls, leaving three feet of space between the beds.

Lexie lay staring at the ceiling, listening to the street noise. "You awake?" she whispered.

"Yep."

"Do you trust Robert?"

"Not at all. Seems decent enough once you stop holding him to a brick wall, but you can never trust a snitch."

"I agree."

For a while after that, there was nothing but the sound of pedestrians chattering and vehicles rushing by. Then, Blake asked:

"Hey, Lexie, what happened to you in South Carolina?"

Lexie froze. She felt her stomach tighten. She opened her mouth, but the words wouldn't come.

"I'm sorry," he murmured. "I shouldn't have brought it up. You don't have to tell me if you don't want to."

"It's a difficult subject for me," she managed.

The outside noises seemed to disappear, making the silence in the room intolerable.

After the quiet had gone on far too long, Lexie squeezed her eyes shut. She knew that Blake couldn't see her, which made what she was about to say easier.

"I went to South Carolina to help the Myrtle Beach office with an undercover case. They didn't have the necessary manpower to support the case, so I didn't have a proper contact agent. The case agent took a few shortcuts when he was setting up the case. I'm not putting all the blame on him, because I should've known better. The case was compromised. I was abducted, held hostage, badly injured, and shot, and an innocent man was killed because of me."

Tears dripped onto Lexie's pillow. She heard Blake roll over in his bed. Turning her head, she could see that he had rolled over on his side and was facing her.

"I didn't mean to dredge up painful memories," he said. "I apologize."

"My therapist says I need to talk about it, but I have a hard time. I feel like everyone is judging me."

"Hey, I'm the last person to feel any right to judge someone."

"Thank you. It's been hard. I 'what if' myself to death."

"You can't do that. Hindsight is twenty-twenty. As agents, we have to make split-second decisions. I'm sure you did what you thought was best at the time."

Haven't heard that *one before.* "I did, but it doesn't change the fact that someone died because of me."

"Listen," Blake whispered, craning closer to her from across the room, "undercover work is all about making judgment calls. Sometimes those calls don't work out as planned."

Lexie rolled over on her side so she was facing Blake. Her eyes had adjusted to the dark so she could see him staring at her.

"It's a hard pill to swallow," she said.

"You can't keep blaming yourself."

"You know, I've thought about leaving the Bureau."

"And doing what?"

"I don't know. Maybe go back to South Carolina and work on a tour boat or something."

"A tour boat? Are you serious?"

"Yes . . . maybe . . . I don't know."

"Everything is still raw right now," Blake said. "Things will get better."

"I hope you're right." Exhaling gently, Lexie said, "Let's talk about something else. Tell me about your daughter."

"Her name is Hannah. She's fourteen years old and just started high school."

"Are you two close?"

"No. Let's change the subject," Blake said, his tone abruptly growing brusque.

"I'm sorry. I didn't mean to pry."

He was silent for a moment, then sighed. "No. I'm sorry. I didn't mean to snap at you. My divorce, let's just say, wasn't amicable. Hannah was caught in the middle. We kind of tore her apart fighting over her in the divorce."

"How long have you been divorced?"

"Three years. That's the reason that I ended up in the Louisville Division. After our divorce, Jennifer, my ex, moved back to Kentucky with Hannah. She and I were high school sweethearts. We married after college. I was only twenty-two years old when we got married, and I had no idea how to be a good husband. When I joined the FBI, she resented having to move away from her family in Kentucky, especially to live in New York City. Jennifer got pregnant with Hannah our first year in New York. I tried everything to make her happy, but she hated the city, and after a while she hated me. I was beginning to work undercover cases, and all that time away didn't help things either."

"I can't imagine trying to live in New York on a new agent's salary with a wife and baby."

"It was impossible. Jennifer didn't want to work. She wanted to stay home with Hannah, but that wasn't an option, which was another reason to resent me. In her mind I couldn't provide for my family."

She could hear the old frustration in his voice. "That's not your fault. New York wasn't your choice for a first assignment."

"I know, but she thought it was somehow my fault. She blamed me for having to move and for having to get a job. I started working long hours to avoid the arguments. In hindsight, that was the wrong way to handle the situation. One day I came home and she had packed her and Hannah's things. She told me that her father was on his way to pick them up. She and Hannah went back to Kentucky."

"Wow. That's harsh."

"Oh no, it gets worse. I thought the whole Kentucky move was temporary and we would eventually work things out between us. I talked to my supervisor, but getting transferred out of the New York office was nearly impossible. I was stuck for a minimum of five years. I decided to make the best of it, so I threw myself into work. Around the holidays, I took some vacation days and flew to Kentucky. Turns out while I was throwing myself into work, my former best friend was throwing himself into my wife."

"What?"

"Yep." He chuckled as if he still couldn't believe it. "She hooked up with my childhood best friend. Josh and I had known each other since the fourth grade. Jennifer served me with divorce papers over the holidays and married Josh before the ink was dry."

"Shit."

"Yep."

"I'm sorry, Blake."

"I'm over it now," he said—a little too casually, Lexie thought. "I've moved on. The sad thing is, Jennifer poisoned Hannah's mind. She told her we were a happy little family before I joined the FBI. She actually told Hannah that I put my career first and my family second."

"What a bitch! What did you do?"

He did his best to shrug while lying down. "I took the high road. I told myself that I would never say a bad word about her mother to Hannah, and so far I haven't. Believe me, it's been hard at times. I'm hoping that one day Hannah will understand and let me explain that I never wanted a divorce, that I never wanted to be separated from her."

"I see why you needed to get back to Kentucky."

"I'm hoping that I can rebuild my relationship with my daughter. The problem is, she's fourteen and more interested in hanging out with her friends than spending time with her old man."

"She'll come around," Lexie said, trying to inject genuine assurance into the statement.

"I hope so." Blake exhaled long and slow, then said, "I guess we better get some shut-eye. Tomorrow is going to be a long day."

"Yes it is."

Before he rolled back over, he said, "Lex, please keep what I just told you to yourself. I'm a private guy, and I don't like people knowing my business."

"Of course," she said, turning back over on her own side and closing her eyes. "I'm the same way."

10

The Gathering—Day One

It was less than a mile's walk to the bus from the hotel, but despite the flat streets of Amsterdam, the weight of the backpacks and the unseasonably warm September left Lexie panting and sweaty. "If I have to cross another canal bridge, I'm going to scream," she said as she stopped to rub her aching thighs.

"Those look like our buses up ahead," Robert replied, pointing forward. "Wait here and I'll check."

Lexie leaned against the wall, not wanting to remove her pack. Pulling to a stop alongside her, Blake tugged the new hemp wallet she had bought him while they were in DC out of his pocket. It was the small things—like carrying a leather wallet, a big no-no among the animal rights activists—that would bring them under extra scrutiny at the Gathering.

"When we text Kate tonight," he said, returning the wallet to his pocket, "help me remember to tell her how much money we need to voucher. It's not like we can get receipts for any of these expenses."

Robert returned. "Those three are our buses. We can go ahead and load if you like."

"Seven euros each, right?" Blake asked.

"Yep."

He thumbed through the cash he'd withdrawn. "Here's twenty-one for all three of us. Ben told me to pay for yours too."

"Great. Thanks."

"He also told me to pay for your 'donation' to the Gathering. When it's time to pay, let me know and I'll give you the money."

Robert nodded, then started for the buses.

Lexie and Blake selected seats near the middle of the bus, with Robert across the aisle. Tattoos and piercings were the norm for the participants boarding the bus—most appeared to be under the age of thirty, though a few looked like old hippies from the flower-child era. Some wore colorful, bohemian outfits while others wore black, militant clothing. Lexie tried to place the various European countries through the languages she heard—smatterings of German, French, something that sounded like . . . *Finnish?*

"Don't worry," Robert said, catching sight of the consternation on her face, "the workshops at the Gathering will be taught in English."

Lexie sighed. "Thank goodness."

The passengers barely noticed the scenic Dutch countryside as the buses rolled toward their destination. The atmosphere buzzed with excitement, old friends busy getting reacquainted and new friends getting to know one another. Two hours passed quickly. Before Lexie knew it, the buses were turning off the main road and caravanning through a small town.

"This is Appelscha," Robert said.

The charming village had a beautiful green park, a small grocery, and a tiny hotel with a windmill in front. The well-tended small businesses had colorful and welcoming displays in the store windows. It was an ideal town for a postcard depicting life in a small Dutch hamlet.

"It's beautiful," Lexie breathed.

The bus turned off the paved road and bounced down a washboard-like gravel road. After about half a mile, they pulled to a stop and passengers began gathering their belongings. Lexie looked out the window and saw a long, rutted dirt road leading back to what she assumed was the campground.

"The buses are too large to get back to the camp, so they drop us here. We'll walk the rest of the way," Robert explained.

The occupants of the three buses gathered their gear from the cargo hold and began the trek toward the distant camp. Lexie watched her feet to ensure that she didn't trip on the rocky dirt road. Dust and grime stuck to her sweaty face and neck. Beside her, Blake wiped at his brow, similarly drenched in salty moisture.

Gradually, their pace slowed, eventually halting entirely. The crowd continued to chitchat while waiting in line and slowly making their way to the entrance. "What's the holdup?" Lexie asked Robert.

"They're checking people against the attendee list and searching bags. Don't worry, I put you both on the list."

Thinking of the hidden compartments in Blake's hiking boots, Lexie chewed her bottom lip. As if her fellow agent had read her mind, he leaned over and whispered in her ear, "If things go south at the gate, keep going and contact me as soon as you can." Then, he separated himself from Lexie and Robert, allowing several people to cut in front of him.

They were almost to the entrance when Lexie heard a loud disturbance—mingled shouts and sounds of struggle.

"What's all the commotion?" Robert asked the people in front of him.

A white guy with a Finnish accent and long dreadlocks turned around and answered, "Security caught someone trying to get in with recording equipment."

A small bead of sweat trickled down Lexie's back.

Breathe. Breathe. Breathe. You got this.

Two brawny men hauled a nearly naked man down the dirt road, each holding an arm. The stripped man, wearing only a pair of boxer shorts, struggled, digging his feet into the grime, but his two captors continued to yank his arms and drag him away. As they passed Lexie, she could see that the captive had blood pouring from his nose. The crowd yelled obscenities at the bleeding man as he was dragged past the queue.

"They mean business," Lexie said. "That gives a new meaning to the term *strip search*."

"Yep. The camp is serious about security."

It was Robert's turn, so he stepped forward and said, "Robert O'Sullivan."

The woman working the gate ran her finger down a list, stopping on a name.

"Welcome, Robert. Proceed forward."

Robert nodded and stepped forward. Lexie moved up. She could feel her heart hammering beneath her ribs. *Don't worry. That guy didn't come prepared, but you did. You'll be fine.*

"Lexie Lancaster."

The woman scanned her list and found Lexie's name. For a moment, she simply squinted at it. Lexie held her breath.

Then, with a flourish, she crossed through the name with her pen. "Welcome, Lexie. Proceed forward."

Exhaling quietly, Lexie started moving. "Thank you."

Before she'd taken more than a few steps, she was greeted by a tall, clean-cut, blond man in his early twenties. "Hello," he said, "my name is Friedrich. I need to check your bag, please, miss."

Lexie handed her pack to Friedrich, who dumped the contents on the table beside him. He opened her small makeup bag and sifted through her food items. "Do you have a cell phone or any other electronic devices?"

"I have a phone," she replied, withdrawing it from her pocket and holding it up.

"Please turn it off and place it in one of the bags on the table. Label the bag with your name, seal it, and place it in the box on the ground. You may reclaim your phone when you leave the campsite at the end of the conference."

While Lexie powered down her phone, she looked around. To her left, she noticed what looked like a smashed piece of recording equipment, a pile of clothing, and a man's wallet lying in the dirt.

She looked back at Friedrich. He unrolled her sleeping bag and ran his hands over it, checking the padding. Afterward, he packed everything back up and handed the pack to her.

"Why are you here?" Friedrich asked Lexie as she shouldered the pack.

"What do you mean?"

He glared down at her, using his seven-inch height advantage as an intimidation technique. "It's not a difficult question."

"I'm here to learn new ways to battle animal abusers."

"That's a canned answer. Why are you really here?"

Keeping her eyes glued on Friedrich's, Lexie answered, "I'm just a do-gooder who wants to stick it to those sons of bitches who hurt animals."

"So you want to learn how to blow things up?"

"Among other things," Lexie answered, careful to retain eye contact.

"How did you hear about the Gathering?"

"Everyone in the movement knows about the Gathering."

"Do you have anything in your pockets?"

"No. My phone is labeled and in the box."

"I need to pat you down."

"Sure. Go ahead."

The Herculean man gently patted Lexie down from top to bottom, being careful not to touch any private parts. When he was finished, he stepped back and brushed his hands off. "Thank you, Miss Lexie." There was still a wary gleam in his eye, but he stepped aside to let her pass. "Welcome to the Gathering."

"Thank you, Friedrich."

"You can call me Fritz."

Lexie took her pack and walked off, wondering how Blake would respond to all the bullshit questions. She found Robert waiting for her a few yards away. "Now what?" she asked.

"We select a camp spot and pitch our tents. There are no assigned spots; it's first come, first served."

Several people emerged from the security area, but no Blake.

"Do you think there's a problem?" Lexie whispered.

"Hard to say. They're pretty thorough around here."

Minutes seemed like hours. Lexie pulled out her water bottle and took a drink. The water was no longer cold, but it quenched her thirst. Finally, a familiar face came into view. Exhaling, she smiled.

"Did you miss me?" Blake asked.

Lexie waved. "Did you have any issues?"

"No. When the guy asked me why I was here, I told him I was here for a girl."

"And that worked?" Lexie asked.

"Yeah, the guy laughed and said, 'Been there, man,' then told me to proceed."

"Let's find a place to camp," Robert said, adjusting his bag across his shoulders. "Follow me."

Robert led the way to an enormous soccer field, where colorful tents were haphazardly popping up all around, some better prepared than others. A fence ran the length of the back of the property, securing the area from outsiders. They passed a manmade firepit with a pile of partially burned tree branches and logs.

Lexie inhaled deeply. "I love the smell of pine needles and campfires."

"Any preferences on where to make camp?" Robert asked.

"The area that looks the most quiet," Blake said.

Robert laughed. "You're kidding, right? This place is party central at night. I don't think there's a quiet spot in the entire camp."

"Great," Blake grumbled. "That corner over there looks good. At least we'll be on the outskirts of the party and not dead center."

Robert pitched his one-man tent in record time and helped Lexie and Blake finish putting up theirs. "You ready for lunch?" he asked, throwing an extra peg to the grass.

"I'm starving," Lexie said, wiping sweat from her forehead.

"I'll show you around, and then we'll eat lunch. This is how it works: Since there's no paid staff, everyone is expected to pitch in and work. You need to volunteer to help in some way, like with kitchen duties or cleaning toilets. Once you finish eating, you'll wash your own dishes. You'll see how it works when you get up to the eating area."

Blake put his arm around Lexie and pulled her close so he could whisper in her ear. "I didn't know I was gonna have to clean toilets when I signed up for this assignment."

"Sorry, dear. I didn't know either."

"You owe me, girl."

Lexie laughed.

Robert showed Lexie and Blake around the campgrounds. It was apparent from the horrible condition of the soccer field and the crumbling playground equipment that this wasn't a setting for families. There were several permanent buildings on the site, all in desperate need of repair. The camp housed a small faction of full-time residents; these permanent inhabitants lived in campers, old recreational vehicles, and rotting mobile homes. Much to Lexie's dismay, she discovered that there was only one set of bathroom and shower facilities for all the campers.

"This could get disgusting," she said.

"I wouldn't plan on using the shower while you're here," Robert said. "It's not worth the wait, and the facilities tend to get pretty gross."

Blake grinned at Lexie. "Having fun yet?" he asked.

"Bite me. And enjoy cleaning them."

Grimacing, Blake turned back to Robert. "What's the deal with the area in the back?"

"That's where the year-round residents live," Robert said. "Mostly anarchists who aren't choosey about their cause, as long as it's antiestablishment."

When they reached the eating area, many of the campers already had heaping piles of food in front of them. Large men stirred the contents of two enormous, black cauldrons of food over open firepits, using wooden spoons the size of boat oars.

"Holy smoke," Lexie said. "Those are the biggest cauldrons I've ever seen. It looks like something a witch would use to make potions."

"Whatever they're cooking smells good, at least," Blake said.

"Everything is on the honor system here," Robert informed them, taking a whiff of the air himself. "You can give the recommended donation each time you eat, or, if you choose, pay for the whole conference at once."

"All at once sounds easier," Blake said.

"That's what I usually do." As they drew closer, Robert recognized the volunteer taking money. "Millie! How are you?"

The girl's long, blonde hair was tied to one side. A natural beauty, she needed no makeup. At Robert's greeting, she broke into a broad smile. "Robert! How are you, my love?"

"I'm good. Millie, these are my American friends Lexie and Blake." Turning back to them, he said, "This is Millie—she's from Denmark."

Lexie extended her hand to shake, but Millie grabbed her and pulled her in for a hug. "We're all family here, Lexie. Family hugs one another."

Lexie noticed that Millie rubbed her back while she was hugging her—most likely searching for a wire, a technique activists routinely used. *Yep, one big lovefest.* Pulling back, she pasted a smile onto her face. "So nice to meet you, Millie."

Millie then turned and hugged Blake. "Is this your first time at the Gathering?" she asked after they'd broken apart.

"It is," Lexie answered. "We're excited to be here with so many like-minded people."

"You are going to have a wonderful time. Did Robert tell you how the food donation works?"

"He did," Blake said. "We'd like to pay up front, for simplicity."

"I will be glad to handle that for you. In the afternoon we have coffee and tea, which are complimentary. Baked goods are available with the afternoon's hot beverages; however, they are an additional small charge. We have found not everyone needs or wants a snack, so it is first come, first served. I will tell you that the apple turnovers are scrumptious, and they always sell out."

The threesome thanked her, paid for their meals for the week, and proceeded through the line. A teenage volunteer server filled their bowls with vegetable stew and gave them each a piece of vegan cornbread. "I wonder what's for dinner," Blake said, motioning toward the second cauldron.

"Greek lentil soup and sweet potato green curry quinoa casserole," the volunteer said. "Serving this many people is a huge job, so we carefully planned the meals for the entire event." The young man had long, straw-colored dreadlocks and steel-gray eyes. His tall, thin body and long arms gave him a willowy appearance.

"This looks great," Blake said. "Thank you for making it for us."

The man smiled at Blake. "You are welcome. Are you American?"

"Yes. We both are," he replied, nodding toward Lexie.

"Thank you for traveling such a long distance to be with us. We are grateful for your presence." The volunteer spoke perfect English, but with a slow cadence, trying to get each word correct.

"Your English is excellent," Lexie said, smiling.

"Thank you. My name is Oskar, and I am from Finland."

"I'm Blake," her partner replied, "and this is my girl-friend, Lexie."

"Nice to make your acquaintance."

A line formed behind them. "I think we're holding up the chow line."

"We will talk later," Oskar said.

Picnic tables were filled with attendees laughing and joking with one another. Lexie, Blake, and Robert found room at one of the tables and devoured their hot meals. Lexie eavesdropped on conversations taking place around her. Most attendees spoke in English, but a few used their native languages. She picked out German, French, and Danish.

After lunch, Lexie and Blake followed Robert through the cleanup line with their dishes. There were three large plastic tubs of water set in a row. When Lexie's turn came, she scraped the excess food from her plate into a large barrel, then moved to the first tub of soapy water, where she scrubbed her plate. She carried her dishes to the second bin to dunk them. Finally, the third bin held what was supposed to be clear water for a final rinse; by now, however, the murky bin water had a soapy and greasy feel to it.

Lexie and Blake excused themselves and walked back to the tent to rest before the start of the opening plenary. A hodgepodge of tents, every size and color, encompassed the soccer field. The two weaved their way through the tent city. Maneuvering proved more difficult than they had imagined; the tents were tiny, but there were a lot of them, and stray possessions were lying everywhere, waiting to be tripped over. When they finally arrived, Blake flopped down on his sleeping bag, the thin pad offering little cushion.

"Well, that was sanitary," he said. "Three hundred pairs of hands submerged in the dishwater. It'll be a miracle if we make it through the weekend without catching a parasite."

Lexie crouched in the corner, trying to organize her belongings. "At least lunch was edible."

"Except for that cornbread," Blake said. "How the hell do you make cornbread without eggs and butter?"

Lexie shrugged and pulled out a schedule of activities that had been given to her at check-in. "Let's plan our strategy for the training sessions. I say we attend the more radical sessions."

"I agree."

"Crap," she said, catching sight of a bold line of text. "The opening plenary starts in thirty minutes."

"No rest for the wicked."

Sighing, she smoothed out the schedule. Blake scooted over so he could see as well. "Should we split up or stay together?"

"If we're trying to sell ourselves as a package deal," she replied, "then we should probably spend most of the time together. However, if anyone shows an interest in either one of us separate from the other, I don't think there's a problem with us splitting up for some of the sessions."

Nodding in agreement, Blake squinted at the schedule. "Looks like the last scheduled activity tonight is the welcome reception from eight to nine thirty. I guess the partying that Robert talked about starts after that."

Lexie looked over at Blake's extra pair of boots tossed in the corner, clothes piled on top.

"Fingers crossed that the equipment works," she said.

Blake nodded. "Let's go get a seat before I get too comfortable in here."

*　*　*　*　*

The crowd shuffled into the main conference room, where the acoustics raised the noise of their chatter to a near roar. Across the room, Lexie spotted Robert, who motioned for them to come over.

"Lexie, Blake, these are two of my dear old friends, Jade and Barnabas." He smiled at Jade and said, "These are the Yanks that I told you about."

Jade's tight, black V-neck shirt emphasized her slender build and perfect figure. She wore her shoulder-length, platinum-blonde hair parted on the side, neon pink streaks adorning the ends. Dark roots revealed that it was not her natural color.

"Nice to meet you," Lexie said as she extended a hand to Jade.

Before Jade could take Lexie's hand, Barnabas grasped it, put it to his lips, and lightly kissed it. "Pleasure to meet you," he said, smiling. He was endearing despite his crooked teeth and thick glasses, which magnified his eyes to an unnatural size.

Robert playfully whacked Barnabas on the head. "Don't mind him, he's harmless."

"Where are you from?" Blake asked.

"We're both from England," Jade answered. "We don't get many Americans for the Gathering. I hope you find it worth the long trip."

"I'm sure we will," Blake said.

From a ways away, the microphone made a sudden, ear-piercing squelch. Fritz, the man who'd searched Lexie's bag, had the mic. "Will everyone please take a seat?"

The crowd quieted.

"Before I introduce the event organizers, I'd like to thank everyone for coming and for showing patience with the queue to enter the campsite. I'm sure you understand that we have to keep tight security at the entrance to prevent infiltrators from entering and destroying the sanctity of our event. My name is Fritz, and if you have any security issues, please come see me. Also, if you see anyone at the camp who is acting strangely or who has a cell phone, please let me know immediately. Our safety and security depend on each and every one of you watching out for one another."

Fritz clicked a remote control—six photographs appeared on the large, white screen in front of the audience.

"Please study these photographs. The photos are of people who have tried to infiltrate our conference in previous years. These individuals are either undercover law enforcement officers or known informants who work for law enforcement agencies. People change their appearance, so if one of these people has slipped past security, you must inform me or one of the other security officers immediately. Now, without further ado, I'd like to introduce the

Dutch activists who organized this amazing event. Please show your love for Nico and Annette, the organizers."

The crowd gave Nico and Annette a standing ovation. Fritz handed the microphone to Nico.

"Thank you. Is everyone ready for a great conference?"

The crowd applauded.

Nico grinned. "That was weak. I'll ask again: Is everyone ready for a great conference?"

This time the applause was deafening, mingled with screams.

"That's better," he said, still smiling. "That's the spirit we hope to see all weekend. We are here to network and rejoice in the company of like-minded people while learning techniques we can use to save innocent animals. My name is Nico, and this is my partner Annette. We are thrilled to host this year's event, and we hope at the end of the weekend we can send you home with some fresh ideas to help you battle animal abuse. We're proud to announce that we have over three hundred participants from twenty-five countries in attendance. Take the time to get to know one another and use this opportunity to build your networks and learn new techniques."

While Nico continued the welcome address, Lexie noticed Jade off in a corner talking to a new arrival. She had her hand on his arm, and he was whispering in her ear. The two shared a laugh, and the man hugged her. Lexie noticed Robert staring at the couple.

"Who's that?"

Without taking his eyes off the pair, he answered sarcastically. "Why, that's the great and powerful Holden."

Lexie gave Blake a little nudge and shifted her eyes toward the couple, mouthing the word *Holden*. Blake followed her eyes and nodded.

Nico introduced the rest of the event organizers and their areas of responsibility. The opening remarks ended, and the audience split up between the two rooms.

"Let's go to Room B," Blake said. "The topic for the session is 'When to Use an Incendiary Device.' Sounds right up our alley."

* * * * *

Training sessions consisted of classroom lectures reinforced through practical exercises. Courses included Bombs and Explosives, Physical Security, Countermeasures, Economic Sabotage, Target Selection, Encryption/Decryption, Vandalism, Poison Hoaxes, Bomb Hoaxes, and Arson.

Lexie and Blake carefully selected their courses and participated in all three afternoon sessions. They walked back to their tent to unwind and compare notes before dinner.

"I can't believe we're being trained to actually build and use a bomb," Blake said.

"I know. It's crazy."

"It didn't take long for word to spread that we're from the United States," he said. "We're like rock stars. I think the only person who hasn't approached us is Holden."

Lexie nodded. "He disappeared after the welcome

address. I guess we'll have to be patient. After all, it's only the first day."

Blake examined the schedule. "There are movie screenings too. That might be interesting."

"I warn you, the movies will be graphic. You might not ever eat meat again after you watch one or two of them."

"You don't know me very well, my dear. Nothing can come between me and my cheeseburger." Flipping through the schedule, he brightened. "There's a welcome reception tonight at eight thirty with free food."

"I wouldn't get too excited. It's probably tortilla chips, salsa, and hummus."

"Speaking of food, let's go to dinner."

*　*　*　*　*

The welcome reception ended at nine thirty. Lexie and Blake were getting ready to leave the main reception area when Robert dashed over and wedged his way between the two, throwing an arm around each of them.

"Ready to meet some people?"

"Definitely," Lexie answered.

"We're going to a private afterparty. Bring a little money with you; there'll be a donation request for booze."

Lexie bent to pick up her water bottle. She'd been carrying it all day—she wanted people to see her carrying it so it wouldn't be suspicious when she needed to use it to make recordings. Luckily, the group was environmentally conscious, so everyone carried reusable drink containers.

The agents followed Robert to a cabin in the part of the camp where the permanent residents lived. Sprawled haphazardly across the outlying area were mobile homes, recreational vehicles, and cabins. Some of the trailers had added porches and awnings to create outdoor living areas. Garden gnomes and flowerpots decorated the makeshift lawns; gravel crunched under the trio's feet as they made their way to the last trailer.

"This is it," Robert said. He bolted up the three rickety steps, opened the screechy screen door, and knocked. The English activist whom Lexie and Blake had met earlier answered the door.

"Hi, Barnabas," Robert said. "You remember my friends, Lexie and Blake?"

"Ah, yes, the Americans. Come in."

They entered the kitchen area and Lexie stumbled over the peeling linoleum floor. There were dishes piled in the sink and cabinet doors that hung askew. The pungent aroma of marijuana filled the air.

In the living room, surrounded by mismatched furniture, sat numerous activists. Perched in a threadbare, overstuffed chair was Holden Graham. Some of the activists stood to meet Lexie and Blake, but Holden remained seated, as if he were holding court with his subjects gathered around him.

Robert walked over and made eye contact with Holden. "Holden, these are the Americans that I told you about. Lexie and Blake, this is Holden. He's also from the United States."

"Have a seat," Holden said, motioning toward a stained, avocado-green couch.

"Thank you," Lexie said as she sank down into the saggy couch cushions.

The sleeves of Holden's perfectly fitted, black V-neck shirt lightly hugged his biceps, emphasizing their shape. With his coiffed hair and GQ style, Holden looked more like a model than an activist. Blake, who was seated next to Lexie, shifted so he could see the man better. "Where are you from?" he asked.

Holden arched one eyebrow. "Why do you want to know?"

Blake's eyes narrowed. "Just curious. I didn't hear an accent, which is unusual around here."

"Where are *you* from?" Holden countered.

"Why do *you* want to know?" A detectable edge had entered Blake's voice.

Oh shit, Lexie thought. *Not the testosterone. This could go bad.*

Holden stared at the other man for several moments; then he burst into laughter. Gesturing at Barnabas, he directed, "Get our new friends something to drink."

Barnabas returned from the kitchen carrying two bottles of beer. He handed one to Lexie and the other to Blake.

"Thank you," Blake said.

Jade came from the back bedroom. "I see the Americans have graced us with their presence. Welcome."

"Thanks for the invite," Lexie replied, taking a swig of beer.

Over in the corner, two men passed a joint back and

forth. "Have you met the Swedes yet?" Jade asked, noticing Lexie's interest in them.

The agent shook her head. Both Swedish men were blond and handsome and appeared to be in their late twenties. They stopped passing the joint long enough to introduce themselves.

"I'm Viktor," said the nearer of the two, "and this is my partner, Olof."

Viktor had short, wavy hair and a matching, close-cropped goatee. Olof had long hair pulled up on the top of his head in a man-bun. He had a long, unruly beard and eyes the color of cornflowers.

"Hello, I'm Lexie and this is Blake. Nice to meet you."

Viktor and Olof pulled their chairs over and joined the circle. "Would you like a hit?" Olof asked, offering the joint.

"No thank you," Lexie said.

"I'm good with my beer," Blake said.

"Robert?" Olof asked, waving the joint through the air.

Robert shook his head. "Maybe later."

Shrugging, Olof took another puff. "More for me."

"What brings you two all the way to the Netherlands?" Holden asked.

Since things seemed tense between Holden and Blake, Lexie took the lead. "Mostly to attend the Gathering, but I have to admit I've always wanted to visit Amsterdam, so this was a great way to do both."

Holden leaned forward, focusing his attention on Lexie. His bronze skin and intense stare vaguely reminded her of someone from her past.

Logan, poor, sweet Logan. Oh my god. Those intense, breath-taking eyes.

"Tell me about yourself," Holden said.

The resemblance unnerved Lexie, causing her to stammer. "Ahh . . . well . . . not much to tell, really. I grew up mostly in the southern United States. I took the common road to activism. I started out as a vegetarian because I love animals, then became vegan. I watched the documentary *Meet Your Meat* five years ago. It made me sick, so sick I knew I had to do something. I became an animal rights activist."

"Do you still live in the South?"

"I do, but I really want to move to the West Coast."

"Why don't you?"

"It's not that easy."

"Sure it is," Holden said, waving his hand dismissively. "You sell everything except what you want to take with you, buy an Amtrak ticket, and go west."

"What about a job? The West Coast is expensive. I would need to find a job before I moved out there."

"Bullshit. You're making excuses. If you want to do it, then you can do it. I have some friends on the West Coast. If you're serious about moving, I can help you. As long as you're not opposed to couch surfing, at least for a while."

"Not at all," Lexie said, calling the bluff. "I'll do anything if it gets me to where I want to be."

Holden turned his attention to Blake. "What about you, hero? You going to move to the West Coast with your girl?"

"I'm giving it some thought," the other man replied.

"How long you two been together?" Jade asked.

"Two months," Blake answered, following the script that he and Lexie had formulated.

"That's not long," Jade said. "How did you meet?"

"At work."

"Where do you work?"

Relaxing a bit as he took his eyes off Holden, Blake replied, "I own a printing equipment and supply business. We do everything from simple print jobs to screen and heat transfer printing. Lexie started working for me about three months ago."

"And now she's banging the boss," Holden said.

"She actually works for my office manager, so technically she's banging her boss's boss."

"You guys have only known each other for three months and you decided to journey halfway around the world together for an animal rights event? That doesn't make fucking sense," Holden said.

"Lexie's been an activist for years, but as you can probably tell, I'm new to the movement," Blake admitted, letting some vulnerability into his expression. "I want to support her, and she's taught me a lot about being an activist. I'm still learning, but I want to do all I can to save animals. I was a meat eater until I met Lexie."

"You seem a little old to change your entire lifestyle overnight." Holden leaned forward, his brow furrowing in skepticism.

Putting on a shit-eating grin, Blake replied, "Haven't you ever done anything crazy for a girl?"

Oh no, Lexie thought. *You didn't just say that.*

Holden shot bolt upright, any trace of warmth gone

from his face. "So, you think our way of life is crazy? Fuck you."

"Lighten up, dude," Blake said, realizing too late what he'd done. "That's not what I meant."

Shut up, Blake. You're making things worse. You're gonna get us thrown out of the camp the first night and we'll never find the missing constable.

"Robert," Holden said. "Take your *new* friends and get the hell out of my camper."

Blake stared incredulously at Holden and then beelined toward the door, forcing Robert and Lexie to keep up with him. "Asshole," he muttered, not entirely to himself. Outside the trailer, he vented his feelings more loudly: "That guy is a total dick."

"Slow down, Blake," Lexie said. "He might be a dick, but he's the head dick, so a little ass-kissing wouldn't hurt."

Blake spun around to face Lexie. His nostrils flared against his crimson face. "I find it extremely distasteful to kiss anyone's ass."

"Well, maybe you need to rethink your approach," she snapped, "before you get us thrown out of the damn camp."

Blake took a breath and ran his hands through his uncombed hair. "Did I just screw things up?"

The truth is, you might've screwed up the entire mission, Lexie thought. "Let's hope not," she said out loud. "Holden is going to be a hard nut to crack. We can't expect a miracle overnight. Let's go back to the tent and relax. We have plenty of time to make this right."

Blake looked at Robert. "What do you think?"

"I think Lexie is right. Today is the first day. Just lighten up some, mate. I'll keep my eyes and ears open and let you know if I see or hear anything. Go back and relax. I'll see you both at breakfast."

"Okay. See you in the morning," Blake said.

Robert peeled off while Lexie and Blake returned to their tent.

* * * * *

Blake remained quiet for most of the evening. They were getting ready to text Kate when Blake turned to Lexie and said, "I'm sorry."

"For what?"

"For screwing things up with Holden."

"Don't be so hard on yourself, Blake. I'll work on cozying up to him. I think I can get him to come around."

Blake handed Lexie his boot. "You want to do the honors?"

Taking hold of the boot, she crawled deep inside her sleeping bag to keep the phone and the telltale light it emitted hidden from any unexpected visitors. She removed the phone from the boot and sent the following message to Kate: *All is well. No issues so far. We have had contact with both Holden and Jade.*

Within twenty seconds, Kate had replied. *Message received. Stay safe and remember to delete this message.*

Will do. Thanks for the reminder.

Lexie deleted the messages, powered down the phone, and put it back in the boot. A few minutes later, Blake's slow, heavy breathing signaled that he was sound asleep. Lexie's thoughts were running rampant, keeping her awake.

Why did Adam pick Blake for this assignment? He clearly has no experience dealing with animal rights activists, and he wasn't ready for this level of scrutiny. I would be better off on my own instead of having to have a babysitter. How the hell am I going to recover from Blake's blunder?

Sighing, she concluded, *I'm going to have to figure out a way to do this on my own.*

11

The Gathering—Day Two

Morning came too soon. Lexie had been kept awake by the wild partying going on all around them. She'd managed to get to sleep around three in the morning but was abruptly awakened by the loud gagging sounds of a partygoer retching outside the tent.

"I have to pee," she said. "I hate having to trudge all the way to the public bathroom."

"I'll go with you," muttered Blake. "I need to brush my teeth."

They emerged from their tent to a chilly, cloudy morning.

Lexie quickly crossed her arms. "Brrr, I need my hoodie," she hissed, her breath fogging in the air. Before she could turn around, Blake was ducking back into their tent, grabbing the black hoodie from the corner, and handing it to her.

"Thanks."

Lexie gasped when she saw the line for the bathroom. As usual, it was much longer for the ladies' side.

"This sucks," she said. "One toilet and shower facility for

three hundred people. No telling how long it's gonna take me. I'll see you back at the tent." Nodding, Blake headed for the men's room.

Lexie was nearly in tears by the time she made it to the bathroom. She bounced up and down and crossed her legs. "You can go in front of me," the young girl with pink hair a spot ahead said to her. "You look like you have to go worse than me."

"Thank you. I'm about to pop. I drank too much beer last night."

"Me too. Please, you go first."

Lexie took the girl up on her offer. Afterward, she washed her face and brushed her teeth. When the pink-haired girl took her spot at the sink to do the same, Lexie turned to her and said, "I'm Lexie."

"I'm Annette."

"I remember you. You're one of the organizers."

Annette nodded.

"Thank you for putting together such an amazing event," Lexie said, though she had to work to make it believable—the wait for the bathroom hadn't exactly left her feeling amazing. "I can't imagine how much work it took to organize something this large."

"It required a lot of work, but I was happy to do it." Sizing Lexie up, she said, "You're the American that I keep hearing about."

Lexie smiled. "I didn't know I was such a celebrity."

"You and your boyfriend came from so far away. It's always nice to have activists from the United States. I would enjoy talking to you at some point about how things work in America."

"Sure," Lexie said. "Any time."

The other woman smiled. "I have to run now, but maybe later today we can sit down for a chat."

"I would like that."

Lexie returned to the tent to find Blake stretched out on top of his sleeping bag, reading a paperback.

"Ready for breakfast?" he asked.

"I am. I had a chance to talk to Annette, the Dutch activist who organized all this."

"Is she the one with the pink hair?"

"Yes."

Blake laughed.

"What are you laughing at?"

"Women and bathrooms. Men go to the toilet to get things done. Women make a social event out of going to pee."

Lexie laughed. "I guess we do." Shuddering, she said, "I can't imagine what the bathroom situation is going to be like by Monday. It's already disgusting, and it's only the second day. Plus there's always a long line."

Blake rolled over on his side and propped his head up with his hand and elbow. "You know what's weird? There was a long line at the men's room as well. All these guys were standing around waiting, and I saw this long communal urinal made out of sheet metal that wasn't being used. It was strange because it was just a few inches off the floor."

"A long, trough-type urinal just a few inches off the floor?"

"Yeah. I guess it's a European thing."

Lexie cocked her head to the side and grinned. "Did you use it?"

"Of course I did. Why stand in line?"

Lexie started laughing.

"What's so funny?"

"You're such an idiot. That isn't a ground urinal, it's a foot wash."

The color drained from his face. "A what?"

"A foot wash. Have you not noticed that we're camping on a soccer field?"

"Oh shit. You mean people wash their feet in there and I pissed in it? No wonder I got some strange looks."

"What? You mean the 'stupid American' look?"

"That's the one."

Lexie laughed so hard she snorted.

"Did you just snort?"

"No. I didn't snort."

"I think you did. You're a snorter."

"I might be a snorter, but at least I didn't pee in a foot wash."

"You're not gonna let me live that down, are you?"

"Nope. Never."

Blake smiled and shook his head. "Let's go eat."

* * * * *

Dried-out vegan muffins and horrible coffee were the morning offerings.

Lexie whispered in Blake's ear, "We need hazard pay for having to drink this coffee."

He nodded. "I'll buy you a good coffee when we get back to Amsterdam."

"I'll hold you to it."

Lexie noticed that even without sleep, Blake's blue eyes twinkled when he gave her his sideways grin.

Stop thinking about his eyes and sexy smile. Stick to the business at hand.

"Any sign of Robert?" he asked, glancing through the rest of the crowd.

"Not so far. Maybe he stayed out late and he's sleeping in." Lexie unfolded her crumpled schedule and smoothed it out on the table. "Let's see what we have in store for today."

They decided to split up for most of the morning workshops and meet back for lunch. Lexie selected a seat in Room B and sipped her coffee, waiting for the session to begin.

"Is this seat taken?"

Lexie looked up and saw the pink-haired woman from earlier. Smiling, she replied, "Hello, Annette. No, please sit."

"Thank you," the other woman said as she slid into her chair. "Much better location for a chat than the water closet."

"I agree."

Leaning closer, Annette said, "I heard your boyfriend and Holden didn't exactly get on well last night."

"Wow, word travels fast around here," Lexie said, unable to keep the annoyance from leaking into her voice. "Why is everyone so concerned with what Holden thinks?"

"Well, without getting too specific, he's kind of the leader of the pack, to use an American phrase."

"I see. Well, Blake's not going to take shit from anyone, including the leader of the pack. Hopefully they can work something out." Lexie ran her fingers through her mop of blonde hair, then tied it up into a ponytail.

"So you got off on the wrong foot," Annette said. "Things will get better."

"I guess I feel like a fish out of water. I kind of thought we would, I don't know—"

"Sit around a campfire and sing 'Kumbaya'?"

Lexie laughed. "Maybe so."

"It's hard being the outsider," the other woman said sympathetically, resting her hand on top of Lexie's. "Most of us know one another. No worries; you'll be accepted soon enough. By the way, where is Blake?"

"He's sitting in on another panel this morning."

"It's kind of a cliché question, but why did you two come to the Gathering?"

"I'm interested in everything they're teaching, but I guess if I had to choose a main focus, it would be to learn better direct action techniques. We don't have anything like this in America. I've already learned so much, and it's only the second day."

"That's good to hear. As an organizer, I wanted to make sure we covered the spectrum of interests."

"What about you? Do you have a specific area of interest in the movement?"

"My passion is animal rehabilitation and placement. I take sick and injured animals and nurse them back to health, then find loving homes for them. I've been doing it since I was fourteen years old. Someday I would love to have enough money to build my own sanctuary."

"Wow, that's wonderful."

Annette grinned, completely unselfconscious. "I love it so much. There's nothing better than freeing a defenseless animal from pain and torture and watching it heal and become whole again. Well, as whole as we can make some of the poor creatures."

"I've bet you've seen so much pain over the years."

The joy faded from her face, then, replaced by old regret. "I have."

"You're a good person, Annette. The world needs more people like you."

Annette looked down and fiddled with the bottom of her shirt. "Thank you."

The speaker entered the room. He was an older man with thinning gray hair, wearing a wrinkled blue shirt with the sleeves rolled up; stained, baggy blue jeans; and floppy sandals.

"Have you ever heard Dr. Adams speak?" Annette asked.

"No."

"You're in for a treat," she whispered as he adjusted the microphone. "He's so inspirational. He's written several books, and he's also a professor of philosophy at the University of Liverpool."

"Good morning," the old man said, leaning a bit closer to the mic. "I'm Professor Gregory Adams, and I'm an animal rights activist like each and every one of you, so please call me Greg. I prefer an informal approach to teaching, so do you mind if I pull up a chair and sit?"

Murmurs from the crowd indicated that no one was opposed.

Leaving the microphone behind, Greg pulled a chair to the middle of the room. Everyone formed a circle around him. Once the general scuffling of moving chairs had died down, he continued:

"We're here to talk about the road to direct action—why we do it and when it's appropriate. If you're of the opinion that illegal direct action should never be used, then I recommend you leave now, because our whole discussion is going to center around actions that some consider illegal."

Greg looked around the room to see if anyone wanted to leave. When no one stood, he continued, "So, am I to assume that you people are the rebels, the lawbreakers, the revolutionaries of our movement?"

"YES," Lexie said loudly.

"WE ARE!" Annette screamed.

The crow joined in cheering and shouting.

"That's what I like to hear," Greg said. "I'm going to teach you how to engage in direct action campaigns to save animals' lives without getting arrested."

Lexie felt the smile stretch across her face.

"I've spent most of my adult life fighting to save animals. I can't think of a better cause than dedicating your life to freeing innocent animals from human manipulation, exploitation, and abuse. You are our next generation of warriors. I'm here to teach you how to fully utilize the array of animal protection laws on the books, how to propose new laws or change existing ones, and how to wage an underground war when laws don't work and people won't listen."

After class, the crowd was pumped up.

"You were right," Lexie said to Annette. "Dr. Adams is so inspirational. I'm ready to go free minks and burn down labs."

Annette laughed. "I wouldn't say that too loudly."

"I wouldn't say it at all if we were in the United States. That kind of talk would have the FBI on my doorstep. I think it's wonderful that we can openly discuss direct action and not worry about getting arrested."

Frowning, Annette asked, "Don't you discuss direct action campaigns when you attend animal rights conferences in the United States?"

"No way. In the States, we always have police informants infiltrating our meetings, so we have to be careful. In fact, any direct action talk takes place after hours and only with extremely trusted individuals. That's part of the reason our movement doesn't make as much progress as we should. We're all scared of our own shadows."

"I see why. I didn't know it was like that in America."

"I'm going to say thank you to Dr. Adams," Lexie said, standing. "Want to come?"

"I have organizational duties to attend to, but I'll catch up with you later. It was nice talking to you, Lexie," Annette said, waving.

"You too. I'll see you a little later."

Lexie approached the professor just as he was leaving. "That was very inspirational, Professor Adams."

He turned to face Lexie. "Thank you, but please call me Greg. You're American." He didn't say it as a question.

"I am. My name is Lexie."

"You came a long way for a conference."

"I was just telling Annette that conferences in the States aren't as open and honest as this one. It's refreshing to be allowed to discuss direct action and other taboo subjects in the open."

"I would love to hear more about animal rights in the United States," he said pleasantly. "I'm on my way to the communal area for a cup of coffee. Would you like to join me?"

"I would."

Greg stepped to the side and waved his arm forward. "After you."

Lexie opened the door to find that the weather had taken a turn for the worse.

"Bollocks," Greg said. "It's pissing out there."

Lexie laughed. "I love English expressions."

The two ran through the rain to the main gathering area. Others had the same idea—the common area was packed with people.

"Would you like a pastry?" Lexie asked. "My treat."

"I would. You buy the pastries and I'll buy the coffee."

"The coffee is free."

"I know," Greg replied, a crooked grin forming on his face, "that's why I offered."

The two found a corner table to discuss their philosophies and views.

"How did you first become an activist?" Lexie asked through a bit of pastry.

Greg ran his hand over his stubbly gray whiskers. "Have you ever had something that happened to you as a child influence you for the rest of your life?"

Lexie thought for a second before answering. "Yeah. Peas. I can't look at a pea. One night at dinner, I think I was seven years old, my sister threw up green peas all over me. I don't mean a little bit, I'm talking covered from head to toe in pea puke. It started a chain reaction at the table. To this day, I can't eat or even look at a green pea."

Greg laughed. "That's hysterical."

"No, not really. I'm still traumatized from it."

"Well, like you with the peas, I had a traumatizing event in my childhood that changed my way of interpreting the world."

Lexie put her elbows on the table and leaned forward. "What happened?"

"When I was ten, my brother and I had an old yellow cat that we rescued. We named him Bingo, and he lived outside. When Bingo became pregnant, we realized that he was a she. My father wouldn't allow us to bring her inside, so my brother and I made sure she was comfortable and had plenty of warm blankets."

"That's sweet."

He took a sip of coffee, then continued. "My brother, Chet, was two years older than me. We really bonded over taking care of Bingo. We were both so excited for the kittens to come. One night, Chet woke me up and told me the kittens were coming. We snuck out to the barn to watch the birthing process. Each kitten came out in its own amniotic sac, which Bingo broke open after delivery. It was the most beautiful thing that I had ever witnessed in my young life. My brother and I stood and watched, both shedding tears of joy."

Lexie smiled and took a sip of her coffee.

"Chet pretended to be sick so he could stay home from school and take care of the kittens. When I got home from school, I found Chet huddled in the corner, crying his eyes out, holding Bingo. The kittens were missing from the box. My father told Chet we didn't need any more stupid cats. He gathered up the kittens, placed them in a burlap bag with a large rock, and threw the sack into the raging river. When Chet tried to fight him, my father beat him with his belt. Chet's face was swollen where my father struck him."

Tears filled Lexie's eyes. "That's horrible. I'm so sorry that happened to you."

"Two things happened that day, Lexie. My brother vowed to never love anything ever again, and I vowed I would protect every animal I could. My father may have extinguished my dear brother's fervor, but he inadvertently lit a fire in me that would become my lifelong passion. I guess, in a way, I'm still trying to save that sack of kittens."

"I can't believe a parent would do that to his sons," she said, shaking her head.

The professor nodded grimly. "I never forgave him for that day. It was bad enough that he killed the innocent kittens, but he also took away my brother's innocence. Those special moments that Chet and I spent together, bonding over our mutual love of Bingo, were gone forever. To this day, Chet has never had a companion animal."

"I feel kind of foolish telling you my pea story now."

Greg smiled. "Don't feel foolish. I'm glad that your childhood trauma involved green peas and not kittens."

"Me too."

After a few moments' pause, the two continued to discuss a wide range of subjects. Their discussion had lasted well over an hour when Holden, who Lexie had seen watching them and sizing things up, finally approached.

"You two look to be engaged in some deep philosophical discussion over here," he said. "Do you mind if I join you?"

"Please do," Lexie replied.

"Yes," Greg said, scooting his chair over to make space for the new arrival, "Lexie and I have been contemplating animal rights, politics, and the reasons Americans don't fully grasp the importance of European soccer."

Holden laughed. "I played basketball in the states, so I can't help you with the last one."

Knowing that she needed to make things right with Holden, Lexie fell back on her undercover training. *Basketball—that's an area of common interest.* "What position?" she asked.

"Huh?"

"What position did you play in basketball?"

"Since I never hit six feet, I played guard. Do you follow basketball?"

She nodded. "I love college hoops. I played in high school, but as you can see, it was never my destiny."

Holden laughed. "Yeah, not a lot of colleges are interested in five-foot-nothing for their team."

"Hey, I'll have you know I'm almost five-foot-two. I really don't think it's proper to make fun of the vertically challenged."

Holden focused his full attention on Lexie, maintaining steady eye contact. His fervor was both appealing and unnerving; she moistened her lips and glanced away. When she looked back, he had a wide grin plastered on his face.

Holden shifted his attention to Greg. "Are you enjoying the Gathering, Greg?"

"I *am* enjoying myself. It's quite a large crowd."

"Yes," Holden said. "The organizers did a great job this year."

"How many more times are you speaking?" Lexie asked the professor.

"I teach again this afternoon, and I'm on a panel tomorrow morning."

"You're an amazing speaker," she told him. "Holden, you should sit in on Greg's next lecture. He has some brilliant ideas."

"I plan to," Holden said. "I wanted to attend this morning, but unfortunately I was tied up and couldn't make it."

"Lexie was sharing with me how different animal rights conferences in the United States are from what we experience in this setting," Greg said, taking a sip of cold coffee.

"Have you been to many conferences in the states?" Holden asked her.

"Quite a few. I stopped going when I realized that most

of the people who attend like to talk big, but when it comes time for action, they—"

"Were all words and no action," Holden finished.

"Exactly. Also, no one openly discusses direct action campaigns like over here. This is so refreshing."

"I didn't realize you felt so strongly about direct action. Why don't you tell me some of the things you've done for the cause?"

He's baiting me.

Lexie raised one eyebrow and said, "You of all people should know we don't talk about that, especially to someone we don't know. Being American, I'm too scared and too smart to talk to anyone about it. At home, if you even mention direct action, the FBI shows up on your doorstep. I've even been followed home from aboveground protests. In fact, that's one of the reasons that I quit going to protests. I didn't want to be on the FBI's radar. If I'm going to do something to garner the attention of the FBI, then it's going to be for something big, not for some demonstration."

After a pause, Holden nodded. "I agree with you. I try to fly below the radar as well."

Greg stood and placed his hand on her shoulder. "It's been nice talking to you both, but I need to get my materials organized for this afternoon. We should talk more. I enjoy getting the American perspective on subjects."

"Anytime," Lexie said.

Holden stood, and the two men shook hands. After Greg had left, the other man sat back down, facing Lexie. "Where's your loser boyfriend?"

"Enough already," she growled, her friendly façade

slipping now that Greg was no longer present. "You claim to be so open and accepting of others, but last night you acted like a huge prick."

"Wow. Tell me what you really think."

"The poor guy said one wrong thing and you act like he murdered a puppy in front of you. He's new to activism and he doesn't know as much as we do. You could've cut him a break instead of humiliating him."

"You might be right. I may have stepped over the line, but there's something about that guy that I don't like. I definitely don't trust him. And I don't think you should either," he said, wagging an index finger.

Lexie rolled her eyes. "You don't even know him. How can you jump to that conclusion so quickly?"

"I've learned to trust my instincts, and my instinct tells me he may not be who he says he is. How well do you really know him?"

"Well enough." Lexie stood to leave.

Holden reached out and grabbed her wrist. "Please sit. I want to talk to you about something. We won't discuss your boyfriend."

Lexie sat back down, hiding her satisfaction. Things were going exactly as she had hoped they would.

"You're sexy when you get all riled up," Holden said with a smirk. "Did you know that your cheeks flush when you get angry?"

"Oh, for god's sake. What did you want to talk about?"

He grinned, then continued. "Were you serious when you mentioned your desire to participate in direct action campaigns?"

Lexie nodded.

"I might be able to hook you up with some people, but we need to get to know one another a little better. I don't really know anything about you other than you're an American."

"I don't know anything about you either. By the way, how did you know I was interested in *participating* in direct action campaigns? We were discussing conferences, not actions."

Holden smirked. "I talked to Annette earlier today. She mentioned that you might be a good candidate for underground warfare. Any interest?"

Lexie leaned in and closed the distance. "You have my attention."

"What I'm going to say next is really going to piss you off, but it's the only way we can continue this conversation."

"Go ahead."

"You can't share any of this conversation with your boyfriend."

"He has a name. His name is Blake."

"Okay, you can't share any of this information with *Blake*. I'm sorry, but I don't trust the guy. You haven't known him that long either."

"I've known him long enough."

"I don't think you have."

She leaned back by a degree, pretending to think things over. "Let's say I agree to your parameters. Then what?"

"Then over the course of the next couple of days, we'll talk. If, at the end of the Gathering, you want to move forward, then I'll make sure you have a team of people who can help you move to the next phase."

"The next phase being direct action campaigns?" Lexie asked.

"Yep."

"How do you propose that I ditch Blake in this setting?"

Smirking, Holden replied, "You're a smart girl. You'll find a way."

"Let me think about it."

Holden stood. "Don't take too long."

She watched as he strode away from the area, not bothering to look back.

* * * * *

Lexie met Blake at the tent before lunch, suggesting that they go for a walk in the woods to avoid anyone overhearing their conversation. A tall fence line protected the camp from the outside world, but, Blake told her, "There's a gate in the back corner. Robert gave me the code for it. If you need to get out, it's 4-2-1-1-#."

The two wandered to the beautiful wooded recreation area adjacent to the campgrounds, silently taking in the scenery as they walked. When they were a good distance from the camping area, Lexie told Blake about her conversation with Holden, being careful to keep her voice low.

"That guy is a total asshole," he said, his own voice rising a bit louder than was ideal.

"Maybe," Lexie said, throwing him a warning look.

"But I have a hook in him, so I'm going to start reeling him in. You have to be cool. I know it will be hard, but you're not supposed to know that he doesn't like you."

"It was evident from the party that he doesn't like me. I can't figure out what I did for him to distrust me, though. I must have done something to set him off."

"Or, he could simply see himself as the alpha male of the group and not like the competition."

"You think?"

She raised her hands in a shrug. "I have no idea, but at this point, I think we should go for it. I'll play his game and meet with him when he wants. It'll be interesting to see how far he'll go over the course of a few days. So far, he's our best lead to find Jonas. We have to follow up."

"He may leave you hanging."

"You're right, but he might help us locate Jonas. In addition, he could potentially set me up with a domestic terrorist cell in the United States. We won't know until we try."

"I don't like you meeting with him alone."

"Me neither, but I'll have my water bottle with me. I'll record all the conversations that I have with him from here on out."

"I guess we don't have a choice," Blake said, though his expression still looked reluctant. "I'm sorry I lost my cool with that guy."

"No worries. You've been doing undercover work long enough to know that sometimes the connection doesn't happen."

"You didn't have any trouble connecting."

"I've swum in these waters before," she said, keeping

her tone reassuring. "Animal rights extremists are a complicated lot. They can sniff out a newcomer pretty easily."

"I hope that's all it is," Blake sighed, staring off into the branches of a distant tree.

She circled around until he was looking her in the eye again. "What do you mean?"

"I don't know. I'm just not comfortable around these people. I'm used to dealing with a rougher, less intellectual crowd."

"I think you're reading too much into Holden's attitude. He's just being cautious. I think you need to stay clear of him and let him come to you."

He nodded. "I'll follow your lead on this one."

"We have time," she said. "It's only the second day."

"Don't remind me," Blake replied, grimacing. "It feels like day ten."

Lexie laughed. "Let's get back. We don't wanna miss lunch."

"That's debatable."

* * * * *

After lunch, Lexie and Blake attended two of the afternoon sessions together. They split up for the third and final lecture of the day. Believing there was a good chance Holden would show up for Professor Adams's second lecture, Lexie thought it might be better if Blake attended a different session. He opted to watch the documentary *Earthlings*. Lexie warned him that the movie used hidden camera footage to detail the graphic mistreatment of animals, but Blake assured her he could handle it.

Lexie arrived early for Professor Adams's lecture, taking a seat in front and off to the side. The room had a moldy smell and several water stains on the ceiling. Holden and Annette walked in together and wandered over to her.

"These seats taken?" Holden asked.

"Nope."

"Perfect," he replied, sliding into the seat at her left. Annette took the one on the right.

"Where's Blake?" the other woman asked.

"He's in the media room watching *Earthlings*."

Annette grimaced. "That's a hard one to watch."

"I warned him, but he really wanted to watch it." Lexie made eye contact with Holden and he winked at her; she felt her face flush. *Oh, this guy is trouble in more ways than one.*

She found it difficult to not stare at Holden. His mussed, honey-colored hair fell onto his narrow but muscular shoulders. With his hair, build, and sun-kissed skin, he could easily pass for a surfer—a look eerily reminiscent of Logan Burkhart. The thought tugged at Lexie's heartstrings.

* * * * *

After the class, Lexie, Holden, and Annette left the classroom together. The morning rain had turned the outdoors into a sloppy mess. Many of the campers elected to trudge through the mud barefoot, wearing trash bags, ponchos, and plastic tarps in a futile attempt to keep dry.

"This looks like the photos I've seen of Woodstock," Lexie said.

Annette laughed. "It does."

"Let's have some fun," Holden said, kicking off his flip-flops.

"What?" the two women asked simultaneously.

The American man grinned, wiggling his toes through the mud with muted squelches. "Come on, ladies. Where's your adventuresome spirit?"

Lexie sat down on the stoop and pulled off her boots and socks. She grinned, then jumped high in the air and landed next to Holden, splashing mud on him all the way to his chin. She stared at him, lips tight, waiting for his reaction.

Holden's eyes widened, a grin of his own slowly creeping across his face. "You're in so much trouble," he said.

Lexie laughed and tried to run, but he grabbed her and picked her up. "Oh no, I think I'm losing my balance," he said as he stumbled around, pretending to be off balance. "If I fall, you're gonna get muddy."

"Don't drop me."

"You're getting heavy. I might not be able to hold you."

"Please," she begged, interspersed with laughter, "please, please, don't drop me." The feel of Holden's muscular body pressed against hers sent shivers up and down her spine. Annette stood on the sidelines, watching and chuckling.

Holden stopped for a second and looked at Annette. "She hasn't joined us."

"I think she should," Lexie said.

Holden gently put her down; they looked at each other, then bolted toward Annette. "Get her!" Holden yelled.

Annette took off running. Lexie and Holden chased her, but she managed to lose them because they were laughing the whole way. The two eventually stopped to catch their breath.

"She's faster than she looks," Holden panted.

"I know. I can't believe she outran us both."

He smiled when Lexie reached over and used her pinky to wipe a chunk of mud from his cheek.

"Yes," she suddenly said, looking him in the eye. "The answer to the question you asked me earlier today regarding direct action is yes. I'm in."

* * * * *

Lexie and Blake sat with Robert and Jade at dinner. Neither of the agents had seen much of Robert, and they suspected that he and Jade had rekindled their romance.

"What was the highlight of your day?" Jade asked the pair of them.

"For me it was Professor Adams's lectures," Lexie said without hesitating. "He makes me want to run out and change the world."

"Did you like Professor Adams as well, Blake?"

Swallowing a mouthful of beans, Blake replied, "I didn't

sit in on his lectures, but it sounds like his discussions were pretty lively. I'm sorry I missed them."

"He's a great teacher," Jade agreed. "I've heard him speak several times."

"I watched *Earthlings*," Blake said. "Joaquin Phoenix did a great job narrating, but man, it was difficult to watch without throwing up."

"I've never made it through the whole movie in one sitting," Lexie said. "I've watched parts of it many times, but never the whole thing from start to finish."

Jade nodded sympathetically. "It's painful to watch."

"Have you guys seen *The Cove*?" Lexie asked. "It's an amazing documentary. I went to see it with some of my friends who weren't activists and it changed their lives. I thought they did a marvelous job showing the dolphin slaughter without being preachy. It really appealed to a more general audience instead of only animal rights activists."

"It's on the schedule for tonight," Robert said. "We should all watch it."

"What's it about?" Blake asked, leaning forward.

"There's a town off the coast of Japan called Taiji. Every year more than twenty thousand dolphins and porpoises are herded into a cove and slaughtered. The meat is sold as food in Japan and other parts of Asia. Dolphin meat contains toxic levels of mercury, but the Japanese government lies to the citizens and passes it off as whale meat. The dolphins that aren't slaughtered are sold to aquariums and marine parks around the world and suffer a lifetime of captivity."

Lexie felt her face flush and her heart race.

"Can you handle watching the movie again?" Robert asked. "You seem pretty worked up."

"Dolphins are my favorite animals. I love everything about them, so to see them needlessly slaughtered tears my heart open. But yes, I can watch the movie again."

"Let's do it," Jade said.

After dinner, the foursome walked over to the media room. People were already gathered, but a few attendees swapped seats, allowing the two couples to sit together. Lexie noticed that Robert and Jade held hands during most of the movie. After the credits had rolled, Oskar, the young Finnish activist, started a discussion on how to end the captivity of not just dolphins but all marine animals.

Rising from her seat, Jade groaned. "Let's go have a drink."

"Where?" Lexie asked.

"A group of us are meeting at the bonfire tonight. We've commandeered some chairs and blankets for the evening. We can stop by my tent and pick up the cooler of beer."

"We want to contribute to the beer fund," Blake said. "Who do we pay?"

"Me," Jade replied. "Somehow I've been appointed the beer girl. Nico has a car, so he drives me to the liquor store every morning to get what we need for the day."

"If you need any help, I'll be glad to volunteer."

"Thanks, Blake. I might take you up on that offer. It gets heavy hauling it back and forth."

"I'm happy to help," he replied, giving a genuine smile.

Lexie hid a smile of her own, pleased to see that Blake seemed to be getting along with most of the activists.

The crowd gathered and people circled the open fire. Holden arrived with Fritz and another blond-haired, blue-eyed male. "Geez, *everyone* here seems to be blond," Lexie whispered to Blake as the three men made their way over to the agents' spot.

"Mind if we join you?" Holden asked.

"Not at all. Pull up a blanket," Lexie said, patting the ground beside her.

Holden did so, sighing as he stretched out on the ground. "Have you met Fritz and Emil?"

"I've met Fritz, but I haven't had the pleasure of meeting Emil."

"Emil, this is Lexie and her boyfriend, Blake. They are from America. Emil is from Germany."

"I like the name Emil," Lexie said. "I don't hear it often."

"Thank you," said the newest blond man. "It means *rival*. Is Lexie short for something?"

"Alexis."

He nodded, contemplating. "Alexis is a strong name. What does it mean?"

"My grandmother told me that it means *helper* or *defender*."

"You look like a defender," Emil replied. "I'm going to call you by your full name."

Lexie smiled.

The night wore on. Only a few people remained at the fire when the topic of documentary films came up.

"Lexie talked us into watching *The Cove* tonight," Jade said. "Have you guys seen the film?"

Everyone had.

"I think if more filmmakers took the approach *The Cove* filmmaker did, then more people would see the movies and make lifestyle changes," Blake said.

"What do you mean?" Holden asked.

"I watched two movies today, *Earthlings* and *The Cove.* There isn't any way mainstream moviegoers would sit through *Earthlings.* Seems to me that a documentary like *The Cove* would appeal to a wide audience and not simply animal rights activists—thus getting more people involved in saving dolphins."

"Are you saying that animal rights activists need to be more considerate of the feelings of the general population?" Holden said. "We wouldn't want to *offend* anyone by showing the world the animal abuse atrocities?"

"I'm not saying that at all."

Glowering, Holden spoke through a face of stone. "I think you are."

"I'm saying," Blake said, fighting to keep his tone level, "that changes can be made in the world without harassing the general population. My momma always said, you catch more flies using honey than vinegar."

Holden threw his hands up in the air. "How can I argue with that down-home logic?" he said sarcastically. "Face it, Blake. When it comes to animal rights, you're a pussy. You claim you want to save animals, but you don't want to get your hands dirty to do it."

Blake stood and glared down at Holden. "You're a

sanctimonious ass. You don't like me because I don't feel the need to destroy property or injure innocent people. Setting off bombs does nothing to further the cause."

"How do you know?" Holden asked, pulling himself to his feet and matching Blake's stare. "You haven't been around long enough to know what does and doesn't work."

Lexie stood and took Blake's hand. "Holden's right, Blake. The lives of innocent animals depend on our activism driving us to destruction if necessary. We have a duty to push boundaries, for the animals."

Blake yanked his hand away from Lexie. "That's where I disagree. We can make changes without blowing shit up."

"Don't you think we've tried other means?" Lexie demanded. "Activists have worked for years to make industry changes with factory farming, but in the end it comes down to money and power. Animal rights activists have neither, which means we don't get a say. Sometimes activists have to take a stand and force people to pay attention any way we can."

"You're a fool, Lexie," Blake replied, looking at her as though he were learning the truth for the first time. "You've let these people brainwash you."

"No, Blake," she shot back, raising her voice. "This is me talking. I'm a rebel, a revolutionary, and an activist. If you can't accept me for who I am, then maybe we should rethink our relationship."

"You're talking like a crazy person. I'm going to bed."

Blake stormed off, leaving Lexie standing in the amber glow of the bonfire and staring into the blackness.

"I should go after him," she said, but her voice was full of reluctance.

Holden took her hand and said, "Stay."

She nodded. Holden's hand lingered in hers until they returned to their spots by the campfire.

The others gradually left, leaving the two of them alone. Mesmerized by the glowing embers and the pulsating rhythm of the flames, they sat shoulder to shoulder, leaning into each other.

"This is nice," Lexie said.

"It is," Holden replied, nuzzling a little closer. "Thank you for staying with me."

Lexie inhaled the smoky air and listened to the soft crackling of the fire.

"Lexie, I know that we've just met, but I feel a kinship toward you." Holden winced. "I'm sorry. That sounded weird."

"No, it didn't. I know what you mean. It's like we were destined to meet."

He turned to face her. "Exactly. We're on the same trajectory. I'm sure that together we can do amazing things."

"Things are complicated for me," Lexie replied, looking back toward the fire.

"You mean because of Blake?"

"Not just because of him. I'm confused—not sure which way to go." She exhaled deeply in frustration. "I want to move forward with my activism, but I'm not sure how."

"You'll figure it out. I'll help you."

"Thank you, Holden. It's nice to be with someone who understands."

He reached over and took Lexie's hand. "I'll help you figure things out. You're not alone."

* * * * *

A couple hours later, Lexie crawled into the tent.

"Glad you could make it home," Blake said.

Lexie laughed. After getting no response, she realized that Blake wasn't joking. "Are you mad?"

He rolled over to face her, his eyebrows lowered and his voice sharp. "Of course I'm mad. Holden is a total ass, and you're buying into his bullshit."

"Keep your voice down," Lexie hissed.

"Everyone here is either drunk or high. No one is listening to us."

"I don't understand why you're mad. Our fight was good undercover work. It opened the door for me with Holden. Wasn't that the goal?"

"In case you've forgotten, the goal is to find the missing cop."

"And to determine if there's a viable terrorist threat to the United States. Which is what we are doing and doing quite well. Don't let those guys get to you."

"I'm not, Lexie. It's . . . oh, forget it. Let's try to get some sleep."

"I need to text Kate," she replied, aware of the sullenness sneaking into her voice but unable to stop it.

"I already did."

"You sure you don't want to talk about this?"

"No," he snapped. "I want to sleep. I haven't slept since we left Amsterdam."

"Okay. Well, good night."

Blake angrily rolled back over so his back was to Lexie. "We'll see."

Christ, she thought to herself. *Acting like a pair of angry teenagers.*

Part of her whispered that maybe Blake was right—maybe she had gone further than was necessary to get Holden on her side. The rest of her angrily dismissed the thought. She'd been with these people, knew far more about them than Blake did. He was being irrational.

Throwing herself down onto her own sleeping bag, she closed her eyes. *Being mad at him isn't worth it. Just try to get some sleep.*

12

The Gathering—Day Three

Blake woke early on Saturday morning, quietly dressed inside his sleeping bag, and left Lexie sound asleep. Neither of them had been sleeping well, so he decided to venture out and allow her some much-needed rest. Besides, he didn't exactly relish the thought of talking to her so soon after what had happened last night.

He found Robert and Jade at breakfast. Remembering that Dutch intelligence showed Jade to be a heavy hitter among the extremists, he decided to try a new tactic.

"Good morning," Blake said. "I see I'm not the only early bird. Do you mind if I join you?"

"Not at all, please do," Robert replied.

Blake grabbed a Danish and a cup of black coffee, then took the seat beside Robert.

The other man put his hand on Blake's shoulder. "Sorry about how things went at the firepit last night, mate. Are you okay?"

Blake gave him a slight smile. "Thanks. Yeah, I'm all right."

"The situation became rather uncomfortable," Jade

said. "You and Lexie have . . . differing opinions about direct action, to say the least."

Sighing, Blake took a too-hot sip of coffee and felt it burn his tongue. "I don't know what we have anymore. Lexie has been in the animal rights world for a long time. I'm trying to catch up. She expected me to jump in with both feet and be as passionate about the cause as her, but I'm trying to find my way."

"That's understandable," Jade said. "Coming to the Gathering is a big step. Maybe you weren't ready for this level yet."

"I probably wasn't, but I'm here now. Don't get me wrong; I'm passionate about animal rights. I want to do all I can to save animals and to make the world a better place for the next generation. I feel like I just skipped several steps along the way." He blew on his coffee, then cautiously took another sip. "I don't have the foundation that all of you have. I think that's why I tend to say the wrong things and offend some people. I don't mean to trivialize the cause in any way. I want to do my part and play a vital role. I guess I'm trying to figure out what that role is."

Jade leaned across the table and surprised Blake by taking his hand. "You shouldn't feel bad, Blake. There is a part in our movement for everyone. You will discover your place in time."

Blake smiled. "Thank you."

Releasing Blake's hand, she continued. "Tell me about Lexie. I take it you didn't realize her level of commitment to the cause before you arrived here."

"I knew she was passionate, but I didn't realize she was

militant. She and I never discussed how far she was willing to go for the cause."

"How far do you think she is willing to go?" Jade asked.

He considered for a few moments. "Honestly, I don't know. Since we've been here, I've seen a whole new side of Lexie. She seems more . . . I don't know . . . more alive. It's like she's finally found herself. I'm happy for her, and I want to be part of her new journey."

"Deep down, are you ready for this kind of lifestyle change?"

Blake locked eyes with Jade. "I am. I really am."

"That's good to hear," she said.

"I just need to make Lexie understand that I'm ready."

"Find her and tell her what you just told us," Robert put in. "Make sure she understands that you're willing to take this journey with her, but you need her help."

"I agree with Robert," Jade said. "But Blake, if you and Lexie are truly on different paths, you must have the strength to let her go. She needs to fight her battle and you need to fight yours. It doesn't mean that she's right and you're wrong. It's complicated. There is no one right way to wage this war. Each person has to ask himself or herself the question: Am I willing to risk my life or my freedom in the furtherance of the cause?"

"I understand. But I love Lexie, so I'm also willing to fight for our relationship. In my heart, I know that we can work this out. If we join together, we can be an indomitable force." He threw an arm wide to encompass the rest of the camp. "Think of all the great things we can do in the United States with what we've learned here."

Without breaking eye contact, Jade took a sip of her coffee, then said, "That's all good, Blake. But you need to decide for yourself how far *you* are willing to go. I think we can all guess how far Lexie will go. Loving her is one thing, but going to jail for her is a different story. Only you can answer that question, my friend. Truthfully, from the outside looking in, it appears to me you're more concerned with trying to keep Lexie as your girlfriend than you are with saving animals." Where her gaze had been sympathetic, it now hardened. "If that is the case, Blake, then I'm afraid you have no business being at this conference."

13

Lexie awoke to an empty tent. She pulled her arm out of the warm sleeping bag to look at her watch. It was almost eight thirty.

Crap.

Hastily rummaging through her bag, she found a clean shirt and threw on her same dirty jeans, then grabbed her small bag of toiletries and trudged to the bathroom. The stench from the bathroom hit her before she arrived—the small facilities were not designed to accommodate this many visitors at one time. Lexie kept her visit as quick as humanly possible, doing only what was necessary. Taking a shower in the malodorous washroom was out of the realm of possibility.

Swinging back to the tent, she dumped her toiletry bag and put on an ALF baseball cap to hide her dirty hair. Since the first lecture of the morning was already in progress, she wandered to the eating area for coffee and a Danish. She found a corner table and picked at her dry pastry.

"Long night?"

Lexie looked up to see Barnabas. "Hi, Barnabas. Yeah, kind of."

"I heard you and your boyfriend got into a kerfuffle last night."

"A what?"

"A fight over differing views."

Lexie nodded. "You could say that. Did I miss the class called 'Surveillance of American Couples'? It seems everyone knows my shit."

Nodding in turn, he asked, "May I sit?"

"Please," Lexie said, motioning toward the empty chair.

Before Barnabas could sit, an earsplitting alarm sounded, causing Lexie to cover her ears with her hands. "What's that noise?" she yelled over the shriek.

"We have intruders at the front gate," he said, already on the move, "probably coppers. Let's go help."

Lexie trailed Barnabas as he sprinted to the front entrance, careful not to trip over tree roots that crisscrossed the path. At the gate, an irate crowd of activists hurled large rocks toward several men in uniforms.

"Throw whatever you can find at them," Barnabas yelled over the alarm's continuing wail.

Lexie gathered a handful of rocks and heaved them in the direction of the police officers who were attempting to enter the camp. She didn't want to hit any of the officers, but she had to make it look realistic. A sense of camaraderie filled her as she joined her fellow activists to fight for a common goal. She didn't want any of the police to get hurt, but she also didn't want them to get into the camp and blow her cover.

After a few minutes of continued pelting, the police gave up and retreated, resulting in a thunderous cheer from the activists. The crowd remained at the gate for a few minutes to ensure no one made a second attempt to raid the camp; finally, the alarm shut down and the group dispersed. Lexie's body buzzed from the adrenaline rush.

Barnabas slung his arm around her shoulders as they began walking back to the main area together. "That was fun," he said dryly.

Lexie laughed. "My heart is still racing."

From ahead, Holden charged up to them. "What's going on?" he demanded. "Is everything okay?"

"Everything's fine, mate," Barnabas assured him, raising his hands. "The police tried to crash our party, but we sent them packing. Lexie here has quite a good arm."

Holden cocked his head and looked at Lexie. "I played softball for many years," she informed him.

"I love Americans," Barnabas said as he gave Lexie a little squeeze, then released her. "Well, I'm off to attend a lecture. See you chaps soon." With a jaunty wave, he departed.

"Softball?" Holden asked.

"Yep. I was pretty good."

"What position?"

"First base."

"Can I buy you a coffee?"

She raised an eyebrow. "You mean the free kind?"

"Is there another kind?"

Lexie laughed. "I would *love* a cup of coffee."

The two took their time as they meandered through the

woods. The dirt path was still muddy and soft from the previous day's rain; the fragrance of moss and decaying leaves filled the air.

Holden touched Lexie on the arm. She felt a shiver run through her. Was it his cold hands or his gentle touch? The memory of their time by that campfire both scared and excited her.

"Are you all right?" he asked. "About what happened last night with Blake—the bonfire turned into a bad scene. I didn't mean for it to happen."

"Sure you did. You don't like Blake and you don't want him around."

"Do you always say what's on your mind?"

She shrugged, keeping her eyes fixed on the trees ahead. "Most of the time."

"I like that. You're right. I don't trust Blake, and I don't think you should trust him either." He tightened his grip on her arm, and she turned her head to face him. "Lexie, you haven't known him that long. You've been in the movement long enough to know that law enforcement will go to almost any extreme to get infiltrators into our cells."

"Oh, come on, do you really think Blake is a snitch? I went to work for his company. He didn't pursue me."

"How did you find out about the job opening?"

"A friend told me."

"A trusted friend?"

She let a hint of doubt slip into her voice, careful not to push it too much. "More of an acquaintance. But that doesn't mean anything. You're being paranoid, Holden."

"Better paranoid than in prison."

"I can't argue with that."

"I'll make you a deal," he said, finally relaxing his grip on her arm. "I'll try to be less confrontational around Blake if you promise to keep anything that you and I discuss between the two of us."

Lexie locked eyes with him. "I guess I can live with that."

"Good. Because I like you, Lexie. I enjoyed our time by the campfire."

An unexpected rush of heat spread across her face. She looked away.

Holden laughed. "You blushed."

"I did not."

"You did. I made you blush. You like me too."

Turning around, she started down the path again. "What? Are we in third grade?"

"I kissed my first girl in third grade."

"I thought you were taking me for coffee, mister."

Jogging a few steps, he caught up to her. "Let's go, then. I don't want to keep a lady waiting when it comes to coffee."

He took the lead. For a while, they strolled in silence, nothing around them but the noise of birds and insects. Finally, Lexie snorted and said, "Third grade? Really?"

"What can I say, I was a ladies' man." Holden turned around and grinned. "Still am."

As they neared the camp, Lexie pondered. *Do things seem to be falling into place for me, or am I falling for this guy?*

* * * * *

After coffee with Holden, Lexie looked for Blake but couldn't find him. Eventually, she headed back to the tent, deciding to send Kate an update on recent events.

She grabbed Blake's boot and burrowed her way into her sleeping bag to hide while she texted. When she finished, she went to the text log to delete the information, but then froze.

It looked like a previous text had been sent late last night—to Adam's undercover number.

What the fuck is this?

Without hesitation, Lexie opened up the text message chain and started to read. As her eyes scanned the words, her lungs constricted, making it difficult to breathe. She felt dizzy and weak.

After she finished, she turned away from the phone. Then, not trusting her eyes, she reread the text sequence again.

Blake: We have a problem with Lexie. You were right, she might not be stable enough to handle this case.

Adam: What's going on?

Blake: She's getting too close to Holden, if you know what I mean.

Adam: Be completely clear. Do we need to pull you guys out?

Blake: Not at this point. I'll keep an eye on her. I didn't want you to be shocked if we have to close this down.

Adam: If Lexie is letting her emotions override her reasoning, you could be compromised. Again: do we need to extract the two of you?

Blake: Not sure, give me some more time.

Gritting her teeth, Lexie moved from shock to anger. She slammed her fists against the ground.

He's a fucking traitor. That's what I get for trusting him.

After copying the entire message chain, she punched at her phone, sending a message to Kate.

Lexie: Read this next message in private. It's meant for your eyes only. Advise when alone.

Time passed so slowly the clock almost seemed to move in reverse. Lexie simply sat there, stewing in her rage. But finally, Kate responded.

Kate: I'm alone.

Lexie: This is what I found on the phone today.

She sent the entire message chain between Blake and Adam to Kate and waited for a response. After several minutes, her phone buzzed again:

Kate: I don't know what to say. Are you okay?

Lexie: I'm fine, but please tell me I can trust you. That you're MY contact agent.

Kate: Absolutely. I hate to ask, but is there something going on between you and Holden?

Lexie: I'm getting close to Holden to help the case. It's just good undercover work. I'm doing what I need to do in order to find the missing officer.

Kate: Do you need to pull out of this case? We can come get the two of you.

Lexie: No. I can do this, Kate. I have everything under control. Should I confront Blake?

Kate: Yes. But do it away from camp.

Lexie: Okay.

Kate: Delete all this. You can't take the chance that someone will see.

Lexie: I'm glad I have you on my side.

Kate: ALWAYS!

Lexie: I'll check in later if I can.

Kate: Be extra careful.

Lexie: Will do. Keep your eye on that snake Adam.

Kate: I will.

As hard as it was for Lexie to delete the evidence of Blake's deceit, she knew she had to do it. Her thumb hovered over the trashcan icon for several moments; then, swearing under her breath, she threw the text chain away.

14

Lexie found Blake at lunch, looking warily at the vegan concoctions that lay in front of him. "Hey there," she said, trying to sound nonchalant.

"Hi," he replied, gingerly dipping a spoon into his bowl.

"Let's go for a walk after lunch," she whispered.

Blake gave her a sideways look but nodded.

Following a meal of roasted sweet potato soup and bread, they left for a walk. To keep appearances up, Lexie reached for Blake's hand. He looked surprised for a moment but then folded her fingers into his. Lexie maintained the charade until they were a good distance from the camp. Then she yanked her hand away.

"What's up?" Blake asked.

"Not yet. We need to get further away."

When she finally stopped far into the dense forest, Blake put his hand on her shoulder. Anger pulsed through her entire body. She knocked his hand away, glowering at him.

Startled, he took a step back. "What the hell is wrong with you?"

"Maybe you should ask your buddy, Adam. I'm sure he has some ideas, since the two of you feel I can't control my emotions."

The color drained from Blake's face.

"I saw the fucking text messages. I thought we were partners, but it turns out you're nothing but a spy."

Raising his hands, he took another step away. "I *am* your partner."

"I've got news for you, Blake—partners don't double-cross one another. You went behind my back and reported to Adam. And the worst part is, you lied. I'm not too close to Holden. I'm doing what I need to do in order to find the missing officer. In case you're unfamiliar with the concept, it's called undercover work. You remember how that works? You build relationships to betray relationships. Oh, wait—you do understand that concept, because you did it to me."

"You need to calm down so we can discuss the situation."

"The situation is called betrayal," she shot back, her voice rising to a shout.

"Lexie, slow down. I can explain."

Lexie looked at Blake and noticed the prominent dark circles under his eyes. Breathing heavily, she forced herself to simmer down a little. "I'm listening."

"Can we sit down?" he asked, pointing at a large fallen tree in the distance. Nodding, she crossed her arms and followed him.

Blake straddled the rotted tree so he was facing Lexie. She leaned against it but stared at the ground, refusing to make eye contact. She pushed around a bright-orange toadstool with her toe.

Out of habit, Blake looked around to make sure there wasn't anyone within earshot before continuing. The only sound was a light breeze rustling through the leaves. Once he was sure they were alone, he exhaled and said, "Adam told me that you've had issues when it comes to getting too close to activists."

Lexie turned and glared at him. "Adam is a lying, two-faced—"

"Please let me finish."

Exhaling loudly, she crossed her arms tighter.

"He chose me for the assignment to assist, but also to keep an eye on you. I saw you and Holden together; you have to admit, you two have some sort of connection."

"It's called undercover work," Lexie seethed.

"You can lie to yourself, Lexie, but I know what I saw. You and Holden have . . ."

"Have what?"

"Have chemistry."

She shook her head violently and stared angrily at Blake. She was so upset that she could barely hear him over the pounding in her ears. "Chemistry? This isn't the fucking dating game. I'm trying to get close to Holden to find Jonas. You make it sound like I'm looking for a boyfriend."

Blake looked at her skeptically. "So, you're telling me that you don't have feelings for Holden?"

"Feelings? I just met the guy. I'm ingratiating myself with him and his friends to get into the group. Are you sure these observations of yours aren't just plain jealousy on your part?"

"Adam told me—"

"Stop it," Lexie yelled, briefly pushing herself off the fallen tree and flinging her arms in the air. "Stop using Adam as an excuse. You made the choice to believe Adam over me."

Blake shifted back and forth on his seat, looking a bit ashamed. "I wasn't sure who to believe, so I went with what I saw."

"And what did you see? Me spending time with the target of the investigation. You're right! That's *so* suspicious."

He shook his head, then looked at the ground.

"How many times have you texted Adam other than the one I found?"

"Only one other time. Look Lexie, I didn't know what to believe. I had Adam in one ear telling me you're potentially unstable. You told me yourself that your last case took a catastrophic toll on you. I'm thousands of miles from home and I haven't slept a wink since we've been in this shithole camp."

"Do you think I'm any less tired than you? Stop making excuses."

"You would've done the same thing if you were in my place," he said, but she could tell from his face that he didn't believe this.

"No way," she replied, shaking her head emphatically. "I would've never done that to you, Blake."

Blake looked down at his feet, then back at her, his expression now fully contrite. "How can I make this right?"

"You can't."

"Look, Lexie, I see now that I handled this wrong. I want to make it up to you. Tell me how."

Lexie absently reached down and picked at the raised edges of the tree bark on the crumbling dead log. She looked up and gave Blake an icy stare. "For starters, stop communicating with Adam behind my back. You and I need to be upfront and honest with one another if we hope to make any progress."

Blake nodded. "I agree."

"Tell me the real reason you accepted this case, Blake."

"What . . . what do you mean?"

"You know what I mean. This case is so far out of your wheelhouse—why did you accept it?"

"Because Adam asked me to, and as you know, a request is the same thing as an order in the Bureau."

"That's bullshit and you know it. I want the truth."

Blake hung his head.

Lexie remained quiet, giving him time to process his thoughts.

Eventually, he made eye contact with her. His blood-shot eyes conveyed exhaustion. "Because I hate going home to an empty house every night. I'd rather be out of town than at home."

Lexie nodded. "I can understand that."

"Also, my supervisor is a real dick. I hate being trapped in the office. This was an easy way to get away from all that."

She raised a corner of her mouth in a sardonic smile. "There's the real reason."

"I'm sorry, Lexie."

"What do you want to do, Blake? Do you want to pull the plug and call it quits? I need to know."

"No. Definitely not. But I need to ask you a question."

"What?"

He locked his eyes onto her own. "Be honest with me. Are you falling for Holden?"

"How many times do I have to tell you? I'm playing a part. I'm trying to earn his trust." *Damn it, does he sense that I'm having doubts? Sitting by the campfire with Holden was amazing, but we didn't do anything,* she insisted to herself. *It meant nothing.*

From the back of her head, a quieter voice spoke: *At least I think it meant nothing.*

"You two looked pretty cozy this morning in the woods."

Any goodwill he'd built back up with her collapsed. "Were you *spying* on me?" Lexie asked, incredulous.

"I thought we had just established that fact."

Once again, she rose from the fallen tree, pushing away from him. "Can you be a bigger ass?"

"Too soon?"

"I don't think this . . . this . . . I don't even know what to call it . . . this relationship is going to work."

The smirk that had been blooming on his face withered away. "I'm sorry. I was trying to lighten the mood. My stupid attempt at humor."

"I'm not in a laughing mood."

Nodding, he said gently, "Take a breath. Let's start over."

Lexie crossed her arms. Her fists clenched so tight that her nails bit into the palms of her hands.

"Lexie, I was wrong to go behind your back. I'm sorry. I'm tired and out of my element with this case."

She let her head fall back and stared at the treetops before speaking. "Maybe I could've talked you through things a little better. Dealing with militant extremists is a little like walking through a minefield. You never know when something's gonna blow up."

"I tried hard to fit in," he said, cautiously trying another smirk. "I thought they would all be drawn to my charming personality." Even in his grungy condition, Blake had a smile that could melt an iceberg.

Lexie rolled her eyes. "What charming personality?"

"Ouch. A dagger to the heart," he said, putting a hand to his chest.

"Let's make some changes," Lexie said. "Starting right now, no more going behind each other's backs. Full disclosure from here on out."

"Agreed."

"If you have any issues with me or how I'm handling the case, you come to me and we discuss the situation."

"Of course. Are we good?"

"We're far from good, Blake." She softened her voice. "But I believe we can work together and salvage this mission."

Blake rose, put his hand on Lexie's shoulder, and gave it a light squeeze. "I think so too. I promise, I won't let you down."

"For the record," Lexie said as they turned to head back to the camp, "Adam is a poor choice of a collaborator."

"Funny, that's what he said about you."

* * * * *

Following an afternoon session, they stopped for a hot tea.

"You're looking rough," Lexie said.

"I'm so tired," Blake said, rubbing at his eyes. "I don't do well without sleep. But I have an idea."

"What kind of idea?"

"Let's move our tent into the woods. We can go far enough away from the camp to escape the party noises, but still be close enough to participate in the evening festivities."

"It's worth a try. Let's do it."

Robert came over while the two were disassembling their tent. "What are you doing?" he asked, frowning at the equipment littering the ground.

"We're moving to the woods to sleep," Blake replied. "I'm a light sleeper and the camp is too loud."

Robert smirked. "Could it be that you two lovebirds need some privacy for your nest?"

"Bugger off," Lexie replied, throwing a tent peg at his feet.

* * * * *

After dinner, Holden approached Lexie and Blake as they were washing their plates.

"Hey," he said as he sauntered over, "if you guys don't have plans tonight, a group of us are getting together at the trailer. You're *both* welcome to come."

Blake glanced over at Lexie before he answered. "Thanks for the invite, but I already have plans to watch the evening movie. Since you've seen the movie, Lex, you should go to the party."

If Holden was surprised by this uncharacteristic politeness, he didn't show it. "How about it, Lexie?" he asked, turning to look at her directly.

"You sure you don't mind?" Lexie asked Blake.

"Not at all."

She looked back at Holden. "I'm in."

The two agents went back to the tent and waited until the start of the evening events. Lexie checked the battery level on the recording equipment housed in her water bottle. She turned on the device and recorded the preamble consisting of her undercover identification number, the date, and the name of the subjects she planned to record; then she turned the recorder off and set it aside.

"You good working on your own tonight?" Blake asked, fiddling with his boot.

"Yeah. I think it was smart for you to turn down Holden's invitation. Less chance of another confrontation."

"I'm trying to do what's best for the case. I know the group would avoid talking about anything substantive if I were there, so I removed myself from the equation. They seem to trust you, Lexie. I'm here if you need me, but I'll gladly let you run with the ball."

"Thanks, Blake."

Stretching his legs out with a small groan, he rose from his sitting position. "I'm off to the media room before the vultures eat all the popcorn."

"I'll walk with you."

"You think you can find your way back to the tent tonight?" he joked.

"I hope so."

The couple walked as far as the media room together. "Enjoy the movie," Lexie said outside the doorway.

Blake bent down and kissed her on the cheek. "Be careful," he whispered.

After he'd disappeared inside, Lexie made her way to the ramshackle trailer. She knocked on the screen door and heard a voice from inside yell, "Come in."

All the regulars from Lexie's prior visit were hanging out in the trailer. The two Swedish men, Viktor and Olof, were even passing a joint around just like the prior Thursday.

"Déjà vu," Lexie said as she looked around the room.

"Have a seat," Holden said, moving over to make room. Lexie plopped down beside him on the stained, threadbare couch.

"Where's your boyfriend?" Olof asked.

"Watching the movie."

"Good. We wanted to talk to you alone," Jade said.

Fritz and Emil emerged from the back room. They moved two rickety wooden chairs from the kitchen to the living room. Everyone took a seat as Holden asked for attention.

"As activists," he began in full declamatory mode, "we have to decide how far we're willing to go to save innocent animals. In addition, we have to determine who, if anyone, we're going to trust. We can do great things if we're willing to work together."

Everyone in the room nodded.

"Lexie," he said, meeting her gaze with his own, "the people in this room are some of the kindest and most unselfish human beings you will ever meet. They have made a commitment to our movement and to each other. It's a commitment that none of us take lightly. We have given up everything in order to change the world. We have forsaken our families, left our partners, and even given up our freedom for the cause. Our movement isn't simply to save innocent animals from torture and abuse. We also believe we need to protect the environment and save the world for future generations. This world wasn't given to us to destroy. It was loaned to us, and human beings have done a shit job of protecting it. It's time we do something, no matter the personal cost. Do you agree?"

"I absolutely agree, Holden." Lexie glanced around the room. "I admire each of you for putting the movement ahead of your own interest and happiness. It's rare to find people of such loyalty and generosity. You have my respect and gratitude."

Holden shifted so he was directly across from her and put his hands on her shoulders. "I know it's risky to trust people, but at some point, we have to take a chance. Lexie, the group has decided we're willing to take a chance with you. With that being said, we don't trust Blake, and we're not willing to include him in any underground plans. We can't have you telling him what we're doing. We understand that this will be a hardship on your relationship, but all of us in this room have agreed to trust you and only you. I think we all believe you'd be better off without him. We completely understand if you're unwilling to proceed, but we need to know now."

Lexie chewed her bottom lip. She looked around the room and made eye contact with each of the activists before answering. "I've been doing some serious soul-searching since I've arrived here. This is the first time in my life that I've felt such a deep kinship with others. I respect your determination, your loyalty, and your indomitable spirit. I understand the cost, and I'm willing to accept your terms."

"This doesn't just mean while you're here, Lexie," Holden said. "We're talking about your underground involvement after you return to the United States."

"I understand."

"Do you? How serious were you about moving to the West Coast?"

"I'll do whatever is necessary for the movement. I'm ready."

Nodding slowly, Holden cautioned, "Think about it overnight. I want you to be sure. This is a decision that will completely change your life. You need to be absolutely sure."

Lexie nodded, hoping no one noticed the death grip she retained on her water bottle.

* * * * *

A few drinks and laughs later, Lexie made her way through the woods to the tent, crawled into her sleeping bag, and texted her update to Kate. She was almost asleep when Blake stumbled into the tent.

"Whoa, you seem like you've enjoyed the evening," Lexie said, looking up at him in bemusement. He was unsteady on his feet and reeked of alcohol.

"Millie from Denmark introduced me to akvavit," Blake slurred.

"What's akvavit?"

"I have no idea, but it was damn good. Funny thing, the more you drink, the better it gets. How was your party?"

"It was good. We can discuss it when you're sober."

"I'm sober." Struggling to remove his boots, he fell over on his side.

Rolling her eyes, she traversed the tent. "Let me help you," she said, then pulled his boots off and helped him get into his sleeping bag.

"Thank you," he murmured, closing his eyes. "You're a good partner."

"Good night, Blake."

15

The Gathering—Day Four

The next morning, both agents woke well rested in their new spot in the woods.

"I need to fill you in on what happened last night at the trailer," Lexie said. "But first I have a date with a tree. I'd rather use that than traipse all the way to that nasty bathhouse."

She returned to find two uniformed Dutch police officers snooping around the tent.

"May I help you?" Lexie asked, startled by the intrusion.

"What are you doing sleeping in the woods, miss?" asked the taller and older of the two, crossing his arms and looking at her suspiciously.

"We're staying at the nearby camp, but it was too noisy, so we moved out here."

"Who is in the tent?" asked the other, younger officer, pointing his thumb at the dwelling.

"My boyfriend. Hold on and I'll have him come out."

Lexie crouched down and shook the door flap. "Blake. Blake, can you come out please?"

The flap flew open and Blake stuck his head out. White

foam seeped from the corners of his mouth, making him look like a rabid animal. Realizing that Lexie was not alone, he spit toothpaste on the ground outside of the tent.

"Sorry. I was brushing my teeth." He returned his toothbrush to a cup and exited the tent.

"Are there others in the tent?" the older officer questioned, looking warily at the remaining flecks of toothpaste on Blake's mouth.

"No," Blake replied. "Just the two of us. The camp was a bit rowdy for our taste, so we moved out here for the quiet."

"You are not allowed to camp in the woods. It is a fire hazard," the older officer said stiffly.

"We're sorry, officer. We didn't realize."

The older officer said something in Dutch to the younger officer, who nodded his head.

"You said you are from the camp?"

"Yes, sir," Blake answered.

"What is going on over there?"

Here it comes, Lexie thought. *The inquisition.*

"Nothing much. Just some friends getting together," Blake said.

"You are Americans?"

"Yes."

"How many friends do you have in the Netherlands?"

"A bunch now," Lexie said.

The two conferred in Dutch again; then the older officer turned back to the campers and said, "Would you mind coming with us to our office? We would like to discuss some of your friends with you."

"I'm afraid we can't do that," Blake said. "We're expected

at the camp this morning. In fact, we better get packed up, or we're going to be late. Thank you for letting us know that we can't camp in the woods. We'll move back to the camp immediately."

"Are you sure you will not come with us? We could take you for a nice traditional Dutch breakfast."

"Thank you for the kind offer, sir," Lexie said. "Maybe another time."

Both officers glared at her.

"Leave this area immediately."

"Yes, sir," Blake said, raising his hand in a salute.

The two officers watched from a distance as Lexie and Blake packed up their belongings and moved back to the campground.

"That was interesting," Blake said. "At least we got one good night of sleep."

As they re-entered the campground, they were immediately surrounded by Fritz, Olof, and Viktor.

"Where the hell have you two been?" Fritz asked.

Blake thrust his chest out and moved toward Fritz. "None of your damn business, Fritz."

Lexie, sensing the need to defuse the situation, stepped between the two men. "The camp is loud, so we slept in the woods last night," she informed Fritz. "When we woke up this morning, we had visitors."

"We saw you talking to the police," Viktor said.

"Yeah, they weren't happy with us camping in the woods. They tried to question us about the camp, but we refused to talk, so they waited around until we left the area."

"What did they ask you?" Fritz said.

Lexie answered, "The usual questions. 'Who are you? What's going on?' They seemed a bit frustrated when we wouldn't talk to them, but allowed us to leave."

"They offered us a nice Dutch breakfast if we would talk," Blake added. "I was hungry, but not that hungry."

Fritz was not amused. "Did you tell them anything about the camp?" he asked, glowering.

"Nothing at all," Lexie said.

"I think it would be best if you two remained in the camp until the end of the conference."

"We will," she promised.

Fritz, Olof, and Viktor stalked away, leaving Lexie and Blake to assemble their tent.

They set up the tent in their original spot. Lexie dug through her backpack, tossing articles of clothing everywhere.

"What are you searching for?"

"I'm trying to find one clean article of clothing. If you haven't noticed, we stink."

"That's because we haven't showered since Thursday morning. I'll wait for you outside. After you get dressed, we can talk about what happened at your meeting."

After Blake had gone, Lexie removed her top and noticed that she had a spot on her chest. Assuming it was dirt, she tried to brush it off, then realized the spot was something else. She stuck her head through the tent flap.

"Blake, I need your help."

"Sure. What do you need?"

"Can you come back inside the tent?"

Unsure what to expect, Blake crawled back inside.

Lexie was sitting in the tent in her jeans and black bra. She held her shirt over her bra.

"This is a pleasant surprise," he said, waggling his eyebrows. "Are you trying to seduce me? If you are, it's working."

"I have a tick on me, and I need help getting it off."

"A tick?"

"Yes. A nasty, bloodsucking tick. They completely gross me out and I can't get it loose. Please, you have to help me," she said, suppressing panic.

"Where is it?"

Lexie looked down at her chest and said in a small voice, "It's on my boob."

"What?" Blake asked with a smile.

"You heard me. Damn it, Blake, please. I wouldn't ask if I didn't need to."

"Sit still. I have a small first aid kit in my backpack. Let me get it."

He located and unwrapped the kit.

"I found some alcohol wipes to clean the wound once we remove the critter," he said.

"I have a pair of tweezers in that pink makeup bag in the corner," she replied, looking down at her chest and wincing.

Blake retrieved the tweezers from the bag, then cleaned his fingers and the tool with one of the alcohol pads. "I'm ready for surgery."

"I can't believe I'm doing this," Lexie said as she lowered the bra on one side, revealing the top part of her breast.

"I didn't picture getting to second base this way," he said.

"Shut up and get the damn thing off me."

Blake steadied his hand, then grasped the tick as close to the skin's surface as possible. With steady, even pressure he pulled upward and removed it, leaving a trail of blood behind.

"Got the little bastard," he said, showing it to Lexie. She sighed loudly in relief.

Blake put the tick in the used alcohol pad wrapper and squeezed it tight. He removed a second alcohol pad and carefully cleaned the small open wound.

"Thank you," she sighed.

"Who's your knight in shining armor now?" he asked, smirking.

Lexie rolled her eyes. "You are, kind sir."

"I hope you don't get Lyme disease."

"Oh, great. Thanks for putting that in my head."

* * * * *

A sense of urgency filled the camp on the last day of the Gathering. Everyone knew they were going their separate ways the next morning. The organizers had saved the most radical training for the last afternoon, escalating the level of illegal activity and possible danger. Lexie and Blake split up to attend as many sessions as possible.

During the last training session of the afternoon, Lexie sat with Jade as they learned how to build a timing mechanism for an incendiary device. The two German activists, Fritz and Emil, taught the block of instruction. Lexie had the water bottle recorder turned on and sitting in front of her.

"I wish we could train like this in the United States," she said to Jade.

"What would happen if you tried?"

"We would all be arrested."

The other woman's brow furrowed. "But we're not actually doing anything illegal."

"Tell that to the FBI. They would find a way to make the charges stick. I've already decided, I'm coming back next year."

"Are you bringing Blake?"

Lexie made a show of looking around her and then saying in a lowered voice, "I think you and I both know the answer to that question. Blake and I are history."

"I'm not surprised. He seems like a nice enough guy, but you two are not a good match."

"This trip has made me re-examine my life. I feel like I'm standing at a crossroads and the direction I take will change the course of my life. I've decided I'm going to move to the West Coast."

"Wow, you really are making major life changes."

"Holden's right. I'm the only person who can direct the course of my life. I'm taking control."

"Glad to hear it. Speaking of Holden, he wants to meet with a small group of us briefly after this session. He told me to invite you."

"Sure. What's it about?"

Jade shrugged. "I don't know. Probably about how

we can stay in contact with one another after we leave this place."

"That's another useful thing that I learned this week," Lexie said. "I'm going to encrypt my computer when I get home, and I'll never send another email without encrypting it first."

After the session concluded, Lexie grabbed her water bottle and followed Jade to the trailer for the meeting. As they arrived, Holden was busy pouring champagne into plastic cups. He handed a cup to Jade and another to Lexie as they entered.

"Don't drink it yet," he said. "We're toasting with it."

Lexie placed her water bottle on the table, hoping she still had plenty of battery power. A few minutes passed and the rest of the crew entered the trailer. Standing in a circle around Holden were Lexie, Jade, Emil, Fritz, Olof, and Viktor. Missing from the group were Robert and Barnabas.

"I've gathered this group because I think we can achieve great things together," Holden said. "As you know, I don't allow many people into my inner circle. I think the people standing in this circle are some of the finest individuals I've ever had the pleasure of knowing."

Holden faced Lexie, then continued. "Lexie, we would like to welcome you into our circle of trust."

The members all nodded and smiled. Lexie's eyes widened and her grin spread.

Holden held his glass in the air. "Let's drink to Lexie, the newest member to our circle of trust. May our circle never be broken."

The group touched their plastic cups together.

Olof made sure to make contact with each person's cup and said, "Skål."

Fritz smiled and said, "Prost."

All eyes fell on Lexie.

"To trust," she said.

The group drank the contents of their cups and gave a hearty cheer.

Lexie smiled and hugged her new tribe members.

Within seconds, the room started to spin. Lexie became nauseous and started to sweat profusely.

She looked at Holden. "What have you done?"

She grabbed ahold of the rickety table next to her, but it collapsed beneath her. She fell, slamming her head on the floor. The room spun around her. As she tried to focus, all she could see were pairs of boots surrounding her. No one moved to help.

The light gave way to darkness.

16

It was getting late in the day, and Blake hadn't been able to find Lexie. He wasn't worried about her until she failed to show up for dinner. He noticed that many of her new friends were also missing from dinner. He spotted Robert across the yard.

"Robert," he yelled.

Robert looked around to see who was hollering his name. He saw Blake, waved, and walked toward him. Blake hustled over and met Robert halfway.

"Have you seen Lexie?" the American agent asked.

Robert thought. "Not since breakfast. Why?"

"I can't find her."

"I'm sure she's fine. Probably hanging out with her new mates."

"I can't find any of them either," Blake said. "I'm getting a little worried."

"I'll help you look for her," Robert replied, frowning. "Come to think of it, I haven't seen Jade all afternoon either. I wonder if they're together." He looked at Blake. "Take a breath, bud. You look as though you've seen a ghost. I'm sure she's fine."

"I have a bad feeling about this. Help me find her. Please."

"Of course," Robert said. "Let's split up. I'll go check Holden's trailer, then meet you at the coffee spot in one hour."

"In one hour. Okay."

Robert put a hand on Blake's shoulder. "I'm sure she's fine."

"I hope you're right."

Blake went back to the tent and searched through Lexie's backpack. Her clothes were missing, but the beat-up copy of *The Prince of Tides* was safely tucked away inside her backpack. He picked up the book and held it close to his chest.

Where are you, Lexie?

Blake saw a folded piece of paper propped against his pillow. He carefully opened and read the note.

Blake,

I am sorry, but I will not be returning to the United States with you. You and I see the world differently and I no longer believe we are compatible. I hope you understand. Please return home without me. I will contact you when I return to America. I apologize for any pain that I have caused you.

Regards,
Lexie

It was obvious to Blake that Lexie had not written the letter. The language pattern was not that of an American and sounded nothing like Lexie. Panic replaced worry. He grabbed his boot and, with shaking hands, removed the hidden telephone. He snapped a photo of the letter, texted it to Adam and Kate, then hurried into the woods so he could talk on the phone.

When he was a safe distance from the camp, he took out the phone and called Kate. He took a deep breath as he waited for her to answer.

"Blake, I have you on speaker phone. Adam is here too. What the hell is going on?"

"Lexie has disappeared. I'm not sure what to do."

He explained to Kate and Adam how Lexie had ingratiated herself with Holden and his crew. He also told them that many of Lexie's new friends were also missing from the camp.

"Where's Robert?"

"He's still here. He's helping me look for Lexie. He thinks Jade is missing as well."

"Is there any chance that Lexie went willingly?" Adam asked.

"No, I don't think so, but it was you who said she gets too close to these people. It's obvious that she didn't write that note."

"The only way to know for sure is to storm the camp and search for her," Adam said.

"If we do that, we risk Lexie's safety," Blake replied. "If whoever has her finds out that she's an FBI agent, then

Lexie will probably disappear like Jonas did. We can't take that risk."

"Blake, what do you think?" Kate asked. "You're the one in the middle of things; we'll trust your judgment."

Blake rubbed his scruffy beard. "I don't know. Can we storm the camp, but make it look like a regular police raid? The more people available to search for Lexie the better, but the activists can't know that we're looking for her."

"That's a good idea," Adam said. "We'll ditch all our FBI insignia and borrow a couple Dutch police raid jackets. Are you in agreement, Kate?"

"Yes. It's our only option. Let's make sure the police know to harass everyone, including Blake. We don't want the activists to know that he's an undercover."

"Get here as fast as you can."

"I'll assemble the team, but given our distance it will be at least an hour."

Blake paced in a circle and rubbed the back of his neck. "Wait. I have a better idea," he said, his head shooting upright. "Why not give me the rest of today to look for her myself. If I don't have any luck, then hit the camp before sunrise. Everyone will be leaving tomorrow, but not until noon."

"That would give us more time on our end to brief the Dutch police to make sure we keep the story straight," Kate said.

"Are you sure this is what you want to do, Blake?" Adam asked.

"Yeah, I think it's our best course of action."

"Would it be possible for you to check in with us every

two hours?" Kate asked. "I know it's an inconvenience, but a quick text would sure make me feel better."

"I can try," he said.

"Then it's settled," said Adam. "I'll assemble the team."

Blake said goodbye and turned off his phone. He heard a twig snap in the distance, then another one.

Someone had followed him.

He dropped the phone beside a large tree and used his foot to cover it with leaves, then quickly left the area and returned to the trail. As he rounded the corner, he nearly ran into Fritz and Emil.

"Hey," Blake said with the best nonchalance he could muster. "What are you guys doing out here?"

"We could ask you the same thing," Fritz said. "Why are you in the woods? You were told to stay inside the camp area."

"Yeah, well, I needed to clear my head."

Fritz placed a hand on Blake's shoulder and gave it a strong squeeze. "I don't believe you."

Blake slapped the hand away from his shoulder. "I don't give a fuck what you believe. Keep your hands off me."

Fritz gave Blake an icy stare. "Why are you upset?"

"I think you know."

"We don't know," Emil said. "Why don't you tell us."

"Lexie left me. She's decided to not return home with me."

"Is that so?" Fritz said.

Nodding, Blake took a step back. "I needed to get away from people for a while, so I came out here to figure out my next move."

"What move?" Emil asked.

"That's what I'm trying to figure out. Do I stay in the country and look for Lexie? Do I return home? I need to find her and talk to her. I'm sure I can change her mind."

"I don't see where you have much of a choice," Fritz noted. "It sounds like she's made her decision, now you have to live with it."

"American men don't give up so quickly," Blake said as he tried to push past the two Germans who blocked his path.

"We're here to tell you to give up. Go home. Lexie will contact you when she's ready," Fritz said, placing a hand of iron on Blake's shoulder and shoving him backward.

"Do you know where she is? If you do, you need to tell me."

"That's where you're wrong. We don't *need* to tell you anything. In fact, maybe you need to make an early departure from the camp."

"I think I'll stay, in case Lexie changes her mind and comes back tonight."

"She won't."

"How do you know?" Blake asked sharply, wrenching himself away from the German's grip.

"You don't get it," Fritz said. "She and Holden are a thing now. She didn't just leave you. She left you for Holden. So, if you know what's best, you will keep to yourself and quietly leave the camp. We don't want any trouble from you."

Blake's nostrils flared as he stared into Fritz's cold, hard eyes. "Fuck you, Fritz." He pushed past the two Germans, nearly knocking both of them off their feet. As he stormed off, he heard Fritz and Emil speaking in German.

* * * * *

"What happened?" Robert asked when Blake returned. "You look angry."

"Those two German goons accosted me in the woods. They told me that Lexie has hooked up with Holden and that I need to leave, peaceably."

"Are you going to?"

"Do I look like a peace-loving guy?"

Robert shook his head. "No. Not really."

"There's your answer. Did you have any luck with your search?"

"No," Robert answered. "Jade, Viktor, and Olof are all missing as well."

"Did you go to the trailer?" Blake asked.

"I did. It was empty. What do we do now?"

Blowing out a frustrated breath, Blake weighed his options. "I don't know. I honestly don't know."

17

Lexie slowly regained consciousness. Her eyes felt as if they had been glued shut. The smell of body odor and sweat filled the air. She listened closely but couldn't hear anything; finally, she managed to open one eye and then the other. She was lying on her side on a cot, still feeling nauseous. The room spun around her.

Where am I? Think. What's the last thing you remember?

The drink. Damnit, I must have been drugged.

"Hey there, sleepyhead."

Lexie tried to focus on the sound of the voice.

"I thought you were going to sleep the rest of the day. I may have given you too much sleeping potion."

Lexie blinked a few times, opened her eyes wide, and saw Holden sitting in a folding camp chair across the room. He got up, walked over, and knelt down beside the cot. He cocked his head to the side, so Lexie could see that it was him, and stroked her head with one hand.

"What . . . what happened?" Lexie's throat felt like sandpaper. "I need some water," she said as the room continued to spin. She made an attempt to sit up, but failed, flopping back to a prone position.

"Let me help you," Holden said gently. He pulled Lexie's legs over the side of the cot, then helped her sit up. He removed the top from his metal water bottle and handed it to her.

Lexie took the bottle and drank greedily.

"How do you feel?"

As her head slowly cleared, she remembered the drink in the trailer. "Like a semitruck ran over me. Did . . . did you dose me?"

"Yeah. Sorry about that. I didn't have a choice."

"What? Are you serious? You fuckin' drugged me?"

Lexie's heart raced as she looked at the water bottle in her hand. She tried to stand up, but her legs were weak and she landed back on the cot.

"There's no need for you to worry. The effects will wear off quickly."

"Where the hell am I?"

"You're at our camp. Drink some more water."

Lexie's eyes widened and she threw the water bottle at Holden, hitting him in the head. Unfortunately, she didn't seem to have the strength to accomplish much. He looked more amused than anything, rubbing at the point of contact. "Ouch. That was uncalled for."

"The champagne last night! I can't believe you drugged me. Didn't you say something about trusting one another during your toast?"

He tried handing the bottle back to Lexie, but she slapped it out of his hands, then attempted to stand. This time she succeeded, and frantically looked around. They were in a moss-colored canvas tent. A battery-operated lantern sat on top of an overturned wooden crate. A small pile of clothing lay in the corner next to the folding chair.

"Where's Blake?"

"He's still at the Gathering."

"You mean we're no longer at the Gathering? Where the fuck are we? What have you done?"

"Calm down. I'll explain everything. Sit down before you pass out."

Lexie's stomach clenched. Beginning to feel lightheaded, she sat down on the hard, uncomfortable Army-green cot.

"Explain," she said angrily.

Holden picked up the discarded water bottle and handed it back to Lexie. "We've brought you to a temporary location."

"We? Who's we?"

"Let me explain everything," he said, maddeningly calm, "then I'll answer your questions."

Lexie clenched her teeth. "Go ahead."

"I need to know if you're ready for the next step before I introduce you to any of our people. Our group works with a very influential person. He makes it possible for our group to force big changes in the world by financing our missions. It goes beyond the animal rights world. We operate in secrecy—no one outside our circle knows the identities of our members. We train together, live together, and work together. Effecting change in the world is our occupation."

"What do you mean when you say *effecting change*?"

"I think you know what I mean."

"I want to be absolutely clear before I commit to anything," she said.

"Fair enough. We engage in underground direct action. We achieve our goals using whatever means are necessary—both legal and illegal, but mostly illegal."

Lexie nodded. "What did you mean when you said you effect changes 'beyond the animal rights world'? How so?"

"Lexie, there are so many atrocities in the world. Mankind is destroying the earth and the world leaders don't care."

"Are you talking about the United States government?"

"Not just the United States government. All the world leaders. Our faction may have started out as an animal rights group, but we've branched out."

Holden stood, pulled over a folding chair from the corner, and sat down. The lamplight cast an eerie yellow glow, but Lexie could make out his strong, chiseled features. His heavily lashed eyes, the color of a stormy sea, pierced right through Lexie. Holden reached over and took her hands. His palms were warm and inviting.

"You and I, Lexie, we're the same. We both see something that is wrong with the world and have a need to change it. I think you know by now that Blake isn't like us. He doesn't understand the need that we have inside us to think of animals and the earth before ourselves."

Lexie looked down at their interwoven hands. "Blake must be worried sick."

"We left him a note."

"A note?"

"From you. The note explained that the two of you were

no longer compatible and that he needed to return home without you."

"Did he believe it?"

"It really doesn't matter. You're here and he's not. Situation handled."

She pulled her hand away from his. "I still can't believe you dosed me. I trusted you, and I thought you trusted me. Why didn't you just ask me to come with you?"

"I couldn't take the risk that you wouldn't say something to Blake. Plus, I didn't want you to know our location. I like you, Lexie, but I have to protect my team."

"If I join you, what happens next?"

"You'll be moved to the main camp headquarters. That's where you'll begin your training."

"Training?"

"You'll learn everything you need to know to survive, do what needs to be done, and elude capture."

"That could be almost anything."

Holden sighed, his face weary. "Lexie, you have to trust me on some of this. I can't give you any more details until you agree to join us."

She leaned further away from him. "It's hard to trust you when you drugged me, then hauled me off."

"I'm sorry you're so upset, but I did what I had to do. So accept it."

Lexie looked away and contemplated her next move. "Are you sure Blake is okay?"

"I'm sure. If it makes you feel better, I'll have a friend of mine check in on him."

"That would make me feel better."

"Why don't you think about our conversation, get some rest. I'll come back for you in a little while."

She nodded. "Can I leave the tent?"

"You're not a prisoner here, but I have to ask you to stay put until I return. Then we'll discuss our next move."

"Okay."

Holden reached over and gently pushed away a stray piece of hair from her eyes. "I'll be back soon."

As soon as he'd left the tent, Lexie searched through the pile of clothes in the corner. She found her bag containing her toiletries among the dirty clothes. Her backpack and sleeping bag had been left behind. None of her FBI equipment, including her water bottle, had been transported with her. She was on her own.

Now what?

Lexie crept over to the tent door and peeked outside. Surrounded by woods, she couldn't see any people or vehicles. Daylight was falling fast as night crept into the forest.

Shall I run for it? If I do, then I'll never get to Holden's main cell. Maybe Jonas is here and being held captive too. I bet Holden has people watching me, and if I run, they'll grab me. I don't have any idea where the hell I am, so I have no idea where to run to.

Lexie closed the flap on the tent and sat down on the cot. She bent over and rested her elbows on her knees, holding her throbbing head in her hands.

Think things through. I must've drank the champagne around four o'clock. By now Blake would know that I'm missing. He'll know that I didn't leave voluntarily and then contact Kate and Adam. The FBI team and the Dutch police will be searching for me. I need to go along with Holden's plan to give them time to find me. Maybe I'll find out what happened to the missing constable. Or maybe I'll end up missing, just like the constable.

How in the hell do I get myself into these messes?

* * * * *

Lexie lay stretched out on the cot, staring at the ceiling, when the tent door flapped open.

"May I enter?" Holden asked.

She turned to face him. "It's your tent. Come in."

Holden had a plate of food in his hands. He placed the dish down on the makeshift table before sitting down in the chair beside the cot. "You missed dinner. I thought you might be hungry."

Her stomach tightened as the smell wafted toward her. "I'm starving. Thank you." Sitting up and reaching for the plate, she added, "Holden, I have a few more questions before I give you my decision."

"I'll answer them if I can."

"How long have *you* been over here doing this … this—"

He interrupted. "Let's call it a campaign."

Taking a bite of food, she repeated, "How long have you been doing this campaign?"

"I've been here a couple of years."

"Have you been with the same team the whole time?"

"For the most part, yes. We've had a couple people move on to different campaigns and we've added a few new faces, but for the most part we've been a cohesive team."

"And you trust one another?"

Holden nodded vigorously. "In our movement we're taught to never trust anyone. However, this is a completely different situation. In our camp we trust one another completely. We train together and learn to rely on one another. I trust my team with my life."

Lexie let her fork *clink* against the plate for several seconds, considering. Then, looking up at Holden, she said, "Yes."

"Yes what?"

"I'm ready to commit to the campaign."

His face brightened, but he cautioned, "Are you sure? You can't return home."

"How does that work? Do I apply for a visa or something?"

Holden laughed. "No. You'll be given a new identity."

"Seriously?"

"Yep. We have a guy who will get you a new passport and other forms of identification. We're not fooling around over here, Lexie. This is serious shit."

"I believe you."

"Do you have any special skills?" he asked.

"Like what? Archery? Fishing?" she asked, pretending to ponder. "I can throw a cast net for shrimp."

"I'm serious," Holden replied, voice growing flat.

"Sorry," she said quickly, "I was trying to lighten the mood. Let's see, I'm pretty good at camping and foraging. I have a black belt in tae kwon do, so I'm a good fighter."

"All good skills that we can use."

"I'm a quick study, so I can learn anything that you need me to learn to further the cause."

"I like that positive attitude." Leaning closer, he said

gently, "I'm going to ask you one more time. There's no shame in not wanting to go further in the movement. I would understand if you said you didn't want to take the next step. I want you to be sure before we go any further."

"I'm sure. I traveled all the way over here to attend the Gathering because I wanted to find like-minded people and learn more about direct action. I believe that things happen for a reason. I knew as soon as I arrived that I'd found my calling. This is what I'm meant to do with my life. This is how I'll help save animals."

"Not just animals, Lexie. You're going to help save the world."

Grinning, she replied, "When you put it that way, how could I refuse?"

Holden broke into a smile. "Eat your dinner, pack your stuff, and I'll be back for you in a little while."

"Do you have a pack that I could use to carry my stuff?" Lexie motioned to her heap of belongings piled in the corner.

"I'll find you something."

"Thanks."

"Enjoy your dinner."

* * * * *

Holden returned within thirty minutes carrying a brown canvas bag.

"You can put your clothes in here."

Lexie crammed her clothes inside, then scanned the

room to make sure she wasn't leaving anything. "Well," she said when she'd verified everything was packed, "ready as I'll ever be."

"Follow me."

She followed Holden down a wooded trail. It was dark, shadows covering slick patches and tripping hazards. She watched her footing to keep from falling. Eventually, the two came to a clearing and a country road.

"Here comes our ride," Holden said as a pair of headlights approached. A white panel van pulled up. Holden opened the sliding door. "I'm going to have to ask you to ride in the back."

Lexie nodded and hopped in the back of the van. Holden followed. An old air mattress and some blankets provided a small amount of cushioning for the journey. "Sorry for the rough ride," Holden said.

"I've ridden in worse."

The lack of windows made the back of the van pitch black. A small amount of light slipped in between the driver's seat and the passenger seat, allowing Lexie to dimly make out her surroundings.

"Good evening," a familiar voice said as a woman crawled into the back from the passenger seat.

"Jade?" Lexie asked. "Is that you?"

Jade laughed. "It's me."

"Great to see you," Lexie said as she fumbled around to find and hug Jade. "Well, sort of."

"It's nice to see you too. I'm glad you joined our little group of renegades."

"Holden made me an offer I couldn't refuse."

"Sorry we had to be so cloak-and-dagger. I'm sure you understand the precautions that we have to take."

"I do," Lexie said. "Who's driving this party van?"

"Olof," Jade said.

"Hi, Olof," Lexie yelled toward the front of the van.

"Hello, Lexie," the Swede yelled back, the sound muffled slightly by the seats between them.

"Where are we going?" she asked, turning back in Jade's general direction.

"We're going to our training center. It won't take us long to get there."

"Is there anything that I need to know before we arrive?"

"The usual rules apply," Holden said. "We operate on a need-to-know basis. We have a strict security policy. We'll provide you with all the equipment you need, so no outside electronics of any kind. No contact with people outside our group."

"Seems pretty straightforward."

"Once you get settled, you'll find we have a wonderful group," Jade said. "There is such camaraderie."

"That sounds nice. I'm looking forward to meeting everyone."

Holden reached over and took Lexie's hands. "Are you ready for your actions to speak for you, Lexie?"

"More than ready," she replied, squeezing the warmth of his fingers back.

"Sentiment without action is the ruin of the soul."

"Why does that sound familiar?" she asked.

"It's a quote from Edward Abbey." Holden squeezed

her hands tighter before letting go. "You're in for the ride of your life. And you're going to love every minute of it."

The three stretched out on the mattress, Lexie sandwiched in the middle.

"I can't wait."

* * * * *

The van turned off the paved road and bounced down packed gravel, swerving to dodge holes in the washed-out path. Lexie sat up.

"The ride is going to be a little rough for the rest of the way," Holden said.

"We're almost at the camp," Jade added. She and Holden sat up next to Lexie.

"I'm a little nervous," Lexie said, her voice bouncing with the van.

"Don't be nervous," Jade told her. "You'll fit right in."

The van finally came to a stop. Holden opened the door and got out, then offered his hand to Lexie and to Jade. After riding in the dark van, it took a few seconds for Lexie's eyes to adjust to the light.

Olof came over and hugged her. "I am glad that you decided to join us," he said. "You won't be sorry."

"Thank you, Olof," she replied, hugging back.

"I must go. I will see you later."

Lexie stretched her back and looked around. "Wow, I was expecting a small campsite, not a compound. This place is huge."

The massive facility resembled lodgings for an army. Several large, olive, military-style tents were scattered around the sizable clearing. Lights strung from poles lit the entire encampment, bathing the tents in a yellow-white glow.

Lexie inhaled a deep, cleansing breath of fresh air, then slowly exhaled. "Ah, I love the smell of pine needles. Is this all for us?"

"Yep," Holden answered. "We're the only ones here."

"Aren't you worried someone will stumble across the camp?"

"Nope," he said, listing off reasons on his fingers. "First, we're on private property. Second, we're in the middle of nowhere, surrounded by a dense forest. On the other side of the forest are miles and miles of farmland. This isn't exactly a tourist area."

"I'm impressed."

"You should be. This place wasn't cheap."

"Who owns the property?"

"Let's just say he's someone who understands and supports our cause."

Lexie looked around in awe at the size of the compound. "It's amazing."

"We have electricity and running water. All the comforts of home. In fact, I think you could benefit from a shower," Holden said, laughing.

"I definitely could use a shower. The bathroom situation at the Gathering was nasty. I haven't showered since I left Amsterdam."

"Oh, believe me, I can tell."

She gave Holden a little shove. "Shut up!"

Chuckling, he said, "Let's get you settled in your quarters. After you get cleaned up, I'll give you the tour."

Lexie smiled. "Sounds good."

Despite everything that's happened, this guy is still charming and funny. Shit!

As she walked to her tent, she took note of all her surroundings. Lawn chairs and wood stumps circled a manmade firepit; she smelled the faint aroma of smoke and stale beer. "Where is everyone?" Lexie asked.

"Most of our team is out on a mission," Holden replied. "They're due back sometime tomorrow afternoon. You'll get to meet the group that's still around tonight, then the rest tomorrow. I have some business to attend to, so I'm going to let Jade get you settled in and show you where to shower. I'll be back to pick you up in an hour or so." He placed a hand on her shoulder for a brief moment, then turned on his heel. "Don't go wandering around on your own until I've had a chance to introduce you to our security team."

"Okay."

After Lexie and Jade watched Holden walk away, Lexie put her hands on her hips and glared. "Did you know Holden was going to drug me?"

Jade's eyes widened. "No. I knew he planned to ask you to join our group, but I didn't know he was going to go about it the way he did."

Lexie crossed her arms and cocked her head to the side.

"I promise," Jade said. "I was as shocked as you were."

"Oh, I doubt that."

"I'm sorry, Lexie," Jade said, casting her eyes toward

the ground. "I know what Holden did must be upsetting to you."

"That's an understatement. He completely disregarded my feelings when he drugged me. It was a violation."

Jade had no response for this. "I understand Holden's motives, but I don't always understand his methods."

"Drugging me was completely unnecessary. I would've willingly gone with you guys. In fact, I would've given consent for him to blindfold me if he felt it was necessary."

"I know. I'm really sorry." Jade continued to stare at the ground, then finally lifted her eyes to meet Lexie's again. "Are we okay?"

Lexie hesitated, then nodded. "Yeah. We're okay."

"Good, because we're roommates. Let me show you our tent."

The two women entered a large canvas tent with a plywood floor. Inside were four army cots, one in each corner. Beside each cot was a small, portable camp chair. Lexie assumed the musty smell came from the gray wool blankets sitting on the foot of each of the cots, most likely purchased from a military surplus store.

"This is my corner," Jade said, extending her arm in a grand gesture. "That's KK's corner over there." She pointed to the rear. "Don't touch any of her stuff. She's a bit on the crazy side. You have your choice of either one of the other corners. There are only three of us in this tent."

"I think I'll take the cot on the same side as you."

"That's probably safer," Jade said. "KK is a good worker, but she's a bit hard to get along with. Unlike me, a peace-loving person"—Jade threw up two fingers in the shape of a V— "she's quite the anarchist."

Lexie chuckled. "Thanks for the warning. I'll steer clear of her."

"The footlocker at the end of the cot is for you to use. Grab some clean clothes, and I'll take you to the shower area."

"I don't think I have any clean clothes left. I'll grab the least dirty."

"We have a place to wash your things."

Lexie followed Jade to the shower. "Hopefully the showering conditions are better here than at the Gathering," she said.

Jade smiled. "There were three hundred people trying to use one bathroom there. Here we only have about thirty people in the whole camp. Much better body-to-bathroom ratio."

They arrived at an area with a row of four primitive shower stalls made from wood. All four doors were open. A metal pipe stretched the length of the stalls, providing water to the shower heads. While nothing was sparklingly clean, they were a far cry from the putrid grime of the Gathering's stalls.

"Everything in our compound is unisex," Jade informed her, "so it doesn't matter which one you use. It's not perfect, but not bad for outdoor living. Enjoy your shower."

Lexie showered and washed her hair, the sensation of hot water pouring down onto her face almost unbearably good. When she'd finished, she found a fresh towel hanging on the hook outside of her shower stall. She dried herself, put on semi-clean clothes, and combed out her wet hair. When she strode outside, Jade waited at a nearby picnic table.

"Thanks for the towel," Lexie said, wringing out her still-soaking hair.

"You're welcome. How do you feel?"

"Like a new woman."

The pair walked back to their tent, Lexie memorizing the path along the way. Holden was waiting for them when they arrived. "You certainly smell better," he joked.

"Yeah, yeah," Lexie sighed, rolling her eyes.

"You ready for a tour?"

"Sure. Let me dump my stuff." She tossed her belongings on her cot, hung her towel over the chair in her corner, and re-emerged from the tent.

"You coming with us, Jade?" Holden asked.

"I have a few things that I need to get done, so I'll catch up with you two a bit later."

Lexie followed Holden around the complex. They came to a large, semicircular Quonset hut made from corrugated, galvanized steel.

"This is the mess hall," Holden said, opening the door for Lexie. "Let's see if Mamma Bear is around."

The mess hall had six long tables, three on each side of a center aisle. Wooden chairs lined both sides of the tables, accommodating approximately forty people at a time. The far end of the building housed the kitchen. Near the kitchen were two long metal serving tables. A metal shelf that held plates, cups, and several round containers of silverware sat to the left of the serving area. Clanging sounds and the sweet aroma of cinnamon came from the kitchen area.

Holden tossed his head back and sniffed the air. "Something smells good."

A heavyset woman in her fifties, who wore blue jeans and a flannel shirt, was preparing something in a giant pot. She jumped when the duo entered the room, and then a huge smile crept across her face.

"Holden, what're you doing sneaking up on an old woman? You nearly gave me a heart attack."

"You're not old," he said as he grabbed her hand and twirled her around. "Mamma Bear, this is Lexie. She's a new recruit. Lexie, this is Mamma Bear, the best damn cook in Europe."

Lexie shook hands with Mamma Bear; the older woman's grip was firm but soft and warm. "He's a sweet talker, this one," Mamma Bear said, jerking her head at Holden and smiling.

Lexie smiled. "I'm finding that out. Where are you from? I can't place your accent."

"I can't say the same about you," Mamma Bear said. "You're definitely an American. A southern one at that."

"Good call."

"I was born in Finland, but lived in England most of my life. My father moved our family to London when I was eight years old. That's probably why my accent is a little different. I actually attended college in America, but that's a million years ago."

"Really? Where'd you go to college?"

"In New York. The Big Apple. I was young, so I loved every minute of it. Too many people for my taste now."

"I agree. I like to visit New York, but after a few days, I'm ready to go home and get away from the hustle-bustle lifestyle."

"Mamma Bear does all the cooking for us here at the camp. She makes sure we're well fed," Holden said, slapping his stomach.

"You have any favorites you want me to make?" Mamma Bear asked Lexie.

"I like almost everything," she replied. "I'm sure whatever you make, I'll love."

"Well," Holden said, "we better get moving. I'm giving Lexie the grand tour."

"That'll take all of five minutes," Mamma Bear said. "See you for breakfast tomorrow. I'm making my famous vegan cinnamon buns."

Lexie's eyes bulged. "I can't wait."

Holden took Lexie's hand as he led her out of the mess hall. They walked hand in hand until they reached and entered a large safari-style tent. Two young men sat at a rickety wooden table playing cards. Both wore ragged shirts and faded jeans. As Holden arrived, they laid down their cards, giving him their full attention.

"Gentlemen, this is Lexie, our new recruit."

Lexie nodded and gave a small wave.

"Lexie, this is Finn and Ryan."

Finn and Ryan looked like opposites in every way. Finn was willowy thin with a wavy mop of auburn hair, freckled skin, and kind blue eyes. A small patch of whiskers under his bottom lip matched his hair. Ryan was pudgy with short, cropped brown hair and deep-set, warm brown eyes. A scruffy beard covered his double chin. The two men stood; Finn extended his hand to Lexie.

"Welcome to Camp Resistance," Finn said. "We're happy to have more help."

"Thank you," she replied. "I'm excited to be here."

Ryan shook Lexie's hand in turn and asked, "Where are you from?"

"The United States. Specifically Louisiana. What about you?"

"Portland, Oregon."

Lexie's head jerked back and her mouth fell open. "You're an American?"

"I am."

"How long have you been in Europe?"

"I've been in Europe for almost two years, but I've only been in the Netherlands for six months."

"Wow. I'd love to hear all about your travels sometime."

"Sure, anytime."

Lexie turned to Holden and asked, "How many Americans are in the camp?"

"Counting you, there are four of us. Does that surprise you?"

"A little."

"Why?"

"I don't know. I guess I never thought about Americans getting involved in activism outside of the United States."

"Think about it, Lexie. We are one world. What affects one country will have consequences in another."

"I get that, but we have so many problems in the states, I guess I thought someone with your experience would be doing direct action in the United States."

Holden cocked his head. "Who's to say I'm not? Think big picture. You're no longer playing in the minor league. You've been called up to the majors, and from here on out your life will never be the same."

18

Blake waited until it was nearly dark before he made his way through the woods to find the phone he had buried in the leaves when Fritz and Emil accosted him, stopping every few feet to listen. Convinced he was not being followed, he started the painstaking task of trying to locate the hidden phone.

I know I buried it near a large tree. Good thinking, dumbass, since you're in a forest. For shit's sake, I'm never going to find it.

Off in the distance, he recognized the bend in the path where he had been harassed by Fritz and Emil. A short distance from the bend, he spotted a familiar tree. He removed a small flashlight from his back pocket and shone it around the base of the tree. He saw a tiny reflection of light. Scrabbling at the leaves, he uncovered, to his relief, the missing phone, dirty but no worse for wear. He knew he should text Kate for security reasons, but couldn't justify the extra time spent texting when he could call.

Kate answered on the first ring. "Are you all right? I've been worried sick."

"I'm fine. The goon squad has been watching me. This is the first time I could get to my phone."

"Any luck finding Lexie?"

"No. I've looked everywhere. I was accosted by two German activists. They tried to get me to leave the camp, but I refused. Kate, there is no doubt that Lexie was taken."

"That's the conclusion that we came to on our end as well. The question is, why? Did they take her because they want her for their cell, or did they take her because they think she's a cop?"

"I'm not sure," Blake said. "I'd like to think it's the first, but the constable is still missing and we don't know what happened to him. Hopefully they haven't suffered the same fate."

"Unless you have a strong opinion otherwise, this is the plan. The police will raid the camp at sunrise. Every person will be identified, photographed, and questioned. The camp will be thoroughly searched. The police know what they're supposed to say; they won't mention Lexie or the FBI. It will appear as if they are doing an intelligence raid."

"What happens to me during all this?" Blake asked.

"You'll be treated like all the other activists. Ben will be the officer in charge of dealing with you. He will attempt to question you, but you'll become upset and take a swing at him. At that point, Ben will arrest you and you'll be removed from the camp in handcuffs."

"Okay."

"Have all your stuff packed so you can let Ben know which tent is yours. We want to make sure all the FBI recording equipment is collected and handled properly."

· "Got it. I'll have everything organized and ready. I haven't been able to find Lexie's water bottle recorder. She had it with her the last time I saw her."

"I'll make sure the police know to search for it tomorrow. Any other questions?" Kate asked.

"No."

After a few seconds of steady static across the line, she asked, "Blake, are you okay?"

Blake swallowed and then sighed. "Honestly, no. I'm worried about Lexie. I should've protected her."

"This isn't your fault."

"Of course it's my fault. I was her partner. This wasn't supposed to happen."

"Blake, listen to me. You're still our best chance of finding Lexie. You have to keep your head in the game."

Blake stared into the dark woods.

"Are you still there?"

Pulling himself back into the present moment, he shook his head and pulled his eyes away from the trees. "I'm here."

"Do you have any other questions about the raid?"

"No. I'll go get my things packed and the equipment organized. Kate, I'm sorry."

"Stop saying that. You have nothing to be sorry about. We'll find her."

"Kate."

"Yes."

"I think Lexie may be in serious danger."

* * * * *

The tent was in perfect order, FBI equipment safely packed away, but Blake still couldn't sleep. He tossed and turned all night waiting for the raid. Darkness had not yet surrendered to the morning light when the earsplitting noise of the camp alarm sounded.

Showtime.

Blake simply lay in his tent for a couple of minutes, listening as all hell broke loose around him. After a suitable length of time had passed, he got up and made his way to the main camp area, pretending to be confused and scared. The shrill alarm added to the disorder as bewildered activists frantically clambered for the exit.

Blake heard the police issuing orders in several languages, including English. He made eye contact with Ben, who rushed over and grabbed him.

"Get your hands off me," Blake yelled.

"Get on the ground," Ben shouted back.

"I haven't done anything wrong."

"Shut up and get down. Now! On your stomach."

Blake obeyed and lay on the ground, turning his head to the side and watching the scene unfold. Police grabbed the scrambling activists and shoved them to the ground. A few tried to run for the woods but were apprehended by perimeter police stationed in the forest.

As the police gained control, all the activists, including Blake, were moved to the main camp area. Robert, barefoot and shellshocked, sat across the room from Blake. A few of the activists continued to taunt the police; others shook with fear and sobbed. Some detainees were half dressed, and most were shoeless. It looked like a congregation of homeless refugees. The police removed each activist one at a time, taking them outside to a processing area where they were interviewed and photographed. Most yelled and screamed about their rights being violated. When it was Blake's turn, Ben approached him.

"Come with me," Ben said.

"Fuck you," Blake replied, sticking as low to the ground as possible. "I have rights."

"Get up and come with me."

When Blake refused, Ben reached down and grabbed his arm. Blake twisted around and took a swing at Ben, purposely missing.

The other man grabbed him and threw him to the ground. A second officer handcuffed Blake while Ben held him. The two officers jerked him to his feet.

"You're under arrest for assaulting a police officer."

"I didn't touch you!" he protested loudly.

"That doesn't matter," Ben shot back.

Activists cheered for Blake as Ben and the second officer dragged him away and took him to a secluded area.

"You should be an actor," Ben said to Blake as soon as they were out of earshot.

Rubbing at his arms, Blake said, "Thanks. That's pretty much what undercover work is."

"We're going to keep the handcuffs on you in case someone sees us."

"I understand."

Blake told Ben which tent was his and which tent was Robert's so they could ensure proper handling of the equipment. It made sense that Blake's tent and belongings would be confiscated since he had been arrested. He then told Ben about the trailer in the outlying area of the camp. Ben sent a search team to the trailer, where they found Lexie's water bottle lying on the floor.

Several activists who had fought with the police were hauled away in handcuffs; since the arrestees were all separated, no one noticed when Blake disappeared. Ben delivered him to the FBI team waiting in the wings.

* * * * *

It was nearly lunchtime, and the only clue that had been found by the Dutch police was Lexie's water bottle. The bottle, along with its recorder, was packaged as evidence and sent to the tech department for its contents to be downloaded. Connor called the FBI team every hour with updates on the search.

Blake paced the floor of the operations center like a caged panther. "Can you please sit down?" Adam asked after this had gone on for several minutes. "You're driving me crazy."

"What are we going to do?" Blake snapped. "We have to do something."

"We will," Kate said. "When the Dutch finish at the camp, we'll get the entire team together and figure out our next step. We'll know more once we get her recorder downloaded."

"Holden has her. I know that son of a bitch is responsible

for her disappearance. I warned Lexie about him, but she refused to listen. She fell for his whole stupid act."

"You're being unfair to Lexie," Kate said from across the room.

"You're her contact agent, Kate. Of course you're going to take her side," Blake shot back angrily.

"I'm not taking anyone's side," she replied, her normally even tone growing heated. "And I'm *your* contact agent as well."

"Everyone calm down," Adam said. "I think we can all agree that Holden is definitely involved. But we need to figure out where they've taken her."

"Holden is an American," Blake said. "He wouldn't own property in this country. He has to be working for someone else, but who?"

"That's the million-dollar question," Adam said. "And is this connected to the missing Dutch constable?"

"Fuck!" Blake yelled. "We can't just sit around here doing nothing."

Kate walked over and gently put her hands on Blake's shoulders. "Sit down and breathe," she said.

Reluctantly, he sat.

"We're all worried about Lexie," Kate told him. "We have to be patient for a little while longer. We're not leaving this country without her. We're going to find her."

"I wish I had your confidence, Kate," Blake replied, shaking his head bitterly. "After all, she's not the first undercover to go missing."

"I know, but when Jonas first went missing, he didn't have the FBI searching for him. Lexie Montgomery does."

She pulled away from him, her face sympathetic but determined. "We're going to find her and bring her home. I promise."

"Don't make promises that you can't keep, Kate."

Kate sighed. "I don't."

19

Camp Resistance

Lexie woke the next morning, her body stiff from sleeping on the hard cot. Despite the darkness, she could make out a body-shaped lump under the blanket on Jade's cot. Lexie pulled her arm from under the blanket to check her watch.

Ugh, it's only six thirty. What in the hell have I gotten myself into? If I don't find a way out of this mess, my career, and maybe my life, is over. Holden is witty and charming, but he's running with some dangerous people. I have a feeling that this isn't going to end well for me. How did I let this happen?

Unable to go back to sleep, she lay awake and contemplated her next few moves. She had to find a way to contact the FBI. But how? She knew she had to act like this extremist life was what she wanted. If anyone suspected her, she was in deep trouble.

A few minutes later, she heard the rustle of a blanket. Jade sat up and looked around the room. "You awake?" her tentmate asked.

"I am," Lexie said. "Good morning." She sat up, stretched, and ran her fingers through her mop of blonde hair.

"I'm glad KK was gone on the mission," Jade said. "It was nice having the tent to ourselves on your first night."

Lexie nodded. "So, what's on the agenda for today?"

"Breakfast," replied Jade. "I'm starving."

"Me too."

The two women dressed. Lexie put on the same clothes she'd worn the night before. "Hey, Jade, could you show me where I can do some laundry?" she asked.

"Sure. There are a couple of compact washers near the shower facility. Bring your clothes and I'll show you."

Lexie gathered up the rest of her dirty clothes and put them in the canvas bag that Holden had given her. The two women chatted as they walked the short distance to the laundry area. Jade showed Lexie how to operate the small washers. Luckily there were two, so Lexie was able to wash all her clothes at once. Next to the washer was an economy-size tub of generic washing powder. The clothes rotated through the wash cycle while the two women washed their faces and brushed their teeth, and then Jade helped Lexie hang her clothing to dry on the clotheslines.

Lexie genuinely liked Jade; she had been nothing but kind, helpful, and sympathetic. Watching the other woman as she helped her with laundry, Lexie had to remind herself that while Jade seemed friendly toward her, she or anyone in the camp could turn on her at any time if they suspected her of anything. *No attachments.*

"Let's go eat," Jade said. "We'll come back for your clothes later."

Because the main team hadn't returned, there were only a few people having breakfast in the mess hall. Lexie saw Holden sitting with Finn and Ryan. Holden smiled when he saw her and Jade approaching. "Good morning, ladies," he called, waving.

"Good morning," Lexie and Jade said in unison.

"Finn and Ryan, right?" Lexie said.

"That's correct," Finn replied. "How did you sleep?"

"Like a rock. I think I was exhausted from all the excitement."

"Go get some breakfast, then come join us," Holden said.

"Mamma Bear's cinnamon buns are the best," Ryan added.

The self-service buffet had a variety of covered trays, keeping the food warm. The two women selected utensils from the round canisters, put them on their trays, then proceeded to the food. Lexie lifted the lid on the first serving tray. The aroma of warm spices emanating from the hot, fresh cinnamon rolls invaded her senses, causing her mouth to water. The smell made her think of Christmas, which caused her to miss her family. She realized it was the first time that she had thought of her real family since she left the United States.

Lexie and Jade each took a cinnamon bun and a cup of coffee. Bypassing the brown-spotted bananas and apples piled in a fruit bowl, they joined the group of men at the table.

"What's on the agenda for today?" Lexie asked.

Holden answered. "The team should be back sometime before lunch. I want to introduce you to the entire crew. Tomorrow, you'll begin your training regimen."

Lexie took a sip of the bitter black coffee, then took a large bite of the gooey pastry. The sweetness was overpowering. "Ryan, you weren't lying when you said these are the best cinnamon rolls," Lexie said. "I could get fat living here."

"Don't worry, Dusty will make sure you don't gain any weight," Ryan said with a slight edge to his voice.

Holden gave Ryan a disapproving look.

"Who's Dusty?"

The lightheartedness of the conversation instantly became veiled and cautious, reminding Lexie of where she was—this wasn't summer camp. The altered mood induced a feeling of nausea within her.

Ryan looked down at his empty plate. "I need to get going," he said. "Catch you later, Lexie."

"I need to go too," Finn said. "I have a ton of work to finish before the group returns."

After the two men left, Lexie turned to Holden and asked again, "Who's Dusty?"

"He trains the ground team," he replied—too quickly.

"Why did Ryan react the way he did when he brought up Dusty?"

"No reason."

"Come on, Holden, be honest with me. I need to know what to expect."

Holden glanced over at Jade, who remained silent.

"Let's just say Dusty doesn't have many friends. He has an intense personality and can be a bit overzealous when it comes to the movement. He trains his team hard and demands perfection."

"Okay. Good to know."

"Don't get your feelings hurt if he's rude to you," Jade said. "He might be a wanker, but he's also the best in the business."

"What kind of training?"

Holden answered, "Your training at the camp will cover everything from recon to covert entries. Camp Resistance is divided up into three factions: the planning/targeting team, the computer/tech team, and the direct action/ground team. Each faction has a leader. The computer/tech team is led by Finn. He might be young, but he's brilliant. The planning/targeting team is led by Jonas. And the direct action/ground team is led by Dusty. The three faction leaders report to Greg. He has the final say of who we target and how hard we attack."

Hearing the name *Jonas* sent Lexie's brain into overdrive.

Could this be the missing constable? Jonas is a fairly common name in Europe; maybe it's a coincidence.

What if it is him? What do I do if I see him? How could he be a faction leader?

Calm down, don't get ahead of yourself, Lexie. It's probably a different Jonas altogether.

"So you're not a faction leader?" Lexie asked Holden.

"No, I'm in charge of recruitment. Once I'm back in camp, I'm a worker bee just like everyone else."

"Where will I be assigned?"

"It depends on your strengths and weaknesses. How good are your computer skills?"

"Not great," she admitted, then added, "but thanks to what I learned at the Gathering, I now know how to encrypt and decrypt my e-mails and computer."

"Probably not the tech team, then," Holden said, laughing. "You look like you're in good condition. Can you scale a fence?"

"I've never tried, but I'm sure I can."

"Then I'm guessing you'll be assigned to the ground team. Listen, I've told you too much already. Just watch and learn. You need to earn people's trust here, and asking a bunch of questions is not the way to do it."

Jade reached across the table and took Lexie's hands in hers. "Lexie, you seem nervous. This is serious business. Are you sure you're ready? There is no shame in saying no."

"I'm more than ready, Jade. I can do this."

"That will happen soon enough," Holden said. "You gonna finish that cinnamon roll?"

Lexie picked up the remaining pastry and stuffed it in her mouth. "Yep," she said with her mouth full.

"What a little bitch," he said, then laughed.

* * * * *

While Lexie folded her clean clothes, she listened to Jade chatter on about American books and television. Most of Jade's knowledge about the United States came from her obsession with television reruns.

"I would love to live in New York City," Jade said.

"Why?"

"I've seen all of the episodes of *Friends*. It seems so romantic."

"Believe me, it's not. It's a dirty, loud, and expensive city."

Holden stuck his head through the tent door flap. "You ready to meet the rest of the group?"

Lexie stowed her freshly laundered clothes in her footlocker. "Ready as I'll ever be."

The three entered the main camp area, where two men were unloading a van filled with equipment. Other vehicles soon arrived carrying people. Lexie didn't recognize the vehicle drivers, but she did recognize some of the occupants.

Someone grabbed Lexie from behind and twirled her around in a circle. As he put her down, Lexie spun around to see Barnabas smiling at her. His hazel eyes twinkled behind his black-framed glasses. Despite his need for braces, his smile radiated charm.

"Barnabas! So good to see you," Lexie said.

Barnabas hugged her, then kissed each of her cheeks. "You too, love. Has this prat been taking good care of you?" he asked, nodding toward Holden.

"Nice," Holden said, rolling his eyes.

"Just kidding, mate. You know you're my second favorite American, after Lexie, of course."

The two men hugged and slapped each other on the back.

"Where's my hug?" Jade asked indignantly.

Barnabas grabbed Jade, picked her up off the ground, and squeezed her. "I've missed you, darling Jade."

"You've only been gone a couple days, so you couldn't have missed me too much."

"Every second away from you is like being stuck in hell," Barnabas said theatrically.

"That's total crap," replied Jade, laughing.

A tall, muscular female with razor-sharp features approached the circle of friends. "Dusty wants everyone assembled in the main hall in fifteen minutes," she said gruffly.

"How did things go?" Holden asked in a low voice.

"Dusty will cover everything you need to know in the briefing," she said sharply, then left abruptly.

Barnabas rolled his eyes. "She's such a peach."

"Who was that?" Lexie asked.

"That's KK, our lovely cabinmate," Jade said.

"You weren't lying when you said she was intense."

"Try to stay on her good side," Holden said. "Let's get to the briefing. I'm curious to hear how the operation went, and I want to introduce you to everyone."

"I need to stow my gear," Barnabas replied. "I'll see you at the meeting."

Lexie followed Jade and Holden to the main hall.

* * * * *

Lexie, Holden, and Jade sat on folding chairs and waited for the meeting to begin.

"That's Dusty," Jade whispered to Lexie, motioning across the room.

Dusty's long, wind-swept, salt-and-pepper hair and matching stubbly beard gave him the look of an old Western movie star. His skin was beginning to take on a leathery appearance, causing Lexie to estimate his age as late forties.

Barely visible above the neckline of his shirt was a portion of a tattoo.

"I need everyone's attention," Dusty said in a loud, authoritative voice. The room immediately quieted. "I'm happy to report that our mission was a success. We start training tomorrow for our next operation. Are there any issues that need to be addressed while we're all together?"

Lexie took this opportunity to look around the room. She estimated that there were close to thirty people gathered, ranging in age from late teens to early fifties. About 70 percent of the group were men.

Finn stood and said, "George will be arriving in a few minutes with provisions, so I need volunteers to help unload the truck."

Members of the group nodded.

Holden stood up. "I'd like to introduce everyone to our new recruit, Lexie." Turning, he motioned for her to stand.

Smiling, Lexie did so. She felt a flush creep across her cheeks.

"Lexie is from the United States, and she's here indefinitely."

The crowd clapped and cheered.

"Thanks," Lexie said. "I'm looking forward to getting to know everyone."

She gave Dusty a darting gaze before sitting down. He continued to stare at her, his arms crossed, evaluating her every movement.

Be cool. You got this.

Jade patted Lexie on the back and smiled. "We're glad

to have you with us," she said, her grin accented by the silver ball on her pierced lip.

"Thank you. I'm glad to be here."

Lexie peered around the room and recognized some of the people from the Gathering. Standing in the corner were Viktor and Emil.

I'm all alone here. I've got no backup. This is way more serious than the Gathering. I can't afford a single slipup, or I'm dead.

The meeting adjourned, but most of the people mingled in the tent instead of leaving. Lexie desperately wanted to leave, but she knew that she had to stay and act like she was enjoying herself. In addition to her life being on the line, she had a job to do. She needed to meet Jonas, the faction leader in the camp, to determine if he was the missing constable. A strange mixture of emotions raced through her—excitement and terror at the same time.

"I see some familiar faces," she said to Holden, motioning toward the corner. "Are they new like me?"

"No," Holden replied. "Those three have been involved with this group since before I arrived."

"Were you at the Gathering strictly to recruit?"

"Not strictly. Like you, we were also there to learn new techniques. But we're always looking for like-minded people to enlist."

"How many did you recruit from this session?"

"Only you."

"I feel special."

Holden turned to face her, placing his hands on her shoulders. "You should feel special. Our mission is important and dangerous, so we're vigilant when bringing new people into our inner circle."

"I didn't mean to trivialize it," Lexie replied, her voice softening. "I realize how important this mission is, and I won't let you down."

"I know you won't."

Wow, this guy is one hell of a recruiter. He used his looks and charm to seduce me into joining the movement. I'm nothing but a fellow activist to him. Someone to help complete his mission. I definitely can't rely on him for help if the shit hits the fan.

"How come the main leader didn't address us?"

"He keeps a pretty low profile. In fact, he's hardly ever here. His main job is to ensure that we have what we need to accomplish our missions. He leaves the three faction leaders in charge of the day-to-day camp operations."

Lexie nodded. "As members of the cell, do we have a say in what kind of missions we accept?"

Holden's eyebrows drew together, causing a deep crease in his forehead. "Why did you call us a cell? That's a law enforcement term."

Oh fuck.

Holden crossed his arms and waited.

"That's how I heard it described on TV and in the trainings at the Gathering. Should I not call it that?"

Holden continued to stare.

"I'm sorry if I offended you. I'm not actually sure what to call us. A camp? A group?"

"How about a family? Because that's what we are. We depend on each other for everything. We might bicker and fight on occasion, but we know we can depend on one another. Isn't that the true essence of a family?"

"I like the sound of family."

Gradually, his wariness started to dissipate, though Lexie remained on edge as he spoke again. "To answer your question, most of the target decisions are made by the planning and targeting team, but we do sometimes make decisions as a group. You're always welcome to voice your thoughts and suggestions for future undertakings."

"That sounds great. I do have some ideas."

Holden smiled and shook his head. "I'm sure you do. Maybe you should wait until you've been here a while before you start making suggestions." Before she could reply, he tipped his head to the right. "Here come some of your old friends."

Olof, Viktor, and Emil approached her.

"Hello, Alexis," Emil said. "What's a nice girl like you doing in a place like this?" His German accent made the line especially funny.

Lexie chuckled. "I was about to ask y'all the same question."

Barnabas walked over to the group. "Hello, mates. Now that the gang is all here, it's time for a drink."

"When is it not time for a drink with you?" Holden asked.

Barnabas pretended to think. "Never. What is it you Americans say? 'It's five o'clock somewhere.'"

Before the group could leave, Dusty approached Lexie.

"You've been assigned to my team," he said brusquely. "Be in the main tent at eight o'clock in the morning. Wear workout clothes and don't be late."

As suddenly as he'd appeared, he stormed off without waiting for questions from her.

Lexie's heart thumped against her ribcage as a trickle of sweat ran down her spine.

"He's a personable chap," Barnabas joked.

"You'll get used to him," Emil said. "He's a great trainer."

"Are you on his team as well?" Lexie asked.

"I am. So are Viktor and Olof. We're all comrades now."

"What about you three?" she asked, motioning to Holden, Jade, and Barnabas.

Holden answered for the trio. "I'm on the ground team with you guys, but Jade and Barnabas both work on the planning team."

"I don't like all that physical stuff," Barnabas said. "Jade and I deal with more sophisticated techniques. We make the plans and you carry them out."

"We are all spokes in a wheel," Viktor said.

"And hopefully the wheel doesn't fall off the wagon," Barnabas joked.

There's more at stake here than wheels falling off a wagon, Lexie thought. *Way more at stake.*

20

Assen, the Netherlands

The Dutch police debriefed Blake, then gave him all his and Lexie's belongings. With the search complete and the activists fully identified, the police and FBI could not justify remaining at the camp and grudgingly left the area. No longer needed in an undercover capacity, Blake joined Kate and Adam to help search for Lexie. He stared out the window during the thirty-minute ride to the small town of Assen. Night had fallen, so he couldn't see the countryside, only blackness.

Upon arrival, he rented the room adjacent to Kate's, then stowed his and Lexie's possessions in his room. He desperately needed a shower but had no clean clothes to change into; luckily, the hotel had a small laundry room with a detergent dispenser. His filthy clothes had a dank smell that he was sure would be permanent. As they rolled around in the dryer, Blake showered away the grime and sweat from his hair and body. It took the entire complimentary bottle of shampoo and several washes to remove the dirt and grease from his hair. He dried himself with the fluffy white towel, slipped on a pair of sweatpants, and retrieved his warm clothes from the dryer.

When he opened the door to his room, the pungent odor nearly knocked him over. The soiled clothing, dirty sleeping bags, and well-used tent filled the room with a foulness he'd become accustomed to until he'd put some space between himself and his belongings. Opening the window to let in some fresh air, he smiled. Lexie would think it was funny that their gear smelled so bad.

He missed her so much.

The room was quiet and cozy, but sleep eluded him. At first light, he wandered to the comfortable hotel lobby and helped himself to a cup of coffee. He sat and stared out the window as he sipped from the steaming cup.

"You couldn't sleep either?" Kate asked.

Blake jumped at the sound of her voice.

"Sorry, I didn't mean to startle you."

"No worries." He tipped his head toward the coffee pot on the counter. "The coffee is fresh."

Kate poured herself a cup of coffee, added cream, and sat down beside Blake. "Did you get any sleep?"

He shook his head. "No. You?"

"Not much."

"What are we going to do?" he asked. "We have no idea where Lexie is, and right now we don't have a single lead to follow."

Kate took a sip of her coffee. "Lexie will contact us."

"How? She doesn't have a phone. God only knows where they've taken her."

"She'll find a way. I know Lexie. She's bright and

innovative. She'll find a way to contact us, and when she does, we'll find her and bring her home."

"We can't just sit around and wait," Blake said. "We have to do something."

"We will. Connor said he would have Lexie's recorder downloaded and ready for us to listen to this morning. With any luck, it will offer some leads. Plus, we still have Robert helping us."

Exhaling in frustration, Blake took a too-large gulp of coffee and scalded his tongue. "Where is he, anyway?"

"Ben gave him some money to stay in Appelscha for a couple of nights. He's going to keep his ears open and see if he can contact Jade."

"That's a good idea," Blake admitted. "According to Robert, Jade disappeared about the same time Lexie did. Chances are they're together." Pausing, he rotated his neck from the left to the right.

"You all right?" asked Kate.

"Yeah. I have a kink in my neck. Probably from tossing and turning all night."

"Blake, you do know that none of this is your fault, don't you?"

Blake lowered his eyes and stared into his cup of coffee. "She was my partner, Kate. I was supposed to keep her safe."

"*Is.* Don't use the past tense. She *is* your partner."

Further conversation came to a halt as Adam strode through the door and announced, "Connor is on his way over with the recording from Lexie's water bottle."

21

Camp Resistance

Lexie woke bright and early the next morning, ready for her first day of training. A fluttery feeling rolled in her stomach, hunger or nerves. KK was missing; Jade stirred under her covers. "You going to breakfast?" she mumbled.

"Yep. Want me to wait for you?"

"No. I drank a bit too much last night. You go ahead."

"Okay. See you this afternoon."

"Hey, Lexie," Jade said, raising her head an inch or so off her pillow, "good luck this morning. Stand your ground and don't let Dusty get under your skin."

"I will. Thanks."

After a stroll over to the mess hall, Lexie had a light breakfast and a cup of strong coffee. Her stomach churned too much for her to want a heavy meal. When she was nearly finished, Olof, Viktor, and Holden arrived, filling their trays with food and joining her.

"You ready for your first day?" Holden asked.

"Bring it on," she said, trying to sound confident.

Viktor grinned. "I like your attitude."

After everyone finished their breakfast, the group

walked together to the main hall. KK and Dusty were in the corner stretching and talking. "Stretch out," Dusty yelled across the room. "We're going to start out with some hand-to-hand drills today."

"That's weird," Viktor said. "He usually saves the physical training for the afternoon."

After a few minutes of stretching, Dusty had everyone circle him. "We're going to practice some basic fighting skills this morning. Everyone pair up."

KK, being the only other woman, walked over to Lexie.

"Morning, KK," Lexie said.

KK nodded.

Dusty demonstrated several moves using Holden as his partner. After he finished, the pairs spaced themselves out and started practicing. Lexie immediately sensed KK had some sort of an ax to grind with her; she was overly aggressive on each move that they practiced together, throwing punches without pulling any. Lexie remembered the advice that Jade had given her and matched KK's ferocity move for move.

If she wants to go hard, then I'll go hard right back.

At the end of thirty minutes, Lexie dripped with sweat. Chunks of hair had escaped from her ponytail holder, causing her to look like a character from a comic strip who had touched a live wire.

"Everyone gather around," Dusty said. "Form a large circle around me. We're going to do some light combat fighting. Go hard enough so your partner knows they've been hit, but don't do any permanent damage. One pair at a time. Holden, you and Viktor go first."

Holden had removed his shirt. A tattoo of a fire-breathing dragon stretched the breadth of his chest. Lexie admired the intricate work of art as sweat dripped down his muscular body.

He and Viktor faced off. They exchanged glancing blows, both careful to pull their punches, before Holden swept Viktor's leg and took him to the floor. When he had him pinned, Dusty called the match.

Lexie watched as KK sat on the sidelines, alternately stretching her arms across her body from left to the right. When Dusty looked over at her and gave her a slight nod, she came to life—a menacing grin crept across her face as she rose to her feet.

"KK, you and Lexie are next," Dusty said.

There is no way this is going to go well.

The two women faced off in the center. Before Lexie had a chance to get her bearings, KK punched her hard in the jaw. Pain radiated through Lexie's face, her eyes watering with the blow.

"What the fuck was that?" she yelled.

Smirking, KK charged Lexie a second time. This time Lexie parried the blow, then delivered a powerful counterstrike to KK's gut. The other woman sucked in, trying to catch her breath, and then spun around to face Lexie, clearly infuriated.

KK grabbed Lexie around the neck, trying to gain a choke hold. Lexie punched her in the stomach and pushed away. Her eyes were still watering from KK's initial punch, but her mind and muscle memory were summoning all her years of tae kwon do training.

When the other woman charged a second time, Lexie dispatched a roundhouse kick to her stomach with a loud *thud*, causing KK to double over. Instead of finishing her opponent off like her years of training had taught her, Lexie opted to stand down, hoping they would be finished.

Instead, KK charged Lexie and tackled her to the ground. While ground-fighting, she landed a solid punch to Lexie's right kidney.

"Get off me, you bitch," Lexie yelled.

"Fuck you. You gotta learn your place, Yankee."

KK pinned Lexie to the mat, but Lexie remembered her ground-fighting training from the FBI academy and used her hips to toss her opponent off balance, allowing her to escape. Learning from her previous mistake, she charged KK and grabbed her around the neck.

KK had twenty pounds on Lexie, so the FBI agent wasn't able to hold on. Before the other woman had another opportunity to grab her, Lexie jumped to her feet, throwing herself back before the other woman could seize her legs. KK jumped to her feet and attacked again, tying up Lexie and landing a barrage of blows to her abdomen and ribs. Lexie kept her grip on KK and pulled her body in close enough that none of the blows packed any power.

"Break it up," Dusty said. He grabbed each woman by the back of her shirt and yanked them apart, nearly ripping Lexie's shirt. Lexie pushed past Dusty and charged KK for another assault.

Releasing KK, Dusty grabbed Lexie around the waist, violently hurling her away. "I said break it up."

Lexie kept her fevered stare on KK, who was bent over with her hands on her knees, trying to catch her breath.

"We're all on the same damn team," Dusty said.

"The bitch is crazy," KK protested.

"I'll show you crazy," Lexie sneered, and lunged again.

"Enough," Dusty said, pushing Lexie away from KK. "Sit down. Olof and Emil, you're up."

Keeping her posture stiff and shoulders squared, Lexie sat cross-legged on the opposite side of the circle from KK. She used the neck of her T-shirt to wipe sweat from her face. Olof and Emil looked like professional prizefighters, weaving and bobbing from side to side, each landing jabs and punches.

With her jaws clenched, Lexie glared across the circle at KK. She wanted her to know that she wasn't scared of her.

After Olof and Emil finished sparring, Dusty dismissed the group for a lunch break.

"I need a shower," Lexie told Holden.

Holden leaned over and took a whiff of Lexie. "You definitely do."

Lexie elbowed him in the ribs. "You don't smell so great yourself."

* * * * *

After lunch, the direct-action faction reconvened in the main hall. Lexie's right cheek throbbed where KK had punched her, but she was ready to learn. A variety of tools and pieces of electronic equipment were systematically displayed on the long table. The group gathered around, awaiting Dusty's instructions.

"After our last mission, we destroyed most of our old tools. As you know, we do this so the cops have nothing to trace. It's much safer to start each mission with new equipment. We will all train on each piece of equipment until everyone is comfortable operating the gear. Have a look at the table and raise your hand if there is a piece of equipment that you are unfamiliar with."

On the table were a variety of tools Lexie knew to be used by animal rights extremists. She saw crescent wrenches, bolt cutters, crowbars, infrared scopes, a parabolic dish, radios, and cell phones. The latter made her heart begin to race—an opportunity for rescue, if she could get her hands on one. Lexie raised her hand to ask a question.

"Go ahead," Dusty said.

Careful to not sound like a law enforcement officer, she said, "I know that dish-looking thing is a bionic ear, but I don't know how to use one."

"I'm going to teach you and everyone else how to use it."

Lexie nodded. "I've never used night-vision equipment either."

"You'll learn. Any other questions?"

She peered around the group, but no one else asked any questions.

Dusty continued, "Since all this equipment is brand new, we need to get it prepared for covert operations. Everyone grab a crescent wrench and tape it up with black electrical tape."

Lexie watched Holden wrap a crescent wrench, then did the same to hers.

"Do you know why we're wrapping the wrenches?" Dusty asked her.

"So they don't reflect light?"

"That's one of the reasons. The other reason is to limit the noise we make when carrying them in a bag."

Lexie nodded.

Dusty picked up one of the packages of large black socks sitting on the end of the table. "Anyone know what we use these for?"

"To cover our shoes so we don't leave distinctive footprints," Viktor answered.

"Exactly. Either use these socks or tape up your shoes with duct tape. We don't want to give the police a clear footprint to use against us."

"These are nice two-way radios," Olof said, picking up a walkie-talkie.

"The best money can buy," Dusty said.

As the team members were handling the new equipment, Dusty approached Lexie. "Since you're new, I'll work with you one on one."

Oh, great. My day keeps getting better and better.

* * * * *

As the rest of the team exited the hall, Dusty grabbed her by the arm, causing her to jump. "I need to talk to you," he said. "Alone."

248

Holden turned to see if Lexie was behind him. "Go ahead. I'll catch up with you at dinner," she said.

When everyone was out of earshot, Dusty tightened his grip on Lexie's arm and sneered at her. His nearly perfect appearance was marred by a chipped front tooth and a thin, white scar just above his right eyebrow. "Who the fuck are you, and why are you here?"

Lexie jutted her chin in the air and locked eyes with Dusty. "Back off, asshole. I'm here for the same reason you are . . . to help change the world." She struggled to free herself from his grasp, but his fingers dug in.

"You might have the others fooled, but I don't trust you."

"I don't give a shit," she said, refusing to break eye contact.

Finally, he released his hold on Lexie's arm. She rubbed her tricep where he had squeezed. "Why do you have such a problem with me? I haven't done a damn thing to you."

He crossed his arms over his chest. "Where did you learn your fighting techniques? You fight like a cop."

"That's crazy. I'm a good fighter because I've spent half my life training in tae kwon do."

"That's a good story."

Lexie shrugged her shoulders. "Whatever. Believe what you want to believe. Can I go now?"

Dusty gave her a disparaging look, moved to the side, and motioned with a sweep of his arm. Clenching her teeth, she brushed past him, making a point to knock his arm out of the way with her shoulder.

* * * * *

Lexie showered, then returned to her tent to get ready for dinner. As she opened the tent flap, she realized it was already occupied—KK was there, rummaging through her footlocker.

"What the hell are you doing in my shit, bitch?" Lexie yelled.

KK jumped and faced Lexie, one of the agent's shirts clutched in her hand.

Lexie charged over and ripped the shirt from her grasp. "Answer me."

"Who the fuck are you?" KK asked.

"None of your damn business. What's the problem with you people? You recruited me, remember?" Lexie slammed the lid of her footlocker. "I told you who I am. You know as much about me as I know about you. Keep your hands off my stuff."

"Something about you doesn't feel right," KK seethed. "I'll find out who you are." She spun around to leave and ran into Jade, who had just entered the tent.

"Oh," Jade said, confusion entering her voice as she took in the women's aggressive posture, "hi, KK."

"You better stay far away from this one," KK said, motioning toward Lexie. "She's trouble." Warning given, she pushed past Jade and left the tent.

"What's her problem?" asked Jade, turning her head to watch KK storm off.

"I have no idea," Lexie growled, examining a hole where she'd ripped the shirt away from her tentmate. "I caught her rummaging through my footlocker. Oh, and this morning, she tried to kill me."

"What?"

"Dusty partnered us up to spar and she tried to take me down. The bitch even kidney-punched me."

"Are you all right?" Jade walked over to get a closer look at Lexie. "You definitely have a swollen cheek."

"Yeah. She punched me in the face right off the bat. Don't worry, I managed to get my share of punches in on her. I let her know that I wasn't taking her shit."

"That's good. I guess. Aren't we all supposed to be on the same team?"

"That's what I thought," Lexie said. "I guess KK didn't get that memo."

"I've always thought that KK was a few sandwiches short of a picnic. Why didn't Dusty stop the fight?"

"Because he wanted it to go bad for me. I saw Dusty give KK a nod before he paired us up to fight. Both he and KK want me to leave the camp. For some reason they don't trust me."

Jade shrugged helplessly. "Stand your ground, and hopefully they'll both come around."

"I guess that's all I can do." Lexie took a deep breath. "Hey, can I ask you a delicate question?"

"Of course you can."

"Do you communicate with anyone outside the camp? Do you ever call your mom or any other family members to let them know you're alive and well?"

Jade sat down on her bed before answering. "Just

between you and me, I call my mom a couple of times a year."

Lexie pulled over a camp chair and sat down in front of her tentmate. "What do you tell her you're doing?"

"She thinks I'm working for a group similar to the Peace Corps. I told her that I travel all over the world, and I call when I can."

"And she believes that?"

"She really doesn't have a choice."

"I guess that's true. Where do you call from?"

Wariness crept into the other woman's expression. "Lexie, you know it's against the rules to contact people outside of our camp."

"I know," Lexie replied, scrambling for some cover, "that's why I'm asking you. As far as my mom is concerned, I've disappeared off the face of the earth. My relationship with Blake was new, so he had never met any of my family. He doesn't have any way of contacting my mom and vice versa. At some point I need to call her and let her know I'm okay. That's the only reason I'm asking. I'm not going to do anything stupid."

Her face softening, Jade replied, "After you've been here a while and people trust you, then you can ask Dusty to help you contact your mom. But wait until you've been here for a few months."

"That makes me feel better. I don't want my mom worrying about me. When I do contact her, I think I'll use the same story you told your mom. I hope you don't mind me asking you questions like this. I don't want to do anything wrong."

"I don't mind at all. I know it's a bit weird being here at first, but you'll get used to it."

"Thank you, Jade. You're a good friend."

"No problem. Let's go get some dinner."

"Why don't we ever see Jonas?" Lexie asked as Jade started to slip out of the tent. "I think I've met everyone in the camp except him."

"That's a good thing," Jade replied. She glanced at Lexie, then quickly looked away, putting her hands in her pockets and staring at the ground.

"What's that mean?"

"Nothing. Let's go."

"No, Jade, tell me," Lexie said, leaning closer and frowning. "What's the deal with Jonas?"

"I just meant that, well . . . Jonas usually handles any problems that arise. When there are no issues, then Jonas keeps to himself."

"Is that all?"

Jade looked around, then lowered her voice to nearly a whisper. "You don't want to get on Jonas's bad side. He has the final say as to what happens in this camp, and he can be extremely domineering. Believe me, you don't want to cross him. Do you understand?"

"I do."

"Don't tell anyone that we had this conversation."

"I won't," Lexie assured her. "What happens between us stays between us. I promise."

"I'm serious, Lexie. Don't mess with Jonas."

"I won't. Thank you for giving me a heads-up."

Finally, Jade nodded. "Okay. Let's go eat. I'm starving."

What the hell is going on in this camp? Who is this Jonas and why is Jade terrified of him? Ducking under the tent flap and into the daylight, Lexie thought, *This place isn't simply an animal rights extremist camp. Something else is going on here. I'm sinking deeper and deeper into a dark abyss.*

22

Assen, the Netherlands

Connor lugged a large laptop into Adam's hotel room.

"Have you listened to the recording yet?" Kate asked.

"No," he replied, setting the system up on top of the room's wooden dresser. "I came here as soon as the tech agent gave it to me." Preparations finished, he looked around the room. "Everyone ready?"

All three of the agents nodded.

"It appears that the recording has a little over four hours of conversations on it," Connor said as he examined the screen.

"Can we skip to the end?" Blake asked. "We can listen to the whole recording later, but the end is what we need to hear now."

Nodding, Connor jumped ahead in the recording, skipping around until he found what sounded like Lexie chatting with another woman. Blake's chest hurt when he heard Lexie's voice on the tape.

"That's Lexie and Jade," he said.

The group gathered close to the computer. They heard Holden greet Lexie and Jade, then offer them champagne.

They listened to Holden's speech welcoming Lexie into the inner circle, followed by a toast. Just a few moment later, they heard Lexie utter the words, "What have you done?" followed by a loud crash.

Kate grabbed Blake's forearm and unconsciously squeezed. The longer the silence, the harder she gripped, her other hand clutching at her necklace with equal strength. Blake noticed the gold St. Michael pendant she was fingering. He placed his hand on top of hers, partly to offer support and partly to keep her from drawing blood.

"What now, boss?" a male voice on the recording asked.

"Tie her up and blindfold her. Throw her in the back of the van. I'll take care of the rest."

Blake's shoulders tightened, and cold sweat ran down his back. "That's that son of a bitch Holden," he said.

"Grab her feet, I will get her arms," a man with a thick German accent said as the recording continued.

"Why the hell did you do that, Holden?" a female voice asked.

"I did what I had to do. You know we can't take any unnecessary risks."

"There were other ways to handle the situation."

"Jade, you need to back the fuck off and remember who's in charge here."

"So much for teamwork!"

There was the sound of a door slamming, then nothing.

Connor checked his computer. He tried skipping ahead, but there was only silence. "That's the end of the recording."

"Other than Holden, did you recognize any of the other male voices?" Connor asked Blake.

"Yes, it was definitely Emil. He's a German activist and was in charge of the security team at the Gathering. I'm not sure about the other male voice. It could be one of the Swedes, but I can't be sure."

The investigators listened to the recording several more times.

"Any ideas?" asked Kate.

"I wish we knew their last names so we could run background checks," Connor said.

"Hell, we don't even know if the first names they used are real," said Blake, shaking his head. *We should have prepared for this. Somehow, we should have planned for what to do.*

"What do we know?" Connor asked.

Blake answered. "Lexie was definitely taken against her will. Holden, Emil, and Jade were all involved."

"Do you have any idea where Jade lives?" Kate asked Connor.

"No. In fact, we asked Robert about that yesterday. He has no idea where she stays."

Blake jumped up and flung his chair across the room. "Fuck! We've got nothing." As the others looked on, startled, he tore open the hotel room's door and headed outside.

23

Camp Resistance

Lexie woke the next morning to sore muscles throughout her body and a painful bruise on her face.

Fucking KK.

She dressed quickly and stopped by the mess hall for a cup of coffee and a muffin. As she ate, a shadow fell across her. Looking up, she saw a familiar face smiling at her.

"May I sit down?" Holden asked.

Lexie smiled back. "Please do." *Damn, the guy still looks amazing despite the shit he's dragged me into.*

"How're you feeling this morning?" he asked as he reached over and gently touched Lexie's bruised face, his long, slender fingers lingering on her cheek. His smoldering eyes and infectious charm reminded her of Logan.

"I'm a little sore," she said, "but I'll be fine."

"You handled yourself well yesterday. Against KK, I mean."

"Thanks."

"She can be a bitch at times," he said, voice laced with sympathy.

"Oh, really? I hadn't noticed."

They finished breakfast and walked to the training hall together. Holden nonchalantly took Lexie's hand. The stares from the other participants penetrated Lexie's skin like arrows zeroing in on a target; she politely pulled her hand from Holden's and smiled at him.

"Listen," she whispered. "It's not that I mind holding your hand, but I've got enough people riding me to prove myself without them thinking you chose me because we're involved."

Smirking, he replied, "They know me better than that, Lexie." Fortunately, though, he did not reach for her hand again.

Finn waited up front for everyone to settle into their spots.

"Good morning, gang," he said. "Today is a full day of computer training. This morning, we're going to talk about computer sabotage; this afternoon, we'll break into small groups and go over encryption and decryption techniques."

"Good," Lexie whispered to Holden. "At least the computer training will give my body a chance to heal before I have to take on the Amazon bitch again."

Finn continued, "There are three kinds of computer sabotage that we're going to discuss: hardware sabotage, records sabotage, and software sabotage. Since I'm not sure who has done what as far as computer sabotage, I'll cover all three areas this morning. It might be a review for some of you, but please listen closely—it's good to keep up with new ideas and techniques."

With his wide eyes and bushy auburn eyebrows, Finn looked more like a cartoon character than a real person. His thick Irish accent coupled with his animated movements reminded Lexie of a leprechaun. After the lunch break, he worked one-on-one with Lexie. Since she was the only new member, he told her, he'd decided to train her himself.

"You're a fantastic teacher," Lexie told him.

"Thank you. I enjoy teaching."

"You seem so young. Do you mind if I ask how old you are?"

"Not at all," he said. "I'm twenty-two."

"Did you study computer science in college?"

"I have a bachelor of computer science. I skipped a couple years in school, so I finished college when I was twenty."

"Wow. That's impressive," Lexie said, genuinely meaning it.

"Thank you. I've always loved technology, so computer science came easy for me."

"Not so much for me," she admitted. "I'm afraid you have your work cut out for you."

"I'm sure you'll do fine," he replied with a reassuring smile. "Encryption and decryption are actually pretty easy as long as you practice them a few times. You'll get the hang of it."

"Do you ever go with the ground team on missions?" Lexie asked him as he tapped away at the computer in front of them.

"Not often. I do most of my work here at the camp. I recently designed an encrypted communication app for our group to use. I believe the future of the animal rights revolution lies in technology. I think if we put more of our resources toward computer intrusion, then we could make greater strides in the movement." Some of the warmth left his face. Sighing, he said, "I wish I could get Dusty to understand that you don't necessarily have to blow up buildings to get people's attention. He's such a brute."

"You're right about that," she said. "He and his wicked bitchy second."

"I heard you had a little run-in with KK."

"Actually, my face had a run-in with her fist."

Finn chuckled. "You Americans are a gas."

"Do you get along with Dusty?" Lexie whispered.

Shrugging, he answered, "I have to work with him, so I try to keep our relationship amicable. I have to admit that I find him a bit rumbly."

"A bit what?"

He let out a cough of laughter. "I forget we have different slang. Rumbly means dodgy."

"I find him a bit rumbly too," Lexie said, smiling.

The two continued to work until the sun neared the horizon. "I sometimes lose track of time," Finn said, rising and stretching. "Shall we wrap up for the evening?"

"Sounds good to me," she replied, groaning slightly at the stiffness in her muscles as she stood.

"You're a quick study, Lexie. Maybe you should consider switching over to the technology faction. You might end up with fewer bruises."

Lexie nodded. "Are you working on any other apps?" she asked as they gathered up and put away equipment.

"I have a couple more ideas after I finish testing our communication app. We're going to use the app on the next mission. I want to make sure it's ready."

"You're brilliant, Finn. Have you ever considered working in the private industry? I can only imagine how much money a person with your talents could make."

"I'm not interested in money. I want to make this world a better place for the next generation. In fact, before I joined Camp Resistance, I relied on skip diving, squatting, and shoplifting to survive."

Lexie raised an eyebrow. "Is skip diving what Americans call dumpster diving?"

"Yes. In Europe we call it skipping or totting."

"I've had friends who dumpster dove for meals, but I never had to it myself. You must've been living completely off the grid. What was it like?"

"It wasn't bad. I lived in a community that actually posted a schedule of when restaurants and grocery stores dumped their trash. I mostly collected fruit, vegetables, and bread from the trash receptacles. You'd be surprised how much society wastes."

"I respect people who can live like that," Lexie said. "I recycle everything and I never waste food, but I've never climbed in a dumpster for provisions." Suppressing a small shudder at the thought of digging her vegetables out of the trash, she quickly changed the subject. "So how did you end up here?"

"I was living in an abandoned building when I met Barnabas. He's the one who talked me into joining the group and using my talents for change."

"So Barnabas introduced you to the group?"

"Yep. I've been here eighteen months. It feels like home."

Something about that statement saddened Lexie. Finn

was a decent looking, highly intelligent young man who seemed lost and lonely. She could tell he possessed a pure heart and truly wanted animal liberation without violence.

"You guys about done?" an unseen voice asked.

Lexie jumped and looked at the door where Holden stood.

"Yep, we're done for the day," Finn answered.

"I didn't see you come in," Lexie said to Holden.

"Didn't mean to startle you. I thought I'd see if you want to go to dinner, then maybe take a walk."

Lexie desperately needed to get her hands on a phone—Blake, Kate, and Adam must have been going insane by now not knowing her whereabouts—but she'd had little opportunity to explore the camp thanks to Holden wanting to spend time with her. She could tell his feelings toward her were growing. That worried her, but she knew it could also present her with future opportunities she might not get from a strictly platonic relationship.

"Sounds like a good plan," she said.

As she reached the door, Lexie turned, smiled, and said, "See you later, Finn."

"Later, Lexie."

Holden draped his arm over Lexie's shoulder, and they walked out together.

"It feels nice being close to you," she said, careful not to sound as though she were rejecting him outright, "but let's not do the public displays of affection. I need to prove myself first."

"If that's what you want," Holden said, removing his arm. "How was your day?"

"Great. Finn really is a wonderful teacher."

"Yeah. He's scary smart."

"He could make so much money in the corporate world."

"I know. I'm glad he's on our side."

"And how was *your* day?" Lexie asked.

"It was good. I worked on some logistical problems with Jonas for most of the day."

"What's his story?"

"What do you mean?"

"I keep hearing about Jonas, but haven't met him yet. I guess I'm just curious."

"Jonas is a natural leader. He's very intuitive, especially when it comes to law enforcement. He always seems to know their next move, which keeps us out of jail."

"That's good to know. I certainly don't want to land in jail in a foreign country. Speaking of that, what would happen if we did get arrested over here?"

"We won't."

"But what if—"

"Chill, Lex," he said, his voice suddenly hardening—it was a command, not a request. "We're not going to get arrested."

Lexie stopped abruptly and stared at Holden. He sighed loudly, then grabbed her by the shoulders and spun her around so the they were face-to-face.

"I'm sorry," he said. "I'm not used to someone asking so many questions. I didn't mean to piss you off."

"You didn't. You kind of hurt my feelings, though," she said, trying to sound sincere.

Holden touched her face and grinned. "I'm sorry. I'm not used to working with sensitive people, either."

Drawing back from his fingers, Lexie said, "I want to make sure I'm prepared for any scenario that we might face, and getting arrested is always a possibility."

"You're right. You should know what to do. As in the United States, if you get arrested here, you simply ask for an advocaat. That's what a Dutch attorney is called."

"Do we have an advocaat?"

"Yes. You'll be briefed on the advocaat and how to contact her before you're sent out on a mission."

"That's fair."

His voice softened, lowering to a more intimate timbre. "Lexie, I won't let them send you out on any kind of dangerous operation until you're ready. Do you trust me?"

"Of course I do, Holden."

Holden's eyes sparkled as he peered longingly into Lexie's eyes. Without warning, he leaned over and touched his lips to hers. The kiss, soft and delicate, lasted only a few seconds, but the adrenaline rush shocked Lexie, causing her pulse to race.

Slowly, he pulled back, keeping his gaze locked on Lexie while looking for some kind of a sign. Lexie had to think fast. If she pushed him away, she would lose the opportunity for inside information. If she didn't, then she knew the relationship would go further than she was comfortable with, and definitely further than the FBI would allow.

But this wasn't an ordinary FBI undercover operation. She was on her own. She would have to break some rules in order to survive and get home.

Fuck it.

When Holden leaned in for a second kiss, Lexie circled her arms around his neck. His tongue entered her mouth, causing a tingling pleasure to flood her body. He tasted like coffee and mint. She quivered in his arms as he whispered in her ear, "I've been dying to do that since the first time I laid eyes on you."

Shit, I'm in big trouble. What's happening here? Am I doing this for the case or for myself? Or both?

24
Assen—the Netherlands

After long hours of listening to the entire recording from Lexie's water bottle, the investigators finally took a break to eat. Opting for a quaint local restaurant, Connor sweet-talked the waitress into seating them at a window table. The sunshine streamed through the window and warmed Blake's face.

He perused the menu, but nothing sounded good. He was too worried about Lexie's safety to bother with food. The realization that he was powerless to help his partner left him feeling hollow inside.

Before the waitress could take their food orders, Connor's phone rang, and he left the table to take the call. Less than a minute later, he rushed back to the table, his face shining. Tossing some money on the table for their drink orders, he told the others, "Come on. We have to go. Ben has a lead."

Blake and Kate jumped in the back seat of Connor's tiny vehicle, allowing Adam the front passenger seat. Blake reached for the seatbelt as Connor punched the gas pedal, causing the tires to squeal and Blake to slam into Kate.

"Damn, dude," he yelled. "Who taught you to drive?" He pushed himself away from Kate, who had a death grip on the handle above the door. "Where are we going?"

Connor answered, "We're meeting Ben and the rest of the team at our hotel. It's only a couple of miles from here."

"Do you know any details?" Kate asked.

"No, only that there's a possible lead. Ben asked us to come quickly."

Connor wheeled into the Van der Valk Hotel parking lot and found the closest spot to the door. The group quickly made their way to the entrance. The lobby was ultra-modern, with a beautiful wood floor and exposed brick walls.

The FBI team followed Connor down a short hallway and into a small but comfortable conference room. Ben was waiting for them. "Good morning," he said. "Glad you made it here so fast. Help yourselves to coffee and danishes."

A coffee cup and an empty plate sat in front of Ben. Beside him, nearly hidden under a baseball cap, was a tiny, pale-skinned female with large, ebony eyes. A silver stud protruded above the woman's upper lip. Her right eyebrow was adorned with two smaller studs.

When everyone was seated, Ben spoke. "Thanks for joining us this morning." He motioned toward the unknown female. "This is undercover operative Tess Haas. She goes by Bug. Tess, this is the FBI team that I told you about. This is Adam Harper, who is a supervisor at FBI headquarters in Washington, DC."

Tess nodded and placed her clasped hands on the table. A delicate dove tattoo decorated her inside wrist.

"Nice to meet you," Adam said.

"You too," she replied quietly.

"This is Kate Summers," Ben continued. "She's a detective from the Los Angeles Police Department who is assigned to the FBI's Joint Terrorism Task Force. She is the handler for the two undercover agents. And this"—he directed his head toward Blake—"is Blake Bennett. He's the undercover agent assigned to this case."

Tess cocked her head to the side. "So, it's your partner who is missing?"

"Yes."

"I'm sorry. I'll do everything that I can to help you find her."

"Thank you," Blake said. "Any help would be greatly appreciated."

"What have you got?" Adam asked Ben.

"Three days ago, a large incendiary device exploded in a laboratory in Tübingen, Germany, destroying the entire lab. The lab is affiliated with Huntingdon Life Sciences, which uses animals for experimentation."

"So you believe it was an ALF action?" asked Adam.

"We know it was."

Ben clicked on his laptop, which was connected to a large video screen. A photo popped up depicting a spray-painted message on the side of what was left of the lab. In large red letters the sign said, *Experiment on yourselves. We're free— The Animals.* On the pavement leading to the lab, also in red paint, was written, *We will never give up—ALF.*

"As you can see," said Ben, "they left their ALF calling cards all over the crime scene. Their message was written in English because it's the language European countries use to communicate amongst themselves."

"There's no denying this was an ALF attack, but why do you think it's connected to Lexie's disappearance?" Blake broke in. "It could be someone who got inspired at the Gathering and did it on their way home."

"Not likely," Tess said. "This operation took precision timing and knowledge of the facility. The action was carefully planned and expertly carried out. It had to be a cohesive cell who trained together to pull off this kind of destruction."

"Do you know of any such groups?" Blake asked her.

"I've heard about a cohesive cell of activists who move around all over Europe. Supposedly the cell has a weapons specialist who can design and build an incendiary device for any scenario. The animal extremists refer to them as 'the ghost regiment.' They suddenly appear, do immense damage, then disappear without a clue. I've been trying for two years to make a connection with the group. A couple of weeks ago, I finally caught a break."

Blake and Kate both leaned forward, focusing their attention on Tess.

"I met a charismatic English bloke named Barnabas. I'm not sure if that's his real name, but that was the name he gave me."

Blake's heart thumped like a horse galloping to the finish line. He made eye contact with Kate and nodded. "Can you describe Barnabas?" he asked.

Tess's eye narrowed and she cocked her head to the side. "He's close to six feet tall, but rail thin. He wears glasses and has a bit of a receding hairline. I would guess he is in his early thirties."

"What kind of glasses did he wear?" Blake asked.

"Black, thick frames, like the hipsters wear."

Blake's eyes met Kate's again. "Sorry to interrupt," he said to Tess, "but I may know Barnabas. Please continue, and then I'll tell you what I know about him."

Tess nodded and continued. "Over the past year, I worked my way into an underground group who specializes in treating and relocating rescued animals. Up to this point, I've only cared for the rescued animals, but I know the leader of the group has participated in liberation operations in the past."

After pausing to take a sip of coffee, she resumed, "Barnabas approached me in a pub. He was charming and bought me a drink. At some point he told me that our meeting wasn't an accident. He was extremely cryptic, but reading between the lines, I believe he was planning a direct-action attack and needed a team who would be willing to take responsibility for a large number of liberated animals and not ask any questions."

"Where did this meeting occur?" Kate asked.

"In Eindhoven. It's a city in the Netherlands, a couple of hours south of here."

"How difficult is it to travel from the Netherlands to Germany?" Blake asked.

Ben answered. "Thanks to the Schengen Agreement, most of the internal border checks have largely been abolished. So to answer your question, not difficult at all."

"I told Barnabas that his friend was correct," said Tess,

"and that I knew of some people who could assist with the animals. He gave me his cell phone number and I told him that I would be in contact."

"Then what happened?" Kate asked.

"I told my leader, Jeanne, about the meeting. Jeanne wanted Barnabas's phone number, so I gave it to her. I also told her that if our group took action, I would like to participate. I waited around in the area and missed the Gathering because I didn't want to pass up the opportunity to participate in an illegal action. I tried calling Barnabas, but he must have been using a burner phone because it no longer worked."

"We ran the number but came up with nothing," Ben said. "This Barnabas guy knows how to cover his tracks."

"We need to pick up Jeanne and question her," Adam interrupted.

Tess's eyes widened with stunned surprise. "That would blow my cover," she said angrily.

"I understand, but we have a missing agent and we need to find her."

"*Both* our countries have missing operatives, Agent Harper," Tess said. "I might be your only hope of finding either of them. It's imperative that you not compromise my alias."

"I disagree," Adam said in a much louder tone. "We need to move quickly. This Jeanne is our only link to Barnabas."

Tess slammed her fists on the table and rose to her feet, nearly knocking over her chair. "You don't know shit about undercover work. You're going to fuck the whole thing up, Harper!"

Kate stood as well. "Let's calm down," she said in a soft voice. "We're all on edge, and we need to think this through in a logical manner." Kate smiled at Tess and gave a slight nod toward the chair.

Tess drew in a long breath, held it, then slowly released it before sitting down.

Kate continued. "I think Tess is correct. Compromising her undercover identity should be a last resort. Let's see if we can come up with a plan using Tess instead of burning her."

Adam gave Kate a hard stare. "Okay," he said. "Let's think this through."

25
Camp Resistance

Lexie woke the next morning pondering the kiss she'd shared with Holden. What did it mean? Was she falling for him or, as she would like to think, just doing her job? Either way, she couldn't keep him at bay for long.

Opening her eyes, she stared at the tent ceiling. She needed to find a way to communicate with her FBI team fast.

"So," Jade said. "You disappeared after dinner last night."

Jade was fully dressed. Lexie sat up and looked over to make sure KK was gone.

"You're up early," she said, rubbing at her eyes.

"I saw you with Holden last night. How did that go?"

Lexie wondered if Jade was actually interested in her romantic life as a friend, or prying to see what she was up to as an activist. "What about Robert?" she asked, attempting to steer the conversation away from her. "You two seemed rather chummy at the Gathering. What's going on there?"

"Robert is a nice bloke. We dated for a bit, but he's not part of our community, so we really can't have much of a romantic relationship."

"Would you ever ask him to join the group?"

"That's not up to me."

"Then who?" Lexie asked. "How does the group decide who to recruit for our little band?"

"If someone in our group knows someone who they think would make a good recruit, then that person's name is given to Jonas and Greg. They run a background check to make sure there are no red flags. If the potential recruit passes the initial phase then, like we did with you, we spend time with them to feel them out. We need to make sure the new candidate will fit in and get along with our established members."

"There's a lot that goes on behind the scenes," Lexie said.

"Yes indeed. We take our security seriously."

"So why not Robert?" Lexie asked. "Did you ever recommend him for the group?"

"I did, but something in his background spooked Jonas."

"Really? What was it?"

Jade shrugged and said, "Jonas told me that Robert had been arrested and would be on the police radar. He was too much of a security risk to join our group."

"That's harsh. Especially if you really like him."

"I do," replied Jade a bit wistfully, "but my loyalty is to our group. You're lucky that Holden is in the circle. As you'll learn, loyalty to the group comes first—everything else is second."

"That sort of makes me nervous."

"Why?" Jade asked.

"What if things go bad with Holden? It could lead to some serious awkwardness. Not to mention, I'm the new person, so if it doesn't work out with us, I'll be the one who has to leave."

"But what if it does work out?" Jade countered. "He could be the love of your life."

"You're right. But I'm scared. What if I make a mess of things?"

"If it's meant to be, then it will be."

"That's it? That's your advice?"

Jade laughed. "That's all I've got. Trust your instincts."

Trust my instincts.

*   *   *   *   *

Finn, Ryan, and Holden joined Lexie and Jade for breakfast.

"What's on the agenda for today?" Lexie asked.

Holden answered. "More tactical training with Dusty."

"Oh boy," Lexie said, rolling her eyes.

"Better eat a good breakfast," Holden told her, smirking. "You'll need the energy."

After breakfast, the group went their respective ways. Lexie and Holden took their time walking to the training tent. The morning was peaceful, the only sounds coming from the crunch of dead pine needles and twigs underfoot. Clouds kept the sun from making an appearance. Before they could reach their destination, Holden spontaneously grabbed Lexie's hand and pulled her behind one of the tents.

"Where are we—"

Before she could finish her sentence, Holden took

Lexie's head in his hands and pulled her into a fiery, passionate kiss. She surrendered and wrapped her arms around his slim body, her heart racing as her breathing became deeper and more irregular.

They pulled apart and opened their eyes. Lexie could see the burning passion and desire in Holden's eyes—it terrified her, but it was thrilling. He pulled her into a firm embrace. With her head resting on his chest, she could smell the bayberry soap that clung to his skin from his morning shower. The soap combined with his natural chemistry to produce a smell that was soft yet masculine.

"I couldn't wait a single second longer," he told her. "I had to kiss you."

"I'm not complaining," she whispered breathlessly.

Holden squeezed Lexie and kissed the top of her forehead. "I think I'm addicted to you, Lexie."

She felt a tingle down her spine as a smile crept across her face. "We might have to put you in rehab."

"I don't wanna kick this addiction," he said. "I think I like it."

He released her from his clasp. They stared deep into each other's gazes. "You have the most beautiful eyes," he said.

Lexie glanced down, breaking eye contact. "We, ahh . . . we better get moving, or Dusty is going to kick both of our asses for being late for training," she said.

"You're so practical."

"When it comes to Dusty, I'm in self-preservation mode."

"Let's get to training," Holden said, throwing an arm around her shoulders as they strode ahead.

There has to be another way to do this. Screwing around with Holden's emotions is stupid and dangerous. If he was crazy enough to drug and kidnap me, what would he do if he finds out I'm using him? Or worse, what if I'm not using him? Could I really have feelings for him?

No! Stop thinking like that. I'm doing what I have to do to stay alive.

* * * * *

Lexie unboxed the new GPS while Dusty stood behind her, his arms crossed and feet planted shoulder width apart. He had decided to work one-on-one with Lexie to bring her up to speed on the operation of the equipment as quickly as possible.

"Do we get new equipment after every mission?" Lexie asked Dusty.

"Not always, but we were due."

"This is nice stuff," she said.

She paid close attention to Dusty's instructions, so he wouldn't have to repeat himself. He wasn't exactly a patient guy, and she didn't want to press her luck with him.

After she'd done as he told her, he examined the GPS. "You're not completely stupid."

"If that's a compliment, I'll take it."

Dusty gave Lexie a hard smile, then showed her how to operate each new piece of equipment. "Have you ever participated in any underground direct actions?" he asked as they worked.

"If I had, I wouldn't talk about them."

He raised an eyebrow. "Good answer."

"I know you don't trust me, but I'm here for the right reasons. I'll be loyal to our cause and to our group."

Dusty took two steps forward, using his superior size as an intimidation technique. "We're not just a group, we're a family. I'm immensely protective of my family."

"And now they're *my* family," she said, refusing to cower to him.

Dusty grabbed her slender shoulders, digging in with his callused, meaty hands. He bent his knees so he was eye to eye with her. "Then you must protect your family at all costs. Do you understand me?"

"I do, Dusty. I'll serve and protect my family."

As soon as the words left her lips, Lexie knew she had made a huge mistake.

Leaning closer, his nose nearly touching Lexie's, Dusty hissed, "Hmm, that's an interesting way to phrase it, *serve and protect*. That's the police motto. Are you a fucking cop?"

Lexie felt a catch in her throat. "That's ridiculous," she said. "I simply meant I'll serve our cause and protect my family. I'm not a cop."

Dusty licked his lips and squeezed harder, causing Lexie to flinch from the pain.

"You better not be, or I'll kill you myself. They'll never find your body out here."

Lexie forcefully shrugged loose from his grip and pushed away, regaining her personal space. "Damn, dude. Lighten up. I'm not a fucking cop. How many more times do I have to say it before you believe it?"

"Words mean nothing to me."

"Okay, how about actions, then? What do I need to do to prove it to you?"

"The time will come when you will be asked to put your life on the line. We'll see what you're made of at that point."

"So until I do that, you're going to be nasty and distrustful of me?"

"You'll be lucky if that's all I do."

"Great," she said, turning away from him and back to the equipment. "More good times to look forward to."

"Are you fucking Holden?" Dusty asked.

Lexie whipped her head back around. "What? Where did that come from? It's none of your damn business."

"It is my business. I'm in charge of ground operations, and if the two of you let your emotions get in the way of—"

"We won't. Holden and I both understand the mission comes first."

"Holden is a good soldier. I don't want you fucking that up by messing with his head."

"I'm not. We're just friends."

Dusty gave a chuckle that was devoid of any real amusement. "You can lie to yourself, but you can't lie to me."

"I'm not lying. We haven't slept together."

"It's only a matter of time before you do, and emotions cloud judgment."

"How would you know? Have you ever had an emotion?"

Dusty's brows drew closer and his face tightened. "Don't push your luck, bitch. You mean nothing to me. I can make you disappear any time I like."

Lexie's eyes narrowed as she glared at Dusty. "Aren't we on the same team? This seems counterproductive."

Dusty crossed his arms and expelled an audible sigh. "I'll ease up on you under one condition."

"What's that?"

"You go slow with this relationship between you and Holden. I mean snail pace."

A light went off in Lexie's head, and she felt her chest loosen. This could be the answer not only to winning over Dusty but also to alleviating the Holden problem.

She took a step back and nodded. "I see your point. I'm not an unreasonable person. I'll agree to go slow with my relationship with Holden as long as you ease up on me and give me a chance to prove myself."

Dusty took a step forward and glared down at Lexie, who was a good eight inches shorter than him. "Agreed," he said. "But don't even think of double-crossing me." Stepping back, he resumed the lesson.

After another hour of instruction, he gathered the tools. Lexie picked up an armload of equipment and followed him to another tent full of cabinets and footlockers.

"All the storage units are labeled," he said. "Make sure you put everything in the proper place."

Lexie nodded and located the footlocker labeled *Night Vision*. She gently placed the night-vision goggles in their proper spot, then located the cabinet labeled *GPS/Two-Way Radios*.

As she put away the GPS devices, she noticed a box in the back corner of the cabinet that held cellular telephones.

Her heart rate spiked. *If I can get my hands on one of these, I can contact the FBI.*

However, to do it, she would have to get away from Holden, sneak into the tent, steal a phone, and make the call without anyone hearing her. No small feat, but she didn't really have a choice.

26

A little after two in the morning, Lexie crept from the tent, careful not to wake Jade or KK. Relying on the full moon to light her passage, she cautiously picked her way through the forest to the tent with the cell phones. The earthy smell of decomposing leaves filled the night air. It was strangely peaceful.

That peace was shattered by a sudden rustling noise. Startled, Lexie abruptly stopped and listened. Nothing.

It's just the wind. Don't let your imagination get the best of you.

After her pulse slowed, she continued. When she arrived, the tent, dark and gloomy, smelled of must and dust. She inched her way inside and stood quietly. Positive she was alone, Lexie beelined to the box that held the cell phones. She pulled one out and held the *on* button.

Please be charged.

The phone chimed and the screen lit up like a beacon.

Oh shit, she thought, quickly ducking under a tarp in the corner. She texted Kate:

Kate, it's Lexie. I'm alive. Being held in a terrorist training camp. Drugged and dragged here. Don't know my location. Not my phone. Don't call or respond. Can't talk. Someone might hear.

Lexie hit the send button, then continued.

Training with the group to maintain cover. In a wooded area with military-style tents and buildings but no idea how far from the previous location. Got to go. Will try to contact you soon. Please find me.

Saying a silent prayer that the texts had been received, Lexie erased the messages from the phone, wiping the contact from the call log as well.

Certain that she'd covered her tracks, she turned off the cell phone and placed it back in its proper place, then left the equipment tent and hustled toward her quarters. She was almost back to her tent when a man's deep, brusque voice penetrated the night air.

"What the fuck are you doing?"

Lexie jumped and her legs weakened. The sound of her heartbeat pounded in her ears. *Shit, perimeter guards. I should have thought of that.*

"You the new recruit?" the man asked as he stepped from the tree line and stood directly in front of Lexie.

"I ... I am."

He moved closer, invading Lexie's space. A gun protruded from his waistband.

"What are you doing out here in the middle of the night?" His voice was gruff and ominous.

"I, ahh ... I couldn't sleep, so I went for a walk." Lexie's voice sounded thin and strange to her ears. "I thought a little fresh air might do me some good." She clenched her hands into fists to make them stop shaking, then extended her right hand and said, "I'm Lexie."

The gangly man lowered his head and stared at her. His deep-set eyes were nearly hidden by his wrinkled brow, and the darkness made it impossible to see facial features. He took Lexie's outstretched hand without breaking eye contact.

"I'm Jonas."

Holy shit!

Lexie felt a rush of adrenaline surge through her body. She released his hand. "You're the leader of the planning team, right?"

"That's correct."

Staring at Jonas, she tried to remember the photo of the missing constable that Connor had shown her. *Too dark to tell.*

"Wandering around the camp in the middle of the night is dangerous," he said. "You may have been mistaken for an intruder, and intruders don't fare well here."

"I'm, ahh . . . I'm sorry. I didn't realize that I had to stay in my tent."

"It would be best if you didn't venture from your tent at night. Not until everyone knows your face. Let's just say we have some trigger-happy security personnel. I would hate to see you end up a victim of friendly fire." Jonas spoke in a slow, deliberate manner, his voice soft but menacing.

"Understood. I'll make sure to stay near my tent the next time I can't sleep."

"You do that. By the way, where's your flashlight?"

"I left it in my tent. The light attracts bugs."

"I would suggest you carry your flashlight and watch where you step. We only have one poisonous viper in the Netherlands, but it does inhabit this region."

Lexie swallowed hard. "Snakes? I hate snakes."

"Then you should be extra careful. I think it's time you get back to bed."

"Will do," she said, trying to sound nonchalant. "It was nice meeting you. Sorry it was in the middle of the night. I'll be more careful from here on out."

Jonas moved to the side, allowing Lexie to pass. "Pleasant dreams, Ms. Lancaster."

She stopped briefly at the mention of her undercover surname.

How the hell does he know my last name? I haven't told anyone in camp. These guys are good. They've done their research.

She looked over her shoulder and gave a quick wave. "Good night, Jonas."

Lexie could feel his stare as she hurried off.

27

Assen—the Netherlands

BAM. BAM. BAM.

Blake sat straight up in his bed. He instinctively reached for his gun, then realized he didn't have one.

BAM. BAM. BAM.

"Blake, it's me, Kate."

Vaguely conscious that he was wearing only his boxers, Blake yanked open the door. His mussed hair stuck out on one side, glued flat on the other. He rubbed his eyes and tried to focus on Kate.

"What's going on? Come in. Come in."

Kate opened the door, looked down at Blake's boxers, and said, "Do you need a minute to, ahh . . ."

"Oh shit. Sorry."

Grabbing the jeans that were draped over the chair, he slid them on, zipped them, and turned to see Kate looking the other way. "You can turn around, I'm dressed." He grabbed a crumpled-up T-shirt lying in the corner of the room and pulled it over his head.

"You've lost weight since we left the states," Kate said.

Blake looked down at his waistline; his jeans sagged on

his hips. "I guess I have. Not much of an appetite. What's going on?"

"I got a text from Lexie!"

Blake's mouth fell open.

"Say that again. My mind is still fuzzy."

Kate handed the phone to him. "Here. Read the messages."

When finished, he sat on the edge of the bed and read the messages again. He lowered his head and covered his eyes. "Lexie's alive."

"Now we have to find her," Kate said.

"Have you told Adam?"

"Not yet. I came to you first."

Blake looked up and saw that Kate was wearing a pair of oversized sweatpants, a long T-shirt, and pink fleecy socks. He assumed it was what she wore to bed. She had dark circles under her red-rimmed eyes, which made him wonder how long it had been since she had slept. *Something we're all a little short on these days.*

* * * * *

The investigative team assembled at the Van der Valk Hotel at sunup. Connor had attempted to trace the cell that Lexie used, but as they suspected, it was a burner phone and untraceable.

Blake studied an aerial photograph spread over most of the conference table. A sudden coldness hit his core.

"She could be anywhere," he said, throwing up his

hands. "Since that son of a bitch drugged her, we have no idea if they traveled thirty minutes or thirty hours from the Gathering. Hell, they may be in another country by now."

"Do you have any ideas, Tess?" Kate asked, trying to keep everyone focused.

Tess joined the others and examined the map, the top of her head barely reaching Blake's shoulder. "I've been racking my brain trying to come up with something," she said.

"Wait a minute," Blake said. "How old are these maps? If Lexie's being held in a camp with military-style tents, maybe we can locate the camp using Google Earth or a FLIR system."

"Using a FLIR is a great idea!" Kate said.

"I've been undercover most of my career," Tess cut in. "I guess I've lost touch with the latest technology. What's a fleer?"

Blake explained. "F-L-I-R. Stands for forward-looking infrared. Basically, it's an infrared camera that detects heat. The operator can look at the thermal image on a video monitor and perform temperature calculations to see if the image is a human being."

"Wow, so the operator can actually tell the difference between an animal and a human?" asked Tess.

Blake nodded. "Yeah, it's a very sophisticated system."

Connor spoke up. "It's a great idea, but we still need to find a way to limit our search area. We can't search the entire country."

"We can start with the area around the Gathering and then make the circle larger," Kate said.

Blake nodded. "I agree. We know she's alive and that

she's being held in a terrorist camp. We can't sit around and wait. We need to start searching."

Hovering over the map, Kate asked, "If we rule out all the populated areas, how much area is left?"

"A lot," Connor said from across the room.

"How many FLIR systems can you get your hands on?" Adam asked.

"I can probably get two helicopters and maybe a drone."

"That's a good start."

Clapping his hands together, Connor stood and reached for his phone. "Let me make some calls."

Kate looked at Blake. Her face shone as a wave of optimism filled the room.

28

Camp Resistance

Lexie stared at her cup of black coffee. The rhythmic ping of the rain on the roof of the mess hall, gradually intensifying, made her eyelids droop. All she could think about was her encounter with Jonas in the middle of the night.

Holden burst into the mess hall wearing an army-green rain slick. He removed it, shook the excess water from the jacket, and draped it over a chair to dry, then grinned when he spotted Lexie.

Hurrying over, he leaned down and kissed her on the cheek. Sagging in the chair, she didn't move or offer any encouragement.

"What's for breakfast?" he asked.

"Coffee."

"Did someone wake up on the wrong side of the bed this morning?"

"You mean cot. I don't have a bed."

His teasing smile faded into vague concern. "You seem a little down. What's wrong?"

"Nothing," she said. "I'm tired. I didn't sleep well last night."

Holden pulled out the chair next to her and sat. "Talk to me. What's wrong?"

"Nothing. Maybe it's the weather. I'm not a fan of rain."

"Come on, Lexie. Are you having second thoughts about being here?"

Lexie faced Holden. "Of course not. I love being here. I think I literally have cabin fever. I know it hasn't been that long, but all we see is this camp, nothing else," she said, hoping he would take the bait.

"Well, I have some good news for you. You and I are going on a supply run later today."

Lexie bolted upright in her chair. "You mean we're going to leave the camp?"

"Yep. Dusty needs some equipment picked up from town, so I volunteered the two of us."

"That's great!" she said, feeling her face burst into a smile. "Can we buy a few personal items while we're out?"

"Sure," he said, chuckling at the sudden enthusiasm. "What do you need that the camp doesn't have?"

"Honestly, the harsh soap is giving me alligator skin. I have to get some better soap. And maybe some lotion."

"Seriously?" he asked, shaking his head.

"I might be a badass eco-warrior, but I'm still a chick. And chicks need a few indulgent items."

"Understood. I think we can take a few minutes out of our busy day to pick up some girly soap."

"When do we leave?"

"As soon as you eat a decent breakfast."

"Deal," she said, and shoved a giant bite of tofu scramble in her mouth.

* * * * *

Holden carefully navigated the panel van down the narrow, rutted path. The morning rain had subsided but left the dirt road a muddy mess. The creases in Holden's forehead told Lexie that he needed to concentrate while driving; she remained silent until the dirt path gave way to a paved road.

"That was nerve-racking," she said, patting him on the shoulder. "Well done."

"Thank you. It's easy to get these stupid vans stuck in the mud. I don't know why we don't pick up another Jeep or two."

"Maybe they're too expensive," she suggested.

"If you haven't noticed, money is not a problem."

"I *have* noticed. Where does all the money come from?" Lexie held her breath after she asked the question, wondering if she had gone too far.

"We're lucky to have a few generous backers," Holden replied

Since he didn't seem unnerved by the line of questioning, Lexie pushed a little further. "What do the backers get out it?"

"What do you mean?"

"No one just gives money away. At least not the amount of money that it takes to keep our camp going."

"These people do. They believe in our mission."

"Wow." As they cruised down the road, she leaned closer to him. "Think about it, Holden. If you and I could get this kind of financial support in the United States, there would be no boundaries to the good that we could do. It would be interesting to know how our group found these supporters. Maybe you and I could do the same thing at home."

Without warning, Holden slammed his foot on the brake, causing the van to slide sideways and stop. He pounded his fists on the dash, then jerked around in his seat to face Lexie. His red face and flared nostrils let her know that she had pushed too far.

"Shut the fuck up about the backers, Lexie! You're here because of me, which means I'm responsible for you. Quit acting like a fucking cop."

The hair on the back of Lexie's neck lifted and she broke into a cold sweat.

"Are you crazy?" she asked, watching his whole body move with his deep, angry breaths. "Why would you say that?"

"Because you ask too many questions. The people we work for do not like questions. You need to stop with all the fucking questions before something happens."

Knowing that she had made a devastating mistake, she reached over and placed her hand on his as a small tear rolled down her cheek. She needed him to calm down so he would take her to town.

"I'm sorry," she said, her chin quivering. "I guess I got caught up in my vision. I've been thinking the two of us could set up a version of Camp Resistance in the United States. We could be an eco-version of Bonnie and Clyde."

Holden looked down at Lexie's hand resting on his.

She continued, "I know I ask too many questions. That's my nature, but I'll try to control it."

"Curiosity killed the cat, Lexie. Don't be the fucking

cat." Holden jerked his hand out from under hers. His eyes cold and hard, he slammed the van into drive and continued the journey.

* * * * *

Lexie remained silent for the rest of the trip but stayed alert, looking for road signs or anything that would help direct the FBI to her location. She knew this might be her only opportunity to narrow down the camp location.

Holden kept to the small country roads. Most of the area was rural farmland filled with dark green pastures of grazing cattle and sheep. She could relay this fact to Kate, but it wouldn't be helpful—rural farmland comprised large regions of the country. She needed the name of a nearby town.

"The countryside is beautiful," Lexie said, testing the waters to see if Holden was still angry.

He glanced over. "The Netherlands is a beautiful country. Tourists make the mistake of not venturing further than Amsterdam. The country has so much more to offer than merely the red-light district and coffeeshops of the city."

The two slid back into a semi-comfortable silence. Flicking occasional glances at Holden, Lexie watched the red slowly drain from his skin.

A few minutes later, a tiny town appeared. Lexie hoped the beautiful image wasn't a mirage. The streets in the town were made of red brick; townspeople wandered around carrying grocery bags and going about their daily activities. The quaint village looked like a scene from a postcard.

"We'll stop at the drugstore before we meet with Dusty's contact. We only have a few minutes to spare, so don't dawdle."

"I'll be quick."

Holden parked the van. The green and white sign above the door read *Exloo Apotheek*.

Exloo must be the name of the town.

Holden remained at Lexie's side as she picked up a bottle of shampoo, liquid soap, a shower scrunchie, and deodorant.

"Oh, please, don't forget the deodorant," he said.

Lexie glanced up and saw his mischievous grin. She picked up a stick of the male deodorant and tossed it to him. "It wouldn't hurt you to buy some for yourself."

He laughed and put it in Lexie's handbasket. When they approached the register, Holden took the basket and paid for Lexie's items.

He placed his arm around her and pulled her close as they walked back to the van. Part of Lexie wanted to think this meant everything was back to normal, but she knew the display of affection was probably to prevent her from running.

"Thanks for the girly things," she said as she put her arm around his waist.

Looking down at her, he smiled. "You're welcome."

Holden drove a few minutes outside of Exloo, then turned onto a long, dusty gravel road leading to a deserted farm. The remains of an old tractor rusted in the field; a long-abandoned, decaying tire swing hung from a giant tree beside the dilapidated farmhouse. Holden pulled the van to the back of the farmhouse and up to a surprisingly intact barn, then gave a short honk of the horn.

Two bearded men opened the barn doors, allowing Holden to pull forward. One man wore a baseball cap concealing most of his face. The two men closed the doors behind them. A chill ran up Lexie's back.

"Stay here," Holden ordered.

Lexie watched him deal with the two men. They shook hands and half hugged one another. Both men stared at Lexie in the van; Holden glanced in her direction, then said something indiscernible to them.

The men nodded their heads and continued talking. Holden handed a large brown envelope to one of them, who opened it and looked inside. After the transaction was complete, the van door opened and the men loaded the first of two large wooden crates into the back.

As the men loaded the second crate, Lexie overheard part of the conversation.

"Be extra careful on the ride back," one of them said to Holden. "I'd hate to see you go boom."

"That's reassuring," Holden said.

"Hey, I get paid either way."

The van door slammed, preventing Lexie from hearing any more of the conversation.

Fuck. We're hauling some kind of explosives. What the hell are they going to blow up?

Holden hopped back in the driver's seat and smiled at her. "That wasn't so hard."

The two men opened the barn doors, allowing them to exit. Holden waved, and he and Lexie were off again. He cautiously steered the van on the horribly eroded gravel road, then took an alternative route back to the camp.

"Since you're driving with such vigilance, I assume our cargo is delicate. What are we hauling?" Lexie asked.

Holden gave Lexie a sideways glance and remained silent.

"I know, I know. It's a need-to-know basis, and I don't need to know."

"Actually, you do need to know. I've been told that you're going to be included in the next mission, and it's a big one."

"Really?" Lexie asked.

"Evidently, Dusty is impressed with your progress."

"You're kidding, right?"

"No. He said you've come a long way and you're one tough cookie."

"I thought Dusty hated me."

"Dusty hates everyone," he said. "Don't take it personally."

Lexie grinned.

"Are you ready for the next step?" He asked.

Lexie thought a few seconds before answering. "I am. More than ready." The van rattled as it hit a bump. Sitting right next to the explosives, she thought, *Not ready at all.*

29

Lexie silently made her way to the tent with the cell phones, keeping close to the tree line in case security guards were patrolling the area, jumping at every late-night noise she heard. She sneaked into the tent, grabbed the phone, then picked her way through the woods to a secluded spot to text Kate.

The screen came to life, emitting a bright light. Lexie quickly covered it and made sure the phone was set on silent.

Kate, are you there? It's Lexie. I'm in the woods. Can't talk but if you're there text back.

Almost immediately, she received her answer.

I'm here.

She smiled, knowing that Kate must have been sleeping with the phone next to her pillow.

Held in a camp thirty minutes from Exloo. Only way in and out is a rutted dirt road. Group uses a white panel van for supplies. Possible Jonas sighting. Will try to confirm. Text back.

The seconds she waited for a response felt like hours.

Working around the clock to find you. This info will help.

Lexie exhaled and typed, *Use caution. Large amount of explosives on site. Text back.* A single tear ran down her face. She missed Kate so much.

Good info. Great job, Lex. Stay strong.

Lexie wiped away the tear. *Got to go. I'll contact you when I can,* she typed, and then erased the messages and the information from the call log.

Just as she turned off the phone, a large hand wrapped around her face and covered her mouth.

Gasping, she reached for the arm that tightly held her, adrenaline flooding through her body. She began to struggle as her body slipped into fight mode. The hand clamped harder against her mouth.

"Shhh. Stay quiet. It's me, Finn."

Lexie stopped struggling. She relaxed her grip on Finn's hand and turned slightly so she could see him.

"I'm going to let go of you," he said. "Please remain quiet."

She nodded.

Finn released his grip, allowing Lexie to turn so the two of them were face to face. "What the hell are you doing?" he whispered.

Lexie looked down at the cell phone resting in her lap. "I was texting my sister. My mom has been sick, and I was worried about her."

"Outside contact is against the rules."

"I know. But I couldn't take it any longer, Finn. I had to know if my mom was all right."

"Did you tell your sister anything about the camp?"

"No, of course not. I told her I've joined a group similar

to the Peace Corps and that I'm living in a remote village in Africa without modern communication."

"Lexie, Dusty would kill you if he found out you stole a cell phone."

"I didn't steal it. I borrowed it. I planned to return it after I finished." She let a trace of desperation, only partially faked, into her voice. "She's my mother, Finn. I had to know if she's okay. I promise I won't do it again. Please don't tell Dusty. I love you guys so much and I don't want to leave. This is my home now."

Even in the dark, she could see that Finn was torn.

"Please, Finn. I'm begging you."

Slowly, he exhaled. "Okay, but you have to promise never to do it again."

Lexie vigorously nodded. "I promise. Thank you."

"You almost gave me a heart attack," he said, rubbing a hand over his forehead.

"What are you doing out at this hour anyway?" she asked, careful not to sound accusatory. "How did you find me?"

"The light from the phone gave you away," he told her. "I have a raging headache and couldn't sleep. I was on my way to the infirmary to get some ibuprofen when I saw a strange light flicker. I wasn't sure what it was, so I investigated. You're the last person I expected to find out—"

"Who's there? Identify yourself," a deep voice shouted, startling them both.

Finn snatched the phone from Lexie and shoved it down the front of his pants. "Follow my lead," he whispered.

Standing, he yelled back, "Don't shoot. It's Finn. I'm here with Lexie."

Lexie stood, and Finn used his arm to move her behind him.

Emil approached, carrying an assault weapon and moving with military precision. "What the fuck are you two doing?"

"Ahh, well . . . this is a little embarrassing," Finn said.

Emil pointed the AR-15 directly at Finn. "You better start talking."

"I invited Lexie out here. I needed to talk to her."

"At three in the morning?" Emil said.

Finn stared at the ground, nervously scraping at fallen leaves with his foot. "Yes, well, I, ahh . . . I didn't want anyone to overhear our conversation. I have feelings for Lexie, and I wanted to tell her before she and Holden became more involved. I knew if I didn't tell her, I would always regret it. I brought her out here because I couldn't risk Holden finding out."

"So, you two are out here playing grab-ass?"

Finn's head jerked up and he frowned at Emil. "No! It's not like that. I needed to tell her how I felt. We weren't doing anything else."

Emil moved so he could see Lexie. "Is this true?"

"Yes," she said. "Finn was trying to be discreet, but so much for that, I guess."

He turned back to Finn. "You and her?"

Finn nodded. "I like her. Well, more than like. I needed to know if I had a chance with her."

"And do you?"

Finn bowed his head. "No. She told me that she cares about me, but not in the same way that I care about her."

"Frankly, I'm surprised you like her," Emil said. "I figured you and the chubby guy had something going on."

"What? No. I'm not gay. I'm just shy."

"Man, you're playing with fire by messing with Holden's woman. Especially at three in the morning."

"Hey!" Lexie snapped. "I'm not Holden's woman. He doesn't own me."

Finn closed his eyes and shook his head before speaking. "Look, Emil, can we keep this between the three of us? I don't want any hard feelings with Holden. It would make things uncomfortable with the group if this gets out."

"Yes, please?" Lexie added. "I don't want Finn to feel uncomfortable. He and I have worked it out between the two of us, and I don't see any reason the rest of the camp should know."

Shrugging half-heartedly, Emil said, "It's none of my business what you two do out here in the woods. I'll have to report this to Dusty, but I'm sure he will keep it to himself."

"Not Dusty," Lexie said. "He hates me, and he'll use it to embarrass us both. He'll definitely tell Holden, and that will cause all kinds of problems. Please, Emil. We're all on the same team."

Emil gave Lexie a hard stare and huffed. "All right. I won't tell anyone."

"Thank you," she said.

"Yes, thank you," Finn said, his face going slack with relief. "We're in your debt. If you ever need anything, just ask."

"I think you two better get your asses back to your tents before anyone else finds you."

"Yes, of course."

The two made their way back to the path. Emil followed them to the tent area. Unable to retrieve the phone from Finn, Lexie returned to her cabin and crawled under the covers.

* * * * *

Sleep-deprived and dressed in yesterday's clothes, Lexie crawled out of bed. Jade and KK were gone; she was alone.

Sitting on the edge of her cot, she rubbed the sleep from her eyes. Memories of the early-morning encounter with Finn and Emil came flooding back to her. Her instincts about Finn had been correct. Now she had to hope that Emil would be true to his word.

Lexie tied her hair back and trudged off to breakfast. Before she reached the mess hall, Dusty caught up with her.

"I need your help with something," he said.

She froze in her tracks. Her legs muscles tightened, her body ready to run. Trying to act normal, she crossed her arms and jammed her hands into her armpits, suppressing their shaking. "Can I eat breakfast first?"

"No. I need you now."

"All right. Lead the way."

Lexie followed Dusty along a dark trail that meandered into the woods. The hair stood up on the nape of her neck. *This can't be good.*

After a few minutes, she yelled, "Where are we going?"

"Almost there," Dusty yelled back.

Someone or something moved behind her. She turned quickly, but couldn't see anything. Her instincts told her to run hard and run far. However, this could be her opportunity to find out what Dusty planned to do with all those explosives. *Besides, where would I run to?* Unsure what to do, she concentrated on her breathing and trudged forward.

Eventually, they emerged from the thick forest into a small clearing. Lexie was relieved to see Ryan sitting on a massive log, engrossed in conversation.

Then she saw the man he was talking to and stopped in her tracks. In the morning sunlight, she instantly recognized the person sitting on the log and conversing with Ryan.

Constable Jonas Hummel. His hair was longer now and he had grown a beard, but Lexie was sure that he was, in fact, the missing constable.

Jonas has been here the whole time? What the hell is going on?

"Wow, this is a pretty area," she said, trying to sound nonchalant.

Dusty grunted, then motioned for her to join the group.

A few minutes later, Emil and Finn emerged from the trail and joined the group. Finn looked pale, drawn, and very uncomfortable.

"I think the gang's all here," Jonas said. "Everyone have a seat."

Lexie, Finn, and Emil joined Ryan on the log. The morning dew on the moss dampened Lexie's pants, giving her a slight chill. Dusty remained standing behind the group.

Jonas stood in front and began to speak. "I suppose you are wondering why I called you here. We're preparing for a new mission. This operation is of the utmost importance."

Holy shit! He's the fucking leader of the group. This changes everything. There was no kidnapping—this guy's become one of the terrorists! A dirty cop makes this situation even more dangerous. What now?

She forced herself to control her breathing. *Stay calm. Keep your head in the game. Think things through.*

Pacing in front of the group, Jonas continued, "It's my job to assess the personnel in our camp and to choose the proper people for each assignment. This can be a daunting responsibility at times." He paused and stared at each person sitting on the log.

"We are a family," he continued. "We have all made sacrifices to be here. We have given up our families, friends, and lovers to be here to wage our war. We fight for the animals and for the people who have no voice. The freedom fighters in this camp are heroes. I have been entrusted with the arduous responsibility of ensuring the safety of this band of heroes. It is a task that I do not take lightly."

Jonas paused, looked to the sky, and deeply inhaled the morning air. He closed his eyes and slowly exhaled.

No one made a sound. Even the birds had quieted.

He opened his eyes and scowled at the troop.

"It has been brought to my attention that one of you has betrayed our circle, jeopardizing the safety of all."

Lexie's stomach lurched.

"The traitor was caught stealing a cell phone from our inventory."

Okay, shit, just run—

The sudden, deafening explosion that followed sent excruciating pain rushing through Lexie's ears.

She felt a warm splatter on the left side of her face and watched as Finn plunged forward, slamming face-first into the emerald green grass. Lexie grabbed her ears, unable to hear the shriek that escaped her own throat. She tried to make sense of the situation, her brain processing each second as if it were an old-time frame-by-frame movie. She looked at Finn's motionless body and saw a gaping gunshot wound to the back of his head, then turned to see Dusty holding a still-smoking gun. His eyes were empty, as if all the humanity had been drained from his body; an emotionless smirk covered his face.

Lexie blinked and looked around the group, seeing spots before her eyes, unable to focus. Another muffled cry escaped her throat. Ryan jumped to his feet but remained still, staring at the body of his dead friend. Emil remained seated on the other side of Lexie, seemingly unfazed.

Ryan abruptly turned and vomited, emptying the contents of his stomach on the bank of the pond. He wiped the puke from his face with the back of his hand and turned to face the group.

Lexie's chest pounded wildly as she tried to catch her breath. Jonas's lips were moving, but she couldn't hear what he was saying. She dropped her hands from her ringing ears and touched her face, then looked at her fingers. They were covered in Finn's blood.

Dusty put the gun in his waistband and walked over to the body, rolling it over with his foot. Finn's eyes were open, but the sparkle and life were gone from them. A cavernous exit wound had replaced his forehead.

A small, involuntary moan escaped Lexie's throat. She dropped her blood-soaked face into her hands and sobbed, trying hard to catch her breath.

"Ryan," Jonas yelled.

She dropped her hands and watched Ryan. Vomit covered the front of his shirt; a deadpan stare locked on the body of his friend.

"Ryan!" Jonas yelled louder.

Shaking his head, Ryan tore his eyes from Finn's lifeless body. His voice cracked as he answered. "Yes."

"Ryan, you're in charge of the tech team now," Jonas said. "Can you handle it?"

"What?" Ryan asked, not comprehending what was happening.

Jonas calmly walked over and stood directly in front of the man, blocking his view of the body. "I said, can you handle being in charge of the tech team? I need an answer from you right now."

"Yes," Ryan said in a quivering voice. He cleared his throat and stood up straight. "Yes. I can handle it."

Jonas stared at him as if he were determining the man's fate. Lexie held her breath watching the exchange, wondering if she or Ryan would be Dusty's next victim.

"All right then," Jonas said. "What happens in the woods, stays in the woods. It's a need-to-know situation, and I will inform anyone in the camp who needs to know. Is everyone clear on this matter?"

Lexie felt her head nod up and down.

"There are some shovels under the tarp," Jonas said, motioning off in the distance. "Bury the body, then return to camp."

Lexie started toward the tarp with the others when she thought she heard her name through the ringing. She turned to see Jonas motioning for her to come to him.

Still dazed, she lethargically walked toward him. He waited until the team was busy digging before he spoke.

"I understand that you and Finn had a *special* relationship," he said.

The words were muffled, but Lexie understood the meaning. She spoke louder than necessary when answering. "What do you mean? We were friends."

"Emil told me that Finn wanted a romantic relationship with you."

For a second, this failed to make sense—then, through her still-dazed mind, she remembered that early-morning confrontation and nodded. "He did, but we never did— have a romantic relationship, that is. We were only friends."

"Looks like I took care of a potential problem for you, then."

Lexie's eyes widened. "Did you have Finn killed because he had feelings for me?"

"No, of course not. That would be cold-hearted. I had him killed because he betrayed all of us. He was caught stealing a cell phone by our security team. It was a blatant act of disrespect of our guidelines. If we are to succeed in our mission, we have to have total commitment to the cause." He looked at her with eyes hard as flint. "We cannot tolerate any acts of betrayal. Do you understand?"

Lexie nodded.

Finn must have been caught returning that cellphone to the tent. Oh my god! What have I done? Oh, shit. Not again.

"I never thought Finn had the stomach for eco-warfare," the former constable told her, "but I kept him around because he was brilliant with computers. His latest project is going to help us achieve a major goal."

"What goal?" Lexie asked. "I don't have any idea what you want me to do."

Jonas leaned down and spoke into Lexie's ear. She could feel his hot, rancid breath on her skin. "You'll find out soon. You're going to be an enormous asset for us in the next phase of our revolution. Can I count on your allegiance, Lexie?"

This guy is a complete psychopath. How did this happen? He's turned into a monster. He ordered Dusty to kill Finn. There's nothing left of the law enforcement officer he once was. He's a deranged killer.

She nodded. "You can count on me, Jonas."

"I hope so," he said. "I would hate to see you suffer the same fate as your friend."

She glanced toward Finn's body, blood pooling underneath.

Nodding stiffly, Jonas told her, "You can return to camp."

"I'll help them bury him."

"No need. They have enough hands. Go back to camp."

"Okay," she said.

She turned to leave, then felt Jonas's hand on her shoulder.

"Lexie, don't forget to take a shower and wash your

clothes. It might be difficult to explain to your tentmates why you're covered in blood."

She nodded without looking back. He gave her shoulder a small squeeze, then removed his hand.

* * * * *

As Lexie stumbled back through the woods, tears flowed freely down her cheeks. She grabbed a tree for support, her blood-smeared fingers digging into the ridges of the rough bark, and rested her forehead against the cool tree moss, trying to stop the world from spinning around her.

Finn was just a kid trying to help me. Another innocent person is dead because of me. How did things spiral this far out of control?

She dropped to her knees and sobbed.

What now? I have to stop Jonas. I have to get word to Kate. They need to know what Jonas has become.

First things first. I have to get out of this fucking camp before I wind up like Finn.

30

Assen—the Netherlands

The Dutch police moved the command center from the conference room to the thirty-foot mobile command post parked behind the Van der Valk Hotel. The command unit was engineered for easy deployment and featured state-of-the-art communication technology, six workstations, a conference room, and a bathroom. Maps were spread on the conference table and hung from the walls. The busy hub buzzed with exhilaration and hope following Kate's report of Lexie's texts from the camp.

Kate, Blake, and Tess huddled over a newly acquired aerial map of the countryside surrounding the town of Exloo.

"I can't believe she's so close," Kate said. "I guess I thought she would be clear across the country or even in another country by now. Exloo is only thirty minutes from here."

"The area around Exloo is densely wooded, so it's still going to be difficult to find her," Blake said as he relayed the maps.

"I grew up in this area," Tess replied. "I may be able to further narrow the search area."

"It would be great if you can," Kate said. "At least we have a general location—and, most importantly, we know she's alive."

"We're going to find her, Kate," promised Blake. "If you and I have to hike every square inch of this country, we're not leaving the Netherlands without her."

"You mean the three of us," Tess said. "I'm not leaving until we find your partner. Besides, this is my backyard. I can help with the backroads."

"Can I have everyone's attention?" Connor said from the front of the room. "Thank you. I appreciate all the hard work and long hours that each and every one of you are contributing to this mission. We have two helicopters and one drone equipped with FLIR systems ready to fly this evening. Since Exloo is so small, we won't move the command post closer until we've pinpointed a location for the camp. No need to tip our hand yet. This matter is top secret, so please be discreet."

Once he'd finished, the command center buzzed with multiple conversations. Adam squeezed through the crowd and approached Kate, Blake, and Tess, slapping Blake on the back. "How are you three doing?"

"Excuse me. I have to talk to Connor about something," Tess said, then abruptly left.

"I don't think she likes me," Adam said, his lip rising in a faint sneer.

"I can't imagine why," Blake replied, shooting Kate a wink.

Adam shrugged. "Anyway, the Dutch equivalents of our bomb squad and SWAT team have arrived. The teams are coming over for a briefing in an hour."

"The waiting is the hardest part," Blake said. "I feel like we should be out there searching."

"Lexie helped us narrow the scope with her last text," replied Adam. "But we're still looking at a large area of land."

"Hopefully the thermal imaging systems will zero in on the camp," Kate said.

"Since we know the group has explosives stored at the camp, we need to be careful with our entry," Adam said. "The area could be booby-trapped. The Dutch are taking all the necessary precautions to extract Lexie in a safe manner."

"And Jonas," Kate added.

"Yes," Adam said. "Now that we know there's a real possibility that Jonas, the missing constable, is in the camp, our mission is to rescue two law enforcement officers."

Connor approached the three FBI agents. "Shall we discuss our plan of attack?"

"Yes, of course," Adam said.

The agents followed Connor over to a quiet corner and sat down.

"Where's Tess?" Kate asked.

"She and I have already talked," Connor replied. "She's helping the logistics team with the drone deployment plan."

"Before you begin, I'd like to say something," Blake put in. He looked down at his hands in his lap, then back up at Connor. "Thank you for everything that you've done for us, and for Lexie. You've given us exceptional support the whole time we've been in your country."

"You don't owe us any thanks," Connor said. "We appreciate the support of the FBI. We are especially thankful for the sacrifices that you, Lexie, Kate, and everyone else have made to try to locate Jonas. You and Lexie put your personal safety in jeopardy to help save a fellow law enforcement officer. The possibility that Jonas is in the camp gives us hope. The ultimate goal is to rescue two missing undercover officers."

A young officer approached Connor carrying a large box. "The items you requested have arrived, sir." He set the box on the table. "Is there anything else that you need?"

"No, that will be all. Thank you."

"Yes, sir."

"The items in this box are actually for you to use for the remainder of the time you are in country." Connor opened the box using a small pocketknife. "The chief constable has granted permission for each of you to carry a weapon. Given the fact that this terrorist group is in possession of explosives, he wanted to make sure that each of you be issued a handgun, a holster, and body armor for the raid on the camp."

"Thank you," Blake said. "We appreciate it."

Connor gave each of them a Walther P99Q pistol, a holster, and a ballistic vest. He gave the smallest vest to Kate. "Might not be a perfect fit, but it should get you through the next few days."

Kate tried on her vest. "It fits fine. Thank you."

"Have you handled a Walther?"

"I have."

"I haven't," Adam admitted.

"Me neither," Blake added.

Connor gave the agents a quick safety briefing for handling and firing the weapon. After he walked away, Adam addressed Kate and Blake. "Just because we have a firearm does not mean we will use it. We will continue to support the Dutch police from a distance. Is that understood?"

Kate and Blake stared incredulously at Adam.

"Look, I don't want to have to explain to the director how an FBI agent and an LAPD task force agent ended up in a shootout in a foreign country. The weapons are for self-defense only."

"Yeah, you having to go before the director is definitely our biggest concern at this point in time, Adam," Blake said, rolling his eyes.

31

Camp Resistance

Lexie scrubbed her face and wept as the last of Finn's blood swirled down the shower drain. Her mind flashed back to Logan, killed during her last undercover mission in South Carolina. The image of Logan, and now Finn, caused her to fall to her knees. Her spine bowed and her shoulders quaked.

What the hell is happening? What have I done? I've gotten Finn killed is what I've done. First Logan, now Finn. All because of me. All because Holden drugged me and dragged me to this place.

Holden! How could I ever have thought that Holden reminded me of Logan? They're nothing alike. Holden's been using me all along. I thought I was playing him, but he's been playing me. Unbelievable! I couldn't see what a selfish prick he is. This has got to stop. I've got to get the fuck out of here and put an end to all of this.

The tightness in her chest refused to loosen. She covered her face with her shaking hands and wept for both Finn and Logan—both young men dead because each had tried to help her.

As the water in the shower slowed to a drip, Lexie

realized it was only a matter of time before Dusty put two and two together. She knew she only had one option left. She couldn't wait on the FBI any longer. She had to run for her life.

She dressed in fresh clothes and stashed her blood-soaked clothing in a bag under her cot. As she stepped out of her tent, she collided with Holden.

"There you are," he said. "I've been looking all over for you."

Oh shit, this is the last thing that I need. I'm not ready to deal with this guy yet. I'll have to fake it until I can escape.

"Oh, hey there," Lexie said, trying to sound casual.

Holden grabbed her by the shoulders and stared at her. "What's wrong?"

"Nothing. Why do you ask?"

"Your eyes are swollen and red. Have you been crying?"

"I'm fine, Holden. Have you had breakfast?"

"Breakfast? It's almost noon. Tell me what's going on."

"I meant lunch. Have you had lunch?"

"Lexie, talk to me. Have I done something wrong?"

Lexie touched Holden's freshly shaven face. His skin felt soft and warm.

"You haven't done anything wrong, Holden. I'm having a bad morning. Don't you ever miss your family?"

"Sure, sometimes," he said. "Is that the problem? You miss your old life?"

"Not my old life, but I do miss my family. I'll be fine. I need some time to myself. It has nothing to do with you, or with us."

Holden reached up and placed his hand on top of

Lexie's, which remained on his face. "I don't want you to be sad," he said. "I'm here to take care of you."

Leaning over, he softly kissed Lexie, barely brushing her lips. As his mouth left hers, he whispered the words, "I love you."

* * * * *

Lexie attempted to go about her daily activities, trying hard to forget that earlier that day she had washed her friend Finn's blood and brains from her hair. Her knotted stomach would not allow her to eat. She refilled her water bottle, forcing herself to stay hydrated.

After the mess hall emptied, she snuck in and made two peanut butter sandwiches. She put the sandwiches, a granola bar, and three apples into her canvas bag. It was decided. Tonight, she would run.

On her way back to her tent, she ran into Jade. "I haven't seen you all day," the other woman said. "What's up?"

"Oh, you know," Lexie said. "Dusty has me working on a project."

"He can be so demanding," Jade sighed.

"Yep. But I'm trying to prove my worth, so I'm okay with it."

"Want to go eat dinner?" her tentmate asked.

Lexie's stomach lurched at the mention of food, but she smiled and answered, "Sure. I'm gonna toss my bag in the tent. I'll catch up with you."

After dumping her bag, Lexie caught up with Jade, who was now walking with Holden.

"Hey, Lexie," Holden said, not making eye contact with her.

Trying to act natural, Lexie took Holden's hand and gave it a little squeeze. He glanced over and smiled.

"Hi, Holden," she said. "Anyone know what's for dinner?"

"I don't know about the main course, but I know Mamma Bear made a dark chocolate cake for dessert," Jade said. "We can't dillydally or we'll miss out."

"Well, let's put the pedal to the metal," Lexie said. "I might skip dinner and go straight to dessert."

She was grateful that Ryan, busy with his new duties, entered the mess hall late. He briefly made eye contact with her, but instead of coming over he joined the food line. His slumped shoulders, vacant eyes, and deathly pale skin confirmed his deep sorrow and misery.

"Where's Finn?" Jade asked. "I haven't seen him all day."

"I don't know," Holden said. "Ryan is in the chow line. Maybe he knows."

Hearing Finn's name made Lexie nauseous. She stood. "Hey, guys, I'm gonna call it a night."

"So soon?" Holden asked.

"Yeah, I'm beat. I didn't sleep well last night, and I need some rest. You guys have fun and I'll catch you later."

"I can walk you back to your tent," Holden said.

Lexie looked down at Holden, smiled, and placed her hand on his shoulder.

"No need. You stay and have a second piece of cake. I'll

see you in the morning." She bent and gave him a quick peck on the cheek. "Good night."

"Good night," he replied.

"See you back at the ranch," Lexie said to Jade.

Jade smiled and flashed her the peace sign.

Lexie refilled her water bottle on the way back to the tent. Relieved to have the tent to herself, she added the bottle of water and a hoodie to her pack that contained food and a flashlight. Fully clothed, she crawled under the covers and waited.

When Jade came in, she feigned sleep; she did so a second time when KK entered the tent roughly an hour later. Now she had to wait until it was safe to make her escape. She planned to run along the rutted road she and Holden had traveled while she had the cover of darkness. Come daylight, she would need to stick to the tree line. She knew it wouldn't be long before Dusty realized she was missing and came searching for her with his goons. Time was not on her side.

* * * * *

The scratched-up Timex on Lexie's wrist told her it was a little after two in the morning. *Time to run.*

She pulled back her wool blanket and slowly sat up. Heavy breathing emanated from both corners of the tent, reassuring her that her tentmates were both sound asleep. Easing out of bed, she grabbed her pack and quietly tiptoed out of the tent. She stood still, waiting to see if either one of the women stirred.

When neither did, Lexie took off at a brisk walk. She ducked into the tent that housed the cell phones, but found all the equipment containers were now locked.

Shit! Guess I should've seen that one coming.

With no means of communication, she exited the tent and quietly crept down the trail that led to the dirt road, staying as close to the tree line as possible. In the dark, she could barely make out the lone patrol keeping watch over the only road into and out of the camp.

She crouched among the trees, making herself as small as possible while keeping an eye on the guard. She needed to come up with a new plan of escape. She couldn't go through the woods, because she would make too much noise.

As she considered her options, the unthinkable happened. The patrol officer suddenly stopped, turned, then moved at a brisk pace in her direction.

Oh fuck. Did he hear me? If he finds me, I'm dead. What do I do?

She remained completely still, trying desperately to control her breathing. Her legs were numb from crouching.

As the patrol officer moved closer, she recognized him. She knew she was no match for Viktor's superior size and strength.

Please don't stop. Please don't stop.

Viktor charged up the trail, holding an automatic rifle. He stopped a few yards from Lexie's hiding spot and cocked his head as if listening for sounds.

He knows I'm here. What am I going to do? He's armed. I may be able to outrun him, but I can't outrun his bullets.

Viktor looked around, then slowly continued on his way.

Lexie gradually released the air from her lungs, slightly light-headed from holding her breath. She stayed put in the tree line, listening for Viktor to return. When she was sure that she was alone, she crawled from her hiding place and quietly made her way to the road. She reached the rutted path and picked up her pace, trying to avoid holes. The last thing she needed was to break an ankle.

Lexie periodically paused, cocked her head to the side, and listened. When she was certain nobody was following her, she fished out her flashlight and used it to light her way. She ran as fast as the terrain allowed. Despite the cool night air, sweat poured down her back and face. Her calf muscles burned, and her breathing became forced and raspy.

She ducked inside the tree line to rest and take a few sips of water. Knowing that she didn't have a second to waste, she wiped the sweat from her face and resumed her trek.

The smell of wet earth and decomposing leaves filled the night air. She jumped when she heard rustling in the woods.

It's just an animal. Stay calm.

The crack of a tree branch caused her heart to leap.

A big animal. Keep moving.

On the brink of total exhaustion, Lexie snared her foot in a root and plummeted face first onto the rocky road. The bone-jarring fall left her bleeding and rattled. Her hands caught the brunt of the fall, the flesh ripping from both palms. Her chin scraped the ground. Despite the severe pain, she continued, knowing that her captors would hunt her until they found her and kill her with no hesitation. She felt blood oozing from her knee. When she glanced down to check, she lost her footing and fell again, knocking the breath from her lungs.

She lay on the ground, gasping for air, wondering how badly she was hurt. Taking several moments to catch her breath, she rolled to her side, then pushed herself up. There was a huge rip in her pants where her knee had hit the ground. Blood poured from the cut knee and both palms. Sweat seeped into the wounds, intensifying the pain. Her body and mind were completely exhausted, but she knew she needed to put as much distance as possible between herself and the camp.

It was nearly four thirty in the morning when Lexie stumbled across an old farmhouse with a light burning in the window.

Okay, Lexie. Life-or-death decision. Trust whoever is in the farmhouse and ask for their assistance, or try to keep moving on.

Your body is beat to hell and about to give out. You have no idea where you are or how much further it is to a town. On the other hand, you know nothing about the occupants of the farmhouse. It's fairly close to the camp you just ran from, and who knows who may be living there.

She waited a few minutes, and then thought to herself, *Fuck it.*

32

Assen—the Netherlands

Blake and Kate remained in the command center, Connor translating the radio transmissions for them. After Connor had realized that Tess had an intimate knowledge of the area, he'd assigned her to ride in Helo One to help plot the search areas. This duty would also ensure that her identity would not be exposed. The two helicopters and the drone were dispatched to start their search patterns; the pilots were ordered to fly as high as possible to avoid alerting people at the camp.

Blake wanted to scream. Idly waiting was the hardest part for him. He checked his watch, then walked over to Connor's work station. "Any word?"

"The answer is the same as it was two minutes ago when you asked."

"Sorry, the waiting is killing me."

Connor pointed toward the far wall. "There are cold beverages in the refrigerator. Please help yourself."

Blake had just popped open a can of soda when he heard the radio come to life. Dashing back, he watched as Connor talked to the helicopter pilot.

"Helo Two is landing to refuel," Connor announced.

Blake's shoulders sank.

"We're going to find her," Connor assured him. "It's a large area to cover, but we will find her."

Hours passed. An exhausted Kate fell asleep in the corner, holding her cell phone in her hand. Blake joined Adam, and the two poured over the maps and examined the quadrants left to be searched.

"Where are you, Lexie?" he mumbled to himself.

"Do you want a sandwich?" Adam asked.

"No."

"Are you sure? There's a sandwich tray in the refrigerator."

Blake turned and glared at Adam. "I know there's a sandwich tray in the refrigerator. I don't want a fucking sandwich."

"All right, all right. I'm just trying to help. Why don't you sit down and try to relax?"

"Relax? Are you shitting me? My partner is being held hostage by a madman in the middle of nowhere. I don't want to relax. I want to find Lexie."

"We're going to find her."

"Everyone keeps telling me that, and yet, here we are." Blake rubbed the back of his neck, rolled his shoulders, then checked his watch for the hundredth time.

Suddenly, the radio blared to life, quickening Blake's pulse.

Connor picked up the mike and responded. A slight grin spread across his face as he scrambled to find the correct map in the pile, talking in rapid succession. Blake wished he could understand the conversation. Kate woke and joined him, putting her hand on his forearm and giving it a little squeeze. He gave her a hopeful smile.

Scribbling longitude and latitude coordinates on a piece of paper, Connor put down the receiver and smiled. "Helo Two has located what he believes is the camp."

A cheer went up inside the command post. The crowd gathered around the table with the map.

"This is the area of interest," Connor said, pointing to the map. "The helicopter has picked up at least twenty different heat signatures in this one concentrated area."

"That has to be it," Kate said.

"I agree," he replied. "There are no known legitimate campsites in this area, which leads me to believe it's our group of eco-terrorists. I'll alert the bomb team and SWAT."

"How soon before we move?" Blake asked.

"We'll get as close as we can tonight, then hit the camp with our full complement at daybreak."

"We're coming with you," Blake said.

"I figured you would," Connor replied. "Get suited up. The FBI team will ride with me."

33

Lexie crept cautiously toward the farmhouse. She didn't want to startle the owners, but she couldn't afford to wait for dawn. She knew Emil and his security team would track her as soon as they realized she was gone.

She knocked on the door, but received no response. After a few louder bangs, a voice on the other side of the door yelled something in Dutch.

"I'm American," Lexie shouted through the door. "I need help."

The door flung open to reveal a man in his early forties, wearing only a pair of jeans. His thick, dark hair looked like a porcupine ready to throw its quills.

"Hello," Lexie said. "Do you speak English?"

"I speak a little English," the man replied hesitantly.

"I'm so sorry to bother you. May I use your phone? I'm in trouble and I need to call for help."

The man cocked his head to the side and glanced past her. "Are you alone?"

"Yes, I've had a car accident. I need to call my friend to come get me."

"Where is your car?"

"About a mile down the road. May I use your telephone? Please."

"You poor girl. You look like you are in pain. Please come in and sit."

Lexie entered the dimly lit farmhouse. One meager lamp sitting on an end table illuminated the room.

"I'm sorry to bother you this early in the morning."

"Not to worry. Farm life starts early. Please relax, and I will bring you a telephone." The farmer spoke in a slow, deliberate cadence.

"Thank you."

Lexie looked at the jagged tears in her blood-stained, muddy clothing; at her hands, both palms caked with mud and blood, dirt and tiny rocks embedded in the wounds.

When the man did not return immediately, she stood and walked to the hallway. That's when she heard him talking.

"*Ik moet Dusty te spreken.*"

The only word Lexie understood was *Dusty*, but that was enough.

Fuck! The guy has ratted me out. I've got to get out of here.

She glanced around the farmhouse looking for a cell phone, car keys, or a weapon, but didn't see anything of use. Not wanting to waste another second, she ran toward the front door.

"Wait," the man yelled in English. "I will help you."

Lumbering footsteps sounded from behind her, and then she was violently knocked to the floor. The farmer hauled himself to his knees and straddled her. Lexie brought her knee up as hard as she could and connected with his groin—he gasped, yelled something in Dutch, and grabbed his crotch, loosening his grasp. As he made a second attempt to seize her, Lexie unleashed a violent kick, landing with a sickening thud. Her attacker's head snapped back, blood spewing from his nose and splattering over the hardwood. Lexie slipped in the fluid but managed to maintain her footing as she ran out the front door.

I can't stay on the road. Dusty will be coming from the camp. I have to go back to the woods for shelter. It will be light soon. I have to get to town or find someplace safe to hide.

She veered off into the forest. At first, she tried to parallel the dirt road, but the thick vegetation forced her off track; she trudged through the dense foliage, hoping she was moving in the right direction.

A faint pulsating sound came from high above her—she paused, listening.

Could that be a helicopter?

You're imagining things, Lexie. Why would it be flying in the dark?

Lexie stood motionless for several moments. Whatever had made the noise was gone.

Suddenly, she heard the crunch of gravel under car tires.

There's more than one vehicle. Dusty must have alerted Emil and his security squad. I'm too close to the road. I have to move deeper into the woods.

Lexie needed to put as much distance as possible between her and Dusty's men before daylight. She knew that if Dusty found her, she would end up with a bullet in her head, just like Finn. She only had one option. Run for her life.

34

Staging area in the vicinity of Camp Resistance

The caravan of blacked-out SUVs moved surreptitiously over the gravel road toward the target location. The helicopter flew high overhead, ready to lend air support if needed. In the lead vehicle, SWAT members, dressed in black fatigues and body armor, double-checked their weapons and waited for the signal to move. The bomb squad and parameter teams followed. Blake, Kate, and Adam rode in Connor's vehicle at the rear of the caravan. A few miles away, tucked into the densely wooded countryside, was Camp Resistance.

Connor spoke into the radio, listened to the response, then translated for his American passengers. "Sunrise is 6:45. SWAT will conduct a dynamic entry into the camp at exactly 6:30, and the follow-up teams will fall in behind to assist with prisoners and searching. We're on radio silence. The next sound you hear will be the command to execute."

Blake could feel Kate's knee bouncing up and down. His throat felt like sandpaper.

"EXECUTE. EXECUTE. EXECUTE," blared from the radio, startling everyone in the vehicle.

Connor slammed the car into drive, and the team barreled toward what they hoped was the eco-terrorist campsite.

Officers advanced on the camp from every direction, spreading a wide perimeter to ensure no one could escape. The single perimeter guard did not see the skilled SWAT operators approach. Within seconds, they'd swooped in and put the guard on the ground and in handcuffs.

SWAT members yelled commands as they pulled activists still in their night clothes from their tents. Blake, Adam, and Kate guarded the detainees, freeing SWAT to continue securing the area. Commands to *get your hands up* and *get down* were given in several languages. A couple of the campers tried to run but were tackled to the ground by Dutch officers.

In the middle of the chaos, Blake heard the unmistakable sound of gunfire—two shots rang out, then a sequence. Kate glanced over at him, her eyes wide.

"Stay here," Connor ordered. He ran toward the sound of the gunfire.

Blake heard the crunch of dead pine needles and twigs underfoot. He turned in time to see a figure sprinting through the woods. "Runner!" he yelled. "Stay here. I've got him."

"Blake, no!" Kate yelled. It was too late—he was already in pursuit.

Blake picked up speed, keeping the fleeing figure in sight. The man in the woods stumbled, trying to cover as much distance as possible. Blake's lungs felt as if they would explode, but when he recognized the person he was pursuing, he pushed himself to run harder and faster.

When only a few feet separated him from his target, he lunged and tackled Holden, both men slamming into the ground. The impact jarred Blake's teeth. Fueled by rage, he dug his fingers into Holden's scalp, then drilled his face into the dead leaves and pine needles.

Holden rolled to his side, struggling to free himself from Blake's grip. He tried to get to his knees, but Blake had him pinned under his weight. He yanked the other man's head back, maintaining a death grip on a chunk of hair.

"I should've known it was you," Blake snarled.

Holden's eyes widened with sudden recognition.

Blake grinned mirthlessly. "Didn't expect to see me again, did you?"

Holden delivered a powerful elbow strike to Blake's rib cage, causing the FBI agent to cry out and grab his side. The terrorist swiftly rolled from Blake's reach, then scrambled to his feet.

"Oh, I was hoping you would resist," Blake growled, struggling upright.

In an instant, he landed two bone-crushing punches to his opponent's face. Holden gasped and collapsed in a heap.

Blake hovered over him. "Where's Lexie?" he demanded through clenched teeth.

"Who?" Holden asked in a thin and raspy voice, trying to get to his knees.

Taking a step forward, Blake savagely kicked Holden in the ribs. The other man cried out in pain as bones cracked.

"I'm going to ask you again. Where's Lexie?"

"She's in her tent," Holden said, his voice barely audible.

Blake reared back to kick him again.

"No! I swear. She's in her tent. Or at least that's where she said she was going after she kissed me last night."

Blake pulled out his gun. "Get up," he said. "Keep your hands in the air."

Holden slowly got to his knees, gasping and holding his ribs.

"Hurry up."

"You broke my ribs," the other man wheezed, wincing as he clutched at his side.

"I didn't break your ribs, you pussy. That would be against FBI policy. You probably broke them when you fell in the woods."

"I knew you were a fucking cop," Holden hissed.

"I'm not a cop," Blake said, keeping his gun centered on his target. "I'm an FBI agent, and you're going to prison for the rest of your life."

The other man spat. "Fuck you."

Blake saw a figure running toward him and realized it was Kate. When she reached him, she took a second to catch her breath.

"Kate, this piece of shit is Holden. He claims Lexie is in the camp."

Kate pulled out a pair of handcuffs from her vest pocket. "Turn around," she ordered.

Holden gave Kate a puzzled look, then slowly turned. As Kate approached, he took a step, but she immediately grabbed him by the wrist and twisted it.

Holden cried out, then crumpled to the ground. Kate secured the handcuffs on his wrists, double-locked them, then searched him for weapons. "Let's go," she said, keeping a firm grip on the handcuff chain.

Blake holstered his weapon and grabbed Holden by the arm. The two agents walked their subject back to the camp, where Connor waited.

"Connor, this is Holden. He tried to run, but we caught him," Blake began, but stopped. From the look on Connor's face, he knew something horrible had happened. "What's wrong?"

"Put him with the rest of the prisoners and come with me," Connor said.

Blake hauled Holden over to the SWAT members guarding a group of detainees. "Watch this one closely, boys; he's a runner." He shoved Holden to the ground, then leaned close to his ear and whispered, "If Lexie's been hurt, I'm going to kill you."

Holden stared straight ahead.

Blake caught up with Kate and Connor. Adam made his way over to the group from another direction.

Connor cleared his throat. "I'm sure you heard the gunfire. SWAT encountered an armed gunman in one of the tents. The gunman opened fire on the SWAT team and shot one of the team members; luckily, his vest saved his life. The team returned fire, killing the gunman."

Connor took a second to gather his thoughts. "The gunman was . . . ahh . . ." His voice cracked. He cleared his throat and tried again. "The gunman was Constable Jonas Hummel."

Kate instinctively reached out and touched Connor's shoulder. "Oh, my god. I'm so sorry," she said.

"Shit. Me too," Blake added.

"I don't know what to say," Adam said.

"We set out to rescue Jonas, and now he's dead," Connor said, his voice numb.

"I'm sorry," said Adam, sounding sincere. "I know he was your friend. Does this mean what I think it does?"

"I'm afraid so," Connor replied. "It appears that Jonas went completely off the rails and was working with the terrorists."

A young Dutch officer ran up to the group—becoming aware that he might be intruding on a private moment, he slowed down and waited for an acknowledgment.

"What do you need?" Connor asked the junior officer.

"Sir, they need you at the main site. There's been a development."

Connor nodded. "Let's go."

The group made their way back to the main camp-site. The Dutch evidence team, dressed in white Tyvek protective coveralls, blanketed the area, taking photographs and carrying bags of collected evidence. One of the evidence members broke away from his team and approached Connor.

"Jonathan," Connor said.

"Hello, Connor. I'm sorry to hear about Jonas."

"Thank you." Gesturing with his arm, Connor said. "Jonathan, these are the three FBI agents who I've been working with on the investigation. This is Jonathan Franke, the evidence team leader."

"Nice to meet you," Adam said.

"You as well." Jonathan, like most of the Dutch officers, spoke perfect English.

"Any sign of Lexie?" Blake asked.

"So far, there is no sign of her. My team has found some disturbing evidence in one of the tents."

Blake let out an audible sigh. "What? What have you found?"

"Stuffed under one of the cots, we found female clothing. The clothing items are covered in blood."

Blake's shoulders tightened.

"Are you sure it's blood?" Kate asked.

"We field tested the substance, and the presumptive test indicated blood. It's impossible to know whether it's human or animal, but it is definitely blood."

"May I see the clothing?" Blake asked.

Jonathan nodded. "Come with me."

The four followed him to the tent. Spread out on a water-stained, stripped cot were bags of evidence, some items packaged in plastic and others in paper. Jonathan tore off his latex gloves and replaced them with a fresh pair. He located a paper bag, opened it, then cautiously removed a woman's shirt, careful not to contaminate the item.

Blake's voice cracked as he uttered, "That's Lexie's shirt." Hanging his head, he tried to regain his composure. His pulse quickened, causing a deafening pounding in his ears.

"I'm going to kill that son of a bitch!"

Blake started toward the door, but Kate jumped

between him and the exit. "You can't, Blake," she said as she tightened her grip on his arm.

He peeled her fingers from his arm. "Watch me."

Adam stepped in and put his hands on Blake's shoulders. "Calm down. We don't know that the blood on the shirt is Lexie's."

Knocking Adam's hands from his shoulders, Blake snarled, "I know someone who does, and he's gonna tell us or I'm going to beat it out of him."

It was Connor's turn to intervene. "I know you're upset, Blake, but we'll get to the bottom of this. We will interrogate every person in this camp until we know what happened to Lexie. I promise you, we will leave no stone unturned."

"Start with Holden. I know he knows where she is."

"We will," Connor said. "I'll conduct the interview myself."

"I'll join you," Blake said.

"I don't think that's a good idea," replied Connor, raising his hands. "There is too much bad blood between the two of you. It will jeopardize the interview. We want him to talk. If you are present, he may refuse to tell us anything."

"I agree," Adam said. "I'll go with Connor."

"Fuck it, then," Blake said, turning abruptly. "Who am I with?"

"You and Kate will assist Ben with interviews."

Blake stormed off.

As Kate turned to follow, Connor touched her on the shoulder. "I put you with Ben because he's located another American in the camp. Ben said the young man seems distraught, so we thought a softer presence might be helpful."

"I understand," Kate said.

"The two helicopters have started a search pattern of the area," Connor said. "SWAT members are fanning out and searching the surrounding forest. We will find Lexie."

* * * * *

Blake and Kate located Ben at the top of the hill. "Thanks for assisting with the interview," he said to them.

"Of course," Kate replied. "We're happy to help."

"The young man we're interviewing has been separated from the rest and is being held in the mess hall. It's up this way."

The three walked up the hill together, arriving at the large Quonset hut in the center of the camp. "This is it," Ben said.

"I'll let you two take the lead during the interview," Blake told them. "Apparently I'm not a very soothing person right now. I'll wait until you need a *bad cop*, then I'll deal with him."

Ben cocked his head and opened his mouth as if to say something, but nothing came out.

Kate lightly tapped his arm. "Before we go in, we want you to know how sorry we are about what happened to Jonas. I can't imagine what you're going through right now."

"Thank you. I'll work now, mourn later."

The three entered the mess hall. Instead of finding a tough eco-terrorist, they found a scared, heavy-set young man with large, glassy eyes sitting alone at a table.

"You're free to go," Ben told the officer standing guard. He nodded and quickly left the structure.

The three law enforcement officers approached the young man. His bottom lip trembled when he looked up at the agents.

"Hello," Ben said solemnly. "My name is Sergeant Benjamin Eldridge. I'm with the Dutch National Police Agency. This is Officer Katherine Summers and Special Agent Blake Bennett. They are my international partners from America who work for the Federal Bureau of Investigation."

The prisoner's head sprang up. "You're from the FBI?"

"We are," Kate said.

Ben cleared his throat and continued, "Before we begin the interview, I need to make you aware of a few things." He gave the young man the Dutch equivalent of a Miranda warning, letting him know that he did not have to submit to an interview and that if he decided to talk, he was doing so of his own free will.

"I'll talk to you."

"You're obviously American," Ben said. "Let's start with your name, age, and where you're from."

"My name is Ryan Fletcher," the young man said, his voice tremulous. "I'm twenty years old, and I'm from Portland, Oregon."

"Ryan," Kate said softly. "I'm not going to insult your intelligence by telling you how serious this matter is. I'm sure you already know. I *am* going to tell you that this might be your only opportunity to help yourself. It's not an accident the FBI picked you to interview. We want to help you."

Ryan bowed his head and stared at the table.

The interview team remained silent, allowing the words to linger in the air. Seconds seemed to pass like hours during situations like this, but a good interviewer knew silence at the right moment was important.

Ryan lifted his head, tears welling in his deep-set, dark eyes. A drop of moisture escaped and trailed down his dirt-stained cheek.

"Please help me," he whispered.

"Can we remove his handcuffs?" Kate asked Ben.

He nodded and stood. Looking down at Ryan, he asked, "If I take off the handcuffs, you're not going to do anything stupid, are you?"

"No, sir."

"Okay, then."

Ben removed the handcuffs. Ryan shook out his arms and rubbed the red marks around his wrists, then politely placed his hands on the table in front of him and looked at Kate.

Blake knew that Kate had made a connection with the young man, so he kept his word and remained quiet. He wanted to jump right into questions regarding Lexie, but he knew Kate needed time to gain Ryan's trust and Ben needed Ryan to provide the framework of the organization. As hard as it was for him to contain himself, he knew there was more at stake than simply locating Lexie—though to him, finding her was the only thing that mattered.

Kate made Ryan comfortable by getting him a bottle of water and continuing to talk to him using a soft tone. The frightened young man responded to the gentle touch. Blake could tell this was the first time Ryan had ever been in trouble. He wasn't the typical extremist who told law enforcement to fuck off; he was terrified and wanted a way out of the horrible situation.

Ryan drew a diagram of the organizational structure to include the three factions and the people who worked within each one. He also provided a description of each and every person in the camp.

"Let's take a five-minute break," Ben announced, looking over the drawing.

Kate cocked her head and furrowed her brow.

"I'll be back in a couple minutes," Ben said, taking the outline of the camp and descriptions with him.

Blake watched Kate fiddle with her phone, killing time until the sergeant returned.

Several minutes later, Ben came back and took his seat. "We can continue."

Kate turned her phone around and showed Ryan a photo. "Do you recognize this person?"

Ryan jerked his head back, his eyes widening. "That's Lexie."

"How do you know Lexie?" she asked.

"She's one of us. She's here in the camp."

Blake was unable to contain himself any longer. "Lexie is missing from the camp. Where is she?"

Ryan looked at him. "What do you mean she's missing? She was here last night."

"I mean she's missing, and there are bloody clothes in her tent. What happened to her?"

Ryan began heaving for air. Blake's hands trembled as

he moved away from the man, terrified to hear the words that might come next.

"Ryan," Kate said. "Please tell us what you know about Lexie."

"Yesterday..." Ryan sucked in another breath, then continued. "Yesterday, Dusty shot and killed my best friend. Lexie was sitting right beside him when it happened."

Trembling, he ran both hands through his hair and interlocked his fingers behind his neck. "I don't know why they killed him. He was my best friend. His name was Finn. He's buried in a clearing not far from here, I can show you where."

Kate nodded. "Continue with your story first, then we'll go there. Tell us exactly what happened."

Ryan told the interviewers of getting summoned to the clearing by Emil and the events that followed.

"Tell us more about Jonas," Ben said.

"This guy Greg is supposed to be in charge of Camp Resistance—that's what we call this place. However, we hardly ever see Greg, only Jonas. We take orders from Jonas, and he has the ultimate say over what we do and don't do."

"So, in your mind, Jonas is in charge of the camp?" Ben asked.

"Yes."

"Is Jonas violent?"

"I've seen him carry a gun, but mostly Dusty is the violent one. I think Dusty is a sociopath."

"Why do you say that?" Kate asked.

"When Dusty killed Finn, it didn't seem to bother him at all. He showed no emotion whatsoever. Finn was kind and gentle. He wouldn't hurt a soul, and Dusty shot him in the back of the head without blinking. Emil didn't even move when the gun went off. I'm sure that no-good German bastard knew Dusty was going to blow Finn's head off."

"Was there anyone else in charge of security besides Emil?" Ben asked.

"Not that I know of. Emil and Dusty handled most of the security matters."

Ryan put his forehead down on the table and lightly thumped it a couple of times. He looked back up at the interviewers. "I wanted to leave the camp a long time ago, but I was scared. Between Dusty being a sociopath and Jonas having a god complex, I knew it was only a matter of time before things got out of control. I never thought it would get this crazy. I was ready to leave when I saw the explosives."

"What explosives?" Blake asked, his voice sharpening.

"Dusty had Holden and Lexie pick up a van full of explosives to use on our next mission. That's when I really got worried. I told Finn I was scared and wanted to leave. He was the only person I trusted. He told me to be patient, that he would figure out a safe way for both of us to leave. After Dusty killed Finn and Jonas put me in charge of the tech team, I knew I had to find a way to escape. I hope that's what Lexie did. The blood on her clothes was Finn's blood, not hers."

Letting his head fall back, Blake exhaled a long sigh.

Ben's phone rang. "Excuse me, I have to answer this." He stood and walked over to the corner. "Eldridge here."

A pause while the person on the other end reported. "Are you sure?"

Another pause.

"Okay. Organize a reactive team and let me know when it's ready to roll."

Ben walked over to the table. All eyes were glued to him.

"Dusty and Emil are missing from the camp as well."

Blake jumped up from the table.

"Oh, no. They've gone after her," Ryan said, what little blood was left in his face draining away. "You have to find her. They'll kill her. She knows too much."

"Do you have any idea where Lexie might've gone?" Blake asked.

"No, but there's only one road into this camp. My guess is she followed the road as far as she could. She only left the camp one time, so it would be the only way she would know to run. Unfortunately, that's the same direction Dusty and Emil would take. They're driving a white panel van or a black Jeep."

"That helps," Kate said.

"Can we get this information to the helicopter?" Blake asked.

"I'm doing it now," Ben replied, pressing numbers on his phone. "Stay here with Ryan. I'll be right back."

"We need to go with you to search for Lexie," Blake said.

"Okay. Wait here until I can find someone to guard Ryan. I want him in protective custody."

Ben dashed out of the tent, leaving Kate and Blake alone with Ryan.

Kate reached across the table and took Ryan's hands in hers. "Thank you for telling us the truth. You may have helped us save Lexie."

35

Briars tore at Lexie's flesh. Exhausted, she trudged through the woods and pushed through the overgrown brush. The morning air smelled different from the night, less mossy. The strap of her canvas bag cut into her shoulder. She stopped long enough to finish the last of her water and switch shoulders with her pack. She desperately wanted to rest, but light had returned to the woods and she knew she couldn't afford to lose any time. Dusty and his crew were closing in, and if she stopped, they would catch her.

In the distance, she could hear the *whup, whup, whup* of helicopter blades. This time it sounded closer to the ground. Filled with hope, she took a few quick, shallow breaths and pushed her fatigued and burning muscles forward. She looked to the sky as the noise grew louder.

The helicopter barely cleared the treetops, but she knew the tall trees would obscure the pilot's vision. She needed to make herself more visible. Quickly removing a white T-shirt from her bag, she jumped in the air and began feverishly waving the cloth.

The helicopter sped past, unaware of her presence.

Exhausted and disheartened, she collapsed to the ground. Numbness spread through her body.

No. No. No.

Lexie dug her fingers into the thick cover of decaying leaves and suppressed a scream.

It's gone. I'm never going to get their attention. I'm alone.

Too dehydrated for tears, she rested her forehead on the cold ground. Feeling hopeless, she wanted to close her eyes and curl into a ball. Every muscle in her body ached. She didn't know if she could continue.

She thought about Finn. She formed a mental picture of his smiling face, then forced herself to remember the gaping hole in his forehead where the bullet had exited his lifeless body.

I will not give up. I owe it to Finn.

She grabbed the rough ridges of the bark on an old weathered tree to help pull herself to her feet. Taking a deep breath, she pushed forward. The air had warmed, and sweat trickled down her face and back; she used her shirt to wipe the sweat from her eyes. Her empty water bottle was a constant reminder of her agonizing thirst.

The thick forest gave way to a clearing. She peeked out from the woods, carefully looking for signs of Dusty and the others.

Where is that damn helicopter?

While she considered her next move, she heard a car engine off in the distance. *Must be near a road.* She began walking toward the noise. Sound carried differently in the woods. She hoped she was heading in the right direction.

Her instincts proved correct when she found a footpath,

which eventually led to a road. She stayed hidden in the tree line and waited. A large area of thick brush provided the perfect concealment.

Lexie heard the crunch of gravel under tires. Her heart raced. As a cloud of dust cleared, she could make out a black Jeep. She watched as the Jeep skidded to a halt. She caught only a brief glimpse of the driver through the windshield, but knew instantly it was Dusty.

Shit.

36

Barreling down the dirt road, Blake listened as Connor communicated with Tess on the police radio. From her vantage point in the helicopter, she kept her eyes glued to the black Jeep as she directed Connor to their position.

"There he is," Blake yelled from the passenger seat. "He's coming straight at us."

"I see him," Connor responded.

Kate and Adam were in the back seat, both clinging to the grab handles as the vehicle bounced down the dirt road.

The Jeep, which had been heading toward the car carrying the FBI agents, suddenly spun around and sped off in the opposite direction. The helicopter swooped down and changed directions, stirring up the road dust.

"Don't lose him," Blake said, his muscles rigid as he maintained a white-knuckled death grip on the handle above the passenger door.

"There's nowhere for him to go. He can't escape the helicopter."

The Jeep suddenly skidded to a stop. A second later, both the driver and the passenger fled the vehicle, running toward the woods. A Dutch police SUV arrived from the opposite side. Two shots rang out, then a barrage of gunfire, as Connor skidded to a halt and all the occupants poured out, weapons drawn.

One man lay motionless on the ground; the other had his hands high in the air.

Blake's body tensed as he recognized the man surrendering. He gritted his teeth and watched as SWAT grabbed, cuffed, and searched Emil.

SWAT team members used a ballistic shield to slowly approach the body on the ground. Blake watched as one officer kicked a weapon to the side while another officer handcuffed the lifeless body. Even from a distance, Blake could see the pool of blood forming around the figure and assumed the man was dead.

SWAT moved in and meticulously cleared the Jeep to make sure there were no other occupants hiding or waiting to ambush law enforcement. "All clear," the leader announced.

"Come with me," Connor said.

The three FBI agents holstered their weapons, then fell in behind him. Before they reached the body, one of the Dutch police yelled, "There's someone in the woods."

All the law enforcement officers pulled their weapons and trained them on the tree line.

Blake heard Kate gasp. His eyes widened, his heart thumping with the abrupt surge of adrenaline.

"WAIT!" he yelled. "Put your guns down. It's Lexie."

He ran as fast as he could to the opening. He could hear someone running behind him and didn't have to turn to know Kate was hot on his heels. Connor translated to make sure all the officers understood it was a friendly in the forest.

Lexie emerged from the tree line and collapsed.

37

University Medical Center Groningen

The rest of the day and night was a blur for Lexie. She vaguely remembered Blake stroking her hair and Kate speaking to her in soft, soothing tones. An endless number of doctors and nurses paraded through her room, each asking questions and checking her IV. She drifted in and out of sleep, listening to the constant sounds of staff being paged over the intercom and the beeps of hospital equipment.

The morning light warmed Lexie's face from the nearby window. She wasn't ready to face the pain that the morning would bring, and chose to enjoy the dreamy feeling for a few last minutes. She had survived on pure adrenaline for so long, not allowing herself to feel the inevitable physical and mental pain she knew she was going to have to face. She knew the day would be filled with painful questions and emotional subjects.

Finally, she took a deep breath and her eyes fluttered

open. She turned her head away from the window and saw Blake slumped in a chair, sleeping.

As if he knew someone was watching, her partner woke and sat up. He rolled his neck and smiled. "Good morning, sleepyhead."

She tried to speak, but only a raspy croak came out. Her throat felt like sandpaper.

"Let me get you some water."

Blake raised the head of Lexie's bed, then poured ice water from the pink plastic container into a glass. He inserted a straw and held it to her lips.

She drank greedily, the cold liquid soothing her throat and satisfying her thirst. When she finished, she managed to croak, "Have you been in that chair all night?"

Blake put down the water, then moved his chair over next to the bed. He took Lexie's hand in his. "Yeah, I didn't want you to wake up and be alone."

Lexie smiled. "Thank you. That was sweet of you."

"How are you feeling?"

She looked over at the IV sticking out of her arm. "This stupid IV hurts, but other than that, I think I'll live. How do I look?"

"You look like you've been in a fight with a wolverine and lost."

"That good, huh?"

"You've been through hell and back, girl."

"I have so much to tell you."

He nodded. "I know. But you're going to have to go over the whole story when Adam and Connor get here. For operational purposes, they need to be the first to hear it. Feel free to relax and rest for now."

"Blake, I'm sorry."

Wrinkling his brow, he asked, "Sorry for what? You didn't do anything wrong, Lexie. If anyone should be sorry, it's me. I didn't protect you. I let them take you from right under my nose."

She squeezed Blake's hand. "It wasn't your fault. They separated us on purpose and drugged me. There was nothing you could've done to prevent it."

"I don't believe that," he said. "I was your partner and I let you get hurt on my watch. I should've kept a closer eye on you."

"Neither one of us knew what Holden was capable of, nor the lengths he would go to. No one could have predicted what he did. You did everything right. What happened to me is the cost of working undercover. I knew the risks when I signed up."

"I was so worried about you, Lex," he confessed, his voice cracking. "I thought I would never see you again."

"You didn't give up on me. You stayed and searched until you found me. Thank you for not giving up."

Blake used the back of his hand to wipe a tear from his cheek. Then, clearing his throat, he grinned. "The next time we work an undercover case together, I get to pick the assignment."

Lexie laughed. "Next time?"

"Yeah, next time. I've grown accustomed to your nagging."

"I don't nag."

"Yeah, you do."

"No, I don't. Well, maybe just a little."

"I brought you something," he said, reaching into his backpack and pulling out her copy of *The Prince of Tides*.

Lexie's lips curved into a smile when he handed her the book. "Guess it didn't bring me any luck after all," she said as she ran her thumb over the battered cover.

"It brought me luck," Blake said, taking her hand. "It helped me find you."

Slowly, gently, he kissed the back of her hand. A second later, a knock on the door caused them both to jump, then smile.

"We can finish this conversation later," he whispered.

Kate stuck her head inside the door. "May I come in?"

"Please do," Lexie said.

Tossing two bags on a vacant chair, Kate hurried across the room to hug Lexie. "I've never been so glad to see anyone in my life," she said, sobbing into Lexie's neck as the two embraced. "You scared the daylights out of me."

"Well, if it makes you feel any better, I scared the daylights out of myself."

"It does."

Both women laughed; Kate released her embrace on Lexie and took a good look at her friend. "How are you feeling?"

"Much better than yesterday. What's in the bags?"

"Oh, I picked up some toiletries and clothes for you."

A relief so intense it was physical swept over her. "You're a lifesaver, Kate. Literally! Thank you."

"Don't mention it. Do you know when you're getting out of here?"

Lexie shook her head. "I haven't talked with the doctor yet, but it better be today. I'm ready to go home."

"Adam wanted me to call him after I talked to you," Kate said. "We need to do a formal debrief with the Dutch police."

"I guess that depends on when I get released from here," Lexie said.

The door opened and an attractive, middle-aged nurse stuck her head around the corner. "Knock, knock," she said before entering. "I'm Karen, your nurse."

"Hi, Karen," Lexie said.

"I need to take your vitals."

"We'll go get a cup of coffee so you can have some privacy," Blake told her.

"Are you coming back?" Lexie asked, sounding more anxious than she intended.

"Sure," he said, before kissing the top of her head. "We'll be back in half an hour."

Karen took Lexie's temperature, checked her blood pressure, then examined the wounds on her face, arms, and legs.

"Do you have any idea when I can leave?" Lexie asked.

"The doctor will be in to see you in a few minutes. She will make the determination, but I don't see any reason why she wouldn't release you today. Your wounds look good and you're fully hydrated. From looking at your chart, you were a mess when they brought you in yesterday."

"I don't remember much about yesterday."

"Do you have any pain?"

"Just some sore muscles, but nothing major."

Two loud raps on the door made Lexie jump. The doctor entered, carrying a patient chart. She spoke with an Italian accent. "Good morning—I'm Dr. Costa. How are you feeling today?"

"Much better than yesterday," Lexie said. "I'm ready to leave."

"That's good, because I'm going to let you," the doctor said, smiling. "We cleaned your wounds while you were in and out of consciousness. You were suffering from exhaustion and extreme dehydration. Make sure you continue with your fluid intake, and please take a few days to rest and fully recuperate."

"I plan to do that, Doctor."

"Yesterday you said a gun was fired close to your head and that you were experiencing ringing in your left ear. Do you still have the ringing?"

"Not now. It seems to be gone."

"Well, I would recommend that you follow up with an audiologist when you get home. You may have some degree of hearing loss in your left ear."

Lexie nodded.

"I'll start the discharge paperwork. We should have you out of here in a couple of hours."

"Thank you, Doctor."

"My pleasure. Take care, Ms. Montgomery."

Lexie was surprised to hear her last name. She hadn't used it since she arrived in the Netherlands. It made sense that Adam would have checked her in under her true name for insurance purposes.

* * * * *

Stretched out on the couch in the posh hotel room, Lexie watched as Blake opened a bottle of wine and Kate dished out food from takeout containers to fill three plates.

"How did you ditch Adam?" Lexie asked.

"I told him that you wanted to be alone and that he needed to go to dinner with Connor and the others."

"Thanks. I'm glad it's just the three of us. I know the debrief tomorrow will be stressful, so tonight I want to relax."

"We can do whatever you like, Lexie," Blake said. "If you want to talk, Kate and I are here to listen. If you want to chill and watch TV, we can do that as well."

Lexie smiled. "Thanks. Right now, the only thing on my mind is that bottle of wine."

Blake laughed and handed a glass of wine to Lexie. He picked up two more glasses, handing one to Kate while raising the other in the air. "To getting the hell out of this country and never coming back."

"I'll drink to that," Lexie said.

They clinked glasses, and Lexie inhaled the fruity bouquet of the fragrant wine. She smiled and savored the luscious liquid.

38

Nightmares plagued Lexie, robbing her of restful sleep. She finally gave up trying to sleep, showered, and hobbled to the hotel lobby to satisfy her caffeine addiction. She was bandaged from head to foot, and every muscle in her body ached.

An hour later, Kate appeared in search of coffee. She jumped when Lexie called her name. "How long have you been up?" she asked.

"An hour or so."

"Why're you up so early?"

"Nightmares," Lexie said simply.

"You want to talk about them?" Kate asked as she sat down beside her friend.

Lexie contemplated for a second, then turned her body so she was facing Kate. "I think so. Maybe it will help make them go away."

"I'm listening."

Lexie took a deep breath and sighed before continuing. "I'm sitting on a log with Finn. We're talking and laughing when suddenly, he turns to me and I see a gaping bullet hole in his head. He tells me it was me who put the bullet in his head. I try to apologize to him, but then someone touches my shoulder and sitting on the other side of me is Logan. He has a huge gash in his head, and his skin is pale and drawn, like he was just pulled from the water. He keeps asking me why I've done this to him."

Lexie's bottom lip quivered, and a tear ran down her face. Kate reached over and took her hands in hers but did not speak.

"I tell Logan that I'm sorry and that I didn't mean for him to get hurt. Logan replies that he didn't get hurt, he got killed. He seems really angry."

Kate gave Lexie's hands a little squeeze for reassurance.

"Then Finn tells me he shouldn't have covered for me and that I'm the reason he's dead. He asks me how many more people have to die. I tell him that I'm sorry, but he doesn't believe me."

With a deep breath, Kate said, "Lexie, I don't think Finn or Logan would blame you for what happened to them. Neither one of their deaths was your fault."

"How can you say that, Kate? If Logan hadn't been involved with me, he would still be alive. If Finn hadn't tried to help me, he would still be alive."

"Both are dead because of the investigations, not because of you."

"We both know that I'm the common denominator. Both men are dead because of their affiliations with me. Both were innocent people."

"Lexie, Logan helped you and ended up in the wrong place at the wrong time. Finn took the phone from you to keep you safe. He had to know that he was putting himself at risk, yet he did it anyway." Kate's eyes ached for her friend. "Neither Logan nor Finn would want you to blame yourself for what happened."

"How do you know?"

"Because both men cared for you. Maybe not in the same way, but each had a connection to you. They helped you *because* they cared. Due to the actions of evil people, they both died."

Lexie chewed her bottom lip as she considered Kate's words. "Dr. Levering, the therapist that I've been seeing in New Orleans, told me there's a difference between responsibility and fault. Do you think that she's right?"

Kate pondered the question before answering. "I guess I've never thought about it, but yes, I do think there is a difference."

Slowly nodding, Lexie felt a sudden lightening within her, as though something had unlocked. "During our sessions, I didn't grasp what she was trying to get through to me, but I think I understand now. I have to take some of the blame for what happened to Logan and Finn, but I didn't kill them. I inadvertently put both men in the path of danger, but their lives were taken by psychotic killers. In the end, Finn is dead due to the actions of Dusty, Jonas, and Holden. Holden brought me to the camp, which set the chain of events in motion. Jonas gave the order to kill Finn, and Dusty pulled the trigger."

Kate sat quietly for a minute, allowing Lexie time to process her emotions.

"Kate, I want to be my old self again, but the world

seems so dark and I don't know which way to turn. I want to cover my head and stay in bed until everything is shiny and new like it used to be. Remember those days?"

Shaking her head, Kate replied, "That's not how the world works, Lexie. You can't stop living because things get hard. You still have to drag yourself out of bed every day and carry on with life. One day you'll look back and this will all be a distant memory—life will be new again. But it doesn't happen overnight. You have to allow yourself time to grieve and work through the pain."

Lexie nodded. "You're right. I've been blaming myself, stuck in victim mode. It's time that I take responsibility for my emotions and put my life back together. I understand that healing my heart and finding happiness is my responsibility and mine alone. This darkness will pass."

"Your feeling dark is understandable. Finn was your friend."

The two sat and sipped their coffees for a few minutes, both lost in thought. Kate broke the silence. "Are you ready for the debrief this morning?"

"Ready as I'll ever be."

"It's going to be difficult, but be strong. Take as many breaks as you need. Everyone can work on your timetable instead of the other way around."

Lexie nodded.

"I'll be right there with you. If you need to stop and catch your breath, give me a signal and I'll ask for a break."

"I will. Thanks, Kate."

"That's what I'm here for."

"No, I mean thanks for everything. For not leaving me lost in this country, or lost in myself."

"My god, Lexie. I would've never left here without you. Job or no job, I wasn't going anywhere without you."

Lexie smiled.

"Besides, there was another person who wasn't going anywhere without you. The director himself couldn't have gotten Blake back to the US without you. He was obsessed with finding you. The poor guy hardly slept or ate the whole time you were missing. He worked around the clock studying maps of the Netherlands and the surrounding countries. He was a man on a mission."

"Ahh," she said, waving her hand dismissively, "he felt guilty because I disappeared on his watch."

"It wasn't just guilt, Lexie. There's a whole other level of feeling involved here. So that begs the question, how do you feel about him?"

Lexie looked down and picked at a jagged part of her fingernail. "He lives in Louisville and I live in New Orleans."

"I didn't ask where you lived, I asked you how you feel about him."

"That's tricky. We started out like oil and water. I didn't think we were going to survive the mission without killing each other."

"And?" Kate prodded.

"I don't know. Something happened along the way. We started trusting one another. He's really a sweet guy once you get to know him."

Kate raised an eyebrow.

"Okay, okay. I think he's pretty damn incredible. He's sweet, and funny, and really hot. There, I said it."

"That wasn't so hard, was it?"

* * * * *

The investigative team sat around the large conference table at police headquarters, the usual coffee and pastries arranged on the small corner table. Everyone knew one another from previous encounters, so there was no need for introductions. The investigators agreed to allow Connor to conduct the debrief of Lexie with limited interruptions. Questions would be saved for the end.

Lexie explained how she'd befriended Holden, how he'd drugged her and taken her to the camp. She explained that she'd only known the activists by their first names due to their security culture. As expected, Connor was interested in Jonas's role in the terrorist cell.

"Did you ever learn the intended target for the explosives?" he asked.

"No. Dusty told me that I was going to be involved in the next attack. He said the mission was big and that it was important to the cause, but he never disclosed the target. I'm sorry, I know that's an important detail."

"It is, but at least we stopped the attack by seizing the explosives. The bomb tech told me that the amount of explosives the group had stockpiled could've leveled a small town."

"You mean I was literally sleeping next to a ticking bomb?"

"Exactly."

Lexie pressed her lips together and exhaled slowly.

"How much interaction did you have with Jonas?" Connor asked.

"Not much. He was a little on the scary side. Kind of a cross between Jim Jones and David Koresh. I'm sorry," she added hastily when she saw his eyes fall, "I know that he was one of you before—"

"No need to apologize," Connor interrupted. "You don't have to sugarcoat any encounter that you may have had with Jonas for our sakes. We have come to terms with the fact that he was no longer one of us. He made a choice and crossed over to the dark side. Any insight that you have on the matter would be greatly appreciated. It might help us to understand why he did what he did."

Lexie nodded, then continued. "From my interactions with Jonas, I found him to be incredibly passionate about the cause. His zealousness and charismatic personality made him a naturally strong leader. Jonas referred to the members of the cell as his family and as freedom fighters. He believed in waging a war to fight for the animals and for the people who have no voice. I think he truly believed that what he was doing was for the good of the planet. That being said, Jonas gave the order for Dusty to kill Finn."

"Why do you think that?"

"Because he told me so."

"What a minute, Jonas told you that he had Dusty kill Finn?"

"Yes. Jonas told me that he had Finn killed because he betrayed us all. According to Jonas, stealing a cell phone was a blatant act of disrespect for their guidelines."

Connor closed his eyes, shook his head, and continued. "Tell us about Holden. Why do you think he recruited you?"

Lexie took a deep breath and rested her head on the back of her chair.

"Can I give my input?" Blake asked.

"Of course," Connor said as Lexie turned her head to look at him. "We don't mean to leave you out. Please feel free to jump in at any point."

"Lexie sold herself to them as an activist. She used her training and experience to make everyone in the camp believe that she was a hardcore activist. She's a talented undercover agent."

Lexie smiled at Blake. She knew he was trying to protect her.

"But why her? There were other hardcore activists at the Gathering. What made her stand out from the rest?"

"Holden liked me," she said. "He made it clear that he respected my activist background, but he also wanted a romantic relationship with me."

"I'm sorry to have to ask this question, but we need to know for prosecution and trial purposes: Did you have relations with him?" Connor's face flushed when he asked the question.

"No. He kissed me a couple of times, but it never went any further than that. He wanted to have a sexual relationship, but I managed to keep him at bay."

"I'm sorry, Lexie. I know some of these questions are uncomfortable."

"I understand that you're doing your job," she assured him. "I also understand that for the prosecution purposes, you need to know all the details."

"What were your feelings concerning Holden?"

Lexie took a sip of her coffee, buying some time to gather her thoughts. "We became friends. I thought he was handsome and charming. I pretended to be interested in him romantically to stay alive, but he was merely a target to me." Staring into her coffee cup to avoid eye contact, Lexie knew she was giving the right answer for law enforcement purposes.

"Did anyone hurt you while you were in the camp?"

"KK beat the shit out of me while we were sparring. She had a toxic hatred of me. In the end I gave her as many bruises as she gave me, so I would call it even."

"What about sexually? Did anyone hurt you sexually while you were in the camp?"

"No. As far as that goes, everyone respected one another."

"That's good. I'm glad you came away unscathed," Connor said without thinking.

"Unscathed?" she asked, her voice catching in her throat. "Oh, I wouldn't say I'm unscathed. I watched a young man get his brains blown out while he sat beside me. His blood and brain matter splattered onto my face and hair. I lost my hearing for nearly two days, and I might have permanent injury to my left ear. *Unscathed* is not a word that I would use."

"I'm sorry," Connor said hastily. "Poor choice of words. Please forgive me."

"Can we take a short break?" she asked, rising to her feet.

"Yes, of course. Whatever you need."

Lexie went to the bathroom, splashed water in her face, and stared at her reflection. The deep cuts on her face were dark red and angry looking. The circles under her blood-shot eyes made her look old and haggard. She splashed more water on her face as Kate entered.

"Are you okay?" Kate asked.

"Yeah, it's just . . . harder than I thought it would be. Reliving it all over again."

"You're doing a great job."

"I'm snippy. I owe Connor an apology."

"I'm sure he understands."

Turning away from the mirror, she asked, "What am I going to do, Kate?"

"Do you want to end the interview and continue tomorrow?"

"I don't mean about the interview, I mean about life. What am I going to do? I feel broken."

Kate walked over and put her arm around Lexie's shoulder. The two women looked at their reflections in the mirror.

"You're not broken, Lexie. You're hurt and you need time to heal. It won't happen overnight, but it will happen. So, to answer your question, you're going to do what you always do. Pick up the pieces and start over."

"What if I can't?"

"You can and you will. You are one of the strongest and

smartest people that I know. It won't be easy, but you're going to heal and move forward."

"How?"

"You'll start by swallowing your pride and going back to your counselor. The one who told you not to take this assignment," Kate said, smiling ruefully.

"Ugh, she may not want me back after I walked out on her."

"Well, then, find another therapist. Any way you slice it, you have to see someone and talk through all this trauma. I would also suggest that you walk away from the under-cover program. For good this time."

"I tried. You saw how that worked out for me," Lexie said, attempting a smile.

"It's hard to walk away from the program because you're one of the best damn undercover agents in the FBI. I under-stand that you want to do what you're good at, but Lexie, you have to put your well-being first. For once, you have to do what's best for *you* and not what's best for the Bureau."

Reluctantly, Lexie nodded. "I understand, and I know you're right."

"I'll be here for you whenever you need me. I'll come visit you in New Orleans, and you can come stay with me anytime you like. You know my phone will always be right beside me."

"Thank goodness for that," Lexie said. "I guess we better get back to the interview."

"You sure you're ready? You can take as long as you need."

"I'm ready. Let's do this."

The two women returned to the conference room. Most of the investigators had fresh coffee and pastries sitting in front of them. Blake handed Lexie a cup of coffee.

"Thank you," she said.

"You're welcome." He leaned over and whispered, "You're doing a great job."

Lexie smiled and took a sip of the coffee. "Ready to get started?" she asked Connor.

"Whenever you are."

* * * * *

As Lexie was leaving the conference room, Connor touched her arm. "Can I talk to you in private, off the record?"

Lexie nodded and followed him to a quiet corner.

"I still can't believe Jonas turned," he said, his voice dull. "How could it happen? I feel like I should have seen it coming."

"Connor, no, it's not your fault. You couldn't have known."

"But I was his friend. And contact agent. It was my duty to know he was in too deep."

Lexie shook her head. "Undercover agents are excellent at hiding their true thoughts and feelings. That's what makes them good at their job. I should know—I'm one of the best at not telling people what I'm really feeling. Plus, it's so easy to get lost in a role. Especially when dealing with impassioned activists."

"They're terrorists, Lexie," he corrected her, his voice edging toward scolding.

"We label them as terrorists, but they are also people. Even people who do bad deeds can be good inside. A lot of the animal extremists get involved in the movement for the right reason but then escalate to illegal activities. It doesn't happen overnight."

Connor shook his head. "This wasn't simply animal rights. These were full-blown terrorists. They murdered an innocent man to cover their tracks. Jonas ordered that hit."

"You're right. I'm not trying to justify Jonas's actions. He became the person he started out impersonating. It's a danger of long-term undercover work. He was too far gone to be saved."

Connor stared at the ground before speaking. "I can't wrap my head around what happened."

"When I was working my first undercover assignment in Los Angeles, most of the targets were genuinely good people. Only a few stepped outside the law. One night, we were on a mission to liberate a large number of beagles who were bred to use in experiments. They were mistreated and lived in horrible conditions. While we were rescuing the dogs, the FBI raided the place and arrested everyone. When it was happening, all kinds of crazy thoughts ran through my head. I wished that I had never told my contact agent what I was doing. I remember thinking that because of the FBI, these poor animals were going to go back to the despicable conditions that we rescued them from and ultimately die a horrible, painful death. At that point, I would've changed sides in an instant. I was so damn angry.

What I can tell you is that when you're living a lie, it's easy to become that lie. What we pretend to be, we become."

Connor put his hand on Lexie's shoulder. "Wanting to save beagles and killing a man are two completely different situations. You would never consider doing something so horrendous as killing a person. I would never in a million years have guessed that Jonas was capable of such atrocities."

"You are not responsible for Jonas's actions, Connor. He was a grown man who chose his path. He deliberately kept his innermost thoughts and feelings from you. There was no way for you to know his intent. None of this is your fault."

He sighed, looking down at the floor. "Thank you, Lexie. I appreciate it."

39

Nearing the end of the second full day of debriefings, Connor brought two colorfully wrapped packages into the conference room and set the boxes down in front of Lexie and Blake.

"This is a little thank-you from our agency," Connor said. "You have no idea how much we appreciate your assistance. I don't think we would've ever known the truth about Jonas without your help."

"We're glad that we could help," Blake said.

Lexie gripped her hands together and grinned. "May we open the boxes now?"

"Please do."

"You go first," Blake told her.

"No," she said, "together."

The agents carefully unwrapped the heavy box in front of them and simultaneously removed a stunning, teardrop-shaped, crystal recognition award. The Dutch police logo was beautifully etched on the top.

"Read what it says," Adam said.

Blake tipped his head toward Lexie, who teared up as

she read the engraved message out loud: "'In recognition of outstanding excellence. Honoring FBI Special Agent Alexis Montgomery. With great appreciation for your dedication and commitment. Thank you.'"

"Thank you," she said. "It's beautiful, and I will always treasure it."

"You're welcome. I wish we could do more."

Blake ran his hand over his award's smooth edges, its text identical to Lexie's except for the name. "Thank you," he said. "We didn't expect anything, so it means a lot that you took the time to do this for us."

"Have some more coffee," Connor said, motioning toward the back of the room. "Eliene just restocked the table with fresh pastries."

"I bet I've gained five pounds in the past two days eating pastries," Lexie said.

Connor smiled. "After all that time eating vegan food, you deserve it."

"Actually, the food at the camp wasn't bad. Mamma Bear was a good cook. Speaking of the camp, did you get everyone identified? What's going to happen to them? Is anyone besides Ryan cooperating?"

"We've fully identified everyone in the camp. Mamma Bear's real name is Myrna Duffy. She's fifty-three years old and only has a few minor arrests for vandalism. She hasn't cooperated so far, but we're hopeful she will."

"I hope she cooperates, but I'm not sure how much she actually knows," Lexie said. "I never saw her outside the mess hall."

"That's good to know," Connor said, making a note on his yellow pad.

"What about KK?"

"She's a handful," Connor said.

"*Bitch* is the word you're looking for," Lexie said.

Connor laughed. "Her name is Katrina Katrien. She's twenty-eight years old and has a lengthy arrest record, mostly for disturbing the peace. Apparently, she likes to stir up trouble."

"I wouldn't count on her cooperation," Lexie said.

"That was the impression our investigator got. When he attempted to interview her, she spit on him."

"What about Jade?"

Connor shook his head. "She's still missing. Somehow, she was able to evade capture. Do you have any idea where she would go?"

"I'm afraid not. Robert was the only person she mentioned from outside the camp. I wonder where she hid while you searched the camp?"

"We went back the next day with a team of search dogs but came up with nothing. She seems to have disappeared. We'll find her, eventually."

"How is Ryan?" Lexie asked.

"He's doing as well as can be expected under these circumstances. I think the poor kid is still in shock over seeing his friend murdered and then being forced to bury the body. He's a vital person in our investigation, and we will make sure that he gets the proper psychological counseling."

"Thank you. He's a nice young man. He was definitely out of his element at that camp."

"Ryan took us to Finn's grave. We recovered the body, and his parents have been notified."

"I didn't even know Finn's last name," she said, grief twitching within her.

"It was O'Brian. He didn't have an arrest record, but Ryan knew his last name and how to contact his parents."

Lexie lowered her eyes and shook her head.

"We identified Dusty through his fingerprints," Connor said. "His full name is Dustin Eugene Perkins, age forty-eight, originally from Crescent City, California. He had quite a lengthy arrest record for violent encounters."

"I hope he rots in hell," Blake said.

Lexie looked at Blake and nodded. "Me too. What about Holden?"

"He's still being a *lastpost*."

She cocked her head and raised an eyebrow. "Translation please."

"It is what you would refer to as a nuisance or a pain in the neck."

"That's Holden all right," she said.

Blake grunted. "He's an asshole."

She gave Blake a look.

"I'm sorry, but I really dislike that guy."

"Is there anything that I can do to help?" Lexie asked. "Maybe I can persuade him to cooperate."

"I don't think that's a wise idea. He has requested a lawyer."

"You need Holden's cooperation," she insisted. "With Dusty and Jonas both dead, Holden may be the only person who knows the intended target for the explosives as well as the identity of Greg. Just because you dismantled this terrorist cell doesn't mean Greg will stop his vendetta. You have to find him and stop him from assembling another cell."

Connor scratched his head then nodded. "Okay. I'll take you to see him, but you can't discuss the case at all. You can only talk to him about cooperating."

"Does he know that I'm an FBI agent?"

"We haven't disclosed that fact yet."

"Good," she said. "The shock might work to our advantage."

"Or torpedo any chances of gaining his cooperation," Blake said.

"Only one way to find out," Lexie said. "I need to go in alone. You can monitor us on camera, but I need to see him by myself."

"Agreed. But remember, do not discuss any facts related to the current investigation."

"If possible, we need to use an enclosed room. The conversation will go better if we have the appearance of privacy."

* * * * *

Seated alone at a bolted-down metal table in a small, windowless room, Lexie waited. The solid metal sliding door remained open, allowing her to experience the daily sounds of prison life. Buzzers going off, mechanical iron doors sliding open and shut, locks snapping into place—all gave her an uneasy feeling deep in her stomach.

The jangle of leg chains warned her of Holden's arrival. A burly, clean-shaven guard appeared in the doorway with the eco-terrorist in tow.

Holden's appearance shocked Lexie. The red prison jumpsuit washed out his normally tanned complexion; the leg chains clanked as he took small steps and shuffled in the room. His hands were cuffed to a band around his midsection, forcing him to walk hunched over like an old man.

His pale skin regained some of its healthy color when he saw who waited to see him. "Lexie." His eyes lit up and a smile crept across his face.

Lexie smiled on the outside, but on the inside she wanted to flee and never return.

The guard pulled out the chair and helped Holden sit.

"Can you remove the handcuffs?" Lexie asked the guard.

"No, ma'am. It's against the rules. Are you comfortable being left alone with the prisoner?"

"Yes, sir."

The guard nodded, then slid the heavy metal door closed, the reverberation adding to Lexie's feeling of vulnerability.

Holden leaned forward. "Lexie, it's so good to see you. Are you all right? I couldn't find you during the raid. I asked, but they wouldn't tell me if you were okay."

"Holden, before you say another word, there is something that I need to tell you. I know that you have retained an attorney, so you and I are prohibited from discussing the case against you."

Holden shook his head. "What are you talking about, Lexie?"

Well, once again I'm living the motto of undercover agents: I've built this relationship, now I have to betray this relationship. It never gets any easier. Lexie took a deep breath and continued. "Please let me finish. This is going to be hard for you to hear, but you need to listen carefully. I'm not who you think I am. I'm actually an undercover FBI agent. I was sent to the Netherlands to search for a missing person."

"What? No way. What?"

"I'm sorry that I deceived you, but I had a job to do. Now, you have to listen closely. You need to cooperate with the Dutch police. It's your only way out of this situation."

Holden's eyes were wide; Lexie could see a vein in his forehead pulsing. "Wait. What? You're serious? You're an FBI agent?"

"Yes."

"So, you don't really care about me? All those intimate moments together meant nothing to you?"

"Holden, I like you, but—"

"Fuck you." Holden jumped to his feet and glared down at Lexie. "You're nothing but a lying, manipulative whore."

The guard's face appeared at the window in the door. Lexie shook her head to let him know that she didn't need help. "Holden, sit down. You need to listen to me."

"No. I'm done listening to you. I felt something when we kissed. I know you felt it too. You can't fake that kind of emotion."

"Please sit down. Just give me two minutes."

Holden slowly sat back down.

"I do care about you. That's why I'm here. I didn't want you to find out about me in some police report that your attorney reads to you. I wanted to tell you face-to-face. You need to save yourself and cooperate with the police. They can help you."

"I'm supposed to believe you? After you lied to me. You pretended to be in love with me." Holden exhaled loudly. "And they call us terrorists. I've heard of some low police tactics, but for the FBI to stoop to this level is unbelievable."

"I didn't mean for you to fall in love with me. It just happened."

Holden stood and gave Lexie an icy stare. "Tell yourself whatever you need to in order to get through the day, but I *know* you loved me too."

Lexie hung her head.

Holden shuffled over and screamed through the door. "Guard."

She looked up at him. "I'm sorry, Holden."

He spat at her feet. "Fuck you!"

40

Lexie took advantage of the final opportunity to hit the restroom before they boarded the airplane for home. On her way back to her gate, a small female who looked vaguely familiar caught her eye. From the distance, Lexie could barely make out the streaks of blue woven through her blunt-cut, raven-colored hair. The woman's eyes connected with Lexie's for a brief moment. She smiled, flashed a peace sign at Lexie, then slipped away into the crowd.

Lexie shook her head and smiled.

Jade.

She strolled back to her gate, where a line formed to board the plane.

"You okay?" Kate asked Lexie. "You look like you've seen a ghost."

Lexie grinned. "Maybe I have."

"Huh?"

"Nothing. Let's go home."

Kate volunteered to sit beside Adam on the airplane so Lexie and Blake could talk. "Can you believe we're finally on our way home?" Lexie asked him.

"It seems like we've been gone for months."

"I know what you mean."

"Lex," he asked, "are you doing okay? You've been through a lot of shit lately."

"That's putting it mildly," she said.

"You know you can talk to me."

"Are you going to report my condition to Adam?"

Blake's eyes widened with shock.

"I'm kidding, Blake. Too soon?"

He laughed. "Maybe a little too soon. I feel terrible about what happened between us at the Gathering."

Lexie reached over and took his hand. "We're okay. You didn't know me, and Adam put all that crap in your head. He can be pretty damn persuasive."

"I still should've trusted you."

"You trust me now, right?"

"Of course I do," he said. "We're partners."

He squeezed her hand and continued. "I'm sorry that I let you out of my sight at the camp."

Lexie turned so she and Blake were eye to eye. "Understand one thing, Blake Bennett—none of what happened to me is your fault. Besides, in the long run, we achieved our goal. We found the missing constable."

"I guess we did, but—"

"No buts. We had a job to do, and we did it."

"At what expense, Lexie? Are you really going to be okay?"

"I admit that I have a lot to process. But I'll promise you one thing: I'm going to take some time for myself. I'm assuming responsibility for my own happiness. I'm going to resume my therapy sessions, and I might actually follow my shrink's advice this time around."

Blake laughed. "I bet you're a pain in the ass in therapy."

Lexie grinned. "Maybe a little."

"Maybe a lot," he said.

She elbowed him in the ribs. He feigned injury, eliciting another burst of laughter from them both.

*   *   *   *   *

Lexie opened her eyes. She had been sleeping on Blake's shoulder.

"Good morning," Blake said.

She sat up and stretched. "Where are we?"

"Almost home. We're landing in less than an hour."

"Wow, I took a long nap."

"You needed the rest."

She dug around in her backpack until she found a package of mints. "Mint?"

"You trying to tell me something?" he asked.

"Yeah," she said, laughing.

Smirking, Blake took one.

Lexie popped a mint into her mouth, stretched, then ran her hands through her tangled hair. Blake lowered his voice and whispered to her. "Before we land, there's something I want to tell you."

She stopped fidgeting and paid attention.

"I, ahh . . . I'm . . . I'm not sure how to say this." Any trace of his smartass qualities was gone from his expression.

"What is it, Blake? After what we've been through, you can tell me anything."

"Lexie, I can't stop thinking about you. When you were missing, I was so afraid that I would never see you again and wouldn't be able to tell you how I felt about you."

Taking her hands in his, he continued, "I'm not sure how things will work out or even if you're interested in me, but I knew that I had to tell you. I would like to see you when we get home. We can take things slow and see what happens."

Not realizing that she had been holding her breath, Lexie exhaled. "I care about you too, Blake. I was worried that you thought that I was in love with Holden. You have to know that he didn't mean anything to me. He was a means to an end."

"Well, as long as we're being honest, I was a little worried. I really hated that son of a bitch. I wanted to punch out his perfect white teeth every time I saw him."

"You have nothing to worry about. I feel bad that Holden had legitimate feelings for me, but that's part of undercover work. We build relationships to betray relationships."

"So, you really never had feelings for him?" Blake asked.

"Maybe at first, but in the end, the bastard drugged me and kidnapped me. Normal people don't do that to one another."

"There goes my plan," he sighed.

"What plan?"

"To drug you and carry you off to Louisville."

Lexie's stomach fluttered and her pulse raced.

"You don't have to drug me," she told him. "I'll willingly come to Louisville."

"Are we talking about a visit or a transfer?" Blake asked.

"How about we start with a visit and see where it goes from there?"

"I can live with that."

Blake placed his hand on Lexie's cheek. His eyes locked on hers. When their lips came together, Lexie felt a sense of safety like a weary traveler who had finally reached home.

* * * * *

The plane bounced down the runway and skidded to a stop. The four weary agents retrieved their bags, cleared customs, and stood in a small circle in the middle of the Atlanta airport. Each person would depart from a different gate, ending their time together.

"I guess I'll go first," Adam said. "I want to thank all three of you for accepting this mission. Kate, I'll have the deputy assistant director send a letter to your chief outlining your achievements and thanking the LAPD for their assistance."

Kate nodded. "Thank you, Adam."

He turned to Blake and extended his hand. "Thank you, Blake. I'll talk to your SAC next week and let him know what an asset you were to the investigation."

"I appreciate that, Adam."

He then turned to Lexie. "What can I say, dear? It's been

another crazy adventure." Adam took Lexie into his arms and squeezed her tight.

Lexie thought about her relationship with Adam. There were times when she wanted to punch him in the face, but there were also times when she felt close to him. This occasion was the latter.

"Goodbye, Adam. I'm going to miss you."

"I'm going to miss you too." Stepping back, he said, "Well, I better run. My plane to DC is boarding now."

The three watched as Adam disappeared.

It was Blake's turn to say goodbye. "Kate, thank you for everything. I can never repay you for all you did." He grabbed Kate and picked her up off her feet as he hugged her. Putting her back down, he smiled.

"No thanks necessary. I'm going to miss you, Blake."

Blake looked down at Lexie. His brilliant blue eyes danced with desire. "I'll see you soon."

"Yes, you will."

Leaning down, he kissed Lexie on the lips. She reached up and put her arms around his neck, pulling him closer for a second kiss—the kind of kiss that creates lifelong memories.

"I think I missed a chapter in this book," Kate said.

After the kiss, Lexie looked over at Kate and said, "It was a long trip home."

"For me too, but you didn't see me kissing Adam."

"Thank goodness for that," Lexie said, laughing.

"Ladies, it's been real. Until next time." Blake winked at Lexie, turned, and walked down the corridor.

At the last second, he turned to see if Lexie was still watching him. She was.

"My gate is this way," Kate said after he'd vanished, motioning to the left.

"So is mine. I'll walk with you."

The two old friends walked through the sea of people to their gates, neither wanting to say goodbye.

"So, what's the plan for you and Blake?" Kate asked.

Lexie hesitated before answering. "I'm not sure. I feel like I'm once again standing at a crossroads in life. But this time the correct path seems clear to me. Maybe I'm getting older, but for the first time in life, I have no desire to rush. I'm going to take time to enjoy this moment in my life. A wise woman once told me that you can't stop living because things get hard. You have to drag yourself out of bed every day and carry on with life.

"That's what I intend to do. Carry on with life and see what happens. Every day is a new discovery."

ACKNOWLEDGEMENTS

I have to start by thanking my extraordinary team at Wise Ink Creative Publishing: Laura Zats, Patrick Maloney, Graham Warnken, and Roseanne Cheng. I first met Laura at a writers conference in 2014. She impressed me then and continues to amaze me with her dedication and brilliant ideas. A special thank-you to Graham for pulling double duty with my last two novels.

I am indebted to my genius editors: Frank Cernik and Graham Warnken. Thank you for challenging me and for giving my characters a whole new level of depth.

Thank you to my ridiculously talented designer, Jay Monroe. Jay has done a marvelous job designing all three book covers for my novels. He constantly surprises me with his illustrious ideas and talent.

To my wonderful publicist Wiley Saichek—thank you for being a pleasure to work with and for your wealth of incredible ideas.

From the first day that I started this journey, I have had the enthusiastic support of my family. Thank you to Mom and Dad for always being in my corner. To my sister, who makes me laugh when I'm having a rough day. To my mother-in-law, who always has something sweet to say. And to my loving husband, who is a constant source of encouragement and coffee. Bill, I can never adequately thank you—please know that I am eternally grateful for your love and support.

Thank you to my devoted beta readers: Mike Lee, Melinda Casey, Terry Palmer, and Bill Endorf. The valuable feedback you provided helped to shape and polish the story.

I am astoundingly grateful for my marvelous friends and writing community. Carol Duckworth travels with me for book events and is tireless in her commitment to making sure each event runs smoothly. Melinda Casey participates in everything from reading the first draft to making giveaway baskets. Patrick Hempfing provides a little spirited competition and constantly challenges me to reach for the stars. Finally, everyone needs a tribe member who can talk them off the ledge when the going gets tough, and Nora Moloney fills that role for me. Thank you, Nora, for always being there for me. Your friendship means the world to me.

In *Below the Radar*, Lexie has the support of Kate Summers, her unwavering contact agent. During my many years working undercover, I was extremely lucky to have three dedicated and enthusiastic contact agents. The character of Kate Summers is modeled after my three real-life contact agents: Bruce Naliboff, Ralph Lima, and Vicki Gizzi. A heartfelt thank-you for keeping me safe and tethered to the real world so I could safely retire and write this series.

In closing, I would like to say thank you to the men and women who serve as federal, state, and local law enforcement officers, and to the fallen officers who died in the line of duty. Thank you for your dedication, courage, and commitment.